Rescu

Thank you for purchasing Rescue Ben
10% of the sale price will be donated to a
Rescue Animal Shelter.

Thank you for supporting the Animals

Sincerely
R.B. Smith
Author
www.rescueben.com

RESCUE BEN

R.B. Smith

abbott press®
A DIVISION OF WRITER'S DIGEST

Abbott Press books may be ordered through booksellers or by contacting:

Abbott Press
1663 Liberty Drive
Bloomington, IN 47403
www.abbottpress.com
Phone: 1-866-697-5310

ISBN: 978-1-4582-0860-6 (sc)
ISBN: 978-1-4582-0862-0 (hc)
ISBN: 978-1-4582-0861-3(e)

Library of Congress Control Number: 2013905142

Printed in the United States of America.

Abbott Press rev. date: 4/8/2013

TABLE OF CONTENTS

OUR DEDICATION

Dedication to those who work tirelessly to save and protect rescued animals. Our hat is off to those that support rescue shelters, animal rights groups and promote animal welfare worldwide.

We hope to do our part to raise awareness within all communities and to work towards a future where all animal owners are responsible and rescue shelters will no longer need to make the choice to put down otherwise adoptable animals simply due to a lack of space and resources.

Support Rescue Shelters

BEN BOOK ONE

Ben – Chapter One

He runs until he gets weary then he walks briskly for several hours.

He has become painfully aware that he's near exhaustion. His firm, powerful muscles are burning, and his body is aching; he is fatigued. Continuing to run at this rate has become difficult. His keen mind is among his greatest assets, and even that is dimming; he has reached his physical and mental limit.

Thirst is starting to make him crave water to hydrate his burning muscles.

Night will soon be here, and it will be more dangerous to travel on these dark roads absent of moon light. So he must find a place to sleep.

It has been too many hours since he ate and slept. Food and a place to settle down for the night are tormenting his mind. His head is drooping. He feels as if he is going to collapse as he cautiously makes his way along the shoulder of the busy highway.

His journey will continue tomorrow. He knows his reward will be worth his valiant effort.

A short distance off the road he spots a small brook with fresh, clear water. This minor detour is crucial as his throat is so dry; the water burns as it trickles down his parched throat. After lapping up the refreshing water he notices almost immediately he is starting to feel refreshed.

Now, he wonders, *where is a safe place to sleep?*

He looks around and by chance is lucky to stumble upon an ideal place where he senses he will be safe and secure. It feels secluded from the elements. He thinks he will be sheltered while sleeping here. The spot he found has a vast green umbrella of trees overhead. The ground level of dense vegetation will surround him and keep him warm and cozy just like his favorite soft green blanket. This will work just fine.

Sleep comes quickly. He sleeps soundly for most of the night. But just before waking there are some nasty disturbing thoughts that remind him of the dangers of yesterday's trip. The hundreds of cars driving too fast and too close were overwhelming. Huge monster trucks came so close they almost blew him off the road.

Regardless of the future risks, he knows that he must push on to reach his final destination.

Daylight came early. He blinks and is immediately aware of the familiar sound of rushing traffic. The patter of light rain bothers him because he knows that when his hair gets wet, people scrunch up their noses because it smells unpleasant. At least the rain blots out the blazing hot sun. Today he feels will be much cooler for traveling. He stretches his stiff aching muscles to get the kinks out. Now he is wide awake, and acutely aware of his need for food. His belly is making gurgling noises.

His nose twitches. *What is that divine scent floating past my nostrils?* Ben points his sensitive nose into the air drawing in the pleasant aroma. Yes, it's the delicious smell of sizzling smoked bacon. He loves bacon. It's his favorite food. Last night when he arrived here, he'd noticed an eating place. It is just across the street. Ben is optimistic about finding a delicious breakfast to fill his empty belly. Just follow your nose, he tells himself.

Crossing the highway to the diner is as treacherous as navigating a car going against traffic. A few near misses and blasting horns make him more watchful. Ben, using his sharp senses tries to judge the speed of the rapidly moving vehicles, but the constant sound of squealing brakes and honking horns frightens him.

Just when he thinks he has crossed the road; he spies more vehicles coming from the other direction. This is a challenge he does not anticipate. His hunger for food is his motivation as he carefully maneuvers his passage through these harried angry morning commuters.

Finally, at the diner he eats ravenously like a hobo who has been without sustenance for an awfully long time. His feast is bursting with the flavors of catsup mixed in the scrambled eggs, over-cooked bacon pieces, clumps of cold, greasy sausage, and toast slathered with butter, peanut butter, and various fruity jams. He loves peanut butter. Just the smallest taste brings delightful memories of home.

Satisfaction and contentment is obvious by the way he meticulously smacks his lips, making sure every last morsel of the delicious meal gets into his belly.

With replenished energy, His thoughts now turn to today's journey. Now that his belly is full, he has renewed commitment and enthusiasm. The kitchen door of the diner abruptly opens and then slams shut causing Ben to look up. A fat man in a dirty, grease-splattered and food-stained white apron approaches him and shouts, "Get out of here you mangy mutt."

Ben – Chapter Two

Insulted, Ben turns and leaves with his tail between his legs and head hanging. Ben thinks, *Yes, I'm a mutt and proud of it. But I'm not mangy. I may not be large, but I am physically and mentally fit.*

Ben now struts, showing off his shiny black coat with a diamond patch of white on his chest and four white boots, giving him quite a sophisticated appearance. His family always tells him he has the look of a formal tuxedo.

Not all breeds would even think to take on a trek like this, nor would they be able to finish it, Ben thinks. *I'm drawn to my human family like I am to peanut butter inside my Kong. I will not give up my quest until I find them.*

He genuinely loves and misses his human family.

They lost me when we stopped at the motel a few nights ago. He often wonders why he ran after that stray cat. Remembering, Ben thinks, *He taunted me. I had to chase him. I fell for it like a magnet to steel. When I returned the next day my family had left without me. I understand that they could not wait.* Hanging his head, he is deep in thought. *I do feel foolish. I know they love me. I remember all the hugs and kisses we always shared. I do not blame them for not waiting for me. They had to keep to their schedule. I was stupid!*

Ben sniffs the air for an indication of which way he should go. The drizzle stops. Seeing the bright red sun in the eastern morning sky with the brilliantly colorful rainbow confirms he is heading east, the direction he must travel. Ben is sure that his steady pace of walking and then running will work out. *I just need to avoid that crazy traffic.*

Soon, I'll get there. It is good that I went with them when they first bought their new house. At least I have a sense of where they are now.

While continuing his hunt for his human family's new home Ben obsesses about Roy and Molly. They are young and energetic and always eager to play with him.

Molly is quite delightful, with her huge brown eyes and very curly black hair. At 16, she attracts attention wherever she goes with her sweet mannerisms, her appealing looks and her engaging personality. She has Mommy, Daddy and I wrapped around her little finger. We are happy to tend to her every need, as she is a wonderful and caring girl, but not spoiled. She just likes lots of attention. Molly really enjoys the older sister role, much to Roy's chagrin.

Roy is an athletic, well-coordinated, energetic boy, with thirteen years of experiences. He wears his curly hair cut close to his head; he says this hair cut is so much cooler in the summer. He also sweats less on his head when he's playing sports. He is only five foot, five inches tall, so his dream of becoming a basketball player, is only that, a dream. He will need to stick with soccer, for now anyway. Ben likes to run around the soccer pitch with Roy chasing the ball. He tries to catch the ball, but it is too big for his mouth.

Roy is also an excellent student and has successfully passed, with very good marks. He says he's not looking forward to attending his new school. He is shy and has always had trouble meeting new friends. Roy is hoping they play soccer at his new school. At least it will be easier to make friends with his new team mates.

These are exciting times, a new job for Daddy, a new house, and new schools for Roy and Molly.

Will I ever find the new house?

JOEY BOOK TWO

Joey – Chapter One

Several days later, Ben is hustling along the gravel shoulder of a country road. There are fields, farm houses, and out buildings for as far as he can see in every direction. With a peppy bounce in his step, he is happy to be making excellent progress.

Today is another warm, dry day, exceptional weather for traveling. He is sure he will make good progress today. He looks up at the now clear blue sky, as the bright sun has risen and no longer shines directly into his eyes. He loves sunny days, best.

This morning he ate a substantial breakfast and drank lots of fresh water from a bucket behind a busy roadside cafe. He is fueled and ready to go as far as he possibly can before nightfall. Sensing he is getting closer to home is likely hopeful thinking, but these thoughts give him motivation to keep going.

Mid-morning Ben feels his heart skip a beat at the sight of a young boy ahead of him. He quickens his step to a trot, as he thinks for a few moments that the boy is Roy. Ben naturally walks quicker than the adolescent boy.

In just a few minutes, he catches up to him. Then his heart sinks because he realizes this young man is not Roy.

The boy, just like Ben, is walking along the shoulder of the road. Every few steps Ben hears the youngster muttering indignantly to himself, and then he forcefully kicks at the gravel with intense anger. Ben wonders why this boy is so irritated.

He cautiously approaches from behind, but the boy is distracted by his grumblings and does not notice him. Ben barks softly in a very friendly way, he thinks, he does not want to startle the boy.

The boy is a teenager wearing blue jeans, a red team shirt, red ball cap, and black high-cut sneakers. After hearing Ben's bark, he turns looking over his shoulder and sees Ben. "Hello," he says, "Where did you come from? Are you running away too?"

Ben brushes the boy's leg with his cheek to show him that he's friendly. Ben thinks the young man looks very sad and angry at the same time. It's unusual to see a young boy walking all by himself on the lonely country road.

Why is the boy not at school? Ben wonders.

Ben determines that the boy is about Roy's age; Roy loves to play soccer. I wonder if this boy plays soccer, too. He has wavy brown hair also but not as short as Roy's hair. Ben sees that he has terribly sad dark brown eyes and dirty streaks on his face from crying. His dried tears have run down his cheeks and been wiped away with his dirty hands.

Ben easily relates to young boys because they like to play games with him. Just remembering Roy makes him miss him so much more. He wonders if his family is at their new house yet.

Ben walks with the boy for a while through the overgrown grass. The boy stops then sits on a tree stump just off the road. Ben lies down and joins him, and they rest for a while.

"Who do you belong to? I haven't seen you around here before," the boy says, "But, I'm lost so that doesn't mean much. I'm not really sure where I am, right now."

"My name is Joey, what's your name, pal?" he asks.

Ben sits up straight so his name tag is in full view.

"Is that your name tag?" Joey takes the tag in his hand and reads out loud, "Ben. That is a different name for a dog. Hi Ben, do you shake?"

Ben offers a paw. The boy smiles, as he takes Ben's paw in his hand, so he can gently shake it. "Good boy, Ben," Joey praises, "You're a pretty smart dog. Why are you here, and where's your home?"

Joey feels very comfortable sitting here on the stump, so he begins telling Ben why he is so upset with his dad and grown-ups in general. “Ben, I know you can’t understand me, but I’d like to tell you anyway. It’s like this; I’m running away from home. Maybe that’s why you’re here, because you’re running away too. I don’t know,” he confided in Ben not holding back his frustration with his dad.

He started his story with the maximum indignation that he could muster, “My Dad does not understand boys or baseball players. We do not want to miss our games because of stupid chores. Chores can be done anytime. In fact, there are always chores needing to be done. Today we have a very important game and my team needs me. We are in the county semi-finals and *I’m* the pitcher for heaven’s sake. Wait until I’m a pro baseball player. Betcha, pro ball players don’t do chores. And even if they did, no one would stop them from playing ball, not just for chores. Why does my dad not know that the pitcher is a hugely important person to the team?”

Ben grumbles something unintelligible, a sound that Joey takes as an agreement.

Joey continues, “My work can wait, but my team cannot. Baseball games are way too important. Adults do not understand kids at all. They say that they do, but when it comes right down to it, it’s just not true.”

Ben rubs his face on Joey’s leg again and whimpers to show his support.

Joey starts walking again. Ben keeps pace with him. There is no particular direction or plan, so they just walk and talk for quite some time, well into the hot afternoon.

A few hours later Ben watches the large red sunset making the whole sky pink. He is aware that it soon will be dark.

Hunger and thirst is taking over Ben's thoughts. He needs food and water before it gets too dark.

Joey follows Ben, as if Ben is the one who knows the right direction.

"Ben, are you hungry? I am. I wish I could eat the lunch Mom packed for me this morning. I left it in the fridge when I ran out of the house. I was so angry at my Dad." His last statement brought back the emotions from earlier today. The tears fill his eyes again, making them pools reflecting the spectacular pink sunset.

Ben realizes that Joey's hurt feelings are still very close to the surface.

"If I knew how to get to the ball park, I would go to the game, but I don't know where I am," says Joey. "I wasn't paying much attention to which roads I took. I think I'm lost," Joey adds, crinkling his eyes making a sad face. He didn't say so to Ben, but he is also getting very worried. He longs for his home, food, and his normal routine. Maybe, even to do his chores.

Joey – Chapter Two

"I do not see him here," Joe Webb, Joey's father said as he anxiously looks around the baseball diamond. Joe manages one of the larger dairy farms in the area. He is over six feet tall, fair haired with a well-toned body, proof of the labor-intensive work of dairy farming. "I'll ask some of the parents and coach Pete," he says to Betty, Joey's mother. Joe walks over to the bleachers. "Have you seen Joey this evening?" He asks several parents sitting there. He cannot hide the tone of urgency in his voice.

"No. Why?" Mary Turner responds.

"Is something wrong?" asks Bud Fowler.

Joe, being a private person, is not ready to share his family problems. No, no, not just yet, he thinks. Instead he says, "Just asking. Thanks."

He spots Coach Pete, who is dressed in his baseball coach's uniform, including his red baseball cap which makes him feel younger; it covers his thinning hair. His rugged completion is partly due to working his land, and partly from coaching kid's baseball for the past five years on very hot sunny days. He is preparing the roster for tonight's game. Pete is deep in thought, planning his game strategies. He is creatively moving around his players for the lineup, hoping for the best result.

Joe approaches the dugout where Pete is waiting for his team to arrive. Joe asks, "Hi Pete, have you seen Joey?"

The coach frowns and hesitantly responds, "No?" He is expecting an explanation.

"Did he show up for practice?" Joe asks the coach.

Pete replies, "No, he was not at practice today. I've been wondering where he is. He is usually here early. It's not like him to be this late." Pete takes off his cap and scratches his head. "Come to think about it, I don't believe in the five years I've coached Joey, I've ever known him to miss a game or a practice for that matter."

"I know. He and I had a little misunderstanding earlier today," Joe adds.

"Has he been gone all day?" Coach Pete asks.

Just then Betty catches up with Joe. "Yes, since early this morning," Betty answers, as she once again, for what felt like the fiftieth time today, wipes away tears from her cheeks with a very soggy, well-used tissue. She's still wearing the same blue jeans and yellow T-shirt she put on earlier today. Changing her clothes to attend the game tonight just did not seem to be important right now. Her short cropped blonde hair is quite untidy and in need of a brushing. Normally she wears makeup, even to Joey's ball games. But not today, how she looks isn't as important to her as finding Joey. She could not remember when they last ate.

"I'll ask a few of the boys if they saw Joey at school today," Joe said to Betty.

Joe wanders over to where the young ball players are gathering and chatting to each other while some participate in horseplay. Seeing the boys having so much fun with each other, Joe thinks. I miss my Joey more than ever. "Hey guys," Joe asks to get their attention, "did any of you see Joey at school today?" Joe questioned each of Joey's teammates.

"No, Mr. Webb. Is he sick?" young Billy responds. The other boys just stare at him.

"No, Joey is not sick. Thanks boys, just checking." Returning to where Betty is sitting, he says, "Sorry honey, but no one has seen him at all today. He did not go to school either. I'm really getting very worried, now."

Betty says anxiously, "I'm so concerned about him. He has never done anything like this before. Where can he be? He doesn't have the skills to take care of himself outside at night in the elements. Why doesn't he come home? What if he's injured or worse? Betty places her hands on her cheeks. "I cannot let myself think such horrible thoughts. It terrifies me." Betty adds, "It will be dark soon. He is all alone and probably scared half to death. These parts have some extremely dangerous coyotes, and they are hungry." She can no longer hold back her tears, and begins to cry again. Her small slight body shakes with retching sobs. She's trying not to think the worse, but she does.

"I know you're scared. I am too. Please don't cry," Joe pleads as he wraps his arms around her. He holds her close and stokes her soft hair. He tries unsuccessfully to console her. His heart is aching too, but he puts on a brave front. She needs his strength right now. He is able to do that, because he is outwardly the emotionally stronger person, inside he is longing for his son's safe return.

Coach Pete trots over to them and says, "I think you should report him missing. Sheriff John would want to know. I hear the first twenty-four hours are the most crucial hours for finding people. Missing kids can get in trouble remarkably fast."

"Maybe, you're right. It'll put a whole different perspective on the situation once the Sheriff gets involved. I guess I've avoided reporting Joey missing. That would've made it more real. And right now it feels very real," Joe responds almost losing control of his emotions.

Joey – Chapter Three

Ben climbs into a big blue dumpster where he searches for dinner. The dumpster is behind a lonely roadside café desperately in need of paint and a handyman. He finds a half-eaten turkey sandwich and carries it very carefully to Joey between his teeth. Ben does not want to risk biting into the food with his sharp incisors.

"Ben," Joey says, "I can't eat that. Yuk!" Joey has a look of surprise and disdain on his face. He sure is hungry, but he never before in his whole life eaten someone else's half consumed sandwich. Especially, one out of a dumpster. "I guess it's different for a dog, eh Ben."

"I am hungry, but no thanks Ben," Joey is quickly losing his desire to run away. "I'm getting tired, too" he says with a big yawn. Lying down on the grass just off the road to rest, Joey realizes how homesick he is and yearns for familiar surroundings.

Ben lies down beside Joey. He wants to reassure the boy, knowing he can guide him and protect him. It's getting really dark. Ben sees that the moon tonight is hidden behind a cloud cover. He knows all too well the dangers that the night can bring, especially in heavily wooded areas like the one that surrounds them right now.

Joey stands up and saunters off along the gravel shoulder of the highway, again.

Ben attempts to keep Joey near the dumpster as there is a bright light in the parking lot shining directly on them. It makes it seem more secure for them. But, Joey will have nothing to do with being corralled by Ben. He pushes past him and continues walking, even though he's not sure this direction is the right way to go.

Ben is not sure how to tell Joey, that night can be extremely dangerous. He begins to bark, trying to get Joey to stop walking.

Joey – Chapter Four

Joe and Betty are in panic mode by the time they arrive at the Sheriff's office. Sheriff John is slender but muscular. He is middle aged with a dark tanned face and arms. After listening to Joe and Betty, he raises his hand and calmly says, "Try to relax. Please. First I need to get some details from you. Let me ask the questions then I can get a handle on just what we are dealing with here."

Joe, ignoring the Sheriff's instructions, nervously blurts in a single breath, "John we are extremely worried about Joey — we had an argument with him this morning over chores — you know how kids hate chores — we were just at the ball park — he did not show up for practice or the game — we spoke to several of his classmates and parents and learned he did not go to school today, either." Joe stops his ramblings, just long enough to take a deep breath.

"Slow down Joe," Sheriff John jumped in to cut Joe off. "Does he have a particular place he would go when he is upset? Like a tree house, an old shack or a place in the woods around your house?" The Sheriff said trying to get some insight into Joey's habits and behavior.

Betty was quick to respond, "No, we have no idea where he would go. He has never done anything like this before."

"Do you have any relatives in the area?" The Sheriff continues asking questions that he knows need to be asked in these situations. It is very important that he assesses both the urgency and severity of the circumstances.

"Yes, I have checked with every family member, plus both our and Joey's friends. No one, absolutely no one, has seen him at all today. I did ask them to call my cell if they saw him or if he shows up at their house," Joe replies.

"Good I was going to suggest you do that," the sheriff says.

"We are so worried about Joey. He is a young teenager that's not that worldly. He has no experience being out alone in the dark, never mind the woods at night," Betty adds.

Sheriff John begins to prepare a plan, and explains, "It'll take an hour or so, but I will organize a search party. It is dark now so I don't know if we'll be successful. Normally I would say we should start our search at the crack of dawn, but a thirteen years old boy out there . . . all alone . . . this is extremely worrisome."

"I'm positive that I can get some help. All I need to do is make a few phone calls," Joe says.

"Good. You start calling. I'll ask my sources to see if anyone saw him today. Otherwise, we will be spreading ourselves pretty thin." Sheriff John is already planning the routes on which each team should concentrate their efforts.

Joe is busily phoning his relatives and friends. "Hi, Matt, when we spoke earlier you offered to help search for Joey. We actually do need your help, right now. It is dark, and Joey is still out there somewhere. All alone, and probably terribly frightened. Would you please meet me at the Sheriff's office within the next thirty minutes, or as soon as possible? Sheriff John is organizing search teams." He holds back his tears while he repeats his request over and over again to friends, neighbors, and family.

The sheriff devotes the next half hour calling folks who have experience with search teams, and also those who are specifically familiar with the wooded areas. "We need your experience on a search team for a lost thirteen-year-old local boy. Yes, the Webb boy. Bring a flash light, flares or any other equipment that will help with the search. Thanks, please meet me at the office ASAP. Appreciate your help."

Joey – Chapter Five

Ben desperately tries to take charge and keep Joey from wandering into the woods. Joey is frantic to find a familiar place or house; it takes a lot of effort on Ben's part to guide him away from the woods, where Ben knows many dangerous hungry wild animals lurk.

"Ben I'm tired. Let's lie here on the grass and take a nap. We can walk further when we're not so tired." He makes himself comfortable, yawns and then closes his eyes.

Ben once again lies down beside him, both to protect him and to keep him warm; the night air is getting chilly. Both slip into a deep sleep.

Ben suddenly sits up; his ears perk up and twitch. He senses the danger more than he hears anything specific. He is not sure what it is but he senses something is not right. He knows he must remain alert.

He nudges Joey several times to wake him.

Joey is so tired that he pushes Ben away and resists. "Go away, I'm tired, Mom. I don't want to get up yet," he whines in his sleepy voice while rubbing the sleep from his tired eyes.

Ben, however, is having no part of that. He pokes hard against him, pushes him several times with his sensitive wet nose, and licks his face with several sloppy wet kisses, insisting they move by tugging at Joey's shirt. At the very least they must stay awake.

There is definite movement in the trees behind them. Ben is now on full alert. *What is that?* Ben wonders to himself.

Now Joey is wide awake too. "Ben what's happening? I hear something out there. Is it a bear? Maybe it's a coyote or a wolf?" Joey keeps imagining all different types of animals, and with each suggestion, he is scaring himself even more.

Ben is convinced Joey is now quite frightened. He does not want him to panic or run. This would give any wild animal the advantage. It would certainly chase them. Ben understands that he and Joey are at a huge disadvantage.

Joey starts sobbing and calling, "Mom . . . Dad . . . where are you? I'm so scared. Help me. I'll never run away again."

Joey – Chapter Six

Sheriff John is experienced and a take-charge kind of guy. He assigns groups based on his knowledge and the experience of the searchers. He appoints his deputies as leaders. "Okay teams A and B take the south side of town and work your way east and west, then north. Teams C and D you start on the north and work your way east and west then south. I'll take the rest of you with me."

He sets them on the right track, using the huge wall map of the county and by waving his arm and pointing on the map the direction he wants the others to begin the search and the areas each team must cover.

"Betty and Joe, go home. When we find him, then we will bring him to you," John insists.

"No, we want to search too," they anxiously reply.

"Absolutely not, I have done this before and believe me the best place for you to be is at *your* house. If Joey wanders home, you need to be there. Now don't argue, go home," John is adamant and will not negotiate.

"Here is my cell phone number. If he does come home, call me," Sheriff John adds.

"Okay, Betty let's go," Joe says. "I guess there is nothing we can do here anyway," he continues as he ushers her to their car. "He might be at home waiting for us." He said this to calm her down but . . . he didn't believe it for a moment.

Joey – Chapter Seven

"Ben what are we going to do? I'm really . . . really . . . scared," Joey says. Darkness and the heavily wooded area, plus hearing strange animal noises and howling wolves, were all making Joey want his own bed in his own house.

"Ben I've never slept outside before. I always sleep in my own bed. Except for the two nights, I spent in the hospital with a broken arm and a concussion when I was eight, after I fell off my pony," Joey said this more to calm his own panicky feelings than anything else.

Ben sees the ominous long pointed nose before the head could be seen between the leaves of the bushes. Ben and Joey watch the animal with eyes like saucers as it moves cautiously from the woods to the edge of the clearing. Now the animal's coal black, steely eyes are visible and glaring at them. Ben identifies the coyote with his thick faun colored fur and snow white belly and chest. He growls deep in his throat, to let the coyote know it is not just Joey who is prey.

Both watch the ferocious animal with terror in their hearts as the coyote cautiously moves a little closer. He is moving very slowly in their direction, but with focus and purpose. The boy and the dog dare not make a sudden move. They do not twitch a muscle. They notice the coyote's ears perk. The animal obviously listens with razor sharp intenseness, making sure he does not miss sounds or unwanted movements in the area.

Unmistakably visible to their enemy, Ben knows that he and Joey are now the coyote's main focus. He understands the scent that he and Joey are giving off, knowing how tantalizing it is to the coyote. Ben's heart is pounding as if it is trying to escape from his chest. He will protect Joey, of that he is certain. He has never fought a coyote before, but he is confident he will do his best to defend himself and Joey against this worthy adversary. This is certainly uncharted territory for him. Although he would not show it, doubts of the outcome of a battle were starting to creep into his mind.

Ben cringes at the eerie unnerving sound of the snarling, howling and growling coming from the coyote. The animal slowly and cautiously moves around them first in a large circle. They watch as each circle brings this vicious animal a little closer to them. Ben hears the ferocity in the coyote's snarl; it feels frightfully angry. This is a new experience for Ben. He has never known an animal or human to show such anger towards him.

The black hair along Ben's back stands up straight like a fan to indicate to his attacker that he is ready for the fight of his life. He is frightened, but he also knows he must fight to the end. Ben accepts the role as protector even if it means his demise.

The coyote is circling them, even closer now. He continues to intimidate Ben and Joey with his spine-chilling growling and howling. He rolls up his lips so his big white, sharp teeth are in full view. His eyes focus on dinner and he will not be deterred.

What to do now? Ben must trust his instincts and develop a plan, perhaps using defensive moves, to at least be ready for the coyote's attack. Ben edges closer to Joey. He stands between him and the coyote. Ben pushes Joey back up against the tree. If only, he could make Joey understand he'll be safer if he climbs up onto the branches of the tree. He will be so much safer up there. How can he make Joey understand?

Ben grabs at Joey's T-shirt with his teeth and tugs at him. This helps to move Joey even closer to the tree. Joey is in full panic mode now. "Ben, what are we going to do?" He begins crying, huge tears are flooding down his cheeks. "I want my Mother! I promise I will never run away again. Mom . . . Dad where are you?" he wails.

The coyote inches even closer to Ben and Joey, and continues his sinister snarling and growling. Ben can only imagine how the coyote must almost taste the tender meat of the young boy.

Joey senses the severity of their situation. He screams at the top of his lungs, “Help . . . help me . . . someone please help us.”

His pleas disappear into the vacuum of a dark menacing forest . . .

Joey – Chapter Eight

Deputy Bob, a slim five foot ten inches tall jock, with bright carrot color hair and a face of freckles to match, is one of the best deputies that Sheriff John has ever worked with, during his twenty plus years as Sheriff. Bob uses his common sense and intuition to work through issues, and solve crimes. Not that there is an abundance of crime in their small county.

"Listen . . . quiet . . . listen." He instructs his team holding his forefinger over his lips.

Gordy, an experienced searcher, says, "Yes! I hear it too."

"Which direction do you think it's coming from? It sounds like a young boy to me," Bob asks.

"Help . . . help me . . . someone please help us," Joey's voice is again heard.

"There it is again. Over by the Ninth Line, would be my guess," Gordy adds. "Let's get these vehicles over there, pronto. "Shine your flashlights into the bushes and woods," Gordy instructs. Please, listen closely, and do not shoot anything unless I give the command."

Gordy points into the woods and says, "There are lots of coyotes around this time of year. The cubs are being born, and parents need food for their offspring."

Bob spots some movement as they approach the Ninth Line. "All heads up folks," he hollers. "We do not want to scare the boy. I do not mind scaring away a coyote though. They can be dangerous when they're desperate for food."

"I see the boy," Gordy shouts, "He's hanging onto a branch of that big Maple over there about, two o'clock." Gordy points in Joey's direction. "I think there's a coyote at the foot of the tree. Get your rifles ready, but do not shoot, yet. We may need to kill that animal lying at the base of the tree. I certainly don't like to shoot the new moms, but this is more about keeping Joey safe."

Joey truly hopes the coyote will not be able to reach him up in the tree. "Ben, I wonder, can coyotes climb trees?" Joey asks as if Ben could answer.

Ben hears the vehicles approaching. He is relieved to see the coyote sprint off into the woods with his tail tucked in between his hind legs. The hungry coyote also heard the men's voices and the noise of the vehicles' tires on the gravel shoulder.

Joey, now aware of the oncoming parade of cars and trucks, hollers again, "Help, I'm over here!" He frantically waves his only free hand as the other hand is still clutching onto a higher branch as if his life depends on it. And it did.

Ben both heard and saw the men with the bright lights on their trucks. He senses danger as he notices the rifle barrels flash as they reflect in the truck lights. Ben does not move. He just listens to the anxious voices of the men. He is not sure what he did to make them angry, but he realizes he needs to be extremely cautious so he doesn't make the men angrier. He once again is frightened. He's not sure what to do next or where to move. But it is more important to protect Joey. This does not feel right. He knows if he moves, they might shoot him.

He lay down playing dead, hoping the humans are not trigger happy.

Bob calls, "Is that you, Joey?"

"Yes, did you come to help us?" Joey's change in tone signifies his relief.

"Joey, please keep still. We need to get rid of that animal lying on the ground below you, before he attacks someone," Bob calls out.

Joey again feels panic rise in his belly as he realizes it is Ben they are about to shoot

"No, don't shoot. He's my friend. He's just a dog. Please don't kill him," he pleads.

"Hold your fire!" Bob says and instructs his team with his hand and arm held up in the stop position. "Don't shoot. Let's see if it's friendly. Hold your fire!"

Ben carefully slinks away mostly crawling on his belly moving as far away from the tree as he can, especially from the men holding the guns, even though he is sensing less danger now.

The men cautiously approach Joey, while keeping an eye on Ben. He does not want to startle them. He freezes in his crouched position, with his head down on the ground trying to cover his eyes under his front paws. He does not move a muscle except to peak up at the men with his big brown worried eyes. He is feeling very exposed, and he wishes he could hide in the tall grass or behind a tree until it is safe.

Bob helps Joey down from the tree, then asks, "You okay? Your, Mom and Dad sure are worried about you."

"Yeah, I'm okay now. It sure was scary when that coyote wanted to fight with Ben. This has been the worst experience of my life," Joey confesses.

"Is that your dog?" Bob inquires.

Ben responds to the more friendly tone in their voices; he's now wagging his tail.

"No, we just met. He kept the coyote away from me, though. He is a really friendly dog and smart too . . . his name's Ben," Joey happily volunteers.

"How did you get up that tree?" Gordy asks.

"Ben pushed me over there until I got close enough to the tree. Then I stood on his back and reached up to that big branch. I climbed as high as I could to the heavy branch, just to be safe. He protected me from the coyote. Ben did it. He saved my life. I have never met a dog as smart as him before," Joey says proudly. Joey is far more relaxed and talkative, now. "Can I go home?" He asks.

"Yes," Gordy says, "I radioed the Sheriff, and let him know that we found you. He called your parents, and they are waiting for you at home. They are very relieved to hear you are safe."

"May I take Ben to my house? I want to tell my Mom all about Ben. I think they will really like to meet him." Joey smiles at Bob while pleading for Ben to accompany him home.

"Well, let's see if he wants to get into the truck." With that Deputy Bob pats Ben on the head and said, "Come on Ben, let's go for a ride."

Ben is feeling safe and is sure there will be food and water at Joey's house. He really enjoys riding on the front seat of trucks. He thrusts his head out of the open window. He smiles, as he experiences the euphoria of the warm soft wind blowing in his face.

Joey – Chapter Nine

Both Mom and Dad are impatiently waiting for Joey at the gate near the end of their long paved driveway. Mom is crying, this time with relief. "We are so happy to have you home safe and sound. Betty and Joe, speaking in unison, ask, "Where did you go? We were so worried about you, Joey. Don't ever, ever do anything like that again!"

They smother Joey with hugs and kisses. "Ugh, Mom, I was fine. You didn't need to send the cavalry out to find me," Joey fibs. "I'm okay." Joey is obviously trying to avoid their apparent display of affection.

"Do you want something to eat?" Mom asks while they walk back to their house, arm in arm.

"Yes, I'm famished. You're not going to believe this but, Ben got supper for me. It was a half-eaten turkey sandwich from a dumpster," Joey chuckles, as he remembers his experience.

"Did you eat it?" Mom asks, with a look of shock and surprise on her face.

"Naw, I guess I wasn't hungry enough." Joey replies, scowling, shivering and shrugging his shoulders.

Joe looks at Ben and says, "I guess when you are a stray dog you eat what you can find. It's all about survival."

Ben wags his tail in recognition of his name.

"See, I was okay. I wouldn't starve with Ben taking care of me," Joey praises Ben. "He's a smart dog. He protected me from the coyote. It was unbelievable how he kept that coyote from coming near me. That animal sure was mad and ready for a fight. He was baring his teeth," Joey pulls a face by rolling his lips and trying to bare his teeth, mimicking the coyote. "And he was snarling and growling really loud at Ben. I think he was mad at Ben for protecting me. I wasn't too scared though," he says flippantly, with a much lighter tone in his voice.

Ben watches Betty and Joe look at each other over Joey's head smiling, nodding, and rolling their eyes. They know Joey is trying to put on a brave front. They also know that he must have been quite terrified.

"Young man, we need to have a long talk about the events of today. You had a lot of folks worried sick about you, today," his dad says as he attempts to warn Joey that his behavior was inappropriate and will not be tolerated.

"Don't worry, Dad, I learned my lesson about avoiding chores. I will never take off like an idiot again," Joey momentarily reveals a little about his true feelings regarding his behavior today.

"Okay, but we will talk more about this tomorrow," Dad states.

Anxious to change the subject, Joey asks, "Dad do you think Ben would have won if he fought the coyote?" Joey is extremely curious now that there is no longer danger. "Just how well do you think Ben would have fared in the fight?"

"Well, I don't know," Joe answers. "A lot really depends on his experience. For example, has he fought other wild animals before? He seems very well groomed. It does not appear as if he has been a stray for very long. It's really hard to say," Joe adds, "We don't even know if he is a stray. Maybe we should check around to see if we can find his owner."

Mom asks Joey, "Would you like us to do that?" She turns to Ben and rubs his ears. "Ben," she says, "I don't know where you came from, or why you were there at that time and place today, but we are truly grateful that you were there to help Joey. I think you are an incredible rescue dog. Thank you, Ben, for protecting Joey for us."

"You are a very good dog," Dad says as he pets Ben's head and tousles his ears. Joe wants to make sure that Ben knows how much they really do appreciate what he has done for Joey.

Ben knows he did an excellent job. He smiles, wags

his tail, and rubs himself against Joey's mom and dad. Then Joey's mom makes him a feast fit for a king. Ben gobbles up recently cooked ground beef and plenty of fresh, clean water. At last, fully satisfied, Ben needs to sleep.

"Joey," Mom says, "You must be exhausted and ready for bed. It has been an awfully long and stressful day for all of us

"Mom," Joey begs, "can Ben sleep with me? Please . . . pretty please?"

"Okay, I suppose just this one time. He did earn the right to be given the royal treatment tonight," Betty says giving in. She is very happy to have Joey home.

Ben follows Joey to his bedroom. Once Joey is comfortable, Ben jumps up and stretches out full length, as he leans into Joey's body on the soft warm comfortable bed. He is totally relaxed and feels very drowsy. Feeling safe, Ben falls into a deep sleep.

The next morning after another delicious meal, Ben experiences a strong anxiety, urging him to continue his journey. This family makes him miss his own even more. Ben feels loved by this family. He wonders, *what would it be like if I should decide to stay here?* What if he never finds his own family?

Joey is kneeling beside Ben hugging him because he

suspects that Ben has a mission and must leave. He says to Ben through teary eyes, “Ben I really want you to stay here. We can be good friends, play fetch and go for nice long walks together.”

“Please stay Ben, please!” Joey pleads.

“I have never had a dog before. I had no idea how much I would like to have a dog for a friend,” Joey says with sadness in his voice as his eyes fill with tears.

Both, mom and dad watch, feeling Joey’s pain at having to say good bye to Ben. They were amazed at how quickly the two had bonded.

Dad offers, “Joey if Ben chooses to leave, later this week, we can go to the animal rescue place in town and see if they have a dog that you would like to make your friend.”

Mom adds, “It will be good to have a dog of our own. Every farm should have at least one dog.”

Ben licks Joey’s face and rubs himself against the legs of the boy’s Mom and Dad. Then, quietly turning with a heavy heart, Ben trots down the long driveway to continue his journey.

That night, Joey cried himself to sleep.

SALLY BOOK THREE

Sally – Chapter One

Ben stumbles just slightly, looks around then takes another step. Much to his surprise, there is a very sharp piercing pain in his paw.

Ouch! What could possibly be wrong with my front paw because it really hurts? He finds it difficult to use his paw to walk. He realizes that he will never be able to walk far with only three paws. The very next attempt to step causes him to yelp again. He really is feeling a great deal of discomfort. He convinces himself, that the pain will go away if he rests for a while.

Looking ahead he spots an area with soft green grass. Using only three paws, and grimacing with each step. He carefully hobbles in the direction of the grass and lies down to rest. During this break he gently licks his paw trying to remove the object that is hurting him so much.

After a short rest, he feels less pain in his paw. He's feeling braver now so he tries to walk once again. *Ouch!* The pain is still there; he hangs his head, whines and whimpers. *What is going to happen to me? If I'm unable to walk, I will never find the new house and my human family.*

He senses he really does need help.

He chooses to sit again and rest longer, maybe he didn't rest long enough. Sitting on the shoulder of the road he raises his sore paw. He looks as if he is waiting to shake hands with the next passerby.

Sally – Chapter Two

"I'll wear what I want to wear. Stop! Just stop telling me what to do," Sally shouts at her mother, "I'll tattoo my body if I want, I hate you!"

"Sally, you do not hate anyone. I know it's difficult to understand. We love you and only want what is best for you," Lil reaches out in an attempt to calm her daughter.

"That's it," She put her hand up to show, stop; "I don't want to hear anymore. I'm out of here!" she shouts and runs out of the front door slamming it shut behind her.

She sprints down the wooden porch steps with peeling paint, almost tripping. She quickly grabs the handrail to prevent herself from falling flat on her face. That would be embarrassing.

"Why don't they just let me be?" She angrily mutters, "I would not argue if they just left me alone. Why do parents think they know everything? The last blowup we had was over a silly butterfly tattoo on my shoulder; this time, my choice of clothing. I don't get it. What's wrong with having cuts and holes in my jeans, everyone else does? Sally kicks hard at the gravel on the driveway to emphasize her displeasure. "After all it is my body. So what if my tattoos are there for the rest of my life. It *is* my life."

"I think I should just run away and start a new life." She gives an irritated sideways glance back at the house with a very angry glare to show her disdain.

Sally continues her musings, "Problem is I'll need money," she pauses for a moment then she says, "I have an idea. Maybe I'll take money from Mom's "rainy day fund." That can be my runaway fund." These musings put a little smirk on her face like she has a devious secret.

"It's time I got serious. I really do need to develop a plan," she ruminates while increasing her pace down the long gravel driveway to the road. Now she is walking with purpose as she wants to put her adversaries behind her as quickly as possible.

Sally continues to mutter emphasizing her points by waving her hands around, as she walks with determination. She soon makes her way to the Fourth Line, her usual route. "Who would not be failing at school? Who cares about school, anyway? So I've got poor marks! So what? Everybody knows school is a waste of time," she rolls her eyes back emphasizing her annoyance. "Just wait until I get a job."

Lil, Sally's mom said to her husband, "It is so hard to reason with her right now. I know we'll get through this. I've heard that rebellious teenagers often test and bend rules." She stood holding the coffee pot. "Coffee?" She asks Rob offering to pour, "You know Rob, we just need to, tell her of how much we love her."

About to pour the coffee, she hesitates holding the pot suspended. "Remember our easy going little girl, with her lovely blue eyes and long blonde curly hair – my how she stole hearts." Lil shakes herself out of her deep thought and pours Rob's coffee, as she thinks about their lives together. Rob has farming in his blood. "Rob, you and I, thrive on planting and harvesting our crops. I am so proud of you. You are such a hard-working person and a good provider for our family," Lil says then blushes at being so open about how she feels about Rob. She didn't verbalize about how much she loves his rugged complexion or his lean, hard body, which is proof of his many long days toiling the land, and operating machinery under the blazing hot sun.

"Lil, you also come from a long line of farmers and have lived on a farm your whole life. We both are down to earth folks. I think this is why we find it puzzling as to why Sally makes such strange choices," Rob says shaking his head side to side, still mystified about Sally's behavior this morning.

Lil says, "Right now we have the biggest challenge of our lives . . . a teenager! When I think about the problems we deal with daily over her behavior, clothing, tattooing, crazy styles and school. How do we prepare for any of this? Who knew raising a teenager would be this difficult?" Lil walks up behind Rob sitting at the table and comforts him by wrapping her arms around him and giving him a loving hug. She stands and sighs, "I'm not sure what to say or do anymore. We always end up in an argument. Here she is with multicolored hair red, green, blue and orange; it looks as if it got stuck in a mix master,"

Rob watches Lil deep in thought slowly making her way to the table, then sitting on the rigid kitchen chair. The old worn table surface scarred with scratches is covered with a bright yellow vinyl tablecloth. Bread crumbs from this morning's breakfast can still be seen scattered about. She brushes the crumbs away, and then places her elbows on their wooden table while hugging her warm morning coffee. She wraps both hands around the green mug more for comfort than warmth.

She is reflecting on the scene from earlier this morning. Absent mindedly she reaches down to her lap, and brings her well-worn apron, with faded red and blue flowers, to her face and wipes perspiration from her brow, "It's going to be a warm one today," Lil offers in a quiet distant voice while half-heartedly attempting to change the subject away from her daughter's awful behavior.

"Lil, you've got to admit she looks ridiculous. That weird makeup makes her look like a clown. Hopefully that will tone down soon," Rob adds as he takes another bite of toast smothered with Lil's fresh strawberry preserves.

Rob sat quiet for a few moments, then states. "I'm probably more worried about Sally than I really need to be, but raising a teenager is all new to us. I sometimes wonder if someone somewhere has written down a way to solve each problem as it happens."

Lil's eyes follow him as he put his dirty dishes in the sink. "Rob, please put them in the sink with the soapy water." Just saying his name brought a slight smile to her lips. She knows he is not a demonstrative man, but he has a heart of gold. All of their neighbors know they can count on Rob to help them.

"So far she does not have too many tattoos, but I hope she is not going to spitefully have more done," Lil worries, She is now standing at the kitchen sink with suds up to her elbows.

Rob asks, "Are you going to feed the chickens and collect their eggs after you finish washing the breakfast dishes?"

"Yes that's my normal daily routine," Lil answers, "It's my social time and I make a few dollars for my 'Rainy Day Fund' by selling our eggs to the neighbors."

Lil isn't ready to leave Sally as the topic, she changes the subject back, "Rob I think Sally spends far too much time in solitary confinement, in her bedroom — her personal prison. At least, she calms down after her walk," Lil ponders, "When she returns, she is much more relaxed and is willing to listen to reason. The walks certainly do her good. We must have faith that with some serious thinking, she will realize we are not the enemy. We need to believe that we have taught her to make smart choices," Lil worries.

"Lil you agonize too much over Sally," Rob adds.

Sally – Chapter Three

Sally's thoughts are interrupted, when she looks up and sees a black and white dog limping towards her. She stops in her tracks. She fears that the dog might be dangerous. Sally can see the dog is hurt so she decides to approach it very cautiously.

Ben is startled by a weird looking girl approaching him. Sniffing the air, Ben does not sense any danger, but he thinks that he'll still need to be careful as she approaches him. He hopes this girl with the bizarre hair, will help him.

This young person as funny as she looks, Ben senses, is sad and in need of a friend.

He limps towards her wagging his tail to show he is friendly. Then Ben sits down, raises his paw and whimpers.

Sally thinks, he appears to be friendly enough. He didn't growl at me. I'll put my hand out to show him that I'm friendly too.

Sniffing her hand, Ben senses safety. Still sitting he moves his body a little bit closer.

Sally says, "Well aren't you are the friendliest little guy? You like it when I pat your head. Yes, you are very friendly."

Sally strokes his head and back until she feels it is safe to move even closer, "I can tell you are a well-trained dog, plus you are thoroughly enjoying this attention, aren't you fella," Sally says with a smile in her voice.

He frantically wags his tail while wiggling his body turning in circles and then he licks her face in agreement.

"What's wrong boy? Maybe you'll let me touch your paw. Let me see what's causing you so much pain. Can I have a closer look?" she asks, as she gently lifts and inspects his paw.

"Your paw looks so sore, "Sally sees the sharp piece of glass then adds, "No wonder you are in such pain, there's glass stuck between the pads. It looks to me like you might be getting an infection too. Good boy, no, I will not hurt you," Sally says in a soft crooning voice trying to make friends.

Ben likes the sound of her voice. He is now rolling over onto his back so Sally can rub his tummy.

"You must belong to someone because you are way too well groomed to be a stray. I think, someone, has been taking excellent care of you. I wonder who you belong to."

Just then she notices the metallic blue tag on his collar. She reads it out loud, "So your name is Ben."

He recognizes his name. Hearing her say, Ben gets him extremely excited. He gets the feeling of belonging. He's back up on three paws so he can wiggle, twist and twirl his body in circles as if his body is being controlled by his violently wagging tail. He is conscious of being extremely careful to keep his injured paw slightly elevated. He gives Sally lots and lots of sloppy kisses, making her face unusually wet.

Sally uses her sleeve as a towel to dry her face.

Carefully she picks him up and cradles him in her arms. Soon she realizes he is getting heavy, and her arms are now aching from his weight.

She amazes herself that she has such stamina. Sally carries him all of the way home.

Ben is comforted and doesn't resist.

Never having been a dog owner or even taken care of a dog before, Sally is unsure what to do next. She is sure of one thing though. Her mom will know what to do.

Sally – Chapter Four

Still carrying Ben in her throbbing achy arms, she burst into their kitchen.

Sally immediately pleads with her mother, “Mommy, Mommy, please help . . . please. I found this poor dog limping over on the Fourth Line near the Simpson’s place. Look he has a piece of glass stuck in his paw. He is in an awful lot of pain. He can only walk on three paws. His name is Ben. Mommy he is very friendly, and he likes me a lot. Please take the glass out.”

Lil is extremely happy, with the surprising, change, in Sally’s demeanor this morning. “Sally, put him down, he must be heavy,” she could see that Sally was straining to carry him, “I’ll try. Please get my tweezers from the bathroom medicine cabinet.”

Sally ran to the bathroom. It took only thirty seconds and she was back, “Here’s the tweezers, Mommy, please take it out,” Sally appeals again to her Mom.

Lil attempts several different times approaching from various angles to remove the glass, but she is unsuccessful. Lil looks closer and notices there is redness where the glass pierced the thick skin of his paw. She worries that this means the beginning of an infection, she suggests, "Sally, I think we should take Ben to town and have Dr. Palmer our veterinarian have a look at his paw."

Sally can see that Mom cares about Ben too. This makes her happy as she feels that for the first time, in a very long time, they have something in common.

Lil is delighted, with the way Sally is taking charge of this little emergency situation. She gets a warm, mushy feeling inside, as tears well up in her warm brown eyes. She smiles inwardly because she likes and misses this Sally.

"Sally, I have a little money I put away for a rainy day; I don't mind using that money to pay the vet. I don't like to see any animal hurt, so let's get this poor dog to the vet," Lil insists.

Sally shrugs and thinks there goes the money for my Runaway Fund. Mother's savings will pay for the vet, and I don't mind one bit. I don't need the run away money, right now anyway.

Sally asks, "Do we need to make an appointment or can we just go to the emergency clinic?"

She knows that she is asking a lot from her family as they are not well off financially. Really she is asking her mom to spend her hard earned egg money, on a dog they don't even know. Sally tries to act as sweet and pleasant as she knows how.

"This looks like an emergency to me," Lil says while scooping up Ben and carrying him to their car. She carefully places Ben on the back seat. Lil smiles at Ben, and then says, "You are a large dog, Ben. You take up the whole seat."

For Sally the drive to the vet took forever, she is anxious to have the vet remove the glass and Ben to be free from pain. She turns in her seat and fondly looks back at Ben. He is happy sitting contentedly on the soft green and blue plaid blanket covering the back seat. Sally watches him and smiles, it is a perfect picture. Her mind's eye took a photo of Ben's head sticking out of the window. He appears to be laughing with his tongue dangling out of the side of his mouth. Wisps of his hair and ears are freely blowing in the breeze. He looks so happy and relaxed. There's something truly calming about this picture for Sally. She is pleased with herself and the good deed she is doing for this unfamiliar injured animal.

"Sally do you remember Dr. Palmer?" Lil asks.

"All I remember about him is how tall he was or maybe that is because I was so small, when he came to the farm, when our cow Bessie had twin calves. We needed his help for the birthing. That was several years ago, I think," replies Sally.

"Goodness me, that was at least 7 years ago. You're right he is all of six feet plus maybe three more inches. He is older now as he is balding, but other than that he is the same good natured Dr. Palmer," Lil adds.

"I do remember how kind he was with Bessie and her twins. She did not want him to touch the twins once they were out of her. She got real mad at him," Sally remembers. "I think she actually charged at him at one point."

"Yes, moms are very possessive of their young ones," Lil was actually thinking, animals are no different than humans in that respect.

At the Clinic they register with the receptionist. They are told to have a seat in the waiting room. Sitting on the uncomfortable metal folding chair makes the wait to see the vet, feel longer than it actually is.

Ben is apprehensive as he has previously been to see his vet with his human family. He remembers the sharp prick of a needle on earlier visits. This thought causes Ben to shiver with fear.

Finally Ben's name is called by the pleasant receptionist with dull gray hair knotted at the back of her head, "Sally, Dr. Palmer will see Ben now."

"Let's go Ben, Dr. Palmer will make your paw feel better," Sally says holding his leash tight and comforting the trembling dog. Sally and Ben walk with varying degrees of apprehension into the examination room.

Upon entering the room, with Dr. Palmer's assistance they lift Ben up onto the antiseptic smelling stainless steel table, "Hello Dr. Palmer," she says.

"Hello Sally, who have we got here?" he asks.

"His name is Ben." She responds.

Sally picks up Ben's leg to show him the glass that is wedged between the pads on his paw. "Can you remove this piece of glass, please?" Sally asks with a very worried frown. She then put his paw back onto the cool steel table, while wrapping her arms around Ben, giving him a comforting hug.

After a cursory examination Dr. Palmer says, "Now that looks painful Ben. How about we fix that paw for you?" he calms Ben with several pats on his head and tousling of his ears.

"I found Ben limping over on the Fourth Line," She adds while patting him.

"Sally, we always worry about unfamiliar animals, so I need to ask some questions. "By any chance, do you know anything about him? I wish I knew if his shots are up to date," he knows the answer, but he asks the question anyway.

"No, sorry Dr. Palmer, I do not know anything about him," Sally replies then remembers, "But he does have a name tag, that shows his Rabies are up to date," she quickly adds picking up the metallic name tag to show the Doctor.

His face lit up at the site of the rabies tag, then states, "With his rabies vaccinations up to date, even though it is a long shot, we should check to see if Ben has a microchip." He takes a small hand held machine out of the top drawer in the examination room cabinet. While holding the device in his hand, he tells Sally, "This is a small gadget that needs to be held close to Ben's neck. Let's see if we can find a microchip," He shows the lit up screen with Sally. "Look do you see that number? This is excellent news. He does have a microchip. These are his personal numbers. His regular vet will give us his contact information so we can let his owners know where he is, and then they can come pick him up. If necessary we can also check his number against the National Registry."

Dr. Palmer puts on his reading glasses and reels off the numbers to his receptionist, Joanne. "The presence of a chip tells us that Ben belongs to someone who actually cares enough about him to have this procedure done," he tells Sally.

Joanne, contacts the listed vet's office who after she identifies herself, willingly gives her the owners name, address and telephone number.

Unfortunately, when she calls the number, the recording states the phone line has been disconnected. She also tries Directory Assistance to see if there is a new telephone number, but there is not.

I am unable to tell them. I know the way to the new house. I was on my way there when I stepped on the glass.

Disappointed with the bad news, Dr. Palmer frowns and refocuses his attention on the sore paw. He looks up over top of his magnifying glasses at Sally and says, "First I will use an antiseptic pad to clean the sore spot. Then I'll use these medium size sterile tweezers to remove the glass. They are sharp and should do the job, but it may hurt Ben. Hold him tight now. I don't want him to try to jump down or pull away too quickly and cause himself more pain or an injury."

Sally tightly holds Ben against her body and speaks softly to him, "It's okay Ben, please be brave." She watches closely as Dr. Palmer easily pulls the glass out.

Ben reacted to the sharp pain when the glass is removed. He tries to pull back his paw from the Doctor's hand. That hurt him and he whimpers to tell Sally. But Sally held his leg tightly in place, with all her strength, just like she was instructed.

Then Dr. Palmer says, "I hope there are no chards of glass left behind. I didn't see any. Now I will apply a salve to the infected area and a wrapping. Watch me carefully, and then you'll know how to change his dressing tomorrow. The bandage is carefully applied, quickly and efficiently by the seasoned vet.

Dr. Palmer removes a few packages from a white cabinet on the wall of the examination room. He turns and hands them to Sally and then says, "Here take these sterile dressings. You will need to change Ben's bandages every day for a few days. Because he is a dog, his bandages will get very dirty."

"Sally, I would like you to carefully check his paw every time you change the dressing, as it might get inflamed or re-infected. That will mean there is either still glass or maybe dirt is in the wound. It is important that you bring him back to me if that happens," Dr. Palmer looks directly at Sally to emphasize the importance of her following his instructions.

The Vet unlocks the other wall cabinet with his key then removes a small bottle of antibiotics. He took out one pill, then turns and says, "Sally this is how you give a pill to a dog." Dr. Palmer holds Ben's mouth open then pops a pill into the back of his throat and with a downward motion brushes the fur on his neck until he sees Ben swallow. "There, did you see him swallow the pill?"

"Yes I did. That looks really easy," she replies, now full of confidence.

"Here take three of these antibiotic pills," he put them in a small envelope and hands them to Sally, then continues with his instructions. "You need to give Ben one each day. With your good care the sore will heal and not get re-infected," he is now confident that the young caregiver is trained to perform the simple procedures.

"Thank you so much for the lessons Dr. Palmer and for taking such good care of Ben," She looks down at him, pats him on the head, and says, "You appreciate his good care too, don't you," Sally smiles at Dr. Palmer and Ben, "I'm feeling confident that nursing him will be pretty easy."

The Vet tousles Ben's ears and says, "Ben you have been an excellent patient. Did you know we give treats to our best behaved patients? I'm happy to say you qualify. Here's a couple of treats for you."

Ben gobbles up the treats, nuzzles the vet's hand, looking for more, and then licks his chops in appreciation.

"Good boy, Ben." Sally praises.

Ben thinks his paw feels better already. He walks almost like normal to the car sporting a bright white bandage on his front black paw. He is able to jump up onto the back seat without pain.

Mom drives them home – the mood is happy and content.

Sally – Chapter Five

Sally's a terrific nurse. She changes my dressings every day and makes sure I have my pills on schedule. I heard her family praise her on her commitment to getting me healthy again.

A couple of days later during dinner Rob chats with Sally, "You are taking darn good care of Ben, Sally, I think you have a natural talent for caring for animals. Maybe you can get a job as a technician that assists a Veterinary Doctor. You might think about that especially if you haven't decided what you want to do when you graduate from High School."

"That feels strange as I have not been planning on graduating. I'm probably failing nearly every subject," Sally confesses, dropping her head in shame and embarrassment.

A few moments later, Sally lifts her head, furrows her brow and asks, "Dad, do you really believe that I will be able to graduate? Hmmm, that is certainly an idea I can consider. I do like nursing Ben. I did get a good feeling making him feel better. You're right. I would like working with dogs and cats, not so much the other creatures like snakes, lizards, skunks, and such," Sally's whole body shivers at the mere thought of treating sick snakes and lizards. She now demonstrates enthusiasm both in her face and voice.

Sally spends most of her free time with me. She rushes home from school, quickly finishes her homework and all of her chores without being asked.

They play every day on the grass in the large yard. She throws a ball, or a Frisbee, sticks, bones or anything that is handy and he runs like the wind trying to catch it before it lands. Most times he grabs it in the air with his strong teeth, and then proudly trots back to her. Then she throws it again. They truly are excellent playmates and are genuinely fond of each other.

After dinner a few days later, while slowly swaying in the green canopy covered swing, Rob and Lil are contently rocking while holding hands and enjoying the star studded sky. Appreciating the mood, Lil shares her thoughts about the recent changes in Sally, "She has changed into a truly likeable sweet gal. I'm so proud of her. I had a talk with her teacher yesterday; he was curious about the reason behind this total about-face in her attitude in general and her studies."

Looking at Rob, she shyly smiles then relates her conversation with Sally's teacher. "Mr. Holmes, as you know, is her home room teacher, he has a good reputation as an outstanding teacher who always has his students' best interest at heart. He's a short, small boned man; I'm guessing this makes him much less intimidating to the students. He tells everyone, his gray hair and balding head was earned, as a result of some of his more challenging pupils. Sally tells me that his trademark is his colorful argyle style sweater vests. She says that he has hundreds of them, an overstatement I'm sure. She says he wears them every day, year round," Lil continues with a little chuckle.

"Mr. Holmes told me that, Sally is now on track to graduate. She's actually working very hard on her school work. Believe it or not, she's doing this all on her own initiative. I like that she is also mending fences with the students that she has been rude to in the past." Lil sits a little straighter as she proudly holds her head high and she shares the conversation with her husband.

"Rob I found this part of our meeting very interesting. Mr. Holmes tilted his head forward looking at me over his cheater glasses," Lil mimics him by looking at Rob over her glasses pulled halfway down her nose. She giggles, but looking very serious now she continues their conversation, "He then asked if I knew that Sally recently met with her Career Counselor? They talked about colleges that offer courses in animal care, and how to prepare for her College entrance exams."

Rob's face lit up as if a light was turned on, and then said, "Oh, okay, that explains why she was checking out colleges on the computer yesterday. I like the remarkable change we are seeing in Sally. This seems to be all as a result of her having her own pet to care for. Amazing! Truly amazing! I never would have thought that having a pet could change someone so much."

Lil continues relating details of her meeting with Mr. Holmes. "I briefly recapped the story of Ben. How, Sally found an injured dog, and is taking excellent care of him, nursing him back to health and so on."

Lil frowns and carefully prepares her next comment to Rob, hesitantly she adds, "I think we should tell Sally that she can keep Ben, if this is something she would like to do, of course. What do you think?" She is not sure how Rob feels about having a non-working animal around the farm.

Rob smiles, reaches over and gently squeezes her shoulder then states, "If having our sweet daughter in a good mood and working hard on her studies is the result, I am in favor of her getting a dog. Heck she can have two dogs if she wants."

Lil, smiles then proudly replies with obvious pleasure, "I knew you would agree with me. Sally is so easy to get along with now. There are no more arguments over silly things, plus she is no longer angry at the world. I cross my fingers," she said, holding up both hands and crossing two fingers on each hand, "I hope that we are past that bump in the road."

"Mommy, I have exhausted all leads on the Internet for state and county animal control, plus dog rescue groups," Sally looking sad shares the results with her mother, "Some people are searching for lost dogs, but not Ben. I did so hope his family reported him missing but every lead just ends up in a dead end."

"Mommy if or when Ben decides to leave I would like to adopt a rescue dog," she thoughtfully confesses hoping her mother will agree.

"I think that would be a good thing to do. You will have your own special pet," Lil says in agreement.

My paw is now totally healed. So once again, I am plagued with those choices; do I stay with this wonderful caregiver and playmate or continue my journey. The pressure to continue my journey is enormous, again.

Later that day, Sally bravely had a tearful chat with him, "Ben, I'll miss you so much if you leave. I realize that you belong to someone else. I honestly hope you find them, she starts to cry. I'm ready to let you go with my blessing." She could no longer hold back the flood of tears that run like rivers down her cheeks. Sally is weeping and blubbering totally out of control.

She hugs him and kisses him, then hugs him some more, soaking his fur and nose with her salty tears.

Ben sits up straight. His ears are standing at attention as he tilts his head to one side then the other trying to understand what Sally is saying, through her heart wrenching sobs. He senses she realizes it is time for him to resume his journey. He wishes he could say, *Sally it's okay. Thank you for taking such good care of me. You are a wonderful caregiver but I must find my family.*

Ben rubs his face against Sally's arm, hand and face several times. He is trying to show his affection for her and appreciation of her love, the best way that he can. Then with a very sloppy wet tongue he licks the full length of her face, covering her chin, cheek and forehead with his saliva, a souvenir. They hug for quite some time as if neither one wants to let go of the other.

Next morning Ben approaches Sally while she is sitting at the kitchen table, eating breakfast. He rests a paw and his head on her lap. He looks up at her with his sad brown eyes. He is trying to say, *I am leaving today, good bye.*

She stokes his head and wonders if he will be here when she returns from school this afternoon.

In a tense silence, Sally and Ben walk side by side down the long driveway. He sits beside Sally on the shoulder of the road while she quietly waits for her school bus. There's no chatting this morning. As she boards the bus, she turns and looks back at him. He sees her eyes are filled with tears. He is confident that she knows. He sits frozen on the spot as he watches the bus drive away and disappear over the horizon.

He stands, turns, and slowly walks in the other direction, to resume his journey.

JENNY BOOK FOUR

Jenny – Chapter One

Ben is trotting along enjoying the morning sun that's playing peek-a-boo with the soft fluffy clouds that are slowly floating across the sky. A very light breeze blows against shiny green trees causing hundreds of leaves to cover the ground dampened by the morning dew. There is freshness in the air that only occurs in the tranquility of first dawn.

Ben is thinking he has had enough excitement to last him quite a while. He just wants a few uneventful days. Although it was hard to leave Sally, Ben's thoughts turn to his human family, which he senses he is nearing.

Ben's thoughts are interrupted by a stressed voice in the distance calling. "Help . . . Help me . . . Please I'm trapped."

He stops, cocks his head from one side to the other side. He intently listens, trying to determine where the voice is coming from.

There, it is again. "Help! Help! Can anyone hear me?"

Curiosity peaked; Ben perks up his ears and listens more closely, and then sniffs the air for something, anything that will guide him in the direction of the stressed voice.

And again, "Help! Please help! I need help." This time Ben gets a bead on the voice and heads in that direction. He thinks it's coming from down the ravine. *Why would someone be way down there*?

Jenny – Chapter Two

Alone in her shiny red car, Jenny had no idea what was in store for her, today. She is singing with considerable enthusiasm to her favorite Allan Jackson country song. "You do not have to love me anymore." The stereo is cranked up and the music is blasting out over the quiet, early morning countryside. Between songs, she is remembering last night's party. She thoroughly enjoyed talking to and dancing with the new guy, Ricky; she likes him a lot. They spent quality time together at the party. She smiles as she gets warm happy feelings when she thinks about him; he is already starting to get into her head. She would really like to see Ricky again.

Suddenly she is blinded by the head lights of a vehicle in her lane heading directly towards her. A thought flashes through her mind; is this how I die?

Her instincts take control of both her physical and mental reactions. Everything seems to be happening in slow motion and completely out of her control. The oncoming vehicle clips the right front fender with a bone chilling crack, which causes her car to swerve towards the left shoulder then totally out of control; it sprints, like a frightened deer, down the ravine.

Jenny fights with the steering wheel desperately trying to regain control of her car, but that proves to be impossible. The journey down the ravine is the most terrifying ride she's ever experienced, much scarier than any roller coaster at the county fair. The continuous bumping, banging, and shaking make her wonder if this will ever stop. The speed of the downhill momentum force bounces her car off trees and bushes. Her car shakes and rattles like a tin can as it zigzags over rocks and shrubbery. Just when she thinks it's over, the car commences rolling again. Jenny totally loses her bearings. She is not sure exactly which direction she is facing.

Most frightening is the uncertainty of what will happen next. Her brain scrambles as she wonders if the gas is leaking and will it start a fire. Praying this will not happen, the car jerks down again. Then an extremely loud crunching sound fills her ears as the car finally hits a large tree which causes a jolt, and the car finally stops. At least it is upright.

Jenny is groggy and not sure if she has lost consciousness. What she does know for sure, is she has fireworks going off in her head. Trying to think, she attempts to guesstimate her location, but to no avail. "Where am I?" she questions, as she hasn't the foggiest recollection of how she got here. "Am I still alive?" she asks herself. She pinches her leg to check. Oh, she's alive all right, and in a lot of pain and bleeding.

She has seen movies showing similar sequences where the car actually exploded. Panic set in. "I need to escape before I'm burned alive. Terror fills her gut as she frantically struggles to get out of the car. She pushes against the driver's door again and again, but it will not open. She struggles to reach over to the passenger door but the seatbelt is jammed. She is trapped.

It takes a few minutes for the reality of the situation to sink into her muddled mind. Her beautiful new red car is firmly jammed between two large Maple trees. She is being held, hostage in her car by both trees.

She has an enormous headache, her vision is blurred, plus her forehead is bleeding from hitting her head against the steering wheel too many times. She wonders why the air bag did not activate and begins to pray for help. She could not see the road from her cracked windshield and wonders how will help find her.

Searching for her cell phone, she discovers that it's not where she placed it. Actually, nothing is where it should be. The jammed seatbelt continues to imprison her.

Jenny manages to wiggle and squirm, the pain reminding her how hurt she is, and finally maneuvers herself so if she stretches out her arm as far as she dare, she can just barely touch her cell phone with her fingertips. Carefully Jenny pulls it closer, first with the tip of one finger, then two until she has it close enough to pick it up between two fingers. Immediately she calls home. No answer. She assumes her parents have already left to work in the fields of their farm. And since they do not own a cell phone, they are no longer reachable.

She tries calling a few friends. But, no one is home. She watches in frustration as the bars on her cell phone fade then completely disappear.

She decides to yell; hopefully loud enough, just maybe someone will hear her and come to her rescue. But who will hear me way down here? She wonders. She knows the area around where her car traveled into the ravine. Knowing no one walks on these county roads, especially this early in the day. And she realizes that this time of the morning, the air is so crisp, most drivers would have their windows rolled up. The more she thinks about it the more despondent she feels.

What do I have to lose? Rethinking her situation and getting her bearings, Jenny begins shouting for help. After calling out time and time again, she feels exhausted and slumps down into her seat. This is hopeless; what will happen to me?

With her last breath, she calls out, “Help! Help! Can anyone hear me?” Her voice is fainter now as she fades into semi-consciousness.

Jenny – Chapter Three

Ben carefully navigates his way through the tall grass and the rough overgrown brush heading towards the location he believes is the source of the pleas for help. A few times, broken branches scratch Ben's side. But bravely he keeps his head up, ducking and darting, trying not to injure his face or eyes. At last, he clears the greenery and sees a red car squashed between two trees near more broken bushes. The stressed voice he heard was barely audible now. However, Ben's sharp senses determine the pleas are coming from the damaged red car. His inquisitive mind overrides any fear he feels.

Ben looks through a broken window where he sees a young girl's pale face with streaky red ribbons of blood dripping down her cheeks to her neck. Of course, Ben has no idea how critical her injuries are, but he does sense from the looks of the sleeping girl, that she is undeniably in serious trouble.

Jenny regains consciousness and blinks. When she looks up she sees a black and white dog. Rolling her eyes back, she is visibly disappointed. Just my dumb luck; my rescuer is a dog. "Well, he is the only help I have right now. My life may depend on making this dog, understand. I must have faith, that he is able to sense the urgency, of my predicament," She mumbles to herself.

Reluctantly, Jenny puts her trust in the dog. She begins speaking to him softly, "Please, boy, bring someone to help me. Go for help, please. Go boy, go find someone to help." Jenny's voice grew fainter. She instantly thought about an old TV show where the star collie understood everything the adults said to him. I wonder if this dog will.

Ben did understand some – at least he recognizes the word help. And he could surmise the urgency – this combination set his senses into high gear. He barks a couple of times to show he understands. Then he navigates his way back up to the road. Earlier this morning he had traveled through a small town. That would be the quickest place for him to get help. He runs as fast as possible, back in that direction. He is not sure what he's looking for, but he believes he will know. One thing he does know; he needs to find a human to help.

Jenny – Chapter Four

As Ben is running along the road, he sees a large black truck. The black truck begins to turn off the road and drives into a garage parking lot. Ben sees the man get out of his truck. Throwing caution to the wind, Ben runs as quickly as he possibly can. He is panting heavily. Upon approaching the stranger, Ben hopes first, that the man is friendly, and second, that he can make the man understand.

Jared does not recognize Ben as one of the local dogs. Now he, too, is cautious at seeing this unfamiliar, but fairly well groomed dog running at breakneck speed towards him. His first thought is to grab something to defend himself. But something about the dog makes him hesitate. Jared does not sense anything menacing from the animal, and somehow the way the dog's ears flap, Jared is no longer afraid.

Ben thinks in order to make it clear to the man that he need not fear me *I'll playfully dance around his legs, furiously wagging my tail. Once I hear friendly tones and words then I'll know the man is friendly too.*

Jared tries to figure out what is going on. Why this dog is barking, running up to me and grabbing my pant leg with his teeth. He's exhibiting such urgency. After watching the dog's performance for just a moment, he recognizes the actions of the dog.

"Okay fella," Jared speaks firmly. "You are certainly a persistent guy. I get the message. I'll follow you."

When he jogs towards his truck, Ben settles down. Jared realizes he has no idea how far the dog is taking him or what he will find when he gets there. In spite of that, he hoists himself into his truck and tries to encourage the dog to get into the cab; but that was not going to happen. Ben barks to the man, letting him know he will lead the truck and not be in it. He trots on the shoulder of the road, just ahead of Jared's truck, and looking back every so often ensuring he is still following him. Ben is taking him out of town about half a mile.

Ben finally reaches the place where he first remembers the cries for help. He leaves the road and starts down the ravine, sniffing all of the way; he is able to follow his own scent. Ben constantly looks back making sure Jared is close behind. His barking and prancing in circles and his body language clearly indicates an even greater sense of urgency. He impresses upon Jared to keep following him.

The seriousness of the situation is now abundantly clear to Jared. He jumps out of the truck cab and calls to the dog, "Hold on fella, I'm coming." Jared plots his route through the broken trees and flattened bushes. Navigation is very difficult but he carefully hurries down the hill.

Jared gasps with horror when he sees the vehicle jammed between the trees. Winded, Jared shouts with sincere concern, “Hello. Are you okay? Are you hurt?”

Silence.

Jared approaches the car where through the broken glass and cracked windshield he sees the occupant. There is blood everywhere and the lovely young girl is unconscious. Jared looks closer at the girl’s face. He takes a step back as he is shocked. He recognizes Jenny, who is his neighbor Jack Wilson’s daughter. My God, she looks fatally injured. He checks for a pulse, but cannot locate one. He turns to the dog, and holding up his right hand he says, “Stay.”

Jared runs back up the ravine to his truck. He pulls out his cell phone and nervously dials 911. Once Jared speaks to the operator and relays the urgency of the situation and the location to the operator, he carefully drives his truck down the ravine to the mangled car. He is hesitant to move the wreck before the EMS team arrives. He wants to be ready if needed.

Ben waits patiently, but paces back and forth.

Jared walks over to the accident scene to check on Jenny, again. He still doesn’t see any sign of life. While waiting for the ambulance, he pats Ben and tells him, "You're a smart dog. What's your name? Let me see your tag." Ben sits up tall to allow the man to read his tag. "So, Ben is your name. Hello Ben. I'm Jared. You're a pretty clever dog."

Ben responds with a happy bark as if to say, "Yes, I know that. Ben licks Jared's face then rubs his face on his arm showing his appreciation. Jared caringly strokes Ben's head and back. Ben is happy.

Remembering Jenny, Jared says to Ben, "I have known her for most of her life. She's been a very happy girl with lots of energy, and a willing helper around her parent's farm. I sure hope they can save her. If not, her parents will be devastated."

Jared fidgets and anxiously waits for help. At last he hears a siren in the distance, and jogs back up to the road. He is certain that he can show the EMS the quickest way to Jenny. They've got to save Jenny's life.

Jenny – Chapter Five

The ambulance screams while red lights flash. Jared flags down the EMS and indicates the need for speed. Two men from emergency grab their gear and stretcher, and quickly follow Jared. "I can't find a pulse on Jenny." Jared calls to them.

"How do you know her name?" one of them asks.

"She's my neighbor's daughter, Jenny Wilson. I believe she is about sixteen year's old," Jared responds.

When they arrive at the wrecked car, everyone is surprised to see that Ben has climbed into the car through the broken window and is covering Jenny with his body in order to keep her warm.

"Is this your dog, or hers?" EMS Ken asks pointing. He explains, "Sometimes an injured owner's dog can be very protective when their master is hurt."

"No, he does not belong to either of us, but he did bring me here. I have never seen him before this morning. By his collar, I learned his name is Ben," Jared explains.

"Thank you Ben," says EMS Ken.

“You did a great job of taking care of our patient,” says Henry, the other EMS. Both men work as quickly as they can. After a cursory examination, they learn that Jenny has a faint pulse and is already in shock. Gently, but quickly, they move Ben from Jenny’s body. And through the same broken window, they administer oxygen, which begins to stabilize her, but she is in grave condition.

Jared hooks his tow truck to the axle of Jenny’s wedged car. The men are talking, trying to come up with the best way to get the girl out of the car. EMS Ken says, “Carefully pull the car, but watch us closely. We must prevent additional damage to our patient.”

Cautiously pulling the car, Jared entices it to freedom. This creates more crunching and tearing of the car’s body. Jared is frowning, and keeps asking, “Everything okay?”

“Yes, just a little bit more,” EMS Ken says. “Pull gently, not too fast. Okay great—stop there.” He motions by holding up his clenched fist and thumb in the upright position. Once free, they have full access to their patient. Ken and Henry start an intravenous drip and carefully, as only experienced EMS attendants can, brace Jenny’s back and neck.

“I’ll pry open the car door using the truck, so it will be easier to move your patient to a stretcher,” Jared offers.

“Thanks. She’s barely alive so the easier it is to move her, the less additional trauma we will inflict,” EMS Henry explains.

Jared said, "If you like, I can help you back up the hill to the ambulance by attaching the truck winch to the underside of the stretcher."

"Wow, that's an excellent idea! We were just wondering how we were going to get Jenny on the stretcher and all this equipment back up that hill." Both EMS Ken and Henry sigh with relief.

Jared adds, "The obstacle course up the ravine will be really challenging with all the bushes and small trees in the way. With the truck bearing most of the weight on the uphill grind, all you need to do is firmly strap in your patient and guide the stretcher. Put your bags and equipment in the cab of my truck beside Ben, then you will have your hands free."

EMS Henry replies feeling encouraged, "We really are grateful for your intuitive thinking and good plan. Now we can concentrate on preventing Jenny from bouncing around too much."

"Right now we are most concerned about possible internal injuries," says EMS Ken, "because so far she's not responding the way we would like."

The trip back up the ravine was hazardous, but with the tow truck taking the full weight by pulling the stretcher uphill, it appears Jenny is not hurt by it.

A few times EMS Ken shouts, "Jared stop! We need to pull branches out of the way of the wheels, de-cluttering the path for the stretcher." The three men could not imagine making this trip without Jared's truck and the EMS equipment, with Jenny securely strapped to the stretcher. Impossible would be the best description!

When they reach the road, Jared and Ben watch as they hurriedly put the stretcher into the ambulance and close the back doors. They speed away, clearing traffic in their path, with their siren shrieking and flashing lights. Speed and safety are their priorities as they transport Jenny to the local emergency hospital, Casper County Regional Urgent Care.

Time is imperative to save Jenny's life.

Jenny – Chapter Six

Jared gets into his truck, and punches Jack Wilson's number into his iPod. After several rings, Jack answers, "Hello Jack, this is Jared. I'm sorry to be the one to tell you, but there's been an accident. Jenny has been taken, by ambulance, to the County Hospital."

"Oh no! How seriously is she injured?" Jack questions nervously.

Jared thinks it would be better if he didn't speculate on the seriousness of Jenny's injuries. Knowing she went by ambulance should be enough to convey urgency. "I don't know. After you see her, please call me at the garage. I'll fill you in on what I know," Jared adds, trying to reassure Jack.

"Thanks Jared, Jack responds. I'll call you later for details, but I need to get going right now. Thank you so much." With concern and anxiety, Jenny's mother, Ester and father, quickly but silently, drive their truck to the hospital, not knowing what to expect and fearing the worse.

Awaiting news from Jenny's parents, Jared takes Ben back to his shop, this time Ben is happy to sit on the front seat of the large black tow truck. "Thanks to you, Ben, we have already had a very busy day, and it is not even noon."

When they arrive at the garage, in a gesture of appreciation, Jared offers Ben half of his lunch, a delicious roast beef sandwich on soft freshly baked bread. "Here boy you probably worked up an appetite with your good deed this morning."

Ben accepts the food which he eats in two gulps. Then he laps up lots of water spraying it in every direction. He slobbers the excess water on the floor of the garage. Feeling nourished, and happy with his newest friend, he finds a cozy place to rest, while watching Jared tinker with a car.

Jenny – Chapter Seven

When Jenny regains consciousness, her parents are at her bedside. Doctor Martin tells Jenny and her parents, "Jenny's injuries are serious but for the most part, non-life threatening, mostly abrasions, bumps and large bruises. You also have a couple of cracked ribs which should be less painful in a couple of weeks. But, you do have a serious head injury from hitting the steering wheel extremely hard, probably several times. You were unconscious and in shock from the trauma when admitted."

Dr. Martin looks directly at Jenny's parents and says, "As a precaution, we want to keep her in hospital for at least a couple more nights for observation in order to make sure there are no lingering effects, from the concussion." He also tells them, "We believe that if she were left there much longer, she certainly would have died due to the severity of the head wound and the massive loss of blood."

"Thank you Doctor Martin," Mr. Wilson said as he shakes hands with him, showing true appreciation in his voice.

Jenny – Chapter Eight

Mr. Wilson calls Jared and reports, "Jenny is going to be okay. Her injuries are serious but not life threatening. She is alive and hopefully there will be no long term effects from her injuries; most importantly she will recover. Thank you so much. How can we ever thank you enough for saving our daughter's life?"

Jared relates his experiences from that morning and about the heroic dog's actions. "According to his tag, your hero's name is Ben."

"Can dogs really do that? If I wasn't living this story I would say you are joshing me. We are very anxious to meet this super hero dog. We also would like to learn more about Jenny's accident. Do you, mind if we come by the garage to meet our daughter's guardian angel?"

"Not at all, I'm here until six today. It doesn't look like Ben has any place to go right now. Though," Jared shares, "He may wander off later."

Mr. Wilson again expresses his appreciation. "We are very grateful and would like to meet Ben to let him know how appreciative we are."

"I'll be here. See ya later," Jared responds and hangs up.

While driving to Matt's Motor Repair Garage where Jared performs his magic the Wilsons chat about Jared.

"You know, Jared is a legend to the folks of Casper County. I have heard that people up to fifty miles away have him on speed dial." Ester said making idle conversation with Jack, mostly to keep her mind off the trauma of this morning's event.

Jack in the same vein of trivial conversation, says, "I know for sure he is a genius with motors of all sizes and states of ill repair. He thrives on trouble-shooting and making motors run like new. Jared tells people that the rhythmic hum of a purring engine is music to his ears." Jack smiles as he thinks about his good neighbor Jared.

"What I know for sure is that he falls into the hero category for me now," Ester adds.

They both fall silent, deep in thought for the remainder of the drive to Matt's Garage. They are emotionally drained.

Ester desperately trying to keep her emotions under control is staring out of the window in a daze.

Jack and Ester Wilson arrive at the garage about twenty minutes later. Their first impression of the garage is organized confusion. Even so, they bet that Jared knows where every wrench, hose, belt and connector can be found. "Hello Jared," Jack shouts over the roaring engine and other clanking garage noises. Jared's sanctuary consists of nineteen foot high ceilings and twelve foot tall roll-up garage doors. The doors display twenty four inch squares of dirty glass panes that let in little sunshine but keep rain out. The multiple rows of fluorescent lights that flicker at odd intervals are the only other source of light.

Alarmed, Jared jumps out from under the hood of an old Chevy, and says, "Hi. You startled me. I'm so happy that Jenny's okay." Jared wears his uniform of khaki grease-stained coveralls and his billed cap, which he wears backwards; it's his trademark.

"That's your rescue dog, Ben," Jared offers, pointing at Ben with the wrench in his grease-smeared hand.

Ben greets the new visitors with his tail wagging. He shares many sloppy wet kisses.

"Ben," says Ester, "That is a name we'll not soon forget. You are a terrific dog and smart too. I bet whoever owns you is desperately looking for you," Mrs. Wilson croons to Ben while patting him and scratching his ears.

Jared shares what he knows about the accident, "I can take you to Jenny's car if you like."

"Yes, that is very kind of you; we're so grateful for your help and prompt actions. You and Ben most likely saved our daughter's life. We are eager to see what's left of Jenny's beautiful new red car," Jack responds.

"Okay let's go. It's not too far. Follow me," Jared said as he hurries to his truck.

Ben barks to say, me too, then runs and jumps up into the cab of the tow truck. He takes his place on the towel covering the front seat beside Jared, as if he belongs there.

Arriving at the accident scene they disembark their vehicles. Jared points and says, "We found her down the ravine; look over there at the flattened bushes and broken branches. You can just see the red of the car over there between those big maple trees."

Ester Wilson let out a loud gasp, "Oh my heavens, poor Jenny, she must, have been terrified. How did this happen? Her car is barely visible from the road." She is clearly shook up; a deluge of tears run down her cheeks. Her tears turn to gut-wrenching sobs.

Jack moves to his wife and places his arms around her shoulders and holds her close while she loses control. "She's going to be okay, Ester. You saw her. Shhh, Ester," he comforts her. He motions to Jared with a circular hand gesture encouraging Jared to finish telling them about the events of earlier today.

"Ben's senses are very fine tuned. He must have heard Jenny's calls for help. Not only did he find her, but he came and got me," Jared shares.

"How did he ever find her?" Mr. Wilson questions.

"That's a mystery to me," Jared responds. "I am even more impressed and grateful to Ben, and truly appreciate the horrible situation. Jenny was completely trapped in her car."

Jared unsuccessfully tries to play down the shocking scene he found upon his arrival, hoping to lessen the raw emotions he sees revealed on both Mr. and Mrs. Wilson's faces. "I've seen worse, it is not as bad as it looks. At one point I went back up to the road to wait for the ambulance so I could direct the EMS to Jenny. When I returned with them, we saw Ben. Somehow, without scratching or cutting himself on the glass, he climbed into the car through a broken window. He had spread his body on top of Jenny's. The EMS said they knew exactly why. He was trying to keep Jenny warm and apparently this helps in delaying the setting in of shock. He somehow knew better than I did what needed to be done," Jared said, "I'm still astonished at Ben's acute senses. Animals truly amaze me!"

"I'm with you on that. Animals use their basic instincts better than most humans," Jack declares, "Jared will you take the necessary photos then tow the car to your garage? We'll pay whatever it costs. Jenny loves this car;

just let us know what your expenses will be for the work that needs to be done. I do not think Jenny will want to see her very special car in this condition," he added.

"Sure thing, that's not a problem. I'll ask Kenny, my apprentice, to come back here with me. He will guide me up the embankment. I'll do it this afternoon," Jared promises.

"Let me, check the car, for Jenny's personal belongings. I think it will be better if you take them home," Jared says as they walk down the hill towards the wreck. He removes her belongings, ownership papers and maps from the glove compartment.

"Thanks, of course, where is my head today?" Ester is flustered. She continues to wipe tears away and blows her nose. She turns to Ben and invites him to stay at her house as long as he wants.

Ben is getting used to the notoriety and is enjoying center stage. He did need a place to stay for a few days as sleeping outside did have its risks. He decides to follow Mrs. Wilson to the car and go home with her.

Jenny – Chapter Nine

Mr. Wilson walks the property with Ben at his side, while he introduces Ben to their ranch. "I hope, Ben, that you will like this place. There are two huge shade trees with a hammock over there that make for a tranquil place for napping on a hot lazy afternoons. If I'm not there you are welcome to sleep there," Mr. Wilson shares.

Ben likes this new home.

"Ben, let me introduce Fluffy, our slightly overweight, ginger and white cat," Mr. Wilson continues.

Ben watches as Fluffy lifts her head and checks him out, sniffs the air then assumes her previous position; she went right back to sleep.

"Fluffy is an excellent mouser, but other than that, she just sleeps her life away. Maybe playing with you will help exercise her plump body. As you can see she is clearly in need of activity," Mr. Wilson says as he concludes his tour, pats Ben on the head, and walks back to the house.

I do like everything about this place, but Fluffy is not too happy about my being here. I will need to make friends with her. I'll make sure she understands that I am just passing through.

Jenny – Chapter Ten

Jenny is astonished and extremely thankful to Ben for saving her life. She recounts her story to anyone who will listen detailing her first encounter with Ben, "I can't tell you how disappointed I was when I saw it was a dog who responded to my calls for help. The accident challenges my belief in animals. I had to put a high level of trust in Ben. What else could I do? I thought for sure I was going to die. It seemed like an eternity waiting for help while trapped in that car."

Jenny tells the local reporter, Willie, who writes for the Casper County Gazette. "Willie, I was driving to work at The Medical Mart. I work there doing stock-keeping, inventory counting and as general helper on weekends and during summer vacation," she adds, "A truck came out of nowhere, swerved into my lane and clipped the right fender of my car."

"Jenny, I'm sure the police have already asked you but I didn't see it in the accident report. Did you see the driver or remember any details about the truck?" Willie asks trying to gather details that were not previously reported in his column.

"No, I could not see the driver or color of the truck; it was early morning and not quite daylight. Their high beam head lights blinded me. I clearly remember that part. I recall swerving in an attempt to avoid the inevitable head-on collision," Jenny says but she is a little vague on some of the details. Her head still aches, and some details that she remembers later, were fuzzy due to the diagnosed concussion.

Jenny recounted, "I may have turned the direction of my vehicle a little too quickly." Jenny demonstrates the swerve, giggles and nearly falls out of bed. "Oops. Possibly that is how I ended up down the ravine between the trees. I didn't realize it at the time, but it has been suggested, that the little defensive move most likely saved my life."

Jenny – Chapter Eleven

Ben laps it up. He likes being in the lime light. They wrote a story about the rescue, front page of the Casper County Gazette. There are lots of photos of Jenny, the accident, and, of course, Ben. The heading read, "Hero Dog Saves Local Girls Life."

I feel like a celebrity with all this attention. People are offering to adopt me and give me a loving home; seems like everyone wants me.

Jared visits Jenny and relates the story of Ben to the hospital staff, "The doctors say this dog saved her life." He sweet-talks the nurses, trying to convince them that Ben should visit. "The doctor said that Jenny would not have survived if Ben didn't respond quickly. The dog did that when he found me and convinced me to follow."

The stout, Head Nurse, wore her silver gray hair in a knot at the back of her head. She sternly said, "It is against the rules to bring a dog into the hospital. For sanitary reasons alone, it is a terrible idea. We have though, on several other times made exceptions for Working Dogs."

Jared continues to plead with the nurses, "Please, Ben is just like a working dog. It would certainly speed up her recovery if she saw Ben. Just for a while. Ah, come on, please make an exception."

The Head Nurse, tiring of his relentless pleading and coaxing, finally gives Jared special permission. "Okay, you can bring the dog into the hospital. Only once and for thirty minutes tops; we can get in lots of trouble if we are reported. I want you to promise me that you will strictly abide by our agreement," insisted the Head Nurse.

"I will. Thank you so much," Jared responds.

When Jared happily conveys the approval to Jenny, she immediately telephones her dad, "The Head Nurse says Ben can visit me for thirty minutes. Please bring him to see me."

Jenny – Chapter Twelve

When, Jenny sees Ben for the first time since the accident, there are tumultuous kisses, pats, licks, quiet muted barks on Ben's behalf, and tears of joy on Jenny's part. Ben absolutely destroys her once neatly made bed. Eventually Jenny calms down then invites Ben to settle into a comfortable spot close beside her on the bed. She continues to pat and scratch his ears much to Ben's delight.

Ben beamed. *I'm feeling pretty proud of myself. I realize from the newspaper articles Mr. Wilson reads to me that my actions played a crucial role in saving Jenny's life. Once again, I did good!*

While shuffling down the hospital corridor during their latest visit, Jenny says to her parents, "I have given this a lot of thought. I'm sure that a higher power sent Ben to save my life."

Earlier that day, Doc Martin thoroughly checked Jenny's vitals and injuries, and then agrees to release her tomorrow but with specific orders. "Jenny, you must recuperate at home for at least two weeks. I do not want you returning to work or school too soon. The last thing we want is a relapse. Head injuries have a habit of reoccurring, sometimes weeks or even months later. I mean it." He looks directly at Mrs. Wilson to reinforce his instructions.

"Don't you worry, Doc, I'm her caregiver and I promise to keep a close eye on her activities," she assures him.

Jenny rolls her eyes back and says, "Thanks Doc Martin. Mom will likely strap me in my bed for at least a month." She smiles at her mom because Jenny understands her mother's motivation is well intended.

Sitting at their chrome and wood kitchen table, Ester, looks over her cup of black coffee and says to her husband of thirty years, "Jack, Jenny's so looking forward to coming home and spending time with Ben. I can't wait to have her home with us. I miss her around the house. It is so quiet without her here." Ester is nervously waiting as she chuckles to herself. "I have dusted the china cabinet at least twice today."

Ben enjoys the great attention he is getting; the Wilsons continue to feed and groom him every day. For some reason, he knows today is a special day. He is sitting at the end of the driveway waiting when Jenny arrives home to begin her recovery.

Jenny and he quickly bond.

With all of this attention and regular grooming I'm looking quite handsome, thinks Ben.

Jenny – Chapter Thirteen

Jenny is haunted, by the person who caused the accident and then left her to die. She wonders out loud, "Who was driving that truck? I can't believe that someone in this county would do such a despicable thing. Everyone knows us," she paces back and forth in the kitchen, she is hoping the walking back and forth will help her work through the details of the mystery.

When Jenny finally feels well enough and her mother agrees to release her, she confides in Ben, "Okay Ben, it's time that we go back to the accident scene. I need to see it for myself."

When they arrive at the accident site, Jenny says to her companion, "Look Ben, here are some pieces from the fender of my beautiful red car." She fights back tears more for remembering the near death experience than the red car. "Look, over here, there are still remarkably clear tire tracks on the shoulder of the road; they clearly belong to a truck. This must be where I went off the road. I will check with Jared and make sure these tire tracks are not from his tow truck, or the ambulance for that matter."

Ben sniffs the ground and watches with profound

interest as Jenny is busy taking photos of the tire tracks from several different angles.

"I think this is extremely valuable evidence. If we can determine more details about the truck it will help reduce the many potential varieties of trucks from this county. We live in a rural population, with numerous livestock farms; there are many more trucks than cars here." Jenny chats away to Ben as if he is listening. Jenny believes he actually understands what she is saying.

Later that day, Jenny shows Jared what she found.

"No, those tracks are not from my tow truck or the Ambulance. These tires in your photos are much larger," Jared shares with Jenny.

"Wow," Jenny exclaims, "I guess these are real clues!" Jenny is very pleased with her investigative skills and findings.

Jared says, "Jenny, I scraped some samples of gray paint off your vehicle before I started to restore the body." He extends his hand holding an envelope, where he has placed the paint scrapings.

Jenny takes the crucial photographs plus the gray paint chips that Jared gave her and drives directly to the police station.

"Come on boy. Let's go see the Sheriff." She excitedly encourages Ben to follow her.

Jenny – Chapter Fourteen

At the Sheriff's Office, she shows the evidence to Deputy Frank. He has a skinny wiry build but anyone that has tangled with him will contest to his enormous physical strength. His tousled curly brown hair gives him the look of a misfit, but that is far from the truth. He is clever and well-educated in criminal forensics, law and technology. "Thanks Jenny we can trace both the tire tracks and the paint through the manufacturer's data bases. We will do a computer search and see if we can find a match. First, we'll search for this specific color of paint, then by year and model of vehicles, and so on.

Deputy Frank walks over to a complicated looking piece of technical equipment setup at the back of the office. He places the paint chip under what looks like a microscope. "Look Jenny," Deputy Frank says, "the paint is named Smoked Gray by the manufacturer. Of course, there will not be any record of vehicles painted at a body shop. We'll just hope it is not a repainted vehicle. Next, we can search by this county and nearby counties for vehicles in that grouping." The deputy is smiling. "See here Jenny, I just located 35 vehicles, both cars and trucks. This is the list of trucks only, twenty-five in total. You did a splendid job Jenny," Deputy Frank congratulates her.

Ben stuck his nose in the middle looking for recognition too.

"Yes, you too Ben," chuckles Deputy Frank.

"Jenny, I don't like telling you this but your accident does not rate particularly high on our list of priorities for the Sheriff's staff this week. We will have to file away the information for next week. The department does not have the manpower to run down these leads, because there is a much more pressing case on the docket. We are hot on the trail of some cattle thieves." He consoles Jenny. "We'll make it a priority right after the missing cattle case is solved, I promise."

"Cattle theft?" asks Jenny.

Deputy Frank says, "Yes, cattle are mysteriously disappearing around our county. The cattlemen and local ranchers are furious over the elusive thieves who are stealing cattle from their pastures at night. They are somehow getting away with taking the cattle without leaving a single trace of evidence. The ranchers are demanding that Sheriff Mitch make this case his first priority. This is an election year, and if Sheriff Mitch wants to be re-elected, he must catch the persons responsible."

Sheriff Mitch walks in. He is rotund from too many sugar donuts and tasting far too many pies baked by his constituency. He does not move as fast as he once did, but he still has a sharp investigative mind. Sheriff Mitch is a fiftyish balding family man. He has been re-elected for several consecutive terms. He is a shrewd, kind, likable man who reads people like his favorite mysteries.

Jenny explains to the Sheriff, “I’m off work until Doc Martin says I’m fully recovered.” She shrugs her shoulders. “I’ve got lots of time to make some discreet enquiries. How can I help?”

“Be careful Jenny. I must warn you that being too nosy can be hazardous to your health. Especially, in this situation, as we do not know who or how many people we are dealing with. Please, just look around do not approach anyone. I cannot emphasize this enough. If you should discover evidence, bring it directly to us. Do not approach anyone! Do you hear me?” Sheriff Mitch tries to impress the seriousness of his order, and the consequences of disobeying. He is reinforcing his instructions by staring straight into Jenny’s eyes and wagging his right forefinger at her.

“I hear you. I hear you. I’ve had my brush with death; that is enough for the rest of my life,” Jenny reassures the Sheriff.

“Come on,” she turns to Ben and snaps her fingers. “Let’s find the culprit.” Jenny and Ben leave the Sheriff’s office with determination and intent. She drives home to make a plan and organize her search.

Jenny – Chapter Fifteen

"Dad, please may I borrow your truck? I want to see if Ben and I can locate a smoked gray truck with damage to its right front fender. It might be the one that hit my car and forced me off the road," Jenny requests.

"Sure, honey, what are you planning?" Mr. Wilson asks.

"My plan is to schedule daily searches and then check off the completed quadrant every day. Will you look at my map and tell me what you think?"

"Sure, let me see," her Dad offers.

"I'm open to any ideas you have that might make my search more efficient. What I need from you is your input. Am I being realistic in my plan to travel these distances each day?" Jenny questions.

Mr. Wilson takes the map and reviews the routes she has marked. "The plan looks reasonable to me," he confidently agrees.

"Great, thanks Dad," Jenny replies, "I sure have my work cut out for me."

Jenny – Chapter Sixteen

Ben and Jenny visit nearly every farm in the county. Both are feeling discouraged and quickly losing their motivation. Near the end of their fifth day, Ben, as usual, sniffs around the truck they are checking out. Ben sniffs again, and then sits down and with a muffled bark brings Jenny's attention to the damaged fender of a gray truck. Jenny looks closer and observes some red paint on the fender looking like it needs body work.

"This is like finding a treasure, because it has the same color of red paint as my red car on the right fender," Jenny cheers softly, not to be overheard by the owner. "Good boy Ben. This is a very good find." Enthusiastically, she gives Ben several hugs and kisses. "Come on Ben; let's go back into town and straight to the Sheriff's office."

In town Jenny parks her father's truck and excitedly jogs with Ben into the Sheriff's office to report her findings to Deputy Frank.

"We're positive this is the truck. Here's the evidence." She places the scraped chips from the truck which show gray paint with streaks of red paint. "It links this truck to the accident," Jenny says.

"Jenny do you have the address of where you found this truck?" Deputy Frank asks.

"Sure do, it is at the Dole place over on Concession Thirteen," Jenny replies.

Deputy Frank said, "Thanks Jenny. We are very grateful to have this information."

"We did good Ben." Jenny gives Ben another celebratory hug and kiss on the head.

Deputy Frank asks, "Jenny would you come with me to Sheriff Mitch's office and tell him your story? I know he will be very interested. This is great news!"

On their way, Ben and Jenny walk past an ominous locked brown steel windowless door; they were told it led to the cells where they hold prisoners until their court dates. She also learns the cells hold more hardened criminals waiting for transportation to the state penitentiary. Jenny shrugs her shoulders, visibly shivering at the thought of being so close to really bad guys.

Ben observes that the Sheriff Mitch's office with faded yellow pine panel walls, it is larger than the others with an oversized desk that wasn't diminished by the Sheriff's large frame. His huge overstuffed chair creaks and squeaks when he moves to stand up or adjust his sitting position.

Jenny communicates their activities of the past week to Sheriff Mitch, "We visited so many farms all over this county, and finally found the Smoke Gray truck with evidence of a recent collision with a red vehicle," Jenny looks down at Ben, "You found the truck Ben, right?"

Ben barks in agreement.

"It took five very long days with a lot of discreet investigating, because we were very careful to not to raise any suspicions. Just like you said, Sheriff," Jenny confirms. "The truck that matches is a surprise, because it is not on the manufacturer's paint list. We found the truck at the new folk's farm. They moved here from a county that was not included in our search criteria. They just relocated to our county four weeks ago after buying Jesse Dole's place over on Concession Thirteen. At least that's what my dad told me," Jenny volunteers. She turns to Ben and smiles down, "We make a good team with your sensitive nose and my curiosity." Jenny scrubs Ben's head.

Ben watches the flurry of excitement at the sheriff's office. I'm not sure why everyone is so happy but they sure like patting me and smiling. There is a lot of "Good boy, Ben" and "Atta boy, Ben." I think I like this detective work.

"Thanks Jenny, you can go home now and we will handle it from here," the Sheriff said.

Jenny – Chapter Seventeen

Ben and Jenny climb into their truck and start driving. Ben wonders why they are not driving towards the Wilson's farm. *Why are we going the wrong way?* Jenny is very quiet . . . perhaps too quiet. Ben senses Jenny is up to something and probably nothing good.

Jenny pulls into the driveway of the Dole place, stops the truck and gets out. She motions for Ben to follow her. They walk over to the gray truck to look at the damaged fender again. *Why?* Ben wonders if Jenny is feeling too proud of her investigative skills.

Just then a two hundred and fifty pound, middle aged man with matted longish dirty blonde hair, leather like sun baked skin, wearing denim dungarees and brandishing a rifle starts running towards them waving his rifle in the air.

Ben whines and nudges Jenny. Jenny stands up; she is startled by how quickly the very large man is moving towards them.

The big man with the rifle begins hollering at them, "Get out of here. This is private property. You're trespassing. I'll shoot to kill."

Ben and Jenny start to run towards their truck but the oversized man is now standing between them and their truck. Jenny is staring at the business end of the rifle; she does not see a way to escape so she panics. She grabs Ben's collar and they run as fast as they can in the direction of the barn. She shouts to Ben, "We'll be safer in here. We can hide until it is dark then we'll sneak out to the truck." This sounds like a feasible plan to Jenny, but not to Ben.

Ben figures there are a few problems with Jenny's plan he has no choice, but to go along with her. They ran into the old barn through the huge wooden doors that were partially open. They find refuge behind a pile of fresh hay bales. Jenny covers Ben and herself with the loose hay. She places her arm across Ben so she can control him should he try to bark at the gunslinger.

Sure does stink in here. Ben is overwhelmed with the stench of cattle and the cow pies, their feces. He finds it very hard to breathe the strong odor. He begins to breathe heavily.

Jenny whispers, "Shhh, Ben." She hears someone pulling open the huge barn doors. They hear the doors creak and scrape the flattened dirt floor, which has been pounded down by the many four legged inhabitants of the barn.

The outline of the scary gun slinger appears massive in the open doorway, "Come out, come out whoever you are," he growls in a sing-song way. "I have the rifle and that gives me the advantage. You can't hide in here forever, my nosy little friends. I'll give you five seconds. C'mon show yourself. I will shoot to kill." The threats are coming from the oversized man with the long blonde matted hair. He carelessly waves the rifle around making his point.

Both Jenny and Ben are shaking with fear as they huddle under the loose hay behind the stack of hay bales. "Ben, please be very quiet. I think he means what he says," she whispers in his ear.

She put her hand over Ben's eyes, and then covered her own with her other hand. She wants to be somewhere else, anywhere else but here in this barn.

Ben notices that there are more than a dozen stalls with several cows housed in each one. The choking stench is incredibly strong and makes it very difficult to breath. He wonders when they will get a chance to leave this stinky place.

The gunman checks several possible hiding places in the barn as well as he can, then shoots. His large body does not permit him to reach into small spaces like the one in which Jenny and Ben are hiding. First place he checks are the stinky overcrowded stalls, and then he makes his way up the rickety wooden ladder to inspect the loft.

A few horses whinny in response to the disturbing sound of gun shots.

Ben looks up and stares at the rough wooden planks the underside of the loft. He can hear the big man's heavy footsteps. From what he can see the loft is filled with huge murky gray bags of feed, plus more enormous bales of hay. He is thinking that would be a great place for trespassers to hide, but not him as he would have a difficult time climbing the old makeshift wooden ladder.

So far, Ben and Jenny successfully elude him . . . for now anyway.

Just then Ben feels the tickle of hay invading his nostrils. He really wants to sneeze. Jenny holds him tight and buries his nose in her lap to stifle his sneeze.

Walking back towards the barn doors the gunman stops, and listens, like he hears something. Then he looks from side to side. Again he shouts, "You are trespassing on my property and the rule here is: shoot all trespassers. That means you and your dog little girl. I will shoot!" To reinforce his threat he fires several more bullets into the air causing the horses to whinny again.

Jenny's body jerks violently with each shot. She closes her eyes trying to block out the gunman, and quietly prays that this impossible situation will not be their final moments on earth.

When the intimidating gunslinger leaves the barn he fires off more shots into the air. Then he pulls the large barn doors and slams them shut with a loud bang. They hear the old rusty bolt being slid into place.

They are locked inside the barn.

When she is positive that the gunman has finally left the barn Jenny says, "Whew that was a close call, Ben."

Jenny patiently waits and waits. Her self-confidence and bravery is waning. She is terrified of moving for fear of giving away their hiding place. Jenny is certain the man means what he said about shooting them. After all they are trespassers. Jenny says to Ben, "I did not think this through before acting. I'm afraid I have gotten us into a very dangerous situation. I hope we're not dead before someone misses us and comes to our rescue." She adds remembering the Sheriff's warning, "Ben, the Sheriff is right. Being too nosy can be hazardous to our health."

Time passes. How long Jenny doesn't know for sure. She isn't going to chance doing anything that will put their lives at more risk. "Ben what have I gotten us into?" she whispers.

"Ben I am really very worried." Now full of remorse Jenny asks, "How are we ever going to get out of here before he comes back?"

Jenny – Chapter Eighteen

Mr. Wilson approaches Sheriff Mitch in the coffee shop across from his office and says, “Have you seen my daughter Jenny and her dog?”

“Sure, she was here a few hours ago. She brought us evidence that shows the truck at Dole’s old place may have been the one that forced her off the road,” Sheriff replies, “She’s probably on her way home now,” he adds.

“Thanks, I’m sure you’re right,” Mr. Wilson replies then he waves good bye, and then leaves.

Jenny – Chapter Nineteen

Ben could hear more angry shouting coming from outside the barn. He too is very troubled. Ben has no doubt that they mean to fulfill their threat and shoot the trespassers. Ben now thinks he is not cut out for the drama of detective work, after all.

"Ben no matter what happens; we need to find our own way out of here to safety. I wish I could make you understand that you must do what is best for you. If we have to make a run for it Ben, look out for yourself first," Jenny says in an almost inaudible quiet whisper.

Ben does not like this situation one bit. An exit plan would be good. But how and where can they find a secure escape route out of here and to safety?

Jenny whispers to Ben, "I certainly don't want to meet that mean dude brandishing the gun again." Jenny adds with genuine concern for their safety. "Yes, we are trespassing, I admit that. Why didn't he just tell us to leave?" Jenny is mystified. "Ben, I think there is something else going on here. What it is, I don't know. Maybe we should look around and see what they are hiding," Jenny confides in Ben. Jenny decides their priority should be to find a way out of the barn. "On second thought, let's first try to find a way out of here," Jenny suggests.

"I have lived on a farm my whole life, my roots are here, and I know lots about barns. During my childhood I spent many hours finding places to hide in our barn. If we quietly look around we just might find an escape route," she again confides.

Jenny looks up at the towering barn walls, absent of windows. The huge gray barn doors are at least twelve feet high with oversized rusty hinges and locking hardware. Cautiously, Ben and Jenny start to search for that elusive breakout place.

Ben wants Jenny to be extra, extra careful as he doesn't like the idea of being shot at, or heaven forbid shot dead.

Jenny – Chapter Twenty

Sheriff Mitch picks up his ringing phone and announces, "Sheriff's office."

"Hi Mitch, it's me again, Jack Wilson, have you heard anything from Jenny? It's been over two hours since we spoke at the coffee shop," Jack says.

"No nothing . . . hmm, I wonder if she went back to Dole's old place to nose around trying to reconfirm her findings. I did warn her to stay away," Sheriff offers as an afterthought. "Jenny will have no idea how dangerous it can be if she did go back to the Dole farm."

"Well, she hasn't come home yet and there is no reason for her to still be out," Jack adds, "Ester and I are getting very concerned. This is just not like her. And she knows since the accident how we worry about her safety."

"I'll tell you what," the Sheriff says, "I'll grab a couple of my deputies and visit the farm where she found the truck. I don't have a subpoena, so legally all we can do is just ask a few questions."

"That would be great, thank you," responds Jack, "I don't know why she would go back there, but you know curious teenagers. Sometimes they don't think things through. I'll let you know if she shows up at home."

"Sure thing, I'll keep in touch." The Sheriff, deep in thought, places the receiver back into the phone cradle. He's thinking about the best approach to take at the old Dole place. He does not want to tip his hand but he must find out if Jenny is there.

Sheriff Mitch and his Deputies are armed and heading to their cruisers, obviously on a mission.

Jenny – Chapter Twenty-One

Ben is feeling badly as he is in an unfamiliar situation, and he just doesn't know how to get free. He wants to trust Jenny, but it was Jenny who got them into this mess. He is thinking that he should also explore the barn some more, and look for a way out. Ben begins his search in the opposite direction of Jenny's hunt for an escape route. He sniffs and moves things around with his paws and nose. Once again he gets hay stuck in his nose; he buries his nose between his paws as he desperately tries to not sneeze.

After considerable searching in, around, and behind walls and hay bales, Ben finds a place where the wood near the ground has rotted away leaving a small open space with jagged edges, just big enough to squeeze through. Just as he starts to move towards Jenny to let her know, he hears angry, boisterous yelling and shouting again, just outside the massive barn doors. He hesitates and waits for some direction from Jenny. He hears nothing from her.

Quickly, he assesses the situation. It is getting increasingly more dangerous in this barn. Then he hears someone lifting the giant rusted latch to open the heavy barn doors. Ben stops dead in his tracks.

Jenny freezes at the pressure of the business end of the rifle being pushed into her back. “Gotcha! C’mon kid lets go,” was hoarsely uttered by a big guy, who was pressing his rifle into Jenny’s back.

“Now just where did you come from?” Jenny puts on what she thinks is her most impertinent demeanor. Even though she was terrified.

“Wouldn’t you like to know? Not that it matters but I have been here all along, just waiting for you to come out of your hiding spot.” This time it was the gunslinger’s friend who spoke.

Jenny, feeling danger, shouts in a loud whisper, “Hide. Ben, hide!”

“Don’t you worry your sweet little head about that dog. We will just lock the door. We’ll deal with him later, maybe even shoot him and put him out our way forever. Ha, Ha,” he adds, while distorting his pock-marked face with a threatening grin.

Ben is sensing the fear now in Jenny’s voice. He is not interested in hiding any longer. He immediately leaves the barn through the escape route he had just found. There were some rough irregular pieces of wood that scratches Ben’s back as he squeezes out to freedom. Better to have scratches, than be dead. Once free he looks in every direction and chooses the shortest route to the corn fields. He runs like the devil is chasing him. His goal now is safety. He hears men running and shouting behind him. Ignoring them he runs even faster disappearing into the tall corn field. There are several hundred acres of dense tall stalks, infinity of planted corn row after row after row.

A dog can be lost in here for days. He realizes how easy it would be for him to become disorientated and lose his direction, but he decides to just keep running until he feels safe.

Jenny – Chapter Twenty-Two

Sheriff Mitch and his Deputies arrive at the Dole farm just as the McCormick family is entering their barn. He hears boisterous shouting and very aggressive shouts. He motions with a wave of his hand to the Deputies to hurry towards the barn with their guns drawn.

No one knows what to expect but they must be prepared for anything.

The Sheriff observes Jenny being escorted out of the barn at gun point. He hears words, such as, “Shoot her. Kill her. She is trespassing on our property.” Sheriff Mitch whispers to Deputy Frank, “We need to contain this situation before it gets totally out of hand.” He motions for his deputies to stay calm and watch. He then announces himself, “Hello, I'm Sheriff Mitch Stevens and these are my deputies. We don't want any trouble. Just, relax and take it easy, guys.”

The elder McCormack says, “We found this thief in our barn. She was trying to steal our cattle.”

“Okay, we can handle that for you. Put your guns down and bring her over here.” The Sheriff tries to stabilize the mob rule mood as he and his deputies are outnumbered by both men and guns.

Mark yells, "She is trespassing and we know our rights. We are only trying to protect our home and belongings." Mark is known to Jenny as the big guy with matted dirty blonde hair, wearing dirty dungarees and most importantly as the gunslinger who made threats about shooting her and Ben.

"I am here now to help you protect your property and animals. So why don't you let me deal out the punishment." The Sheriff asserts the authority his position gives him.

The gunman lets Jenny go and she quickly runs towards to the Sheriff. Once she is safely with the deputies, Jenny says quietly to Sheriff Mitch, "They have lots of black and white cows packed into the stalls, and I mean packed. It sure stinks in that barn; worse than I ever remember our barn smelling."

Sheriff said to the elder McCormack, "Show me where you found her."

"No. It's okay, no harm done," Mr. McCormack replies, waving his hand to indicate that all is well, don't bother.

"I would just like to see where you found her," the Sheriff insists.

They hesitate and look at each other. No one came up with an alternative plan so they sauntered with purpose toward the barn. They all enter the barn through the massive doors.

Sheriff says, "You have quite a large herd of black and white cattle. Did you bring them here from your last farm?"

"Naw, we just bought these guys, they stay in the barn, for acclimatization, ya know, new place and all," the senior McCormack replies as he starts to move towards the barn doors. He encourages everyone to walk towards the exit as well. He knows that the less time they spend in the barn the better it is for him.

"Sure," Sheriff says, as they leave the barn. He did notice the branding was for the farms that were missing some cattle. He adds, "The double 'KK,' and the triple 'WWW' are just two of the symbols I see branded on the livestock in the barn. Both ranchers have reported missing cattle over the past three weeks. I know for sure, none of them sold any of the stock in the past month."

They stroll over to the gray truck. Changing the subject, the Sheriff says, "I notice this truck of yours. Looks like you had a little fender bender. How'd it happen?" the Sheriff probes.

"My son, Mark, had a close call over the north side of town a few weeks ago," he lied.

"It looks a lot like a truck we have a B.O.L.O for," The Sheriff informs them without being too accusatory.

"A what?" Mark asks.

"Be On the Look Out, a B.O.L.O. There was a serious accident on the south side of town and the driver of the offending vehicle left the scene and someone almost died," the Sheriff continues.

Sheriff Mitch looks right at Mark and says, "Mark, I think you were the driver. Am I right?"

Mark shrugs his shoulders as he smugly responds, "Yeah, so what?"

"Mark, you are under arrest for the Hit and Run accident you caused and leaving the scene of an accident. As you just admitted to driving this Smoke Gray truck, license number PMG246. Turn around Mark, so I can put these cuffs on your wrists," the Sheriff says then snaps the handcuffs close with a loud click. He pushes Mark a little harder than he needs toward his deputies.

The Sheriff, in his official demeanor, orders his deputy, "Mirandize him. Then put him in the cruiser."

"Mr. McCormick, you and your boys are all under suspicion for Cattle Rustling. Those cattle in your barn actually belong to someone else as they have been branded by a ranch other than yours. We know where the cattle rightfully belong," Sheriff Mitch pronounces with full confidence, "Deputies, cuff them all and take them to the office. I have lots of questions for them for which I need answers," Sheriff Mitch orders.

Once all of the suspects' hands are cuffed and then locked in the cruisers, Jenny asks, "Has anyone seen Ben?"

Jenny – Chapter Twenty-Three

"No, is he still in the barn?" questions Sheriff Mitch.

"I don't know. I did tell him to hide when that big guy with the pock-marked face stuck the barrel of his rifle into my back. Those guys locked him in and said they were going to deal with him later. They even warned me that they would shoot him. I suppose he could be still hiding," Jenny says as she is starting to worry. "It is unlike Ben to not be in the middle of the activities."

"Frank, will you go to the barn with Jenny, but do not go in or touch anything. That is all evidence and we do not want to contaminate the crime scene," the Sheriff instructs his deputy, "Close and padlock the barn door when you're finished."

Jenny starts towards the barn. She begins calling, "Ben, come, Ben. Come here boy. Where are you?"

Ben is quietly resting in the middle of the corn field gathering his thoughts, when he hears Jenny call him. The tension in Jenny's voice is gone. Ben cautiously works his way back through the endless rows of extremely high corn stalks, towards her voice. Ben barks a few times just as he pokes his head through an opening between the stalks.

He sees Jenny and runs in her direction and that of the Sheriff, and his Deputies.

"Ben I am so happy to see you. How did you get out?" Jenny was full of questions but knew, of course, Ben couldn't tell her.

Back at the Sheriff's office, Sheriff Mitch says, "Jenny first of all we should charge you with trespassing, interfering with a crime scene, plus a whole list of minor infractions. I specifically told you to stay away from the Dole place. What were you thinking?" The Sheriff is showing his angry face to emphasize the severity of the situation. He spoke sternly with his booming voice accentuated by wagging his finger in Jenny's face.

She begins to cry, partly from relief and partly begging for mercy, "I wasn't thinking. I am so sorry. It just all happened so fast. When I saw that big guy with the rifle running towards us, I panicked. I was really, really scared for our lives in that barn. I don't think you ever need to worry about me doing something that stupid again." Jenny wipes her tears with the back of her hand, apologizing to the Sheriff.

Sheriff adds, "Good! Don't ever disobey a direct order again. You caused your parents undue anxiety and this office time and money. The only reason I'm not charging you is because we solved two crimes today. We were lucky that the cattle were in plain sight, and we were able to bring in the McCormacks without an arrest warrant or subpoena." A smile cracks the Sheriff's face. "On the bright side, the evidence that you discovered appears to link both cases," he continues, "The McCormack family are persons of interest, and just as we suspected they are involved in both your accident and the cattle rustling which is our high profile case."

Jenny – Chapter Twenty-Four

Jack Wilson drops by the Sheriff's office the next day to share in the good news. "Got a minute Mitch?" Jack asks as he pokes his head into the Sheriff's office.

"Coffee, Jack?" Sheriff offers holding a mug of black coffee out to Jack.

"Thanks, I can use a coffee break."

"Have a seat Jack, take some weight off your feet," Mitch offers encouraging Jack to sit and chat.

"Everyone's so grateful and happy that Jenny is safely home and these new-comers are behind bars. Now the town people and the farmers can relax and go back to their normal businesses and routines."

"That's what they pay me the big bucks for," the Sheriff chuckles then reaches over his right shoulder with his free hand and pats himself on the back. He is mocking the praise and trying desperately to play down the compliment.

"I'm also grateful that you have arrested the persons that caused our family so much anguish and expense over Jenny's accident." Jack pauses and takes another sip of the overcooked coffee, "I also want to mention that Jenny said that she learned a valuable lesson yesterday."

The Sheriff asks, "What is that?"

"Leave the sleuthing to the proper authorities. She promises no more detective work. It is far too dangerous, quote, unquote." Jack says as they both chuckle, enjoying the relief that it all turned out okay.

"I do hope she doesn't forget that promise. That situation could have had a completely different outcome," Sheriff cautions while furrowing his brow revealing a frown as he remembered the scene when they arrived at the McCormick's ranch.

"Thank you, Sheriff."

They shook hands and Mr. Wilson leaves happy.

Jenny – Twenty-Five

A few days later, Jenny is rocking in her granddaddy's old rickety rocking chair to the rhythm of the squeaking front porch floor boards. Ben is beside her, lying on the freshly painted gray verandah. Ben looks up at Jenny with sad eyes. He does not know how to communicate this to his new adventurous friend. He must move on and continue his journey.

Jenny knows in her heart that Ben is not hers to keep. She doesn't know where he came from or where he is going, but she interprets Ben's sad look to mean it is time for him to leave. Tears well up in Jenny's eyes, and she says, "Whenever you are ready boy . . . go with my blessing, appreciation and love. I will miss you so much. You are a terrific friend; you give so much, but never ask for anything in return." With that, she gives Ben a loving hug and gentle kisses on the top of his head. "Good bye, my dear friend," Jenny walks into the house as she could not bear to watch Ben walk away. She knows she might try to stop him, even though she knows in her heart that he needs to go.

Ben leaves later that afternoon with a heavy heart, since leaving behind such caring people again, is not easy, but, his yearning for his family is much stronger.

Ben knows he must continue his journey.

SAM BOOK FIVE

Sam – Chapter One

For two days now, the weather has been warm and sunny, terrific weather for traveling. Ben was able to find sufficient water, nourishing food, and safe places to sleep.

Today the sunrise is a wonderful painter's delight with ribbons of fuchsia pink, blue, purple, and rose-tinted brush strokes of color, streaking across the sky. The trees in the distance vaguely resemble mountains and the mist rising up ahead of the faux hills appears to be water. The tall trees pushing their tops up out of the mist conjure up visions of sky scrapers in the distance.

The interesting vibrant sky appears lost on Ben; he is indifferent about the magnificent colors. More important to him is navigating the east bound road with ease. Progress is good as Ben takes light happy steps. He is in high spirits as he bounces along.

Next day, a heavy rainfall severely limits his progress. Ben watches the spectacular light show, with streaks of flashing lightning zigzagging across the sky. Each flash is accompanied by enormously loud cracks of thunder; the rumbles and banging imitate someone moving furniture upstairs. Ben trembles with fright every time the thunder roars across the sky. He ducks in and out of several temporary shelters with each loud ripping and booming sound overhead. Holding his head down, he is seeking refuge from the lightning, thunder and the torrential rains.

He searches and searches, bobbing in and out of doorways seeking a more permanent dry place to wait out the storm. Finally he finds protection in an open doorway, which leads to a hallway in an old derelict building. This offers the shelter he is seeking. Sniffing around, he finds an old cardboard box, which he snuggles into, fully appreciating the coziness, dryness and warmth. He licks his fur almost dry as he plans to stay here, have a nap and wait for the storm to pass.

Once he comfortably settles into his safe haven, Ben takes this opportunity to look around the hallway. He observes the discolored old paint and faded peeling wallpaper strips, that are coming unglued from the wall and hanging like wilting leaves from tree branches. Further observation reveals ancient wooden floors that are badly scuffed with dangerous splinters of wood, just waiting to stab a foot without warning. The floors and walls both display an assortment of stains, an indication of many years of wear, neglect and abuse. Several broken bottles and soiled food wrappers are strewn the length of the hallway. His sensitive nose twitches at the very strong odor of urine. It is far from perfect, but it is dry, warm and provides protection from the blowing rain. *This will be perfect for the time being.*

The storm doesn't stop. It continues to cast its furor for several more hours. Ben's shelter is still comfortable and dry, so he hunkers down and commits to staying the night.

A short while later, unexpected company arrives. Ben knows that not all humans like to share their accommodations with dogs. First he thought that he might be chased out of his retreat. Without making himself known, he observes the visitor who is an athletic looking muscular young man in tattered clothing that smells almost a bad as Ben's hair does, when it is wet.

This new dweller came in from the rain just like Ben. His longish hair and oversized clothing dripped water onto the floor. The visitor shivers under his cold wet clothing, then, curls up hugging himself and settles down for a nap.

Just then the visitor sees Ben, and in an almost inaudible whisper says, "Hello my friend. Do you mind sharing your digs with me? It sure is nasty out there."

Ben looks at the man with his large brown eyes and sees caring eyes the color of the ocean, gentle and friendly, looking back at him. He does not sense danger, so he decides to scrutinize his visitor more closely, but he will wait until tomorrow. He closes his eyes, and snuggles down to sleep; as he feels safe, and senses he need not worry tonight.

When Ben wakes up, he perks up his ears then tilts his head, first one side then the other, listening for the storm. The quiet tells him the loud noises have gone. This is good news as he will be able continue his journey. Ben attempts to quietly and carefully navigate his way out of the passageway.

The new friend said, “You don’t need to be running off without some food in your belly, fella.”

Ben looks back at the interesting young man then barks softly signaling that he agrees with him. Ben promptly sits down in anticipation of the drifter joining him.

Together, they wander off side by side, like they have been friends for a very long time. The breakfast hunt today ends behind a nearby all-night eatery, the big blue dumpster around the back is brimming with abandoned food. The visitor and Ben, with the help of a pile of stuffed green garbage bags, climb up onto the edge of the tall steel box that is overflowing with a wide variety of tasty scraps. They search through the discarded food and find an ample feast of half eaten hamburgers, steak and potatoes with hot sauce, and pasta covered in sauce and cheese, all leftovers from last evening’s dinner guests. They eat until their bellies signal they are full.

Ben likes this young man. He wonders how he got here and where he is going. The new friend gently strokes Ben's head and back. Ben is content and enjoys the attention. He feels there is a notable energy about this person. He cannot explain it. And his urgency to resume his journey abates for now.

The drifter asks Ben, "How did you get here, fella, and where are you going? Where do you belong? You don't seem to be lost." He continues to stroke behind Ben's ears, and the dog rolls over to expose his belly. The man laughs. "You certainly are a beauty." Ben sits up and begins to lick his face.

"Hey, fella, my name is Sam. What's your name? You are far too handsome to be nameless."

Just then, Ben raises himself into an upright position. Sam notices the blue metallic tag on Ben's collar and reads out loud, "Ben. Now that's a good name. My name is Sam, Sam Garner. It is nice to have shared your accommodations plus a meal with you." Sam stands and wishes Ben a farewell. "Who knows, maybe we will share another meal, some other time."

Ben rubs his side against Sam's leg and barks, as if to say, "See you, Sam."

The sunrise in the eastern sky is so bright it is almost impossible for Ben to look directly at the huge red and orange ball of fire. The brilliant sun hurts Ben's eyes, but he knows he must tolerate it until the sun rises higher in the sky. He is heading towards the intense sun traveling directly east; he is committed to traveling east because he feels east is the right direction.

Ben turns his head and watches as Sam walks west on Young Street. He drops his head and tucks his tail between his hind legs indicating that he is very sad. He feels like he is losing a friend. Ben takes two more steps then turns to look back again. At that same time Sam stops walking and turns his head to look back at him. Then for no reason, Sam makes a complete about face and starts to walk in the same direction as Ben. He hopes it is because Sam has no reason to be going the other way.

Sam brushes a rogue piece of his brown curly hair back, and mumbles under his breath, "Ben, you might know where you're going, as you seem to be walking with real purpose. I'll go with you today and see where you're headed."

Off they go, making quite the sight. Ben is trotting happily along wagging his tail in what appears to be to the beat of the tune Sam is whistling. It pleases Ben that Sam is joining him on his journey. Even though there have been some interesting adventures, it is nice to have a companion since there have been lots of lonely times, too.

They navigate their way out of town on the highway. Walking in step they look like they have been friends for a very long time. Sam does not feel the need to speak. There is a comfort level that he has not previously experienced, at least lately. They walk in silence until the sun sets creating colorful red and pink clouds. As dusk settles in, once again they search for and find food, water and a safe place to bed down for the night. This becomes their routine for the next few days. They are happily bonding.

Ben studies Sam. He is very handsome with long curly brown hair that continuously falls onto his forehead. Smiling to himself, Ben sees Sam absentmindedly brush his hair back with his hand, and then watches it fall down to his forehead again. Standing over six feet tall, Ben can still see traces of his once firm six pack.

Something very serious must have happened to Sam, Ben thinks, because his face is pleasant, but Ben has never seen such incredibly sad eyes. Ben can see that he is far too thin. When Ben sniffs him, he realizes that Sam probably hasn't bathed in a long while. His bushy brown beard is evidence that he hasn't seen a barber or used a razor for quite some time, either. It's probably time for him to find new clothing, because his oversized, tattered blue and green plaid shirt hangs off his thin frame. Ben wonders at Sam's faded, too large threadbare blue jeans that gather at the waist by a rope, otherwise they might fall down. The cardboard inserts showing through gaps in the soles of his shoes are getting thin; but not completely worn through yet.

Sam – Chapter Two

Next day the sunrise is again a fireball in the cloudless sky. It is amazingly beautiful, as it creates long shadows. The bright sun is a sure predictor of a hot humid day. Ben and Sam mentally prepare themselves for very warm, muggy travel today.

Walking in the hot sun is not and never will be Ben's preference. Stopping frequently for water in streams keeps them hydrated and makes the heat bearable. They are weary but they're toughing it out.

Approximately an hour into their travels Ben notices something in the distance, on the side of the road. It resembles abandoned garbage left to rot. As they get closer, they can see it is a furry animal that appears to be dead.

Sam doesn't want Ben to see the dead animal. He tries to encourage him to cross the road. "Ben, let's cross the road and walk over there. Come on Ben," Sam's suggestion falls on deaf ears.

Ignoring Sam, Ben runs ahead. He is first to approach. The animal looks like a mound of old discarded clothing. He sniffs several places on the body then gently nudges the motionless carcass. A quiet painful whimper is his first clue that it's still alive.

Ben senses an injured dog that is very frightened. Her dingy tangled black and dirty white coat has blotches of red blood. Ben sees her coloring is similar to his, but she is not nearly as handsome.

Sam is very cautious as he approaches the injured dog. He doesn't want to startle her. He thinks an unfamiliar person might cause the dog to shift into flight mode, which could aggravate her injuries. "It's okay," he whispers softly, "We are friendly. Don't worry. Good girl," Sam continues as he bends down and places his hand on her head, in an attempt to reassure her and let her know they will not hurt her.

She does overreact to Sam's touch. She mistakenly thinks she can run to safety, but instead her attempt to stand results in a very loud painful yelp! It is obvious to everyone she is in excruciating pain. Ben realizes her leg hurts too much to move it and she is not able to support herself. She carefully and cautiously returns to her previous prone position trying not to cause herself additional pain.

Sam kneels down beside her, on the gravel shoulder of the road and again attempts to reassure her that he and Ben are friendly. "Take it easy young lady," Sam says as he strokes her head while he tenderly checks her legs. He discovers that her hind leg seems to have been seriously injured. It appears to have received the brunt of the hit.

A cursory examination of her three other legs and torso show no visible sign of wounds. "It'll be okay girl. We will get you help, just hang in there," Sam speaks softly, hoping to reassure her.

Ben wonders. *Can we help her? She really needs our help. She is unable to walk. Ben senses she is in horrible pain. He hopes Sam can come up with a solution. Ben worries, that Sam will be unable to carry her very far. But we can't just leave her here; she might die.*

While stroking her body, Sam turns his head and eyes towards the sky that is when he sees the vultures circling overhead. He points to them and says to Ben, "They are scavengers waiting for us to leave so they can have lunch. We will not let that happen to her, Ben."

Ben's ears twitch and perk up at the sound of clattering from an old truck, driving on a gravel surface country road. He puts his paw on Sam's arm and barks softly to alert him of the approaching vehicle.

Sam jumps to his feet as now he also hears the rickety old truck, before he actually sees it, shaking and rattling along the pot-holed country road. They watch as the faded and paint chipped green truck turns onto the highway heading towards them.

Ben watches Sam, as he stands in the middle of the road, franticly waving his arms. There isn't a lot of traffic on this road in the morning so they need to take advantage of this person and hope he is willing to assist them.

When the truck comes to a stop, an old man opens the passenger door window and asks, "Someth'n wrong?"

Sam pokes his head through the open window and says, "Thank you for stopping. We need help right now. Please, we need to take this injured dog to an animal clinic. Will you help us?"

"Hi'ya fella, Frank's the name. Y'er dog hit by a car? Hmm. Looks'n bad shape." The old man gets out of the truck cab to assess the situation.

Frank appears to be imitating a character from an old western movie with his rugged sunbaked skin looking very much like leather, and sporting a vast collection of wrinkles. Sam figures it's a result of working the fields all day in the hot sun. With further assessment, Sam observes that the old guy has a few teeth missing, made more visible when he removes the cigarette dangling from the right side of his mouth to spit or cough. His khaki overalls are dirty from his labors with patches covering the worn spots.

Sam pleads with Frank, "We are strangers to this area. Please, will you take us to a local animal hospital or clinic?"

"Ya comin' too?" Frank enquires as he removes his cigarette to spit on the gravel."

"Yes, of course we'll go too," Sam responds. He is happy that Frank is willing to take time out of his busy day to help this injured dog.

"Sure, I don't like to see one of God's creatures suffer'n." Frank good heartedly suggests, "We'll be need'n someth'n to carry er on."

They look in the nearby culvert and around the bushes for something that will make a suitable bed. They spot a large soiled cardboard box in the ditch which was damp and flattened from the recent rain. He and Sam carefully lift the patient onto the improvised stretcher.

"On the count of three, we'll lift her together up onto the truck bed. Okay, one – two – three - lift. Good," Sam murmurs, "that wasn't too hard. Thanks so much for your help," he says as they successfully orchestrate the lift.

Sam drags his dirty hands down his shirt removing the mud that was transferred from the cardboard stretcher. He is feeling good about helping this injured animal.

Ben really wants to keep her company because she is frightened and in so much pain. He decides to jump up in the back of the truck and ride with her so they'll be together. Ben is convinced that she will be less fearful with him close by.

Sam sits in the cab with farmer Frank. They chat up a storm, once Sam owns up to being *The Sam Garner*, the ex-professional hockey player. They spend most of the drive discussing hockey, recent trades and the ridiculous salaries hockey players get paid. Their banter continues all of the way to the veterinarian clinic.

Ben gently licks her injured leg trying to clean off some of the blood. There are already signs of matting fur on her pretty black leg.

Upon arrival at the Animal Hospital, Sam turns to Frank and asks, "Do you mind waiting for us here? I need to explain the situation to the folks inside. I'll make it clear this is a real emergency so you can get on your way."

"Sure fella. Check'n ta see what they can do fer her," Frank agrees.

Sam – Chapter Three

Ben observes Sam walking back to the truck with a man dressed in green scrubs. He learns the man is a vet. He displays a firm muscular body that shows his obvious commitment to regular workouts. He walks with a sense of confidence, urgency and determination. Ben learns that it is his job to assess the situation and examine the dog to determine the extent of the damage.

The vet speaks softly to his new patient. "Little lady," he says, "don't you know yet that you can't take on cars? They win every time. No worries; we'll take good care of you. We specialize in making dogs feel better."

Addressing the group, he says, "Hi, my name is John Williams. I am the resident veterinarian here. I came out to your truck because the clinic needs to be very careful about bringing stray animals inside. We need to check her to make sure that she doesn't have a contagious disease or Rabies. This could infect our other patients as their immune systems are compromised when they are ill." John proceeds to do a cursory examination. The John says, "She doesn't present any of the more obvious symptoms and it is unlikely that she has rabies; besides she hasn't made any attempts to bite me thus far." Looking at Sam, he asks, "Will you help me carry her into the examination room so we can take x-rays to determine the full extent of her injuries. Let's use this makeshift stretcher." John proposes.

Smiling John looks directly at Ben and says, "We'll be very careful and hopefully we will not hurt her too much." Then he ruffles Ben's ears as a friendly gesture.

Ben watches as John and Sam carefully carry his new friend into the clinic, then into the examination room.

He did sit and perk up his ears then tilt his head a few times when he heard her whimper or yelp with pain. Ben has sharper hearing than humans, therefore he hears more than Sam or Frank.

John and his crew examine her, and then x-ray the fractured leg and her torso checking for internal injuries. John then appears in the waiting room and addresses Sam, Frank and Ben. Reading from his clip board John reports, "The good news is the only injury that we can find is a fracture of her right hind leg. We are applying a splint and wrapping it, as the break isn't too serious and does not require surgery. I'm afraid she'll be very sore tomorrow from her collision with the vehicle. Of course landing on the ground will have created more bruising. These will hurt, too. Unfortunately she'll be in lots of pain for a few days. Most importantly she needs to rest; this will allow her leg to heal. I believe the fracture will probably take in the neighborhood of three to five weeks to mend."

Now what's going to happen to her? Ben wonders as he looks to Sam then John and back to Sam. She is my new friend and I want her to come with us he thinks as he whimpers, trying to communicate with them.

John frowns and says, "She did not have an identification tag or a microchip. We'll call a few vets in the area to see if they know her, or have any reports of missing dogs that match her description. Maybe they know or can find her owners."

Two hours later - she is still an orphan.

Sam explains to the Vet, "John, we found her lying on the road side. I probably should have told you earlier but we do not have any money to pay you. I hope this isn't a problem."

John replies with a wave of his hand, "No, don't worry about it. I can arrange to have the medical charges covered by our charitable donations so you don't need to concern yourself about paying. But, thank you for your kindness in bringing her here for medical attention. Who knows what would have happened to her if you didn't stop to help. I recommend that you leave her here. The clinic staff will also check for missing dogs in the surrounding areas. Failing that we will find her a new home."

The men shook hands all around, then Sam and Frank head towards the door to leave. Sam opens the door and turns his head to call back over his shoulder to Ben, "Come on Ben. Let's go, she'll be okay."

Ben does not budge. He sits, with his rump firmly planted in place.

Sam tries pleading and coaxing, "Come on Ben. We have to leave now. She'll be okay. They'll find a nice home for her. Let's go."

His words fall on deaf ears.

Sam says, "Ben, it is impossible, we cannot take her. We can't continue our travels with a dog that can't walk. It's just won't work." Sam's tugging at Ben's collar trying to lead him towards the door, that doesn't work either. With increasing frustration Sam continues to plead his case, trying to convince Ben, "She is going to be in splints for at least four weeks. I just cannot carry a dog that size, I'm not strong enough," insists Sam.

Ben just sits there like a statue, ignoring Sam and watching the door to the examination rooms with his sad brown eyes. He whimpers *I do not want to leave my newest friend behind.*

Sam continues to tug at him, struggling to communicate. Ben resists and stands his ground; actually sitting as if he is firmly glued to the floor.

The animal owners sitting in the waiting room are watching with interest as the drama unfolds. Some snicker to their pets or partner. One lady says, "The vote's unanimous. No one here doubts the outcome of this little tug-of-war for one minute. As a dog owner myself, I'm confident; that beautiful dog will not lose this war of wills."

One man in the waiting room watching the performance is outwardly amused with the whole scene, and chuckles as he envisions what he's about to suggest, "Hi, my name is Bert." He walks over to Sam offers his hand and they shake. Then he says, "I couldn't help hearing your dilemma with the dog. I have a suggestion that may solve your problem if you are interested."

Sam says, "Sure Bert, I'll listen to any proposal at this point. What is your solution?"

"There is an old wheelbarrow in the back of my pickup truck. It's not much but it still works. You are welcome to it as transportation for your injured dog. It's yours if you want it – no charge," Bert offers still chuckling.

Sam thinks for a few moments and tries to envision how that situation will unfold. Then he hesitantly agrees, "Thank you that is very kind of you. Your wheel barrel could be the perfect solution to our little dilemma. It's apparent that Ben has made up his mind."

"Frank, do you mind if we take the wheelbarrow with us?" Sam asks, hoping for an affirmative response.

"Naw, seems lik'a solution ta me," Frank responds, shrugging his shoulders and scratching his unshaven face.

"Okay Ben, we will take her with us," Sam says surrendering to Ben's wish. He shrugs his shoulders and shyly smiles showing his appreciation to the crowd in the waiting room.

Ben happily wags his tail and dances around in circles in response to Sam's agreement to include the injured dog in their newly formed family.

After all the pleading, coaxing and cajoling . . . Ben won. His chest swells with pride. The patrons sitting in the waiting room chuckle and lightly applaud. He is happy with his new friend.

Sam explains the wheelbarrow idea to John. He furrows his brow and says, "I'm not sure how it will work out for you. But, I've been around animals long enough to know they often know what is best for them. Obviously, Ben has made up his mind. With his support and care, she should be like new in let's say, four or five weeks. Thank goodness her injuries are non-life threatening. She does need time to heal, though."

"Yes, we understand. Thanks Doc," Sam says.

John then adds, "Because you don't know her history, as a precaution, I think it would be wise to give her some shots, like Rabies and heart worm, before you leave."

"That's great if you are sure you can do that. This treatment is going to cost your charity fund a few bucks," Sam says. He just can't believe that John is willing to take such good care of this non-paying patient, who he has never treated before or will likely see again.

John confidently smiles to himself at the vision of the odd little trio, and then says, "I will prepare a little travel kit with some extra medications for pain and clean bandages. I wish you well. And most of all, I wish you all happy travels."

The shots are administered. She is wrapped in a blanket and brought to Sam in the waiting room. John says as he hands her over, "It's been a pleasure to treat her. I hope she realizes how lucky she is to have both a canine and human friend that cares about her."

Ben walks beside her when they carry her on a soft blue blanket to the back of the truck. Farmer Frank graciously offers to take all three of them and the wheelbarrow back to the highway where they met.

Ben enthusiastically wags his tail to show he is pleased with their choice, then jumps up into the back of the truck with a perky little bark, as if to say, *"I approve."* It is obvious this was his plan all along. He gently nudges his new friend to let her know she's in good hands. *Welcome aboard.*

She slept most of the way back to the highway, oblivious to any discomfort from the rickety old truck as it bumps, rattles and sways. Arriving at the highway, they unload the wheelbarrow and their new charge. Ben and Sam, each in their own way, thank Frank.

"Thank you so much, Frank," says Sam and shakes hands.

Ben licks Frank's face, rubs his cheek on his hand, and barks in appreciation.

Frank takes off his well-worn cap with the frayed bill and begins scratching the bald spot on his head with the same hand holding his cap, as he smiles while watching the trio resume their journey.

Sam – Chapter Four

Ben is aware they are quite the sight with a rough looking drifter in tattered clothes walking on the side of the highway, with one dog trotting alongside, and another in an old beat up wheelbarrow, which is desperately in need of repairs.

This will have to be her mode of transportation, until she is mobile again, thinks Ben. We are going to have so much fun together.

Sam has a discussion with Ben while walking. He is trying to choose a name for their new companion. Sam suggests, "Daisy? - Lady? - Missy? Ben, it seems every name I suggest, you veto with a low growl."

Sam then asks, "What about Molly?"

Ben gave a happy little bark to the name Molly.

Why that name appeals to Ben, Sam has no idea, but Ben knows.

"Okay, that settles it, Molly is her name," Sam says. He likes that she has a name now. "It seems only right. Everyone needs a name," he adds.

Molly slept through it all as if it didn't matter or she

is just too groggy to care. John the Vet did give her a sedative to help her sleep and dull the pain during her unconventional ride.

Ben knows it is time to stop for the night so Molly can rest. He is tired too, as it has been a long action-packed day.

"First we need some food," declares Sam.

A short while later they come across an eatery with a dumpster out back. Ben and Sam both climb up into the big green dumpster behind The Blueberry Hill Diner and find edible food.

"Hey, Ben, this diner has good stuff. Here's the best part of a burger. You can have that one; I found an almost whole chicken sandwich," Sam adds with a smile, while digging deeper into the dumpster. "Now, we need something for Molly and water for all of us," Sam adds, as he is getting to be an expert at dumpster diving. "Here, Molly, have some meat. You really need to eat so you'll get better." Sam tries, but she turns her head away refusing everything he offers her for dinner. "It's okay girl. I understand. I'm glad that you're at least drinking the water," he states.

Sam looks up. "It's almost dark, Ben. We must find a place to stop for the night. Molly needs her rest. It is also essential that I rest my aching back," Sam chats away to Ben. "Today was an eventful and interesting experience. I certainly got more insight into your personality and stubbornness today, Ben. The trip to the vet and now having to push the old wheel barrel is an added feature that nobody would have scripted for us. We didn't travel very far today, my friend," Sam good naturedly chuckles as he reviews their day. "We sure did attract lots of attention though; some people even stopped their vehicles to gawk at us, some actually enquired about our unique story," Sam muses.

"I don't know about you Ben, but I am very weary from walking. Molly is still in a fair amount of pain from her injuries," Sam continues, "Okay, Ben, let's try to find a safe comfortable place to sleep and hopefully stay a few days so Molly can heal."

She whimpers slightly when Sam attempts to adjust her to a different position. "I'm afraid you might be getting muscle cramps girl because there is no padding at all in the wooden wheel barrel, except for the blanket from the clinic that John told us to keep," Sam says to Molly as he alters her position a little more.

They search and search for some time looking for a convenient shelter. Finally they discover an old abandoned building not far from the diner where they ate dinner. Sam is pleased with their find. He says, "This place looks as if it was probably someone's apartment. There are remnants of old cabinets that were once part of a working kitchen." Sam pictures a happy family eating dinner, laughing and discussing the events of the day. This thought makes Sam sad. He quickly diverts his thoughts away from his personal issues and continues his assessment of their new digs.

Other rooms are defined as bedrooms because of a lone mattress left behind. “Wow, Ben, I like this soft mattress; it sure beats the cardboard boxes that we have been using as our bed. This place has potential to be a comfortable place for all of us to sleep,” Sam cheerfully remarks. He is looking forward to having a good night's sleep.

Ben's ears perk up and he barks, as if in agreement.

“It isn't the Ritz, Ben, but it'll provide good protection from the elements and give all three of us plenty of room to stretch out and rest our weary bodies,” Sam declares, pointing out the attributes of their new found home.

Sam turns to Molly. “Here, girl, you need to have your medication. Your bandages are still in place and I don't see any fresh blood. They are looking good.”

Sam has concerns that the pain killers might be wearing off as Molly is fidgeting. He wants to make certain that she is comfortable before they settle in for the night. Sam gently opens her mouth then puts a pill way back in her throat, then rubs her neck with a downward motion just like the Veterinarian showed him.

Just before dozing off, Sam chuckles quietly and wonders what has he gotten into?

Sam – Chapter Five

Sam is awake early. Once again, he takes a few moments to review the events of his life. It seems so long ago now since my prosperous high flying life of a sports celebrity. I was a very well-paid professional hockey player with a huge fan following. The world was my oyster. I had, money, success, lots of friends – male and female – and was engaged to a great woman I loved dearly. All of it gone, because of my personal tragedy. I know now it was an artificial existence, a house of cards that could tumble at any moment. And it did fall apart.

It is so good to have these dogs to take my mind off the past.

Ben woke well rested, but immediately is aware that Sam's dealing with unpleasant memories due to the tears running down his cheeks. He closes his eyes and pretends to be sleeping.

The stirring of Molly brings them both back to reality.

"Here you go girl," Sam said as wipes away his tears with his sleeve, then helps her off the mattress so she can relieve herself. Sam assumes by her awkward movements her body still hurts from the trauma of the impact. "Molly you're still a little groggy from the medications, so be very careful."

She protects the sore leg by delicately hobbling on her three good legs, being very careful to not touch the ground with the injured one, she moves very slowly towards the patch of grass outside the back door.

Molly needs to get her thoughts together. *Where exactly am I? How did I get here? Who is that dog? Oh Yes . . . I'm starting to remember now. . . Ben, he is my handsome hero. He was so protective of me yesterday for which I am grateful. I'm getting hungry now. . . I wonder what's for breakfast.*

Ben tells her to wait here. He will bring her some food even if he has to regurgitate his own breakfast. After all, she needs nourishment to build up her strength. It is obvious she is still unable to walk very far.

He hides his excitement and looks forward to her company. He thinks playing with Molly will be great fun. He is looking forward to the good times ahead with this new companion.

Later they ate breakfast at the same dumpster they found last evening and drank some water. It is decision time. "Ben, I am wondering if it is wise to continue walking. It's very difficult with Molly in a wheel barrel," Sam states. Then continues, "Walking with my six foot, one inch frame while bent over pushing the wheel barrel is just as awkward as it looks; also it's very hard on my back," Sam relates to Ben. Am I talking myself into hanging out here until Molly can walk?

Ben barks in agreement. This place is a very good shelter. There's a door and windows even if they are dirty, plus an old lumpy mattress. Sam and I have slept on some pretty hard surfaces recently.

Sam reminisces. The old mattress is not the most comfortable bed but good enough. Isn't it amazing what you can get used to? It doesn't seem like anyone will bother us here. He thought that he heard some rats running along the old galvanized furnace pipes during the night and wonders if they will bother him with the dogs nearby.

Maybe I can pick up some casual work and earn a few bucks. "Now there's a thought," he says out loud. Perhaps this is an acknowledgement that he is once again feeling positive and looking towards the future. For the first time in two years I am experiencing awareness that I am motivated. For some reason the dogs help to renew his energy. "I like feeling good and looking towards the future. I didn't realize how much I miss this positive side of my life," Sam whispers to himself.

He begins to scratch Ben's ears. "So far we are doing okay without money. What do we need money for? This ritzy hotel certainly doesn't cost anything. The food is free. The weather here is great, very little rain in the scheme of things. Freedom and no responsibilities, we have the perfect situation," he says, rationalizing his current living arrangement and financial position.

Ben barks and cuddles his head into Sam's hand. "Staying put is the right decision. People don't hassle us when they see our trio. Molly's feeling better every day, probably just as much due to your watchfulness, Ben, as to my nursing care," Sam says giving credit to Ben for his help with Molly.

Sam – Chapter Six

Three weeks pass and their routine does not change. Ben is happy and patiently waiting for Molly to feel like playing.

Then one day Sam, Ben and Molly happily walk to the diner on their regular food hunt. Another warm sunny day and all is well. Sam smiles contentedly, "I am so glad we found this place. They always have the best and tastiest food here. Let's eat guys."

After climbing up and looking in the dumpster for food, Sam suddenly stops, and then backs away from the dumpster. He is in shock by the look on his face. Then for no obvious reason that Ben understands, Sam becomes very irritated, muttering incoherent sounds under his breath.

Sam then quickly jogs, with determination, towards the front entrance of the diner.

Ben is curious about this strange behavior. What is happening? Why is Sam acting so strange? He decides to follow him. This behavior from Sam is quite out of character. Ben has never seen Sam so agitated.

Ben watches as Sam, in his tattered unwashed clothes, enters the diner with immense irritation. Ben sees that many of the customers observing Sam in the diner are uncomfortable and pulling faces, but Sam ignores their looks and sneers because he just doesn't seem to care right now. This also is out of character for the mild well-mannered Sam he is familiar with.

Sam remembered seeing a police cruiser in the front parking lot of the diner. With hands on his hips Sam rushes into the diner and with deliberation walks directly up to a booth and interrupts two police officers in uniform having their daily cup of Java. He blurts out, "There's a head in the dumpster!"

Sam quickly gets their attention. They immediately put down their coffee cups; sit up in their seats with their eyes and mouths wide open, and demand, "What did you say?"

"There's a head in the dumpster out back," Sam indignantly repeats.

The officers jump up from their seats knocking their muffins off the plates and spilling their coffee onto the table. They then speak in unison with a wave of the hand, "C'mon show us!"

Ben trots after Sam and the running officers to the dumpster out back.

Molly hobbles as best she can as she tries to keep up with Ben.

Some curious diner customers, plus Tom the owner, overhear Sam's declaration, and follow the entourage to the dumpster. The officers climb up onto a wooden box and reluctantly peek down into the dumpster.

Sure enough, there's a head in the dumpster. Ben watches as one daring officer climbs up higher so he can get a better look at the head, and leans over just a little bit too far; he loses his balance, slips, then falls into the dumpster. He lands right on top of the severed head.

The officer's arm was waving, as he shrieks at the top of his lungs, "Help. Oh my God! Get me out of here! Get me out of here, now!"

The other officer scrambles up onto the stack of garbage bags and helps his distressed partner extract himself from the dumpster. "That'll teach you to be so nosey," he teases him.

The officers immediately radio in the gruesome discovery to their supervisor, "This is patrol officer, Jackson, Badge number Three - Six - Four. We're at The Blueberry Hill Diner and a guy has discovered a severed head in the dumpster. We need a detective here pronto before these folks start wandering away."

The operator's voice was heard on the two way radio asking. "Sure thing; is the person who found the head still there?"

"Yes, he is," responds the officer.

"Please ask him to stay there until the detectives arrive," the operator's voice instructs.

Officer Jackson approaches Sam and says, "We have orders to keep you, here as a witness. When the boys from downtown arrive they will want to take your statement. Probably they will want to ask you more questions." He pauses, looking at Sam again. "Are you from around here?" He asks, thinking he recognizes Sam.

"No, just passing through," Sam responds, realizing he might be made.

"Are you sure? You look very familiar. It'll come to me. I always remember faces," the uniform says as he, deep in thought, slowly wanders away.

"Do you know that guy?" The other officer asks Sam nodding in the direction of the dumpster.

"Nope, never saw him before," Sam responds.

The trio waits patiently as instructed. It seems obvious to Sam that this is a murder.

In the meantime Sam watches with interest as they cordon off the area around the dumpster with yellow crime scene tape. Sam thinks about how he has not, of late, always lived strictly within the law. Being homeless forced him to do what was necessary to survive. For this reason Sam is not motivated to hang around. But, he knows if he leaves the police would increase their suspicions. Sam says under his breathe, "I don't want them digging too deeply into my past either. I don't have many explanations that I wish to share about my time spent as a drifter."

Ben and Molly wait at Sam's side watching the proceedings. An observer might compare their head movements with the bobble heads you see on dashboards of cars or trucks, back and forth, back and forth, following the movements of the people investigating.

When the detectives arrive with the coroner, they put on their Latex gloves and yellow coveralls, and then climb into the dumpster and rifle through the garbage; they do not know it is lunch for Sam, Ben, and Molly.

That is when the detectives inside the dumpster holler to those watching, "We just found a foot – wait, two feet to be exact."

This isn't getting any better, Sam thinks with despair.

The first officer turns to Sam and says, "I know who you are! You're that hockey player that left after your family died. I knew you looked familiar. You were a great right winger. I was a huge fan of yours."

"Let that be our little secret, okay?" Sam whispers to the officer with his forefinger held to his pursed lips. Sam knew there was no sense in denying his past.

Sam – Chapter Seven

One of the detectives that just arrived approaches Sam. "Hello, my name's Detective Michael McCann. I'd like to ask you a few questions if you don't mind."

Sam assesses this fellow to be a very serious, hardnosed interrogator. His rather large physique, wide hips and big belly, pale complexion, and balding head support Sam's thinking, that Detective Mike is a career detective who spends far too much time sitting at his desk, drinking coffee, and eating donuts. "Sure, no problem, ask away," Sam answers.

"I understand you found the head in the dumpster," Detective Mike asks.

"Yes. I did report it immediately after my discovery," Sam volunteers.

"Do you know who that severed head in the dumpster belongs to?" the detective asks.

"No sir, never laid eyes on him before," Sam states almost wishing he hadn't been quite so flippant or for that matter diligent in reporting his gruesome discovery.

"What's your name?" Detective asks.

"Sam Garner," he replies in a more serious manner.

"What's your address?" Detective Mike inquires.

"Well, right now, me and my two dogs kind of live and sleep in one of the abandoned buildings on Sutter Street," Sam offers hoping his response won't cause him trouble or give birth to suspicions.

"What you are telling me is that you don't have a regular address," he presses Sam. Being homeless makes him seem less credible in Detective Mike McCann's mind.

"No, I don't," Sam replies shaking his head negatively but trying to be positive in his response and tone of voice.

"When did you first notice the head?" The detective continues to gather specifics which he writes in his note book. He always includes his observations for future reference.

"Earlier today. I'm pretty sure it wasn't there yesterday," Sam shares as he glances over to the big green dumpster which is now crawling with officers in uniforms and wearing masks due to the stench of rotting food.

Detective Mike's curiosity is peaked so he asks, "What makes you so sure the head wasn't there yesterday?"

"Sir, we have been eating food from that dumpster for almost three weeks now. At least twice a day, we dig through the food for our meals that the diner folks throw out. Believe me, I would have seen it, just like I did today," Sam replies trying really hard to not show his irritation with the questioning. He senses he is being accused of the murder and dismemberment of the body. He's feeling quite threatened.

"So you're a Dumpster Diver?" Detective Mike asks in an unkind provoking manner.

That doesn't sound like a complimentary reference, so Sam thinks it's best to divert the interrogation and judgments away from him. He asks, "Have you identified the person's head?" nodding toward the dumpster.

"Right now, that's a need to know situation and you don't need to know," responds Detective Mike sounding more like a television actor for a detective show than a real life cop.

The detective continues to nail Sam down for details that he will be able to investigate and verify, "Where can I find you, should I need to talk to you again about this case?"

As politely as he could, Sam tries to reinforce his point, "I have no idea who the head belongs to and I do not know him. I have only been in this area for a few weeks. I am originally from out west, Seattle to be exact. I don't know too many people that are anxious to make friends with a drifter. Do you?"

"Just, don't leave town." He orders Sam, while pointing the working end of his pen at him.

"Sure." Sam replies, "I have an injured dog," He indicates by bringing the Detective's attention to the splint still on Molly's leg. "Until that heals, I'm not mobile. I'm here every day. If you don't see me just leave a message with the diner owners. I think they are quite used to my schedule." Walking away, Sam mutters indignantly, "Dumpster Diver! Does he think I eat there by choice? Some people just don't get it." A few steps further, Sam says under his breath, "Don't leave town. Do I look like someone who has the resources to leave town?" He continues grumbling to himself for another block.

Sam knew he wasn't actually wanted by the police, but he's not so sure about Ben and Molly. Maybe someone's looking for them. They might charge me with dog knapping or just take the dogs away from me and send them to Animal Control. Sam thinks about that for a moment causing a frown of deep ridges to appear on his forehead. "I would hate that." He scowls at the very thought of losing them. Ben and Molly certainly can't speak on my behalf.

Sam – Chapter Eight

Tom and Sue Floyd, the owners of the Blueberry Hill Diner, watch the excitement taking place in their parking lot. Many of their customers are overcome with curiosity. Sitting and standing customers crank their necks to watch the flurry of activity. There's an ongoing commentary reporting the activity in the parking lot, to those who don't have a good view.

Sue says to Tom, "I would wager that some of our more curious customers will actually hang around for hours just watching the police at work."

"Casper County hasn't seen excitement like this for a very long time. I suppose they have nothing better to do," Tom tells Sue.

The Blueberry Hill Diner is very popular with locals. They play fifty's and sixty's music all day. The fiftyish-era interior design scheme is mostly shiny chrome. The tables and soda bar are spotlessly clean white laminate countertops. The booths, chairs and stools are shiny polished chrome with turquoise leatherette seat and back covers. The glass display towers on the counter house scrumptious desserts such as pies, donuts, cookies and muffins.

Always floating through the air is the enticing aroma of Tom's delicious baking beckoning the patrons to order, hungry or not.

Each seating area has its own machine where the customer is able to select music to play on the juke box for only a dime. Currently C-14, an all-time favorite is playing, Elvis Presley's Heartbreak Hotel. A few patrons are animatedly singing along and displaying the appropriate guitar strumming actions and the famous hip gyrations.

Tom feels empathy for the hard working police officers and detectives. He prepares a tray of coffee which he offers to them, "Would you guys like a coffee break?" He then suggests, "If, you would prefer to sit, you are welcome to come inside and make yourselves comfortable."

"Thanks, but we have lots of work to do. I will take a coffee though. We need to find out who that guy is and how his head and feet got in your dumpster," Detective Mike responds. "Did anyone ask you if you know that guy?" The Detective as an afterthought questions, Tom.

"Nope, no one has asked me. We've owned this diner a long time; I've never seen him around here, ever," Tom convincingly replies.

"What do you know about that guy, Sam?" Mike questions Tom.

"Not much. He has been hanging around for about three weeks now. He and his dogs eat food from our dumpster every day," Tom said, confirming the information that Sam had told Mike.

Sam – Chapter Nine

Later, Tom said to his wife, Sue, "As an owner of the diner you know I have no problem with that young homeless guy bringing his dogs here to eat food from our dumpster, but it doesn't feel right having him eating kitchen scraps from the dumpster."

"I agree," Sue says. Then she asks, "What should we do now because the dumpster's a crime scene and off limits?"

Tom said, "I have an idea. I'll put out some food out this evening just for the gang. We can use some of our old beaten up cooking pans."

Before the trio left, Tom pulls Sam to one side and says, "We will not be able to put our scraps in the dumpster for a day or two. I know how much you and your dogs depend on that food. When you come back this evening with your friends, we will have a plate for each of you out back."

Sam graciously responds, "You are too kind. Thank you so much – thank you."

When Sam and his gang arrive that evening their food is there alright, along with a little surprise. Sam doesn't know what to think. The surprise has a beautiful, shiny black coat, green eyes and a little pink tongue. It also possesses a nice little set of teeth, which shows when he hisses at them whenever the threesome approach, just like a ferrous Jaguar. The little black beauty's ribs and bones are far too visible. Sam feels bad for him as it is obvious that he is pathetically undernourished and very hungry. The cat is ravenous and eats like he hasn't had a decent meal for quite some time.

Sam smiles at how the cat has taken possession of all of the plates. I guess he's protecting his personal treasure. Upon further observation, Sam notices that the cat is most interested in the big roasted chicken drumstick. So he says, "Here little fella, I'll move your dinner over here then you can finish eating your drumstick, on your own . . . without competition from the dogs."

Sam announces to Ben and Molly, "Okay guys, problem solved now we can eat in peace. The little black beauty does not seem to be afraid of either of you, Ben and Molly. That's very interesting," Sam says out loud.

When they finish eating, each in their own way, they clean their faces making sure that they do not miss any of the delicious food. They all sit for a moment to digest their feast, including the cat, which is perched on a wooden box, close, but just out of reach.

Sam, Ben, and Molly wander around the streets enjoying a post meal walk and checking out their neighborhood. Later they head back to their digs for the night. They are totally unaware that they are being followed.

When they wake up the next morning, there is a little glossy black cat curled up to the warmth of Ben's body . . . sound asleep. Ben doesn't mind one bit.

"I guess this means that we're now a quartette." Sam voices out loud.

Sam – Chapter Ten

Sam watches Molly's progress and observes that she is still hobbling . . . her leg's taking time to heal. He recalls that John the Vet said to expect it to take up to five weeks . . . so they must not push her too soon.

Sam says to Ben, "We should wait another week or maybe two until Molly can walk a good distance without too much discomfort."

Ben barks in agreement. He is in no hurry to move on right now, either. Ben likes the family feeling with familiar animals and people around him.

Sam believes things are going along very smoothly even though their group is growing. He delights at the compatibility of the new friends. Animals are far less discriminating than humans; they just stick together and protect each other. I suppose there are good reasons to be adversarial at times but his impression right now is that would be the exception not the norm. He certainly doesn't feel lonely and is not dwelling as much on the past as he did before he met his new companions.

Tom and Sue get a chuckle when the quartette arrives for breakfast. “It‘s a strange but pleasant sight,” Sue says.

Tom comments to Sue, “I have concerns about that pleasant soft spoken guy’s only food supply being our scraps of garbage.

“I have an idea,” Tom says, deep in thought. “I’ll be back in a few minutes.”

Tom politely and cautiously approaches Sam and asks, “I do not mean to pry and you certainly don’t need to tell me if you prefer not to, but if it’s not a problem, will you please tell me a little about yourself.”

Sam frowns when he looks back at Tom and asks, “Why? What do you want to know? Have I done something wrong?”

Tom said, “No . . . Please, I’m asking you to trust me. Even though it may appear that I’m just being a busy body. I do have a valid reason for asking.”

Sam hesitates for a few moments. He then takes a deep breath, drops his broad shoulders and hangs his head. His Adams apple moves slowly up and down as Sam swallows his pride, then reluctantly but briefly, shares some of the details of his past. “I was a professional hockey player for a Pro NHL Team. I’m originally from a small town out west,” Sam pauses, “I’m sure you are now curious about how I went from that great life to this.”

Sam opens his arms and moves them like he's inviting someone into his living room. They both sit down on a couple of wobbly old wooden boxes, intended to be picked up by the disposal company.

"Very," Tom has trouble containing his growing curiosity.

"Well . . . briefly, because the full length novel is just too painful," Sam takes a deep breath again to gather his courage. "My mother, father, brother and two sisters attended my eldest sister's soccer game. I had promised my older sister that I would go to her championship game, with the family. She was my biggest fan and so competitive, even when we played street hockey."

Tom tried to keep a neutral face even though he is thinking Sam is sharing a gut-wrenching sad story with him. He could see the pain in Sam's face as his eyes fill with tears, making them look like greenish blue marbles in pools.

Sam valiantly presses on, "This is the sad and really painful part of my biography. After the game, while driving home, a drunk driver crossed the middle line coming into their lane and hit them head on. They all died at the scene. I suppose for them that was good because they didn't suffer too long. But it still is so difficult for me, even though it's now two years since that terrible night. I blame myself and carry a lot of guilt because I wasn't there for my amazing family. I always believed that maybe if I was driving, I could have somehow avoided the accident. I completely lost it. I stopped going to practice, then stopped playing hockey. I eventually quit the league and moved away because I found it too difficult to continue to live in my childhood home with all my memories of those very happy days of my youth, with my wonderful family. They were my biggest and most supportive fans."

Sam excuses himself as he now becomes speechless; he tries desperately to choke down his emotions. He is overcome with the urge to be alone so he can let go and have a good cry. Then he thought, that was painful but having said it out loud, I kind of feel a little better. Have I finally put the horror of that night behind me? I will never lose those memories; of course, they are filed away in my private scrapbook, filled with many mental photos of the good times.

When Sam comes back, Tom is still waiting.

"That's a tragic story. I didn't know when I asked you to tell me about yourself that it was such an emotionally painful tale. Thank you so much for sharing your personal nightmare with me. I am so sorry . . . I didn't know," Tom, being a compassionate person, hears many stories, but this is one of the worse ones yet.

"I do recognize you now. You did look familiar but I couldn't place your face. Maybe if you had shaved your beard, had shorter hair and worn your helmet, I would have recognized you straight off," Tom said, jokingly and smiling at Sam. He is trying to lighten up the mood and is excited to personally meet a real celebrity.

Sam – Chapter Eleven

Detective Michael McCann returns to his precinct and proceeds to review the evidence they collected today from the dumpster. He said, "Guys, run that face through the recognition program and see if we can ID him."

Twenty minutes later, Officer Jim announces, "We got a match. His name is George Lamb from Seattle. He has a current driver's license. He also has a few misdemeanors – mostly minor stuff, plus a few DUIs."

Mike calls to a junior officer working on the computer, "Check the DNA of the feet with the coroner. Let's confirm they actually belong to the head."

Checking his notes from his interviews, Mike says, "Wasn't that homeless guy that found the head from Seattle too?" Mike said flipping through the pages of his note book; he felt something might be fitting together, "I don't believe in coincidences. I want to talk to him again."

"Should I know him? He seems very familiar but I just can't place the face." Mike asks Jim, the senior Uniform Officer.

The officer shrugs his shoulders and starts to walk away, then turns his head, speaking over his shoulder, to Mike, "I think he's looks a lot like that pro hockey player. Don't know for sure though, but if I had to guess that's who I think he is."

Mike telephones the Seattle police. "Hi, my name is Detective Michael McCann, Casper County. We have found, so far, the head and possibly the feet of George Lamb. His driver's license shows a Seattle address. Can you transfer me to someone there who can tell me something about him?"

"Yes, please hold. I'll transfer you to the detective in charge here, Frank Ottello," the officer says.

Picking up the receiver Frank speaks briskly in a little too loud voice, "Yeah, Ottello here. Who are you?"

"Hi, I'm Detective Michael McCann, Casper County. I'm calling to let you know that we have found a head and two feet, so far. We have identified them as belonging to George Lamb. His driver's license show a Seattle address. Can you tell me anything about him?" Mike repeats.

"Hold for a second and I'll check our system . . . Yeah! Lamb has several DUIs. We did question him in connection with a serious accident where a father, mother and her three children were killed by what we believed to be a drunk driver a couple of years ago, but nothing ever developed. I remember this case because the only living member of the family was a Professional Hockey Player. Case is still unsolved," Detective Frank explained. "Lamb has not held down a steady job for some time from what we can tell. We don't know for sure, but we hear he has gotten involved with a nasty bunch of low life criminal types," Frank shares some documented information and some unconfirmed gossip he has picked up on the streets.

Mike went silent for a few seconds mulling over this new information. He questions, "What would he be doing here? I don't see the connection, except, the guy who first discovered the body, well the head, in the dumpster is originally from Seattle."

"What's his name?" Frank asks.

"Sam Garner. Is the name familiar to you?" Mike questions while hoping this detail would help to put his case together.

"Hmm . . . maybe . . . yeah, I think he's the hockey player I just mentioned. I'll need to check that case file. I'll get back to you," Frank replies, then he gets that all too familiar twitch on his left cheek, when something sounds like it fits but he just doesn't know how or why. He is unaware that he is tugging at his ear lobe, a sure sign that he knows something. He realizes there is a fact that is not coming to mind, not right now anyway.

Mike adds, "Maybe I need to have another chat with our guy. He may know more than he is telling us about

Lamb. It is early in our investigation. I'll keep digging." Mike is convincing himself this information is a piece of the puzzle. He rubs his fingers across his bristly facial stubble deep in thought.

"Mike if I come across anything at all, I'll call you." Frank hangs up still wondering if there is a connection, and wonders what it could possibly be. Where or how could their paths have crossed?

"Sure thanks, Frank," Mike says to the dead line, hoping the answers he is seeking are in Seattle.

Frank put a big question mark on his notes. He didn't like unsolved mysteries. "I'll do some digging. There's more to this story, and I need to check my sources," he promises.

Sam – Chapter Twelve

Later that evening while sitting in the living room, Tom told Sue, "I'm always amazed when I learn the cards that people are dealt during their lives. Even more interesting is how they play their hands."

He shares with Sue, "We're very lucky; some might even think we're even boring. We have been married now for what about thirty eight years? We have two really great kids, one boy, one girl, the millionaire's family. Yes, we are blessed. We have owned the diner for the past twenty five years. When the kids went off to college, much to my enjoyment you joined me there. I really like working side by side with you and sharing the details of our day and the business."

Sue responds, "Yes, I admit I do enjoy eating your wonderful culinary creations."

While checking her hair in the mirror, Sue asks, "Tom, do you think I should put some color in my hair? It is getting a little dull?"

"Sweetie, I don't care about a little gray hair. It is your dazzling amber eyes that attracted me to you then, and continue to do so, until this very day. You're still a striking gal to me. You look wonderful. Even in your late fifties you are still a great looking woman. I think you would give some of those movie stars a run for the money. I know I'm a little biased but that's how it is."

While we are discussing physical attributes, Sue smiles and teasingly states, "You do know that, we can all see the bald patch on top of your graying red hair. I agree that wearing the big chef's hat does do a good job of hiding the hairless patch. You know sweetie, I guess we aren't getting any younger. We should be happy with our lot. Life has been kind to our family." Sue adds, "I listen to our customers and I hear them confiding in you their most inner thoughts, both fears and the good times. People tell me, Tom's eyes made me do it. You know that I, too, have always loved your bluish green eyes. They are so soft and friendly." Sue chuckles and Tom blushes.

Tom shares Sam's horrific story with Sue. In a very sympathetic manner he said, "You can never make assumptions about why people are where they are, and the events of their lives that influence their behavior and decisions. You know, we have lived quite an ordinary life when you hear the details, events and incidents, in other people's lives."

Sue agrees, "You are right."

Tom says, "Clive, told me today that he is moving out of state. His folks are elderly and in poor health. They need his help around the house. He also confided that he has decided to go home." Tom fidgets a little in his chair as he prepares his speech. "I have something, actually an idea that came to me today. I would like to bounce it off you. Don't get excited . . . just let me finish. Yes I think this qualifies as one of my more goofy ideas, but here it is," he exhales to relax and to gather his courage. "As you are aware, earlier this afternoon I had a long chat with that homeless guy, Sam is his name. Later I got to thinking, after Sam finished telling me his heart-wrenching story. How can I help? Did you know he was a professional hockey player?" Tom asks.

Visibly showing her surprise, Sue exclaims, "No way. He certainly is a handsome guy and still has a pretty good build, but I never would have guessed him to be an athlete."

"I thought I recognized him, but I have only ever seen him on TV. Now that I know he is well-educated and a man about town, I think that translates into way over-qualified, but hear me out . . . let's offer him the job of bus boy. I don't know if he will do it, because it is an enormous step down from a hefty income and the fame of a professional competitor. But keep in mind it is also a huge step up from homeless and eating the food we throw into the dumpster." In his excitement, he is almost out of breath by the time he finishes his little speech.

Waiting quietly for what seems like an eternity while

Sue mulls over the proposal in her mind, he envisions the wheels of her mind turning. He hopes she will see it his way. Impatiently he adds, "Well, well what do you think?" Her response came quicker and more enthusiastically than he had anticipated.

"I think that is a wonderful idea, Tom. He does seem like a great guy and educated, maybe just a little lost for the moment. I would love to be there when you ask him tomorrow morning. I have an idea, too, almost as goofy as yours," Sue replies.

Tom presses her to tell him, "Come on, Sue, share your idea with me."

She shakes her head and will not tell him her idea, not even a hint. Instead, Sue prefers to keep Tom in suspense. Smiling, she quietly develops the plan in her mind.

Sam – Chapter Thirteen

Molly and Ben are indifferent about the cat's name. So Sam alone chooses to name their new feline friend, "Harry." It suits him as he acts almost human.

Observing his pets at play, Sam thinks about the easy going contentment within his little group. We are all friends brought together from various situations but nevertheless comfortable and respectful of each other. I like that. Today is another bright, warm sunny day, their favorite kind. "You guys hungry?" Sam asks.

All four saunter off to see what the diner had served for breakfast today. Harry's off somewhere doing his thing but never too far away, as a cat he had no interest in traveling directly to any place. He is very curious and just likes to explore.

Ben is pleased with Molly's remarkable recovery. She's prancing and frolicking with him. Not showing any ill effects from her fracture. That means we'll soon be able to continue our journey. Ben's not sure he's happy about that prospect . . . maybe he secretly wishes that he could settle down some place, and that he may never find his first people family. He definitely has mixed feelings. He thinks he will need to get serious and assess just which direction he wants to take, the rest of his life . . . especially if he decides to stop looking.

Ben thinks Harry seems very happy as he darts in and out of every nook and cranny. Whenever Sam speaks to Harry, "He meows, back at him." It's as if he actually is responding to Sam's voice and taking part in the conversation. Sam chuckles every time it happens. Ben is not very familiar with cats and their ways, he wonders if this behavior is normal or an aberration. Nevertheless Harry keeps them all amused.

Ben notices that as they arrive at the diner, Tom, who is dressed in his whites with his large food soiled apron blowing in the wind, comes running out of the diner door waving Sam over. The entourage follows.

"Sam, come inside the diner."

Sam is reluctant at first. Then he points to his little group, "What about my family?"

"Yes, of course, all of you." To everyone's surprise a table is set for Sam and three bowls of food, plus water, are all lined up near the back door for Ben, Molly and Harry.

Sam hangs back and shows resistance. "I'm not comfortable with this special arrangement."

Tom says, "Don't worry it's okay. If you would like to wash up the washroom is over there."

When Sam returns to the booth with his breakfast neatly arranged his concerns were quickly shelved. Then Tom and Sue both sit at the booth with him.

"We need your help, Sam," Tom declares with a totally straight face.

"My help . . . what could I possibly do to help you?" Sam frowns bringing his eyebrows closer with an exaggerated frown; he is very curious.

"Clive, our bus boy, told us he is leaving soon, due to family issues, and we are desperate to find a replacement for him. Actually, we need someone immediately. Clive has agreed to stay here to train the new person. We know you are way over qualified but you would be doing us a huge favor. Even if you just took the job for a few weeks until we are able to hire someone else, it would really help us. Please, we would really like you to consider our offer," Tom did a good job of pleading his case. They did make it sound like they were actually trying to get Sam to take the job.

Sam's face lights up, he sits up straight on the bench, and his body language is showing his pleasure. A low pressure, low skills job did kind of appeals to him right now. "I must admit, that I am getting a little weary of sleeping outdoors and always looking for food and the necessities of life," he stops to think for a moment before continuing. "Maybe with a job, I can find a room to rent where they allow pets." Sam's mind is now working overtime, as the proposal of putting down roots with his new friends has merit and feels good.

"If possible I would like to take a few hours to think about the job offer and, of course, talk it over with my family," Sam said, but deep down he was eager to accept.

Sue raises her eyebrow and questions, "Family?"

Sam smiles and points to the trio now resting near the back door.

"Oh! Enough said, "Sue responds and then coyly adds, "I have something else that we would like to add to that offer.

"Oh?" Sam questions. Now it's his turn to raise his eyebrows. He wonders what else they can possibly add, everything being so perfect.

"There is an apartment upstairs," She indicates by pointing her index finger to the ceiling of the diner. "It has been vacant for over a year. Clive stayed there when he first started working here. Then he moved to another place closer to his new girlfriend."

"Are you offering to rent the apartment to me? I have the dogs and now a cat. Will that make a difference? Besides, I don't know what you pay a bus boy, but I'm pretty sure I can't possibly afford an apartment," Sam responds negatively, shaking his head expressing his immediate concerns. "As much as I would like the job, I'm not prepared to give up my four legged friends. They mean way too much to me," Sam adds.

"There are always problems in a diner or restaurant with mice and various bugs. I think you have the best collection of exterminators I have ever seen," adds Tom. "So, we'll call it a wash."

"Wow, you sure make it difficult for a fella to say, no," Sam quickly jumps in, "Not that I have made that decision, at least not yet," He raises his hand palm side to Tom stopping him from drawing a wrong conclusion from his comment.

"My head is whirling at the thought of employment plus a place to live with my pets. I am seriously considering accepting the whole package," Sam adds.

"If you need more motivation, your meals will be free. You'll be able to come straight to the kitchen in the morning, not via the dumpster. Of course, there are always scraps for your family," Tom said with a wink in Sue's direction.

Sam consumes one of the best meals he has eaten in a very long time. He offers his hand and shakes Tom's hand, then says, "I can't thank you enough, I really do appreciate the offer. I will get back to you soon, very soon."

After he leaves, Tom gives Sue a peck on her cheek and says, "I like your surprise and no, not goofy at all. It's perfect."

Sam – Chapter Fourteen

Sam is deep in thought as he; Ben, Molly and Harry leave the diner on their way back to their temporary home the Ben Ritz. He pressures himself to make the correct decision. His entourage plays, romps, and chases each other around the diner parking lot. They are a happy group and Sam isn't inclined to do anything that will upset that chemistry. They have only just reached the edge of the parking lot, when a police cruiser pulls up right in front of Sam, and comes to an abrupt stop.

The officer rolls down the cruiser window then asks, "You Sam Garner?"

Ben moves between Sam and the cruiser. He stands guard shielding Sam. He doesn't like the sound of the officer's aggressive voice. Ben worries about Sam's safety and immediately goes into protection mode.

"Yes I am. Why? What's up officer?" He questions, while patting Ben to calm and reassure him.

"We would like you come with us," The officer adds, "We have some questions we'd like to ask you."

Ben is happy when he looks back at the diner and sees Tom and Sue quickly running towards them.

Tom asks, "Sam you okay?"

"I think so. These officers want to ask me some questions at the police station," Sam says nervously, wiping his sweaty palms on his worn plaid shirt. He is putting on a brave front but he is feeling pangs of anxiety in his gut.

Tom quickly resolves the dilemma for Sam. "We'll watch your family. Don't worry. They'll be fine."

"Thank you so much. I hope this doesn't take too long," Sam adds and gently moves Ben out of the way. "It will be okay Ben, good boy," Sam tries to calm Ben but wonders if he succeeded when he is not feeling very calm himself.

Ben watches as the men in uniform guide Sam into the back seat of their car, with the blue and red flashing lights. Ben feels very uneasy. *What's happening? Why are they taking Sam away? What is going to happen to us?*

Sam – Chapter Fifteen

At the Police station the officer escorts Sam to an interview room and instructs, "Mr. Garner, you will need to stay in here until we're ready."

While waiting Sam takes the opportunity to survey his environment. The interview room is stark; the walls are painted a dreary drab gray, and they are very much in need of touch ups on the scuffed walls. The room is no more than an eight foot square box, almost claustrophobic. It is absent of windows and furniture except for a rough unfinished wooden table with the steel loop adornment for handcuffs, to keep the prisoners from free movement. The wooden chairs are modest and very uncomfortable. In the corner near the ceiling is a blinking red light that reminds the room's inhabitants, that they are being videotaped and recorded. Of course, the wall opposite Sam has the infamous one-way glass mirror, keeping observers anonymous.

Sam wonders, "Who's behind that mirror watching me?" He turns to the mirror and under his breath asks, "What's going on? What do you think I have done?"

"You'll find out soon enough," the officer replies. By the way the officer is wrinkling his nose, it is apparent to him, that this guy hasn't showered recently and he does not smell good.

"Do I need a lawyer?" Sam asks, not wanting to make the situation worse, but he knows he has rights.

"Do you need a lawyer?" The officer responds just as Detective Mike enters the room.

Sam looks up and says, "Who's your decorator?" He is nervous and trying to ease the tension in the room.

The Detective briefly glances around the room, but other than that, ignores Sam's comment. Detective Mike McCann anxiously awaited Sam's arrival. He has lots of questions. "Hello again, Sam, do you remember me? I'm Detective Mike McCann." He reintroduces himself, and then he slaps down a file on the table in front of him making an unnerving cracking sound in the quiet room.

"Yes I do remember you. What's going on here?" Sam is getting agitated as he feels an unfriendly tension developing in the interview room.

"Relax. I just need some answers to a few more questions, and I thought you might be able to help me with that," Mike speaks calmly as he does not want to exacerbate an already stressful environment. Detective Mike points to the flashing red light in the corner of the room and says, "I just want to let you know that this interview is being recorded."

"I have done nothing wrong and I want to know what this is all about, right now." Sam's patience is wearing thin. He really does not want to play this game.

"Okay, let's get right to it. You told me that you were originally from Seattle," Mike reviews the facts.

"Yes, two years ago. I haven't been back since," Sam responds. "There is nothing there for me, anymore."

"What does that mean?" Mike queries.

"Just what I said; I have no reason to ever go back to Seattle," Sam responds.

You also said you didn't know the guy in the dumpster. Is that right?" Mike asks looking at his notes then he pushes a photo of the severed head in Sam's direction.

Sam turns his head away and shoves the photo back in the Detective's direction. "That's right, I have never seen him before," Sam says, responding with an edge in his voice. He is visibly repulsed by the photo. He feels like he needs to vomit.

"I find that odd. You see, I don't believe in coincidences. I'm thinking you had a beef with him back in Seattle," Mike insinuates as he pushes Sam.

"What are you talking about? I told you, I don't know him. I didn't even know he was from Seattle. Seattle is a very large city with several million people," Sam gets more agitated. "I don't see how I can help you. I don't know where you are going with this."

"Sam, we are in the evidence-gathering phase of this investigation. I am just collecting information about facts that seem to be relevant," Mike answers with hand motions that suggest he wants Sam to relax, settle down and talk to him.

"His name is George Lamb. He has a sheet full of misdemeanors and DUIs," Mike shares.

For a split second a flash of recognition or something crosses Sam's face at the mention of DUIs. Mike, a keen observer, sees it and wonders what it means.

"I think you just reacted to something I said. I want to know what that was," Mike says probing for an explanation.

"I'm extremely sensitive to any words about drunk driving. My family was all killed by a drunk driver. That's all," Sam said, now feeling vulnerable.

"Do you think Mr. Lamb was that driver?" Mike proposes.

"No, I don't know who killed my family. I'm sure this is all a vast collection of unrelated details," Sam emphasizes his point by jabbing Mike's file with his fore finger, "that you have wound together. It is a massive assortment of coincidences and conjectures just to create a fable that matches your theories, hoping to snare me in your spider web," Sam replies indignantly. "You are creating a fairy tale from totally unrelated information."

"Sam, this is my problem," Mike pauses, "both of you are from Seattle. Both of you have been impacted by drunk driving. Both of you show up here in Casper County. That in my book is a considerable number of details in common, don't you think?" Mike asks, "I'm sure you can see my dilemma. So, please help me out here."

"I don't see anything of the kind. You are trying to make individual unrelated pieces of information into a case. This has nothing to do with me. Why are you trying so hard to manufacture a link between us?" Sam questions as he is poised to stand up and leave.

"Okay just relax. Maybe it would help me to put the pieces together correctly, if you told me your story." Mike motions with an open palm for Sam to stay seated.

"Believe me my story has nothing to do with your investigation. I want to leave here now," Sam pleads with Detective Mike. He stands with the intention of leaving the interview room, but detective Mike stands and places his hand on Sam's shoulder, forcing him back down into the uncomfortable wooden chair.

"Please, humor me. Let me be the judge, Sam," Mike presses.

"Okay, okay." Reluctantly Sam begins; he takes a deep breath, drops his head and shoulders then begins, "My eldest sister, Karen had a soccer match. It was a championship game and I had promised her that I would be there, but due to a change in my schedule, a stupid, silly photo op, I could not be present. I just could not change the appointment as it involved the whole team. It was one of those beyond my control situations.

"I carry so much guilt for that very reason." He fidgets in his chair and takes another deep breath, then continues. "Karen's team had just won the County Title for Junior Girls' Soccer. They were jubilant, on cloud nine. It was a very happy time for them," Sam recounts, and then his tone changes. "While they were driving home after that soccer game a drunk driver hit them, head on. They all died instantly. In a weird way, that was a blessing. Only, because they didn't suffer for long."

"My wonderful parents whom I loved so much are gone. I don't know why, I just couldn't make any sense of it then or now. I still miss them every single day. I'll never stop asking why," Sam says as his eyes fill with tears; Mike offers Sam a Kleenex.

"Then, there's my youngest sister, Jenny. She was so sweet just three years young and cute as a button with her little turned up nose, clear glass blue eyes like a baby doll and her long curly blonde hair that bounced when she walked. She was far too young to be taken." More tears are shed and another Kleenex is drawn to his face.

"Then, Christopher, my little brother who idolized me so much, a little macho man just six years old but insisted on being addressed by the more grown up version, Chris. He so wanted to be a professional hockey player like me when he grew up. Little did he know he would never grow up," Sam pauses again to take a breath and fights back the hot lump growing in his throat. Sam knows he must continue.

"Last but not least there was my other sister barely into her teen years. She was beautiful, competitive, and talented; Karen was the apple of my eye." Sam's eyes once again fill with tears that overflow and run down his cheeks. "I miss her smile and cheeky smirk she flashed at me when she wanted to win me over."

By now his words are almost inaudible. Raw emotions always seem to linger just below the surface, and now they are totally exposed, like a wound having a scab scratched off.

"All of them gone when their lives were just budding, what beautiful flowers they would have been. Sometimes I wish I had kept my life together . . . but there was no way. I couldn't have continued to play professional hockey. It didn't mean anything to me anymore. That life had lost its importance for me," Sam stated as his body shudders and shakes with deep sobs.

Sam took a moment to compose himself then he adds, "I was a mess. I became depressed and stopped going to workouts. I was a well-paid professional hockey player. I lost my motivation to play. The team owners hung in for me as long as they could. Eventually my manager had to ask the dreaded question . . . when was I going to be mentally ready, to come back to the game? Deep down I knew I never would," Sam said.

Mike asks, "You're an educated man so I assume you were under the care of a doctor?"

"Yes, I attended therapy for a while. Then the doctors offered drugs; but I was afraid that I would forget my wonderful family. Besides becoming an addict was not a solution. I did not like that option," Sam sighs deeply, slumps in the uncomfortable chair and hangs his head showing how helpless and emotionally drained he feels.

"Sam, did they ever charge the driver?" Mike asks.

Sam, now a beaten man, replies in a monotone voice, "Not that I know of. I was a wreck. I left soon after. I became a drifter. I have been wandering around for about two years."

"Didn't you want justice?" Mike taunts him.

"No thanks. I am not in the revenge business. I'm actually in a good place right now," Sam adds getting agitated again about being questioned as if he is the criminal, not the victim.

"Wow, I bet you have a strong civil case, too. You could sue them, and then you might be rich," Mike again taunts.

"Yes, but I was already rich," Sam declares a little calmer now. "I didn't want to then, and now I just don't care. I just wanted to get away. Before I left Seattle I contacted the police, but they had nothing. Check my story out. Check with the police there. When I left two years ago it was an unsolved case."

"You're a smart guy; maybe you solved the crime all by yourself and got your revenge?" Mike seeing that Sam is feeling stronger pushes him again.

"But I didn't! Check it out. I have been here in this county for close to five weeks. Besides I never wanted revenge. I wanted my family back." Sam leans forward and points at Mike with his forefinger and asks in a very aggressive tone. "Do you have any idea what it feels like to lose your entire family?"

"No, not personally," Detective Mike solemnly adds.

"I'm sure the driver responsible is living in their own hell," Sam acknowledges.

"Can you prove that?" Mike asks taking Sam off guard.

“Prove what?” Sam angrily asks.

“That you have been here in this county for four to five weeks,” Detective Mike clarifies. “In other words, do you have an alibi?” Mike calmly continues as he is hoping to trip up Sam.

“Tom and Sue, the diner owners, can testify that I have been eating out of their dumpster at least that long. Also, there is the veterinarian who put the splint on my dog, Molly. I still have the pill bottle. That was almost five weeks ago.” Sam supplies his alibi, yet he feels that everything he says is being twisted and taken out of context.

“Don’t you worry, we will check out everything about you,” Mike promises.

“Are you going to charge me?” Sam inquires trying to hold in his anger.

“I’m not sure yet,” Mike replies.

“If you are not going to arrest me, I want to leave right now.” Sam feels like he is suffocating under the unrelenting accusations of Detective Mike. “I need some fresh air. This room feels like a cage.”

“You look good for this. If I can link you two together I think we will find that you certainly do have motive. I’ve got lots of evidence albeit right now is all circumstantial, that ties you to this case. Wait here. I’ll be back in a few moments." Mike picks up the file and leaves the interview room closing the door.

Sam waits for what seems like hours but was only twenty minutes.

When Detective Mike returns he says, "Okay you can go. You might want to hire yourself a lawyer. Most important, don't leave the county!"

"Thank you. I hope in the meantime you use your resources to look for the real killer, because you're wasting your time trying to construct details that label me as the killer," Sam firmly pronounces. He musters the strength to stand up tall and proud, and then starts to leave the interview room.

Reaching for the door knob Sam looks back and casually informs detective Mike, "I need a ride back to The Blueberry Hill Diner."

"Sure, the officers that drove you here are ready to take you back," replies Detective Mike in a very congenial tone.

Sam – Chapter Sixteen

Ben hears the cruiser arrive. He immediately stands and moves quickly to the large window of the diner he puts his front paws on the window sill and watches the police drop Sam off in the parking lot. Sam looks very sad and worried; he appears to be weighted down. *I hope Sam is okay.*

Sue opens the diner door allowing Ben and Molly to both run to Sam and greet him with furiously wagging tails, barks of happiness and lots of sloppy kisses. They are sure this happy welcome will make him feel better . . . and it does.

Now it is Harry's turn to welcome Sam back this he did by sitting up on his hind legs and reaching up with his front paws, motioning that he wants Sam to pick him up and give him a big hug.

Sam obliged. He loves exchanging hugs with Harry and listening to his soft purring. That soothing sound put Sam to sleep many a night when he had nightmares.

Tom and Sue run to meet Sam as they were concerned. Sue immediately asks, "Are you okay? You look really stressed, Sam."

"I just can't believe that I . . . me, Sam Garner . . . a former all-American athlete, am under suspicion of a vicious murder and dismemberment of a body."

"Come inside, the diner is closed," Tom insists as he sees Sam is not in a good place mentally and needs friends right now, "You look like you could do with a drink. Scotch?" he offers, "How do you want it?" he asks.

"Thanks Tom, on the rocks would be perfect. I haven't had a drink of hard liquor in a long time, but I think this is an appropriate occasion. Hopefully it will calm me down because inside I am so angry," Sam responds desperately trying to keep the quivering out of his voice. His guard drops when he hears the friendly sympathetic voices of Tom and Sue. He feels tears developing and is trying very hard to hold them back because he doesn't want to cry right now. He's afraid that if he lets the flood of tears start he will not be able to stop and will completely lose control. Then he asks, "When is this nightmare going to end?"

"Sorry Sam I wish we did but we don't have an answer for you." Sue says with concern.

"Life can sure throw some crud at you, just when you are not expecting it. There I was on top of the world. I had everything, money, fame and my perfect job. Now I realize it was all a façade, it wasn't real at all. One terrible accident and it is all gone, poof!" Sam motions upward with his hands. He ponders the reality of his previous life.

"Just when I think I see the light at the end of the tunnel, with you folks giving me an opportunity to get my life back on track, something like this happens. I am having a very difficult time with all of this," Sam is trying not to be too emotional, mostly for those around him. He is especially concerned about Molly and Ben, as he knows they are very sensitive to his emotions.

"What do you mean? Murder! Who did you murder?" Tom says as he hesitates holding his glass in midair waiting for Sam's explanation.

"The guy in your dumpster," Sam clarifies.

"I'm in total shock and astounded that anyone would accuse you of such a horrible crime," Tom exclaims.

"Maybe I'm guilty of not fully appreciating my success, but that doesn't translate into me being a deranged killer," Sam says as he is still overwhelmed with the events of today.

"I didn't murder anyone. You are not going to believe this scenario. The head in the dumpster belongs to a person of interest to the Seattle police, my home town. He had several DUIs back there, so Detective Mike is manufacturing a case based on some of our commonalities. Pure fiction, I tell you. Pure fiction is all it is." Sam stops to catch his breath, takes a sip of his drink and then adds, “He is suggesting that I killed that guy as he might have been involved in the death of my family. Welcome to Fantasy Island.” With that, Sam throws his arms up into the air over his head, and then brings his palms down to rest on top of his head. “Totally frustrated, absolutely totally frustrated, that’s how I feel,” he adds.

“I’m stunned. I don’t believe what I’m hearing,” Tom tries to console Sam, “I’m a good judge of character and I do not believe for one minute that you could or would be involved in anything so violent. Cutting a man’s head and feet off? That’s ridiculous! Even if I thought you could commit murder, which I don’t, I would never believe you could do something so gruesome.”

“Absolutely not, I’m with Tom one hundred percent,” Sue adds, shaking her head in disbelief and offering her full support.

Ben is listening to the conversations. He doesn’t understand much of what is being said, but he sure senses the tension, stress and frustration that Sam, Tom and Sue are expressing. This is worrisome.

Ben and Molly are lying peacefully near Sam’s feet.

Molly looks up, gives a little whine, and then returns to her prone position.

Ben seems to better understand the severity of the situation. He sits up, puts his right paw on Sam’s leg, and then rests his chin beside his paw. He gives Sam the big brown eyes look, offering Sam an, *I'm here, how can I help you* look.

Sam stokes Ben's head and states, "This is what true friendship is all about. I so love these dogs and Harry. They help to ground me."

Tom and Sue nod their heads in agreement and say, "You're right. Having all that fame and fortune is great, but it can disappear just as fast as it came. You've got true friendship there with your family of four legged friends."

As if Harry knew what was being said, he senses he is being ignored, so he said "Meow" loudly, and then brushes his face against Sam's leg and purrs and purrs. He is very happy with his new family.

Tom, Sue and Sam all chuckle. Sam pats Harry's head, then picks him up and holds him close then says, "No we didn't forget you're here. You are a very good friend too, Harry."

A few hours later, after much lamenting, Sam said to his new pals, "I should go; you guys need to get up early and I need to calm down and think this through."

"Actually in two hours I will be back here, starting breakfast," Tom teases Sam and winks in Sue's direction,

"See, if you lived upstairs you would be home in two minutes."

"Are you telling me that you are still willing to offer me the job? Even after all this today?"

"Of course, why not, we believe in you Sam," Sue chirps in.

"Thank you. At least this part of my life is working out for me." Sam is elated with the prospect of employment with people that support and believe in him.

"Come on guys, it's time to go home to bed," Sam announces to his family then turns to Tom and Sue offers his hand, and again expresses his sincere appreciation, "Thank you so very much, for everything," They shake hands and the quartette leaves.

Sam – Chapter Seventeen

He really does like both Tom and Sue and from their discussions earlier this evening they are kind and genuine people. Their customers are always happy and joking with one or the other. The Blueberry Hill Diner is a happy place. I think I'm talking myself into taking the job. He hesitates just for a split second to consider how he feels about being tied down. It has been two years since he actually worked and lived in one place for any length of time.

He negotiates with himself. It's not a problem, as it is just a temporary situation, so I can leave any time I get the wanderlust. It's not like signing a two- year contract to play professional sports. It's only a bus boy job. Sam laughs out loud because he realizes he is arguing with himself. Who is he kidding? His mind is made up. We have both a job and a place to live. He cheers, "Hurray, guys, we have a new home!"

Ben likes the sound of Sam's happy voice. This is very comforting for him.

"Now I just need to prove that I didn't murder and mutilate that fellow from Seattle." Sam is more worried about that situation than he cares to admit.

Ben, Molly, Harry and Sam eat breakfast as usual inside the diner. Sam is very aware of Tom's continuous glances over in his direction. Sam thinks Tom is hoping for an affirmative response from him. This helps Sam to believe that he will be welcome with open hearts to The Blueberry Hill Diner.

All the way back to their temporary housing, Sam grows more confident that he has made the right decision for himself. His heart swells with joy and pride at once again being a working member of society. This feels good. I haven't been this happy in two years. I have forgotten how respectable this new situation makes me feel.

Ben cannot understand why Sam is so elated. Something good is happening that he knows for sure. But, what took place? Molly and Harry are no help as they are as confused as he is. Ben really did enjoy seeing Sam this happy. He just didn't understand why.

Later that day, just before dinner, Sam and his followers pack their few possessions into the old rickety wheelbarrow for their walk back to the diner. Upon their arrival Sam says, "Tom, Sue, I would like very much to help you out. I don't know where the investigation will go. I did not kill that man. I cannot stop living my life until this ludicrous mystery gets solved. I have wasted too much time already. We are ready to set up our new home." Sam waves his hand to include his three friends.

Ben hears that they agree that tomorrow morning Sam will start work. Ben likes the vibes he is getting from this happy group of humans.

Tom replies, "I see that you came prepared to move in upstairs this evening. This is good, as you can get a good night's sleep. Then you only need to come downstairs to work in the morning."

Harry and Molly enjoy the excited people around them. There are smiles, lot of pats and happy words.

Ben feels good and leans into Sam's leg, rubs his cheek on his trousers, and then looks up at him smiling, to show his love and support, because Sam is happy again.

Dinner is served in the same manner as breakfast this morning, with the trio at the back door. There's an almost party-like atmosphere in the diner. Sam feels that the other diners are genuinely welcoming him and his animals

He says more to himself than Tom, "Yeah! I'm no longer a Dumpster Diver."

"What did you say?" Tom asks as he didn't quite believe what he thought he heard.

"Detective Mike categorized me as a "Dumpster Diver." Officially, I no longer fall into that category, he proudly states with pleasure and a sense of accomplishment. "I've officially graduated from that way of life," Sam adds in a very light hearted manner.

"Have you noticed that Ben and Molly do not beg?" Tom asks Sue.

"Yes I have. That's quite amazing, considering these animals previously survived on scraps and dumpster food.

Sam – Chapter Eighteen

Harry like most cats is territorial and does not like too much change so he admits he feels a little nervous with the change to a new home. Ben and Molly are with him so he's feeling a little less nervous about the move.

Harry was abandoned a while back – *I did not misbehave and I thought my people loved and cared for me. Everything was good. Then one day they took me out for a car ride. They opened the car door and put me out on the road. To my surprise and shock they just drove away and left me. Why would they do that? Survival was not easy. I had to learn how to hide from some dangerous animals then to find food . . . that is, until I met my new friends, Sam, Ben and Molly. They really protect me, and make sure I have a familiar place to sleep, and food to eat. I now have everything I need.*

I'm almost normal again. Molly's leg only hurts now if she plays too rough with Ben. Her life is the best it has ever been since she left her mom. Born in a culvert with her three brothers and two sisters, life was all about playing and having fun. She was nursed and then as she grew bigger her mother found food and brought it back for her and her siblings. Later their mother took them hunting and taught them what to look for, and how to kill it before they ate. She was separated from her dog family and had to fend for herself. After her accident, she was frightened because she saw the Vultures circling overhead. She thought she'd die for sure. Then she opened her eyes and she saw Sam and Ben walking towards her. They saved my life. Ben tells me that Sam needs a lot of credit for that, because he made sure I got proper treatment. I am also grateful to Sam; he is a very kind man.

Tom gives Sam the key for their new apartment. "Now you'll be able to access your new home from the back of the building. You can come and go without passing through the diner." Tom told him, "Make yourself and your pets comfortable. Sue has had the apartment cleaned and prepared just for you."

It has been very hot for several days in a row and today is a scorcher. The quartette walks around to the back entrance of the diner. Sam sniffs the air and is quickly aware of a horrible rancid odor coming from the big green dumpster. The dogs and cat immediately run to the bad smelling dumpster for another meal.

"Hmmm . . . this habit will need to change. Come on guys, let's be glad, we don't have to eat from there anymore," he happily advises his family.

Sam opens the door with his new key and calls to them, “Let’s explore our new digs. Follow me, we’re going upstairs.” Sam wonders if these guys had ever climbed stairs before.

Sam is pleasantly surprised when he enters the clean, fresh-smelling apartment. The living area is painted a neutral warm soft gray. The furnishings consist of a big overstuffed green leather couch and matching chairs. There are several small wooden tables and a TV. There are even a few knick knacks that give the place a homey lived in feeling.

The bedroom has a queen sized bed, with clean white sheets that smell like a summer breeze, with polished wooden night tables and a period dresser for the new clothes Sam will buy. He knows he made the right decision; he has visions of sleeping in a comfortable bed with clean sheets dancing through his head.

The kitchen also comes furnished with dishes and cooking pots, a stove and a microwave oven. The refrigerator is stocked with the basics like milk, butter, bottled water, a few condiments like catsup and mustard. Upon further inspection he discovers there is even a coffee maker with coffee. “Perfect!” Sam utters.

Sam is preoccupied exploring his new digs and for a moment completely forgot about the dogs and cat. Looking around he sees Ben is stretched out full length sleeping soundly on the couch, and Molly's curled up on one of the overstuffed living room chairs. "Harry, where are you? Hmm . . . he's not in the living room. Harry, where are you?" Sam voices his thoughts out loud talking to the animals and to himself at the same time. He immediately fears that in all the excitement, he has accidently left Harry outside. Quickly he heads towards the stairs, on route to check outside. In passing, he glances into the bedroom and that is when he spots the beautiful black beauty fully outstretched and burrowed between the white pillows on the bed, sound asleep.

"Yep, we are home!" Sam again says reassuring himself.

Sam – Chapter Nineteen

Sam woke from the best sleep he has had in many, many, months. He reminds himself that he must be at the diner by 5:30 am. He feels excited about working again, getting paid, and appreciating his ability to now have better personal hygiene.

Sue had left some toiletries and a few incidentals including a change of white work clothes, for Sam.

Sam found scissors. "Thank you, Sue." He roughly cut his hair to a shorter version. The razor Sue left works well to shave off his overgrown beard and mustache. His face feels strange minus the two-year old beard. He rubs his chin with the palm of his hand while looking in the mirror. He showers and washes his hair clean until it squeaks. The soft fluffy towels feel wonderful as he quickly dries his clean body, and puts on the clean whites. "Good fit, Sue," he mutters to himself.

When he arrives in the kitchen, he is greeted by a cheerful Tom, "Good morning Sam. Sleep well?"

"Good morning to you, Tom. Yes, I had the best night's sleep in ages. Thanks to you guys," Sam says, with the most enthusiasm he could express at this early hour.

Sam notices that Tom has already heated up the grill; as he prepares the eggs and starts cooking the smoked bacon. He watches him cut and prepare fries and hash brown potatoes, for the breakfast crowd. "What time do you arrive to have all of this great looking food ready for breakfast?" Sam enquires.

"I get here in the around three in the morning," Tom responds. He hears the coffee stop percolating so he extends a bright and cheerful, "Coffee, Sam? Help yourself. Clive is on his way and Sue just arrived. Relax for a few minutes because once the breakfast diners get here, it will be hectic."

Sam hears the juke box; it is already whaling out a familiar Connie Francis 60s-style tune. Sam turns to Tom, looks up and points to the ceiling speaker, then says, "Setting the breakfast mood?"

"Yep," he says, "They come here for the atmosphere. If there isn't music playing they give me a razzing."

Sam has no doubt that he will be able to do the job. He is very eager to start this new phase of his life. While sipping his coffee his thoughts turn to his hairy gang. They'll soon be hungry. He did leave fresh water for them – a real luxury.

Tom explains that while Clive doesn't have much of an education, he is meticulous about his hygiene that is why he did well here as the bus boy. He's a quiet man and gets along great with friends and others.

After a while, Clive tells Sue, "Sam sure is a quick learner. I think he knows the whole job already, and it's not even noon."

"Thanks, Clive, for showing Sam the ropes. We really do appreciate your help. It's okay with us if you want to leave any time now. I realize you are anxious to get to your parents. We will pay you for the full day and mail your final check to your parent's house," Sue assures Clive.

Clive says his good byes and leaves by the back door. His car is packed with his worldly possessions ready for the long drive home to Montana.

Sue suggests to Sam, "Take an hour off during the slump between breakfast and lunch. You can take the morning scraps you put aside, to your family upstairs."

Sam feeds the gang upstairs, and then takes them out for a walk. When they return he sees there is about two hours before he needs to be at the diner. He falls into a deep sleep in the comfy green leather chair. He just isn't use to the early hours and working anymore.

Startled, Sam wakes up and for a minute forgets where he is. He looks at the clock and sees he is almost late for the next shift the afternoon diners. He quickly jumps up, getting to his feet he runs to the washroom where he splashes cold water on his face. He must be alert for his job. Arriving in the diner a few minutes late, he apologizes profusely to Sue for his tardiness, "I am so sorry. I 'm usually very punctual. I don't even remember falling asleep. I promise it won't happen again. Sorry Sue,"

"It's okay I understand the routine is very different than your previous life. We'll survive," Sue assures him.

Sam said, "Thank you so much. I can do this job. I feel good about everything in my life, right now, thanks for understanding."

The first work day is finished and he wants to play with Ben, Molly and Harry. He misses them as much as they miss him. "Now, I think we should get some exercise. So how about we all go for a long walk today?" He never tires of chatting with his canine and feline friends. Sam thinks he'll never get used to how our quartette attracts attention wherever we go. Harry walks like a small puppy now in line with Ben and Molly. He only strays when he is absolutely and completely overcome with curiosity. Harry has adopted them and has no interest in leaving his new family. This is his home now.

Sam – Chapter Twenty

A week later Detective Mike McCann visits The Blueberry Hill diner. "Is Sam Garner here?" he asks Tom in his informal but direct manner.

"Yes, he's in the kitchen," Tom warily replies, his face was asking why, but he knew that it was not his place to ask the, burning question.

"Will you get him for me?" Mike requests, pauses then adds as he notices Tom's slight hesitation. "Please?"

"Sure," Tom says. He couldn't read the Detective; he was worried for Sam and really hopes this visit isn't the bad news that Sam has been stewing about.

Tom slowly walks back to the kitchen, compassionately puts his hand on Sam's shoulder and says, "Sam, the Detective's here to see you." Tom is desperately trying to keep his expression neutral.

Fear strikes Sam's gut; it feels like he was just kicked in the stomach. An all too familiar knot starts to grow inside his belly. He surveys Tom's face, looking for a hint or any slight indication of his reading of Detective Mike. "Here we go again," Sam says.

Sam looks directly into Tom's eyes and says, "Right now, I have a tremendous urge to run out the back door and escape. Logic tells me that this would not be a good solution," Sam exhales letting out a deep sigh that shows just how wound up tight he is. He puts down the cloth and pot he is holding in his hand runs his fingers through his hair and then says, "I guess the brave thing to do is go out there and face the music."

Tom says, "He didn't bring any uniform officers with him, if that helps. I think if he is going to arrest you he would have brought a couple of uniforms with him. But what do I know," Tom threw his hands in the air while still trying to be encouraging.

With his adrenalin pumping through his veins Sam gathers his courage and walks slowly towards the front of the diner. When he finally appears in the seating area his fear turns into defensive anger. Aggressively, he asks Detective Mike, "What do you want now?" He could not hide his irritation towards this man.

"Sam I want to let you know we have solved the George Lamb mystery," Mike declares, trying to diffuse some of Sam's annoyance with him.

"Is that so? What does it have to do with me?" Sam flippantly questions with a slightly sarcastic tone in his voice and a stone cold facial expression.

"More than you think. Have a seat, please, hear me out," Mike lowers himself into a booth and invites Sam to join him.

Sam hesitantly sits down opposite to Mike, "I'm listening," Sam states irritably.

"This is what we learned," Mike explains as he sips a cup of coffee placed in front of him by Sue. "Mr. Lamb came to this area just to see you. According to his family this is what he reported back to them. He had finally tracked you down. He wanted to apologize to you," Mike discloses while watching Sam's facial expression change from anger to surprise.

"Apologize to me?" Sam asks while screwing up his face. He couldn't fathom why this guy would apologize to him. "I told you I didn't know him," Sam reinforces his previous statements, still a little defensive.

Keeping a calm demeanor, Mike continues his story, "No, maybe you didn't, but he knew you for just over two years now. He has been tormented with guilt since the accident that killed your family. He has been searching for you ever since. Apparently he caught up to you a couple of times but you moved on before he could work up the courage to approach you."

Mike lets the details sink in then resumes the story, "From all the pieces of information we have, and with everything put together it appears he was the drunk driver that killed your family." He is not sure how Sam will react to this statement so he is ready for any reaction coming from Sam.

Sam is stunned; his jaw drops, his eyes are like saucers. He is at a loss for words, "I'm shocked. I never saw that coming. In fact, I'm . . . I think I'm speechless." Sam visibly displays his emotions as he wipes his sweaty hands on his white work shirt and desperately tries to maintain some level of composure.

"Sorry if I was a little rough on you a few weeks ago," Mike says, "but you can now see why you were our prime suspect in this murder. I can understand your anger with being questioned like a suspect and I do empathize with you."

"Did you find the person who did that horrible thing to him?" Sam asks, his curiosity urges him to ask the big question.

"Mr. Lamb made some really bad friends. He got mixed up with some very nasty criminals who were into drugs, women, and gambling. Apparently Mr. Lamb shared his nightmare with them over drinks one night; he confided in them, his role in and other details about the accident." Detective Mike is happy to reveal the results of their investigation.

"Mr. Lamb's murder turns out to be a revenge killing over drugs and money. His cohorts had gotten the idea to keep track of him; they came here to put their plan in place.

They met up with him here and on some pretense which has not been revealed to the police, they took him back to Seattle. Then his criminal friends killed him," Detective Mike continues.

"They killed him in Seattle?"

"Yes," Detective Mike answered, "Then a plan was devised to make you the perfect scapegoat for his murder. You had motive plus you were a drifter. They figured you would not have an alibi therefore you would be our first suspect. A perfect murder in their pea size brains. Evidence like his head and feet were planted here in the dumpster so you would look guilty. They figured it would take the heat off them. And it did for a while."

"It worked," Sam interjects.

"The cops in Seattle arrested them at a sleazy hotel in Seattle. It was kind of a fluke as the Seattle detectives were following them for another crime, totally unrelated," Detective Mike concludes his story.

"This reads like a mystery novel," Sam said.

"Yes, you know sometimes real life crime is stranger than fictional stories," Mike acknowledges.

"His family said he was a terrible mess. I'm sorry that he didn't get to actually apologize to you directly, Sam," Mike adds apologetically.

"So it's over and done – the case is closed," Sam stated his body language and facial muscles showing visible signs of relief.

"Yup, sure is. You can now close that chapter and get on with your life," Mike said as he stood up, shaking hands with Sam. He smiles back at Sam and waves as he walks to the diner door.

Sam calls after him, "Thank you, Detective, for taking the time to come here and explain the whole drama to me. I do appreciate your kindness even though at our last meeting I wasn't as pleasant as I could have been."

"No problem. I like happy endings and particularly this one. Justice has been served," these were the detective's last words as he strolled to his vehicle and then drove away.

Sam sat motionless looking out of the window in a daze. He is still trying to get his head around the facts and conclusion to his story.

Sam – Chapter Twenty-One

Tom hears the diner door close. He rushes to the front to make sure Sam is still there and not arrested. Then he sees Sam in a daze sitting in the booth. "You okay Sam? You look quite devastated," Tom states and then demands, "Sam, talk to me."

He shakes his head back and forth demonstrating his disbelief, "I can't believe what I just heard. That head in the dumpster was the head of the drunk driver that killed my family. Now I know why they were so focused on me as a suspect in his murder," Sam briefly recaps his conversation with Detective Mike.

"It's almost closing time. I think this is great news and calls for a celebration. How about I open that bottle of Champagne sitting the refrigerator?" Tom offers looking over his shoulder while he is already walking back towards the kitchen.

"I would like that. For some reason I'd rather not be alone tonight," Sam shares. He knows even though the end result was good for him, it is still going to take a while to get all this information digested.

Tom returns with three glasses and an uncorked bottle of champagne. He gleefully says, "I have been saving this for a real celebration and your news qualifies."

"Hi Sam, congratulations on your freedom," Sue quips as she slips into the booth beside Tom.

"You folks have been great friends. Thanks for being so trusting and willing to give me a chance. I really do appreciate you both," Sam says with the utmost sincerity as he reaches across the table to touch their hands. "I feel a real bond with you guys."

"It's a good thing that I didn't run before I spoke with the Detective. I must say, I really, really wanted to get as far away from here as possible." He pauses for that comment to sink in before continuing, "Then, I would have been a fugitive on the run. I might never have known that I was in fact running for nothing."

"It is all about doing what is right, even if it feels like the worst or most difficult choice," Tom interjected into the conversation. "You chose the right option; therefore, you now have peace of mind and closure."

"Here's to good people and great friends," Sue proclaims. A toast, with that declaration all three raise their glasses and have another sip of the bubbly.

She turns to Sam and affectionately says, "Sam it is so good to see your warm smile. By the way, where did you get those cute dimples?"

"I have been hiding them, just for such an occasion as this," Sam says grinning from ear to ear. "My true personality has been overshadowed by my tragedy for far too long. I feel it is now resurfacing. I feel like Sam Garner, the professional hockey player, again."

Tom inquires, "Sam do you think you will ever play hockey again?"

"No. That chapter is closed," he thoughtfully states. "In time there will be another opportunity, what, when, where or how who knows? Until then, I am the bus boy at The Blueberry Hill Diner," he declares by slapping the table with the palm of his hand.

"I'll drink to that," exclaims Sue as she holds her half full champagne glass high in agreement.

They drink and eat for several more hours while continuing their party. Sam entertains them with his many amusing locker room episodes and stranger-than-fiction hockey stories.

Ben trots in and sees how happy everyone is once again. This is good news. He senses the bad stuff is in the past and Sam will have a good future ahead of him. Ben sits beside Sam's chair, puts both paws on his leg and plants several sloppy licks on his face. Ben is happy too.

Sam – Chapter Twenty-Two

A few days later, Sam notices a change in Ben. "Hey big guy are you okay?" Ben appears to be out of sorts.

Ben's torn. He thinks about his current family. But he also thinks about his human family. *Where are my first people family, Molly and Roy?*

I love playing with my dog friend Molly; we chase, wrestle and roll around and then playfully chew on each other's ears. She is a good sport and a fun companion. Harry is okay as far as cats go. He's friendly and I don't mind when he cuddles up beside me to sleep. Sam has been great. I'm happy for him. He is much more content now that we have a nice home. He has always taken good care of us. I think he needs more now. I sometimes wonder if he will stay here or move on to a new house.

I would like to stay, but I get this nagging feeling that it is time for me to continue to move on and find my first people family.

Ben often thinks about his mom, dad, Roy and Molly. They took very good care of him and he really does miss them.

Molly, my people sister, is the real reason that I wanted to call my new dog friend Molly. I like to hear her breathing and that funny little squeaky noise she makes with her nose.

Ben realizes that they must be very worried about him, and feels torn and conflicted. It's not like he's unhappy or ill-treated. It's that feeling that something is missing; it just keeps nagging at him. It will not go away. He realizes it is time to go.

He tries explaining to Molly that he has to continue his search but she just gets angry with him and will not hear him out. She doesn't understand and definitely does not want him to leave the family. He has the impression that she would like to join him, but is not prepared to give up the good life with Sam.

Then he tries his best to convey his need to leave to Sam by being very attentive and affectionate as if he is trying to express enough love to last Sam forever. Ben follows Sam everywhere; he seems to be stuck to him.

Sam wonders why, "Ben, you are certainly being affectionate and so attentive. It's okay we are best friends. I wish I knew what is going on with you."

Sam somehow knows their friendship will not be forever; though he will never forget the journey they shared.

They sleep together for another night. Sam consoles himself by rubbing Ben's tummy and hugging him, hoping he will not leave. In his heart he feels it might be time for Ben to continue his journey. "I hope you find what or who you are looking for fella. I know you will always be loved by someone," Sam says as a lump develops in his throat and tears fill his eyes.

The very next morning Ben went out for a walk all by himself. But, he did not come home that day . . . nor the next day . . . or ever.

Every day during their walks Sam, Molly and Harry search for Ben.

Sam is very sad and cries himself to sleep for several days over the loss of that very special dog. He is emotionally moved by the change in both Molly and Harry as they now sleep with him every night. They miss Ben too.

"Oh how I miss you," Sam cried. "Ben, I promise that I will never forget you. You are the most extraordinary canine friend I have ever known. Ben, you and I have a very special bond that will last forever.

BEN BOOK SEVEN

Ben – Chapter One

Walking away from The Blueberry Hill Diner is the most difficult thing I have ever done. Ben tries to hold his head high and keep his mind on today's travel. He must not dwell on the group he has just left behind. His heart hurts too much, when he remembers Sam, Molly and Harry. He cannot recall ever feeling this sad before. Sam is a terrific friend. He is kind and loving. *Oh, how I miss Sam.*

Ben hopes that Sam finds what he is looking for, now that he is in a good place both physically and mentally.

It seems to Ben his life has been a series of ups and downs. Recently his emotions have run the whole spectrum from extremely happy to devastatingly sad. He wants to be home with his human family. Oh how he longs for them now.

He must trust his instincts that he's going in the right direction but these roads are unfamiliar to him. Just then the sun peeks up over the horizon. Ben is happy to see the brilliant red morning sun and instinctively changes direction. He is now walking towards the bright colorful eastern sky. *I know I'm traveling in the right direction, now.* These thoughts motivate him and put a happy bounce in his step. This renewed enthusiasm has eluded him for the past few days.

I do not want any more adventures. I just want to get to where I'm going. He did make good mileage for the next couple of days.

Ben – Chapter Two

Out of nowhere a leather loop wraps around his neck. Ben is startled as he tries desperately to free himself from the man holding the long pole with the loop on the end. *Why is this happening? Why is this man doing this to me?* He fights like his life depends on him winning, and it might. He frantically rotates his body in all directions trying to get free. The he tries growling fiercely to intimidate the man. That did not work either. He continues his fight by twisting, turning and pulling with all his strength, adrenalin, brought on by fear, is pumping through his veins giving him super strength. He tries again and again to free himself. His attempt to fight off the enemy isn't working. He is being dragged by the neck into the back of a big truck.

Why?

The large man is so much stronger than Ben; his resistance is causing him to choke. Attempts to get air in his lungs are proving to be more difficult as the loop is cutting off his air. He coughs several times trying to get air into his lungs. He panics as his chest tightens with the lack of air. Finally Ben succumbs as he realizes he must stop resisting the man or he may injure himself or die.

Ben, being a fighter, did not give up completely. Once he recovers from the choking episode he refocuses his energy and restarts his futile struggle. Now the man is forcing Ben into a wire cage. Ben resumes his ineffective fight, furiously resisting being put into the big cage by pushing away with his paws using the side walls for leverage. Eventually he loses this battle too.

Sadly, Ben is now a prisoner and feeling claustrophobic and cramped in the locked cage that now feels so much smaller.

All day long, more and more animals are forced into the truck and locked in cages. None of the prisoners are the least bit happy about being captured and confined. No one is more upset than Ben. Sitting upright in the enclosure he whimpers and whines. When the big man comes near his cage Ben snarls ferociously showing most of his strong sharp teeth.

Finally all of the cages in the truck are occupied with frightened unhappy animals. They drive for what seems like days but in reality it is only about six hours. Some of the roads are very bumpy making the animals even more uncomfortable in their prison cells. Ben wonders. *Where are we going? What are they going to do with us?*

At last the large brown truck comes to a stop. The enormous muscular man opens the back door of the truck, letting in what is left of daylight. The man is blasted with an orchestra of barking, meowing, growling and hissing from the reluctant occupants. Some were crying with fear, others whimpering, even growling, as a defensive tactic. The restrained animals are terrified and trembling with fear. They are afraid and very unhappy at being held captive in this unfamiliar place.

Ben and his fellow prisoners are taken from the truck to a big room, and then transferred to larger cages which are fastened to the wall. There's a cacophony of barking and meowing which after a while Ben finds quite upsetting. He lies down on the uncomfortable floor of his cage and put his paws over his ears in an attempt to block out the cries of desperation.

Ben watches a peppy young college age girl wearing a white coat as she signs papers for the mean man who imprisoned him and the others. Her white lab coat is open at the front showing a slim body that is almost covered with her skimpy top and hipster jeans. He observes how affectionate she is with her charges. He watches her as she takes a small kitten out of its cage. She gently stokes its fur, speaks softly to it while she cuddles it up next to her face. Ben can hear the kitten's loud purring from across the room. It is obvious to Ben, she loves animals.

The girl feeds each animal dry crunchy food and then puts a small container of water into each of their cages. She speaks to her new guests in a soft calming voice, "Hello my new friends. I'm happy to see you. This experience must be very upsetting for you guys." As she walks from cage to cage, she speaks calmly to each animal, "Take it easy we'll do our best to find your own home or a nice new one for you."

Ben watches her finish her paper work which she puts in a big cabinet with pull out drawers. She smiles and waves at them as she walks to the door. She reaches for the switch to turn off the lights. As she pulls the door close, she turns and pokes her head back into the doorway and says, "Good night my new friends, I'll see you tomorrow." She disappears through the doorway and the big cold sterile room, feels even colder to Ben as she shuts the door behind her.

Ben feels abandoned in the darkness. Some of the other animals sleep, while others cry or howl with fear all night long.

Ben wonders how he will he ever find his family if he's locked away in a cage. *What is going to happen to me? I must tell them I have to get to my family. I'm not lost. I need to be free. My family misses me. I want to find them. "Help!" He barks. "Please let me out."*

Ben – Chapter Three

As daylight peeks through the windows Ben hears the door open and the girl walk in. In a very cheerful voice she says, "Good morning my little buddies. Did you all sleep well?" She pauses in front of the cages as if she is expecting an answer, "Good, don't all speak at once," was her response to the meowing and barking coming from the wall of cages. "I know you want out but I'm sorry, that just isn't going to happen. Let's have some yummy breakfast, shall we?" She gives each dog and cat food and water, again.

Their caregiver is aware that her voice quiets their complaining. She decides to talk to them by telling them a little about her goal, "Hi guys my name is Maggie. It is nice to meet you all. I'm just here part time while going to school at Bamberg College just down the street. So if I'm not here you'll know why. I'm studying to be a Veterinarian Doctor. I really love my career choice as I will get to work with animals just like you, every day."

She chats away while performing her morning chores, "Hope you guys are lucky and we find your home today." The music on her iPod is blasting a tune while she does little dances entertaining the animals and hoping by watching her, it takes their minds off their current situation.

The girl removes each dog from their temporary home and in turn walks with them to the exercise run to do their business. She throws a ball or stick to see if they are up to playing, but they are too frightened to participate.

Ben thinks, this might be considered humane treatment but it's definitely not where he wants to be. He does not like this diversion at all. He has to think this through and find a way to escape. He wonders how long he will be in a cage. Now he is questioning the wisdom of his decision to leave Sam, Molly and Harry. They are not in a cage. *Why am I? What did I do to deserve this treatment?*

To Ben it seems like weeks, but only three days later, two men in blue uniforms, Wayne and Allen, enter their prison. "Hi Maggie, We are here to see your new recruits," Wayne playfully says.

"Hi guys, we have a couple of beauties this time. Take a look at the black and white 'Heinz 47' dog in number twenty-five. His tag states his name is Ben. He will be perfect." Maggie offers enthusiastically.

"Does he have a microchip?" Wayne asks.

I do have a microchip, Ben wants to shout. He would really like to get out of here and resume his journey.

"Yes, he does have a microchip. But when I looked up his number on the National Registry I can't find the contact person and the information has not been updated for some time. He is really well-trained and a nicely groomed dog I can't see anyone abandoning him. But here he is. It is a mystery to me," Maggie says with concern.

The men walk by the cages looking into them, checking out some of the confined dogs. The officers are friendly and speak to a few of the dogs, but just look at others. Some they even pat, when the dog or cat sticks their noses through the square openings in the wire doors to sniff the new visitors.

Wayne selects a few dogs, only those who seem healthy and alert. Ben in number twenty-five, is one of the chosen few. He is restrained with a muzzle and a leash, and then taken to another room.

This new room looks familiar, Ben thinks.

Allen the other large burley man picks Ben up and puts him on the cold steel examination room table. He says, "Hi Dr. Bob, I hope this one meets our criteria because I really like him. His name is Ben."

"Thanks Allen I'll do my best," Dr. Bob responds as he gives Ben a superficial look."

Ben is greeted by the elderly man with gray hair, and a scruffy beard. He is looking very professional in his white clinic coat. Ben sniffs Dr. Bob, up and down his protective coat and senses this man is kind.

He speaks softly, “How are you today big fella. My name is Dr. Bob. Ben you look healthy enough to me. Let’s listen to your heart – hmmm, good strong heart, no signs of any problems there.” The rest of the physical examination doesn’t reveal any problems either. When Dr. Bob completes the cursory examination, he smiles at Ben and gives him a quick pat on the head.

Allen sees Ben start to quiver as Dr. Bob approaches with a needle all primed to stab him. He pats him on the head and down his back, as a diversion, to distract Ben while Dr. Bob finds a place in the muscle of Ben’s hip. He pinches the skin and punctures it with the needle.

Ben whimpers to let them know he is not happy about the needle.

Dr. Bob, which is his habit when thinking, pulls on his right ear lobe while reading the form. He removes his pen from the left breast pocket of his lab coat and proceeds to check off boxes on the card. Recommending Ben, he confidently states to Allen, “He is a very healthy, clean and well groomed dog. Maggie did find a microchip, when he arrived. Unfortunately the contact information is not current. So he’s all yours.”

Ben is one of the final four dogs chosen. He does not know what he has been chosen for, making him more nervous and hesitant. *Is this a good thing or a bad thing?* Ben wonders.

Ben and the other selected dogs are once again locked in the portable cages and transported to a truck, this time by a different man in a brown uniform, but he was still grumpy and yells at the dogs, "Shut up! Consider yourselves lucky. You could be still left behind in that place. You're an ungrateful lot."

Ben thinks, *Lucky, I wonder what he means? There is nothing lucky about being caged.*

The trip was short but full of uncertainty. The caged occupants are all very frightened. Some shake and shiver with fear. This does not feel good to Ben.

He thinks *if the outcome is to be positive why do they scare us like this?*

More big men arrive and help unload the dogs from the truck. These men take the portable cages with the dogs inside to a large room with lots of people in blue uniforms. Ben's cage is lined up along the wall with the others. The people in charge call out the names of various officers. They come forward and stand beside specific cages. The uniformed officers each take one of the animals in a cage to their vehicle and drive away.

Ben wonders. *Where are they taking us now?*

AMANDA BOOK SEVEN

Amanda – Chapter One

Ben is sitting on the front seat of the vehicle belonging to one of the blue uniform people. He's no longer in a cage like a wild unruly animal. He thinks *she must finally realize that I'm a well-trained, polite and a very obedient dog.*

She introduces herself to him, "Hello Ben, my name is Amanda. I will be your handler and new trainer."

He desperately tries to understand, while sniffing the front seat and interior of the vehicle, looking for some familiar smells. Even with his vast experience he struggles to assess his current situation. He tilts his head from side to side trying to grasp what is happening and what she is saying to him. He is unable to make any sense of anything. *What is a handler?* Ben has never heard of a handler.

Amanda takes him to her home; she has great tasting dog food, a huge backyard and a wonderful soft cozy oversized pillow for him to sleep on. Ben busily sniffs floors, sofas, chairs and especially his new bed the oversized pillow. He is reassured, because there isn't a recent scent of another animal in Amanda's home. This thought makes

Ben very happy as he isn't prepared to share Amanda or this new luxurious home, with anyone. This certainly is a major step up from his last few nights' stay in the wire cage at Hotel Animal Control. Things are getting better, but he still can't make any sense out of it all – yet.

His first impression is that he likes Amanda; she wears a blue uniform that fits nicely over her well-toned body. Her dark brunette hair is tied back in a bun. Most important to Ben is her soft sky blue eyes as they are happy and friendly.

Early next morning, Amanda dresses in tight clothes and running shoes. She attaches a leash to Ben's collar, they walk to the road, and then she proceeds to run . . . *me too. I didn't know why we were running because after all of that running exercise, we ended up at the same place we started. It was fun. When we got back home I was quite out of breath and needed a long drink of water.* Amanda now realizes that he is in good shape because he kept up with her, the whole time.

Next morning she invites him to join her on the front seat again while she drives to a big building with lots of other dogs and more people in blue uniforms. *Now what's happening? Nothing, nothing at all makes any sense.*

"Heel," the head trainer commands. Not all of the dogs know what this means, but I do because I attended obedience classes as a puppy.

Amanda and Ben work together all day with commands followed by treats. She's kind, firm and gentle with him. She's happy when he quickly follows her commands. Amanda is generous with her positive feedback so he knows that he pleases her. They make a good team. The best part is the crunchy cookie treats she gives him when she praises him.

Ben is told that an important part of this training is recognizing specific smells. Ben has a very good sense of smell and like most dogs he can retain the scent in his nose for long periods of time even when there is a mixture of smells. Amanda is proud of him as he learns quickly and remembers his training.

The training continues for a couple more weeks.

Amanda states, "Now it's time to have actual field training. This will be more difficult, Ben. Because in the field, you will find a cocktail of odors, scents, and smells. This will make it very difficult for you to single out the scent that will be most important. I believe you are ready and you can do this."

One of the field exercises that he particularly likes is when they have the bad guy hide in a big box. The field is spotted with at least one dozen boxes that have numbers one to twelve or the number of boxes in the field.

Once the bad guy is fully hidden in the box of his choosing, Amanda uncovers Ben's eyes and says, "Find. Ben, find the man." Twelve times out of twelve Ben finds the correct box, and then, the bad guy comes out with his arm covered in very thick padding for protection. He is holding a gun pointed at Ben.

On command from Amanda, "Ben, get the gun. Get the gun."

Ben jumps up at the bad guy; he snarls and growls showing his most ferocious anger. He tries to intimidate and block the bad guy from escaping. He does this by attacking the covered arm with his sharp teeth and hanging on; this motion causes the man to stumble, lose his balance and sometimes it knocks the gun right out of his hand to the ground. Ben stops the fake criminal in his tracks and prevents him from escaping.

These exercises are always followed by play with a pull toy, and of course some delicious treats.

Ben graduates with honors.

Amanda tells him, "You're really lucky to be a member of the K-9 Police Kennel Brigade. You do a great job at following orders and that's important."

The head trainer rates Ben as superior over the other dogs in his group. He states, "I am confident that Ben will make a difference. He possesses natural abilities and skills that cannot be taught."

Ben likes the idea of catching bad people like thieves, finding lost and abducted people or kidnapped children.

What a great job! He's a real working dog, now. The treats are a bonus.

When they aren't working he has the run of the house and the big backyard. *Life is pretty darn good here.*

Ben really enjoys taking long walks and jogging with Amanda; even when they end up in the same place they started.

Amanda takes Ben everywhere she goes. This team must be ready for action immediately, when needed.

Ben waits patiently for his first call to duty. Maybe he'll be challenged to find a real person in trouble.

Amanda – Chapter Two

A few days later, Amanda summons him with both anxiety and urgency. Ben has not heard this tone in her voice before, "Come Ben, quick, hurry, we need to go *right* now."

They run to her vehicle, she opens the back of her SUV. She guides Ben into the cage.

Wait a minute. Why am I in the cage? He clearly remembers the panic he felt when he was taken prisoner a few weeks back. He intensely stares at her questioning her actions; he is tilting his head and moving it from one side to the other, whimpering and frowning. *What's happening? I normally sit up front with you. Has something changed? I don't think, I did anything wrong. Amanda, it's me, Ben, your best friend.*

Seeing Ben's reaction Amanda realizes she has forgotten to tell Ben about the rule. "It's okay Ben," she stokes his head and reassures him, "I forgot to tell you. Whenever we go to a crime scene, as a member of the K-9 Kennel Brigade, you must arrive in a cage. This rule is for your protection. If we need to move you to another vehicle or a helicopter it's safer for you and much more efficient for us."

It turns out that he didn't need to worry after all. He is officially on duty and this is his first real big job.

When they reach their destination, Amanda opens the hatch of her SUV, puts on his leash, and takes him to the crime scene which is cordoned off with yellow crime scene tape. She says, "C'mon Ben let's catch ourselves a bad guy."

This place is full of strange smells. There sure is a lot of confusion here. Why are so many people mingling around? It is very noisy. He is told, they are at the fairgrounds. Ben watches as people are pushing, shoving and running around every which way. The folks in blue uniforms are shouting directions at people. He recognizes the people in uniforms as police officers just like Amanda.

Amanda is holding a little sweater. She says, "Ben this belongs to a young boy who has been reported missing. He was at the carnival with his mommy and daddy when he disappeared."

"Ben sniffs the sweater," She holds it close to his nose, making sure his nose is full of the boy's scent. Then she commands, "Find. Ben, find the boy."

Ben knows this is going to be difficult, but he's up for the challenge. His record for finding people during practice sessions is one of the best in the department. He is confident that he can do it!

He instinctively knows how to separate the boy's scent on the sweater from any other important scents, which he might get from other people and the various aromas of food cooking.

His training did teach him, there will be at least one other stronger scent along with the boy's.

Once again she orders, "Find. Find, the boy Ben."

Ben sniffs the air and the ground, in several directions before he picks up the boy's smell on the ground. He put his nose to the ground, sniffing he follows the scent. It is very strong here. Now he is picking up another even stronger smell that seems to be mixed in with the boy's smell. Ben takes off pulling Amanda behind him.

Amanda hollers to the other officers, "We've got it . . . follow us."

Ben is very good. In his training once he locked onto it, he never lost the scent. Amanda is in the lead and being tugged by Ben as he strains against his harness. It feels as if her arm, holding the leash is being pulled out of her shoulder socket. The other police officers follow Ben as he guides them along the route he believes the boy and his abductor traveled. He focuses, and continues sniffing the ground with his snout following the scents. Ben leads them past the food booths and the rides. He is not distracted by the delicious aroma of food cooking. He is working. There are so many different scents now, he really needs to concentrate. It is very difficult, but he still manages to keep the boy's scent in his nose. He continues to follow it for several minutes. Ben's running, and the officers are following close behind, as he exits the fairgrounds.

Ben can hear the officers behind him constantly speaking into their radios, reporting their location to someone.

Ben hesitates momentarily as he loses the scent. He runs in a few circles, sniffing the ground and the air checking for the boy's scent. Then he barks, to let Amanda know he is ready to continue. He yanks at his leash tugging Amanda in a new direction. The other smell is very strong and the boy's scent is fainter. He hesitates for a moment then remembers his training. He did learn that this usually means the boy has been picked up, or put in a car. Ben searches in every direction moving a short distance this way, then that way, searching for the route they took; he finds the secondary scent again.

Ben barks, to let Amanda know he has a strong smell again and is ready to follow it as he tugs at the leash pulling her on the path he believes will lead to the boy.

The scent takes Ben and those following to the older section of town, about five minutes from the fairgrounds.

Amanda shares her thoughts with a fellow officer, "These old abandoned buildings with dirty and broken windows are perfect for hiding an abducted child."

"I agree," the officer responds.

Ben is still locked on to the important smell. He is once again running and dragging Amanda with her fully extended arm behind him. She has to jog just to keep up with him. She does her best to stay close so he is not restricted or hindered.

She is getting winded and has a little trouble keeping up with Ben's fast pace. But, she encourages him by saying, "Good boy, Ben, I'm right behind you." She knew she had to keep up and give him free rein.

The officers are running full out now, and shouting back and forth to each other, "He's really locked-on now. Look at him go! I think we're close now, by the way he's focusing."

Amanda tells the officer keeping pace with her, "I think the boy must be nearby."

It took less than five minutes to locate the building in which Ben is sure the boy is being held captive. He stops dead in his tracks, promptly sits and softly barks. An indication to Amanda, the boy is somewhere inside.

"Good boy Ben, you can rest now. We can let the officers do their job. You did your job. Good Boy," Amanda praises him while trying to catch her breath.

A few officers cautiously, with weapons drawn enter the derelict old building. Sean a physically fit, a seasoned officer is in charge. He orders the search team, "Stay alert, we have no idea who or how many suspects we are dealing with."

Ben guesses they are expecting trouble. He and Amanda move back towards the road and wait.

The boy must have been in plain sight because almost immediately, Officer Ken, a tall thin new member of the police force, hollers, "We found him. He's okay."

The good news is accompanied with hoorahs and "high fives."

"There's no sign of the abductor though," another officer reports in a disappointing tone.

"Good boy Ben, you did it, rookie," Amanda praises him, and then hands him a treat.

Ben thinks, *now, this is a great job*. He didn't like to think of the times when he would be shot at or have a knife thrown at him. He is trained for these scenarios, but these would not be among his favorite situations.

Amanda – Chapter Three

Just then, as they are bringing the boy out of the building, Ben got a whiff of something then quickly gets to his feet, sniffs the ground and the air again in several directions, then barking with real purpose, and then he begins to run. Amanda is not ready for this sudden response, and is nearly pulled off her feet, but she never let go of his leash.

"Ben, what's going on? What do you smell?" she questions.

Ben just tugs at the leash. Amanda yells to the other officers, "I don't know for sure, but I think he has just got a hint of the abductor's scent, again. Follow us!"

A few officers follow out of curiosity, others because they believe that the perpetrator must be close by, as he really didn't have time to get too far away. One officer states, "We're counting on your dog knowing what he's doing."

"Don't you worry, Ben knows his job," Amanda proudly states.

"Keep your eyes peeled guys," Sean, the leader, hollers.

Ben is running and barking. He knows the bad guy is in the next building. He is confident he will find him. The scent is overwhelmingly strong now.

He stops at a big rusty, metal roller type oversized garage door, the entrance to another old warehouse. A quiet bark is an indication to Amanda that the perpetrator is very close, maybe just behind the huge door.

"Bang . . . bang. Ben hears the bullets ping off the metal door. He crouches low to the ground, making himself a much smaller target.

"Down boy — stay — good boy," Amanda whispers and immediately goes into protection mode. She gives Ben a reassuring pat as they move hunched down, almost crawling to a safer place behind a huge recycling bin.

"We're okay. We'll stay here behind this bin until you tell me it's safe," Amanda whispers to Officer Sean, who has just joined them, and is hunkered down beside her.

Sean tells her, "I'm guessing either he can see us or he heard us approach."

As Sean moves closer to the large door, he signals to the other officers with his hands, motioning them into position.

"Bang, bang," again, more gunshots are heard from inside the building.

Ben watches Sean, as he approaches a small old wooden door with peeling paint just west of the roller door.

Sean signals with three fingers indicating the count down so they can synchronize their entrance into the building. He shows the count with his fingers. “One — Two —Three — Go,” he quietly whispers, and then motions with his hand for them to move quickly.

Amanda and Ben wait. Their bodies jerk with the sound of every shot fired. She speaks softly to Ben, “This is one desperate kidnapper. I don’t know why he has a gun. Sorry Ben, I guess this is your initiation to gun fire.”

Again, they hear more shots coming from the warehouse. Suddenly, there is a deafening silence. “I don’t like this silence one bit,” she says to Ben, “I worry about the outcome,” Amanda hopes for the best. Then she hears the big door grinding up, opening the deep dark cavity to day light. “Look Ben, the officers are coming out, just a few at a time, but they look pleased with the results,” Amanda says, as much to calm herself as Ben.

Sean is feeling grateful that none of his team is injured, as he and a few officers strut to where Amanda and Ben have taken refuge. “Amanda that is a terrific dog you have there,” Sean praises Ben, with sincere pats on his head.

“I know, he is so easy to train and follows instructions to the letter, he instinctively knows his job. He’s the best

K-9 I have ever worked with," Amanda beams as she proudly praises Ben's attributes.

"I know for sure, we would never have found the abductor, this quickly, without that great nose of yours Ben," Sean smiles down at Ben and strokes him again.

"Is that guy doing the shooting, the same one that took the boy?" Amanda curiously asks.

"Yes, we are positive because he has one of the kid's shoes in his pocket. I'm guessing that it fell off while he was carrying the boy to the other building." Sean looks around at his peers, smiles and says "No one ever said criminals are smart. It's a fact; we count on their stupidity."

Ben watches the group of officers, some chuckle, some just smile, but they are all happy with today's positive ending.

The mood is much lighter now. Ben is feeling proud that he found both the boy and his abductor.

"Why did he have a gun?" Amanda asks as she really wants to understand the criminal mind.

Sean briefly shares some new facts he has been told about the kidnapper, he says, "We identified him by his finger prints. He was in the system, apparently this is not his first, and actually he has had a string of arrests for suspicion of child abduction. He did several stretches of time in the slammer. I 'm guessing he opted for suicide by cop over another stint in a prison."

"How awful life must be when that is your only option," Amanda responds, then disappears deep into her thoughts.

"Amanda, we had no choice, he just stood there in the open, shooting and shooting at us. He was not going to surrender. Sometimes they feel that is their only option," Sean adds defending their actions and explaining the outcome.

"See you guys," she says waving good bye. Walking away she hesitates, then turns and says to Sean, "I need to digest the events of today, plus write up my report. This is not the conclusion I anticipated."

The drive home is somber. She hardly notices or speaks to Ben. He knows he did a good job, so she must be unhappy about something else.

Once home, Amanda surprises Ben with a special meal, "Ben, here's a steak for the champion."

Ben really likes this special treat. He gobbles up his scrumptious meal and swallows it with very little actual chewing.

Amanda proudly looks at Ben and tells him, "Now you have proven yourself. You will be specifically requested when the K-9 group is required again. I am so proud of you, big guy." She is anxious about future assignments, but definitely hoping for less drama. She waits with anticipation for the next call.

Amanda – Chapter Four

The Bamberg Police receive a letter from a local family with a special request. Susan the secretary to the Manager of Public Relations reads the letter out loud to her boss, "We have been reading the articles about Ben, his abilities and his connection to people. Our thirteen years old son, Scott who is Autistic, does not communicate with anyone in the family or his therapist. Part of his therapy is for us; his parents is to read out loud to him as frequently as possible. Up until now he has been totally non-responsive but this past week a miracle happened. Scott actually said 'Ben'."

The Manager is visibly impressed then says to Susan, "That is amazing. I have an idea how the police can get some good publicity out of this letter." He picks up his phone and dials the Chief's office, speaks with his assistant James. "Hi Jim, I would like about twenty minutes with the Chief tomorrow. Can you slip me in between his other appointments?"

"Sure, if you can be here around two tomorrow afternoon. I will fit you in right after his lunch."

"I will be there, thank you, James."

The Public Relations Manager, Ken White said while handing the letter to the Chief, "Chief this would be great press for the K-9 unit as budgets are being prepared for next year. We have heard rumors that the K-9 unit is to be cut or at least reduced in next year's budget. We don't want that to happen as we know the K-9 department has proven to be a great crime solving tool."

The Chief carefully reads the letter

Dear Chief,

Thank you for taking the time out of your busy day to read this letter and for considering our request.

Our ten year old son Scott was diagnosed with Autism at the age of two. We have done everything that was recommended and more to communicate with him.

One of the suggestions made to us by a specialist in this field was to read to him. Our habit is to read the local paper out loud to him; we read the paper anyway, so it has become part of our daily routine.

Scott up until now has never uttered a single word to us or anyone else about anything. We have tried every method available to encourage a response from him but nothing; he's silent. We were thinking that he was unable to speak even though he has been tested and there isn't a psychological or physical reason for his silence.

We read the article about Ben last week out loud as usual to Scott and showed him Ben's photo. Then out of the blue, Scott blurted out, "Ben." The word "Ben" is the very first word he has uttered in his entire ten years. This is deemed a major breakthrough and suddenly the doctors are hopeful that he may someday be able to communicate with us, his family.

His therapist suggested that we ask the police, if Scott could meet the dog, Ben as they would like to observe the interaction between them. We are excited as there has never been any recognition with other dogs or cats. We do not know what is different about this dog but he has something special.

We are not asking your officer Amanda, Ben's handler to come on her own time. We are offering to pay the officer if she will bring Ben to our home or anywhere she chooses. Of course our home is a familiar environment for Scott so that would be our preference but we are definitely not opposed to meeting Amanda at another location.

We are excited, encouraged, scared, desperate and optimistic all at the same time.

Thanking you in advance and hoping for a positive response.

Grateful Citizens

Sincerely

Pam and Lorne Hopper

Then he looks up at his manager and says, "Ken do you know anything about the parents, Pam and Lorne Hopper?

"Chief, I did a background check and they appear to be legit. They are respectable law abiding citizens they have a son with Autism. They own their place, a nice farm over on the east side of town," he offers then adds, "I can do a more in-depth check if you would like me to."

Chief responds with a smile, "Yes, do that. I like to know who we are dealing with before committing public funds to a project. I agree this could be positive press for our K-9 unit."

"I'll get right on it. Thanks Chief," Ken says. He is pleased with himself especially since his boss likes his idea. He scurries off to find a computer where he can do a thorough background check on the Hoppers.

Eddy, editor of the Bamberg Chronicle reads the Hopper's letter to his assistant editor, Jonathon and says, "They say that they also sent a copy of this letter to the Chief of Police for Bamberg County, they go on to say they anticipate this idea will be a great humanitarian story and will help on several different levels, one being hope for other children with Autism although it might be slim hope. Of course they consider the possibilities for further research into understanding Autism. You can bet it will be at the top of this family's list, *if* and I do emphasize *if*, it helps them communicate with their own son."

Eddy reads a post script written to him personally, "They say there is no such thing as bad publicity in this scenario. We believe it is all good. Win – Win for the police, K-9 Unit, Ben and Autism. Please consider reporting this meeting with Ben. Of course, we understand that the Chief will need to approve the meeting first."

Eddy is grinning from ear to ear when he looks up from the letter at Jonathon, and asks, "Well, what do you think?"

"It is a stretch. Who knows if they don't try they will never know. Seems there is some desperation here. I would like to know what they will think if there is no recognition of the dog if he does meet the boy," Jonathon says, "I like to take the skeptical side of any story as there is less disappointment."

Jonathon continues his thought process, "Its right up our alley for a humanitarian story. We've been looking for something, along this line. One could say it's made for us. Shall I call a meeting to discuss how we handle that meeting and who will do what?" he said even though he realizes he has already lost Eddy's attention, because as usual he is two steps ahead of him.

Eddy is so excited about the prospect of this story he telephones the family. He asks them questions to verify some details then says, "I read your letter and I'm offering to send a reporter and photographer to the meeting. We will print the story and any follow-up stories. Regardless of the right results it will be a good story." Eddy for the first time in a long time, got his niggling twitch when he knows a story could be big news.

The Chief weighs the pros and cons. Then a couple of days later after he speaks with his legal people and advisors, plus he receives well over one hundred phone calls urging the Police to participate in the experiment. He calls his staff that would be involved in the experiment to a meeting and says, "I have decided to allow the visit but within very strict parameters. My agreement is for limited access and at a specific and length of time. I can't emphasize enough that *all* and I mean *all* press releases must come across my desk before being put in print. I don't want misinformation and all the celebrity status in the press to spoil the dog for future criminal cases. Every report I have seen so far, states that Ben has exceptional abilities and his trainer give him outstanding recommendations. He appears to be a gem."

Amanda is summoned to a meeting at police headquarters to discuss the matter. She already has an idea, regarding the subject of the meeting, as there are no secrets in the police department. She takes her time and prepares her thoughts and suggestions related to the request. She practices for the meeting by reciting her position while looking in a mirror, she ends her presentation with, "As always, I'm most concerned about the impact this will have on Ben because I want nothing but the best for him."

She attends the meeting the next day armed with her arguments and suggestions that fuel her mixed feelings. She says, "On one hand I see it as a great opportunity for both the K-9 division and the Police department as a whole. The publicity for the force will be tremendous. I can also see the positives for the boy. I would love to be instrumental in assisting the family, but on the other hand I want to keep Ben from being spoiled. He is a smart, alert, well trained useful member of the K-9 Kennel Brigade and I want to keep him focused on his job. This could be a distraction we don't need."

Amanda's supervisor Trevor calls her into his office to relate the decision, "It's a done deal that is their decision. Everyone involved is on board with the limitations and time line. Everyone agrees. Details are signed off by our boss, the Chief, Robert Benjamin. The agreement was drawn up by the police department's legal team to avoid any future law suits and to curb any unrealistic expectations which might occur. The documents have been duly signed by the Hopper family, Scott's Therapist, and the Bamberg Newspaper's editor, Bill (Eddy) Edwards. Of course Amanda as Ben's handler you need to sign also. Each person will receive a copy."

"Amanda you are the front line of the department so you need to know the support everyone has for Ben. After all he is only a dog, a very astute, intelligent dog but, still only a dog. Sometimes these situations start out innocently enough, but then there is an opportunity for problems, and a tendency for misunderstandings, or to be taken out of context," Trevor adds to reinforce his thoughts on the matter.

Amanda says, "I'm comfortable knowing that Ben is being protected. Of course the lawyers have gone to great strides to protect the police first and then Ben."

"I'm anxious, worried and feeling physically ill as my nerves are taking over. I have concerns about Ben's reputation as one of the best K-9 recruits any one has ever seen before. I'm also well aware that there could be a negative backlash. What if Scott does not recognize him or doesn't respond favorably to Ben in real life?" she shares her concerns with Trevor.

Trevor adds, "The *Bamberg Chronicle* our local newspaper, has everyone for a hundred miles in all directions – hyped. They are selling tons of newspapers and there is a rumor that the story could go viral. No, they haven't gone beyond their approved boundaries but their limits sure are bulging."

"I have made a mental note to have a serious conversation with Eddy very soon. He needs my input because I feel that he is getting carried away. Sensationalism sells newspapers but that isn't always the best for the people involved in the story. My heart hurts for Ben," Trevor states. He reinforces his and the department's position.

"Thank you, for looking out for Ben," she says, "I'm sure he appreciates your desire for positive press."

Amanda – Chapter Five

Today is the big meeting for Ben. It doesn't matter where you shop, bank or eat the meeting between Scott and Ben is the subject on everyone's lips.

Amanda says, "Ben you're going on a trip to the groomers today. I bet you are wondering why you're getting groomed and it isn't your regular appointment. Even your nails will look respectable. This is for a very special day tomorrow. We want you looking handsome for your big photo op."

Ben thinks *why is this happening? This must be a very, very special occasion!*

Amanda is anxious too. He can feel it when she comes near him. Ben thinks Amanda is a terrific handler as she takes the best care of him and makes sure he has everything a dog could want. They even work together.

Great! We are going out in the car he has his K-9 coat on but he is not in the cage. Hmmm, he wonders. He can't tell if today is a social day or a work day. He is too handsome and far too nicely groomed to be going to work. Amanda is letting him sit in the front seat with her and the window is open. *I really enjoy when the breeze is blowing in my face.*

The trip today is very short. Now they are turning into a long driveway. This is a new place he doesn't remember coming here for a job. Look at all of these people. *Why are they are waving at us?* Some have flashing light things in their hands.

Ben sees that Amanda is getting very irritated. Maybe we should go back home. It doesn't feel good here. He senses Amanda's apprehension.

Ben barks to tell the people crowding him and Amanda, *we don't like them pushing and shoving us.*

"Inside voice Ben," she reminds him.

Amanda mutters, "I really don't like the edgy feeling in this crowd. Why do they need to take movies and videos? Nothing is happening, yet."

Ben observes that she is getting more irritated with the unruly crowd.

Amanda drives slowly making her way up the driveway pushing the people out of the way with her car. She parks the car near the front door of a big house. When she gets out of her side of the car she commands, "Ben stay."

That usually means she is not sure what is happening. *I'll wait. She knows best what's best for me and I trust her.*

Amanda opens my door, then says, "Here Ben, let's put your leash on before you get out."

Ben sniffs the air for recognition of something, anything.

She then guides him through the crowd directly to the front door. It doesn't look or feel like a crime scene. *I'm confused.*

Just as they got to the porch steps, the front door is flung open by a very happy smiling lady. She introduces herself as Pam. She is very happy to see us. A man who said his name is Lorne stands beside Pam, he is also very cheerful and glad to see us. They invite us inside their house.

It smells different than our house. *I can smell cats. That reminds me of inquisitive little Harry. I wonder if he is still with Sam and Molly. I sure would like to tell them about my job and the people I find. I wonder if they remember me.*

Ben's thoughts are interrupted by the arrival of high pitch nervous voices from new people, just entering the room.

Lorne introduces us to Becky, Scott's therapist.

So this is what a therapist looks like. She looks like a little girl because she is so much shorter than Amanda. She sure is pretty with her dark hair, icy blue eyes and brownish skin. *I like her soft voice, it is very comforting.*

Amanda said, "Ben, go see the boy, go fella."

I walk in the direction Amanda is pointing to find a boy sitting in a chair with wheels. I look then sniff the chair and sniff all over the boy and nudge his hand. He is ignoring me. I'm not sure what they want me to do. He ambles back to Amanda.

Pam hands Amanda a sweater with a very strong smell of the boy. She thinks this might get his attention.

Once Amanda knows that Ben has the boy's scent, she instructs, "Go Ben, find him. Find the boy," Again Amanda commands, "Find. Find him Ben."

This is the same way she does it when we are working. *I obediently trot into the room and bump the boy with my nose. I bark but nothing happens. I'm not use to being ignored; usually I get too much attention. The boy did not even look at me.*

Lorne had another suggestion, "What if I sit beside Scott, and call Ben into the room so Scott could hear his name?" There's an agreement that this might work.

Lorne walks over to Scott and says, "Scott, Ben is here to see you." Then he calls my name, "Ben, come in here. Ben, come see Scott."

I respond but Scott does not. Lorne took Scott's hand and put his hand on my back so he could feel my fur. Nothing!

This little exercise is not great for my ego. *I wonder*

why this boy does not like me. Everyone else does and I am really good looking and especially handsome today.

We hung out for another thirty minutes or so, trying a few more scenarios. He just didn't respond to me. Ben senses a high level of disappointment and frustration in the room. They were not as happy now, as when he arrived.

Amanda made an excuse and said, "Sorry, but we do need to leave."

Amanda attaches his leash and heads for the front door. When it opens, it is obvious she was not prepared for all those people, shoving things on sticks in her face. The constant flashing lights are really annoying for both Ben and Amanda.

They are pushing and talking, all at once? Amanda said many times over. "No comment . . . no comment, please move . . . no comment, watch out for my dog."

Someone in the unruly crowd of people trample on his paw. Ben yelps very loud, and then barks, this seems to interrupt their incessant chatter, just for a few seconds. Amanda is trying hard to keep them from hurting me. Finally we reach our car. Amanda put me in on my side then locks the door. She pushes her way through the crowd to her side. Opening the door was not easy for Amanda, as the crowd is disorderly and still frantically pushing and shoving. *I start to bark loudly as I worry about her safety.*

I want to ask Amanda, who are these crazy people?

Finally we left. The drive home was quiet. Amanda didn't speak to me all the way, she is preoccupied. The events of the morning were a new experience. He didn't understand what it was all about. No matter, it's over now.

Amanda – Chapter Six

Maybe we can go to work today; he thinks that might change her subdued mood.

Amanda didn't go home. She did though, drive straight to work. *Great!* What he didn't realize was that she needs to report to Trevor her boss regarding the events of this morning.

Based on her tone of voice she is not happy.

Amanda reports to Trevor, "It was a frigging circus. Where did all of those reporters come from? It was horrible . . . they stepped on Ben's paws at least once."

"Besides the circus how did it go?" Trevor smugly asks.

"I'll just tell you, no one is happy. The boy totally ignored Ben."

"No recognition at all?"

"None, zilch, notta. The kid never even looked at Ben. I have to give the father credit though. He tried several different scenarios and unfortunately the results were fruitless."

"It was a big hype over nothing, definitely a none event, eh?" Trevor comments, "I guess you should write your report sooner than later so the folks upstairs can respond to the press," he pauses for a moment then motioning to her office he adds, "Why don't you take some time right now to do the report because you're still on the clock?"

Amanda reluctantly agrees, "Okay good idea. I would rather get it done so I don't fret over it."

Amanda walks the twenty or so feet to her office, takes out a pad and pen, sits on her large office chair and begins writing. Ben made himself comfortable too. He chooses a comfy spot to lie down, right next to her desk. He has a little nap while she writes her report. It didn't take long because there wasn't much to communicate. Most of her time now is taken up by her co-workers who keep dropping by to ask how it went; she got to repeat her story several times.

Every time the story was repeated Ben got pats and guarantees that it wasn't his fault. *Of course it wasn't my fault.* He is starting to think that he may have had something to do with the outcome: even though they continue to assure him otherwise.

Betsy, her office buddy waves her over and asks, "Well, how did it go?"

"Not the outcome the family was hoping for," Amanda shares with some disappointment in her voice.

"Amanda, we've been friends for a long time now, right?" Betsy tests.

"Sure, where are you going with this Bets?" Amanda inquires with a small frown.

"When are you going to give Trevor the green light? I see how you each light up when the other enters the area. He talks about you all of the time. He is smitten with you, gal," Betsy states with encouragement.

"Bets, you know the rules, no fraternization, we both like our jobs. It's a non-issue," Amanda adds, "so just drop it!"

"He is a handsome guy. He has a great tan; I love his coal black hair and those eyes. Wow! You guys would be perfect together. I know he is sweet on you. I watch him and you glow whenever he speaks to you," Betsy continues. "He's got a great education. He has a wonderful career in the police force. He is perfect for you. You should grab him before someone else does."

"What part about 'drop it' do you not understand little miss matchmaker. It's all about careers," Amanda continues with a little less enthusiasm. "If it is meant to be, it will happen. I can't imagine not being on the force."

"If I don't leave soon you will have us walking down the aisle. Got to go, Bets see you later," Amanda smiles in her friend's direction then waves goodbye as she leaves.

"Let's go home, Ben."

They drive in silence. Amanda has a lot on her mind.

Amanda – Chapter Seven

Two days after the disappointing episode with Scott. Ben hears Amanda's conversation with the dispatcher Lucy.

Lucy tells Amanda, "A two years old toddler is missing, and the parents said she wandered away about four hours ago. The parents and neighbors did search the whole neighborhood for several hours looking for the child, unfortunately she has not been found."

"Supervising Officer Sean Black asks for the assistance of a K-9 team. You and Ben were specifically requested," dispatch continues, passing the message along to Amanda, 'I'll send the address with directions to your iPhone,"

"Thanks Lucy, my Estimated Time of Arrival (ETA) is fifteen minutes," Amanda replies as she gathers the necessary equipment.

Amanda disconnects, and immediately takes Ben to her vehicle; once again she put him in the cage for transportation to the crime scene.

Ben doesn't resist as he knows now this means work. He is excited about the next assignment too.

Amanda grabs the red flashing light designating her as an emergency vehicle and puts it up on the roof of her automobile with her left hand. This permits her to drive uninterrupted and very quickly to the scene. Amanda knows time is of the essence. She raises her head to look into the rear view mirror. Watching Ben, in the crate she asks him, "Ben, are you ready to go to work again?"

Ben barks in acknowledgment, yes he is ready.

When they arrive at the scene, Amanda parks her vehicle in front of a house just down the street. She walks to the rear and opens the hatch of her vehicle to let Ben out. She attaches his leash this insures that she is always in control.

The sobbing young mother, at the direction of another officer, hands Amanda a toy the young child likes to chew. "Please find my baby," the mother pleaded, wringing her hands and wiping tears from her cheeks.

Amanda agrees, "This should have a good strong smell for Ben. He'll be able to follow it, no problem. We should be able to find the lost child, shortly. Don't you worry. If she's around here Ben will find her."

This case, from the get go was a routine scent search. Ben got the smell and starts searching. He wanders around in circles sniffing and sniffing the ground and the air. He walks a few houses in one direction but nothing. He goes in the other direction but he cannot find a strong enough scent anywhere on the street. Ben is puzzled. He continues sniffing and sniffing but still nothing.

Amanda encourages him to find the scent by offering the toy for Ben to smell again, then commands, "Find the baby. Go find the baby, Ben."

Ben sits down and looks at Amanda tilting his head from one side to the other. He is questioning the instructions. He is confused. There is no scent on the ground past the child's home. The lack of scent just didn't make sense to Ben.

He definitely isn't making a good impression on these police officers.

Amanda pats him and says in a very quiet voice, under her breath, "The non-believers are always there waiting for someone to fail."

A cantankerous officer, shouts, "Get that dog out of here and let us do some real detective work."

Amanda questions Ben, "What happened? Why did you lose the scent?"

He whimpers then barks to tell her there is no scent past the house. Nothing, nothing at all!

Ben wanders towards the house where he did get a faint scent, but the police officer at the door blocks him. He will not let him in the house. The officer on guard says,

"The crime scene lab people are still documenting the contents of the house and the child's room. You cannot enter."

Other officers trying to help tell Amanda, "Your dog needs to go down the street because a witness told them they saw the child going that way."

Ben hesitates because there is no scent on the street. Ben is not convinced. The officer is wrong. He tries going towards the back yard. He is blocked again by another police officer standing on the driveway.

Ben wanders around trying to pick up the scent. He waits for the guarding officer at the driveway, to be distracted then cautiously sneaks past him. Ben runs directly into the back yard pulling Amanda behind him. This is where the scent is really strong, not faint like on the street. He has been trained to follow his nose, and this is exactly what he is doing.

In the back garden he sniffs several places then stops, sits and quietly barks.

Amanda has faith in him. Her training is to trust your dog. The dogs most often know best.

Ben did find a mound of earth in the garden, where the scent is very strong. He knows he is in the right place. He proceeds to scratch and dig very carefully in the earth with his front paws. He appears to be committed to that mound of earth. Ben finds the smell to be overwhelmingly strong. He continues to frantically dig. He hesitates for only a moment as he finds another scent a bad scent, that is very distracting but he continues digging. He must find the baby.

Amanda is right behind him watching. Amanda puts her hand to her nose and screws up her face, as she also smells something very strong and unpleasant. "Whew, what is that odor?" she asks.

She frowns and wonders what is making Ben so driven to dig here in the garden. She asks, "Ben what did you find?" She is shocked when she sees what Ben uncovers. The mound of earth is in fact a grave for the toddler. Right before their eyes, now lays a small motionless body wrapped in a dirty stained yellow blanket.

Amanda immediately summons the detective in charge. When he arrives she points to the disturbed mound of earth in front of Ben. Her voice breaks as she says, "Sean, look at what Ben has dug up. This little bundle might contain the body of the missing toddler."

The detective sighs and declares, "Now, what we have here is a suspicious death case — thanks to Ben." He walks away with his head and shoulders hunched over; he now has the unpleasant task of talking to the parents.

Amanda says, "Good work Ben. This is not the result anyone wants but you did your job. Good boy." She pats and scrubs his ears showing Ben, her appreciation for a job well done.

A few weeks later, Ben is awarded a citation for his service to the K-9 Police Kennel Brigade. Ben the sleuth is a hero, again.

This is proof to Ben that being a working dog is a very rewarding job. He has never done anything that has given him the satisfaction and pleasure that this job has in just a few weeks. His is very motivated. He can't wait until Amanda gets the next call.

He rocks!

It has been a while since Ben seriously thought about continuing his journey or searching for his human family. In the scheme of things right now, the journey is not on the top of his priority list.

Making a choice between being a family pet versus a crime solver, in Ben's mind, there's no contest. He's a crime solver through and through, and loving it.

Sam reads the local paper for news of what is going on around him every day. This is an old habit from his former life. Today's news hit him like a bolt of lightning. He shouts to Tom, "I was just reading an article. Apparently there is a dog in a town in eastern Bamberg County that's making big news. All because of the help he's giving the police to solve cases," scratching his head he continues, "you're never going to guess his name. It's Ben. That can't be a coincidence, can it?"

Sam shows the photo to Tom. "I agree he looks just like the Ben we know and love," Tom adds.

After reading the whole story again Sam pauses and reminisces. Tom watches Sam; he can see his mind is a million miles away. "I always knew he was special," Sam murmurs.

Amanda – Chapter Eight

Bill (Eddy) Edwards telephones Amanda, "Hello Amanda. Eddy, Editor of the Bamberg Chronicle, here, "I had some reporters at Scott's house the other day. I understand the meeting between Ben and Scott didn't go as the Hopper's had hoped." He sighs, and then continues, "It is unfortunate as everyone was so hopeful. It would have been a real breakthrough."

"You're right. Unfortunately, it was disappointing for the parents. I think the whole exercise was a long shot. Maybe they had their hopes set just a little too high. But kudos to them for trying to communicate with their son," Amanda says.

"I want to personally thank you for taking your precious time to see if there was anything to it, which would be something very important to report. I know the Hopper's appreciated you and Ben going to their home," Eddy says graciously.

"I drove straight to my office and wrote my report so you should have access to it shortly. Sorry, nice try. I'm not sure where we would be if Scott had recognized Ben and exactly what that would mean, to Scott or others with Autism," Amanda thoughtfully shares.

"Amanda, would you consider meeting with me at our offices? I have some scenarios for future articles that could have a positive spin for your K-9 Unit. I'm hearing that Ben has been a special dog for quite some time."

"What do you mean?" Amanda questions.

"Even with limited circulation. The stories about Ben have got the attention of people in at least one other county. My nose tells me there are more stories. It's the 'news hound twitch.' I feel it in my bones. I want to share what I know with you, but I would rather be sitting across from you."

"Is this something I need the Chief's approval for?" she asks.

"No, it's all good. Let's just say Ben has acquired a bit of a fan club. I don't want to spoil my story. Let's meet. What's your schedule like this week? You know us news guys, we want to strike while the iron is hot," He excitedly expresses his thoughts.

She agrees. "But I do need to get approval before speaking to the press. If they say yes then I'm in. Ben's previous pursuits are of interest to me."

"Good, the time is set for tomorrow at 10:00 a.m. Looking forward to seeing you Amanda," He happily responds.

Amanda adds, "I am very curious."

She calls her boss, Trevor to fill him in on her phone conversation with Bill Edwards. "Trevor, Eddy just invited me to a meeting at the paper tomorrow. Do you have any advice?

He cautions her, "Choose your words wisely and do not give any statements. Just tell them you need to put it past me first. You know those legal beagles upstairs. You might even think about wearing a wire. All reporters make me nervous. They like to put it in their own words, sometimes there is very little resemblance to the actual conversation. Come to the office before the meeting and we will fix you up with a wire."

She didn't see the necessity of wearing a wire for an informal meeting but she has learned to trust the experienced officers like Trevor. She made her first stop at Police Headquarters to meet with the techie guy.

"Testing One – Two – Three; Testing One – Two – Three," She repeats for the sound check.

Trevor hears the transmission and says, "Loud and clear, thanks Amanda. No harm in protecting your butt." He also gives her a thumb up.

Amanda and Ben drive in silence to the Chronicle.

When they arrive at the offices of The Bamberg Chronicle for the meeting with Eddy, there are quite a few other press people in attendance.

"Thank goodness I'm wired," She murmurs under her breath.

At first it sounds to Amanda like they are trying to salvage the autism boy, Scott's story. Amanda thought it was over, but is told by the reporter sitting next to her, "There are way too many people waiting with bated breath for the continuation of that story."

She thinks that is extremely dangerous at the very least insensitive. Amanda feels better once the meeting starts.

Eddy shouts over the chatter, "Introductions people. May I have your attention? Most of you know each other. To my right here is Officer Amanda and for those who and I can't imagine there will be a single person in this room, not familiar with, Ben. Take a bow a Ben."

He barks to show he recognizes his name. This causes chuckles around the room and Amanda's hand on his back to remind him.

"Inside voice Ben," she whispers.

Immediately Eddy put the guessing and rumors to rest. "I think we should change the focus of the articles just a little, I think the story should be more general. Of course Ben our hero, will still be the subject and at the center of the story. We can make the piece about Ben's crime fighting abilities and his skills for finding people."

They try to get Amanda to buy in because Eddy adds, "The goal here is to promote the K-9 Kennel Brigade. We are looking for a different angle, this way we can keep the Ben story alive, longer."

Amanda agrees with them, but warns, "You will need the Chief's approval, for each article and the parameters set. Everything must be in writing. There could be major issues with confidentiality as you all know; those laws are cast in concrete. Also some legal issues if too many of the evidence details are revealed, or the wrong details are printed that could be a big problem. If this happens, the county prosecutor may have trouble getting convictions. Also for consideration, what will be the defense attorney's objections? Possibly some guilty people will have their cases thrown out of court due to evidence problems."

Amanda is becoming less enthusiastic about the whole concept; because she knows the readers push and keep pushing for more facts and more information because they are hungry for more, always more. She continues, "It's a well-known fact that readers have an insatiable appetite. This worries me and I'm sure it will worry the Chief, the Prosecutors and the lawyers as well."

Eddy animatedly making his point asks, "Ben could be a weekly column. It's a budget year and you don't want your department to make all of the cuts."

Amanda admonishes him, "That's a low blow, Eddy. I cannot ever agree without the Chief's stamp of approval. The argument you just made will never encourage a vote in your favor."

Eddy quickly apologizes, "I'm sorry Amanda I guess I over stepped my boundary."

"Apology accepted," she responds.

"Amanda, remember my conversation the other day about other Ben stories are out there?

"Yes, I do and I am curious," she replies.

"We now know of two families that temporarily adopted Ben. It is possible that he's been adopted by others," Eddy adds.

Ben can't believe the noise level of the chatter from the group, it was out of control. There were so many different conversations and opinions being bantered around the room, at the same time. All based on their limited knowledge and speculation of his escapades.

Eddy tries to speak above the noise. He shouts, "Hold it down, guys. Just hear me out. These people are telling great stories. Somewhat unbelievable in one case but they swear it all to be true and well documented. Ben apparently brought help to someone who had a car accident over in Casper County. Ben actually saved her life."

Ben put his paws over his ears as the noise level increases many decibels, once again. Everyone is talking at once. Each has their own twist on how it should be reported. Ben thinks, Amanda should tell them, *inside voices, please.*

Dollar signs are floating through their minds. Then someone stopped the chatter as if a switch was turned off, by saying, "This story has the potential to go national."

There was a renewed excitement with a consensus among the Newspaper folks, "A National story would benefit all of us." There is also agreement that recognition and publicity will help the paper and some careers. "Yes, let's do it," this is the cry from the majority of the Newspaper reporters.

Amanda wants to hear more, "How do you plan to present this story?" She is interested in learning more about Ben's past too. But she is timid about what a National story or a YouTube video will do for Ben, her department and their sleepy little town.

"I like things the way they are. I'm not big on the prospect of National exposure. I have heard the expression, 'Going Viral' I have this strange feeling about the experience of going viral," she shares with the reporter sitting next to her.

"I'm not sure we are ready for the 'Going Viral' experience," the reporter whispers to her.

Amanda sat quietly, she worries, "What if through all of this publicity, I lose Ben?" What if his previous family locates him through these stories? She didn't like that prospect at all. She has become quite fond of Ben. Who wouldn't be, he is well behaved, smart and . . . an absolute pleasure to have around.

"The meeting is coming apart as there is little or no structure, it is simply out of control. Eddy is no longer in command; there is no order . . . just bedlam," she voices to her neighbor.

Eddy shouts, "Order, please let's have some order," he attempts to take charge, once again.

With a resemblance of order he can now speak normally. He continues, "We need to plan, organize and move as a single unit. We as a group need to manage what is said to and by whom. What needs to be done and by whom? What we and others print? It is important that we do not lose control of our own story."

There is a mumble of agreement from the group.

"Thank you. I think we need to setup interviews with those that have already contacted the paper. We must verify, check and verify again. The last thing we want is to end up with is egg on our face, because we didn't do our homework, research and verify the details; I can't say this enough." Eddy lectures the group. He's a solid news guy and he knows his role as editor is extremely important right now. He's excited as he knows he has to be the head cheerleader and pull the story together.

Amanda got his attention and suggests, "I am very interested in Ben's story. I think this part of the meeting does not need my input. When you have your plan ready to implement, please call me."

"Amanda, I want to thank you, for attending our meeting. There are so many Ben stories out there. We will search and find more Ben stories, I'm sure of it," Eddy says good bye as he shakes Amanda's hand.

She turns and waves to the reporters. Amanda adds, "Thanks for inviting me. It was very interesting."

Amanda – Chapter Nine

Amanda and Ben leave the meeting. Ben is sensing Amanda is not too happy. She is deep in thought, all of the way back to her office.

She wants to talk to Trevor. She goes directly to his office. She says, "Good you haven't left for lunch yet. I won't bore you with all the details. I have not experienced a meeting quite like that, ever before. It was a riot; really they were out of control, with everyone talking at once. The reporters are so excited about the huge potential to go national. They all seem extremely high on the story, I have concerns though, Eddy might lose control and, all hell will break loose."

She continues with her feedback, "Here is the Readers Digest version. Ben wasn't a virgin when we discovered him. It sounds like he has been influencing people's lives for quite a while. I don't know all the details, but apparently there are folks out there with stories to share. Eddy is organizing the interviews so the Chronicle can write their sequels. I don't know where it is all going or how. Someone at the meeting threw out the words 'going viral' and caused a massive uncontrolled and unorganized chattering. Now, that does scare me."

Trevor queried, "You got all of this on tape?"

"Yes, yelling, shouting, group madness is what it was. They were so excited. I hope you can understand and decipher the voices on the recording."

Trevor now has concerns too. He is hoping for guidance from the folks up stairs. "You should wait around for a while just in case you're needed to clarify something. Give me the tape and I will drop it off at legal. Then brief the Chief. You know him. He wants to know everything" Trevor took the tape, starts walking away, then turns and looks back at Amanda, winks then says, "There goes my lunch today."

Ben senses, that Amanda likes Trevor, he is single. He is also her direct Supervisor. Also, Trevor likes Amanda, she is single. She reports directly to him. Ben thinks he would like both as his new human family.

While waiting for Trevor to return, Amanda thinks, *Department Rules say no fraternizing among fellow workers. We both continue to deny our feelings. We do not speak about our feelings for each other. We both love our jobs. If we get together one of us will need to leave the force. That will not be my choice so getting together is not likely to happen.*

Ben does sense the magnetism between Amanda and Trevor. He likes them both. Trevor's a good guy. He's kind, smart and according to Amanda a "Hunk."

Ben likes Trevor's office because he has a great carpet. It is so soft. He doesn't mind having a nap there while Trevor and Amanda flirt.

While Amanda waits she chats with some friends. "What's new Betsy?" Amanda asks.

Betsy said, "I overheard part of your conversation with Trevor. I visited my Uncle Andy in Casper County a month or so ago. I glanced at their Gazette one morning and saw the story about this heroic dog that saved someone's life. He also helped them find a criminal. I didn't put the names together until just now. Is our Ben one and the same as the Casper County Ben?

Amanda nods in agreement, "It appears to be so."

Wow a hero in our midst." She pulls up a chair and settles in for a visit.

"Hey Ben are you a hero?" Betsy kids as she bends down to give Ben a loving pat and scratches his ears.

He likes Betsy she's a good person.

Amanda rolls her eyes and groans, "Here we go. This is exactly the crap I want to avoid."

Trevor came back from his meeting with the Chief. He saw Amanda in his office chatting with Betsy, "Hi ladies, are we having a quilting bee?"

Both chuckle at the unintended insult.

Amanda asks Trevor, "How did it go?"

"No problem, "Trevor replies.

Then she asks, "So am I free to go?"

Trevor nods approvingly, "It's a wait and see game now. Chief suggested you might keep the communication channels open with the editor, Bill Edwards. He wants us to stay on top of the story. Of course a heads up before it is printed, would be best."

"See you tomorrow Trevor," she waves good bye and gathers up her belongings.

Ben dutifully follows.

Amanda – Chapter Ten

Eddy, read an article in the Casper Gazette newspaper. This story involved a sixteen year old whose life was saved by a dog named Ben. The editor of that paper conducted what Eddy thought to be quite a superficial interview. He knows he can do a better job. More importantly he has knowledge about Ben that the Gazette does not.

Eddy telephones the Wilsons and says, "Mrs. Wilson my name is Eddy Edwards, Editor of the Bamberg Chronicle. I would very much like to interview Jenny regarding her experience with the now famous dog Ben.

"Mr. Edwards, Jenny did an interview with our local paper last week. Can't you use that interview? She is only sixteen and we want to protect her from too much publicity," she responds with a slight bit of irritation in her voice.

"I do understand your hesitancy but I know where Ben is and the exciting life he has so I have a very different perspective," he adds.

"Okay, but first let me discuss this with my husband and Jenny. Call me back tomorrow and I will give you our answer," she says putting him off because she wants space to think the whole idea through before agreeing.

"If it would help I will let you read the story before it is printed," he knows how to reel in hesitant prospects.

"I understand that you want to have this interview yesterday. Tomorrow is the best I can do. Call me after five today. I will give you our answer. That's a promise, Mr. Edwards," she said. She was trying not to show her irritation with his pressure. The more he pushes the more confrontational she feels.

"Hello. Yes Mr. Edwards, we did discuss your proposal and we agree with two conditions. We want to see the questions you are going to ask Jenny plus we want to sit in on the interview. Remember she is only sixteen." Mrs. Wilson states the parameters they want for the interview.

"Thank you so much. Your conditions are totally acceptable. Obviously I would like to conduct the interview as soon as possible," an elated Eddy says.

"Jessie grab your gear we are going into the field to conduct an interview. I want full sound and video of this meeting," Eddy instructs his best photographer, "Jessie, get photos of everything. Take ten times more than you think you'll need. This is a onetime opportunity to get the best photos and interview, plus a feel of the atmosphere. Things like this just do not happen very often to folks who live in a small town. This is so very special. None of us can ever fathom the final impact."

He met with Jenny the next day. The videoed interview begins, "Jenny we are recording this interview so I will first introduce you first."

The interview began, "We are here in the home of Jenny Wilson a very lucky young lady. I'm Bill (Eddy) Edwards's editor of the Bamberg Chronicle. We are going to talk about your recent experience with Ben. Is that alright with you?

"Sure Mr. Edwards, that's okay with me," she replies.

"Jenny, please Eddy, that's my nickname. He continues, I have read the police reports and an article in your local paper. Therefore I am familiar with the factual details of your rescue by Ben. I will not spend too much time on the known facts. What I am looking for is the humanitarian details for my story.

"Briefly you were driving to your part time job at the local Medical Mart when out of nowhere a truck driving towards you came into your lane and forced you off the road. Is that close to the facts of the case? He says reviewing the background information.

“Yes, close enough,” she agrees.

“Jenny what were your thoughts when you were bounced and hurled around as if you were in the eye of a tornado, all of the way down that ravine? Tell me about your fears and what went through your head. What were you thinking?” Eddy burrows down for the story.

Jenny said bluntly, “Simply, I thought I would die. I was a goner. At one point after regaining consciousness I remember asking myself out loud, ‘Am I alive’? I tried to call my parents, but they had left to work in the fields. I also unsuccessfully tried to call friends to ask for help. The bars on my cell phone disappeared and the battery died.”

“Why didn’t you call 911?” Eddy asks with curiosity.

“You’re not the first person to ask me that. I don’t know. Maybe I wasn’t thinking straight. I don’t know if I even could‘ve told a stranger to these parts where exactly, I left the road. I just don’t know.” Jenny silently ponders that question, and not for the first time.

She continues, “I have since the accident wondered that maybe the master plan was not to dial 911. Maybe Ben was meant to find me. Maybe it was all about faith . . . testing my faith. Putting faith in an animal you don’t know I think could be very risky. My faith is much clearer to me now. I think if the same thing happens again, and I hope it never does, but if it did, I don't think I would be hesitant to ask the dog for help."

"Please describe to me your first impression when you saw that an unfamiliar dog responded to your pleas for help," Eddy probes.

Jenny's facial expression shows the stress she felt, as she visibly sighs remembering the deep emotion of the frantic uncontrolled ride down the ravine, "Meeting Ben proved to me that putting my faith in him, in this case was a good thing to do. Previously I would never in a million years have believed a dog that didn't know me would or could have done so much for me. He saved my life. Period. How do you, one up that?"

"Please tell me about your thoughts and feelings after the accident when you first saw Ben in the hospital. What did you feel? What were your first thoughts?" He prodded.

Jenny smiles and relates the frantic scene in the hospital, "Ben was as excited about seeing me, as I was to see him. He smothered me in dog kisses. He made a total mess of my hospital bed. He acted like we had known each other for years. Why I have no idea. You would need to ask Ben." Jenny's tears of happiness were sneaking into the corners of her eyes during the reminiscing of the event.

She wipes her tears then continues, "My whole family will always be grateful to Ben. He is the smartest and most wonderful animal. I have come to believe that dogs are smarter than we humans give them credit for. He stayed here with us while I recuperated from the concussion and cracked ribs. He was my constant companion for a few weeks.

"Jenny I understand you and Ben also did some crime solving. Would you please tell me about that?" Eddy continues to probe.

Jenny coyly smiles, makes a face that everyone read as, 'I was so foolish,' and then looking over at her parents says, "I got curious about the person who left me there to die. When my mother, the warden, finally felt I was well enough to be allowed out of the house and to drive. Ben and I drove to the accident scene where I found tire tracks on the gravel beside the road."

"There must have been lots of other tracks on the shoulder of a gravel road? What made you so sure they belonged to the culprit that forced you off the road?

"I took photos of them. Then I went to see Jared our local mechanic and body shop guy. He confirmed that they were not from his truck or the ambulance. Jared fixed my car. He also saved me some paint chips that belonged to the truck that side swiped me," she clarifies for Eddy.

"Jared is the person that Ben brought to your accident scene, yes? He is also the person that called 911, and then telephoned your parents, right?" Eddy says to clarify the sequence of events for the record.

"Yes, I guess I'm getting ahead of myself," Jenny smiled in agreement.

"What did you do next?" Eddy asks.

"Ben and I drove to the Sheriff's office. They did the research based on the evidence I collected. They determined that it was a Smoke Gray truck that had forced me off the road.

"I always wondered how they zeroed in on that type and color of truck. Thanks for clearing that up for me. What happened next?" Eddy is getting the story he came after.

"Then the sleuthing began. Ben and I found the truck, and then reported back to the Sheriff, but I the curious one, didn't stop there. I went back to the farm where I found the truck. That's where the real drama began." Jenny pauses takes a deep breath and frowns remembering the terror of that day.

"Are you okay? Jenny, do you want to stop or take a few moments to compose yourself?" Eddy could see how deeply she was affected by those events.

"Thanks, I'm fine now. Whenever I think of the time Ben and I spent in that barn I feel tinges of the panic I experienced, all over again. My sleuthing days are finished, done, never to return," she recovers and is ready to proceed.

“Ben and I didn’t know the people who lived on that farm were also cattle rustlers. But, they thought we were going to reveal their illegal activities. One huge man became very aggressive, threatened to shoot us. Fortunately, Sheriff Mitch and his deputies arrived just as I was being escorted out of the barn at gun point. That was a very, very scary situation. I never want to be in that predicament ever again, she said with facial expressions hinting at the fear she felt back then.

“Where was Ben during this drama?” Eddy needs to know how Ben fits into this part of the story.

Jenny grins showing her dimples, and then says, “Just before the pock marked face guy found me hiding behind hay bales, Ben and I were looking for an escape route because they locked us in the barn. Then he instructed me, at gun point, to leave the barn. As we were leaving I shouted to Ben that he should hide. Apparently Ben was *not* interested in hiding so he escaped through an opening he somehow had found. I don’t know exactly where it was. When it was all over the Sheriff asked me where Ben was hiding. I called Ben several times. That is when we discovered that he had left the barn and found refuge in the massive corn field.” Wrapping her arms across her chest and giving the appearance that she was hugging herself for comfort. She said, “That was the end of my short lived career as an investigator.”

“How long did Ben stay with you after that incident?

"It seems like once he knew I was well he began distancing himself from me. Then one day he got really attentive and affectionate. The next day he just walked away and never came back. My parents and I were all very sad that day. But his job was done here."

Jenny asks, "Do you know where he is now? Do you think there is a chance I can see him?"

Eddy said, "As a matter of fact, I do know where he lives right now. I keep thinking that I should arrange a reunion for the people, that Ben has had an impact on their lives."

"I would really like that. Sort of like closure for me. Will you let me know when you have this re-union?" Jenny felt a warm mushy feeling in her gut or her heart, somewhere inside, when she thought she would be able see Ben, again.

"Sure I will put you on the list," Eddy agrees. Eddy's brain is spinning with ideas and how to make the most of all of the new Ben stories.

"What it's like living on the farm? Do you have a dog of your own?" Eddy inquires.

Jenny shares many details about living, and the hard work that is required, when on a farm your whole life. Then she adds, "No I don't have a dog as yet. The idea is not foreign to me or my parents we have been to the animal rescue place a couple of times. We just haven't seen the right one for us, yet. We just have Fluffy my cat. I do think though, when I settle down like maybe get married, a dog would be good. It would complete my family." She gets pensive for a moment then says, "I think right now I would expect too much from a dog. Ben would not be easy to replace."

Eddy asks, "Do you think everything happens for a reason?"

This question brought a thoughtful smile to Jenny's face. "Absolutely, I am not the same person that was run off road that morning. I believe I matured . . . very quickly I might add. There's nothing like a life changing experience to catapult you into reality. My reality check is appreciating how life can be snatched away in an instant." Jenny the philosopher snapped her fingers to emphasize the speediness that change can happen.

"Well done Jenny. I very much enjoyed your take on the story. Thank you so much. I wish you well no matter what you choose to do in life. It doesn't sound like being an investigator in is the cards for you.

Jenny smiles and sighs with relief that the interview is coming to an end. "I do think that I have some life decisions to make about where do I go from here," she says pensively

"Yes, before you ask again, you will receive an invite to the reunion once we have the details in place." Eddy's chuckles and smiles as he is very happy with his approach to the story it is from a very different angle than the local guy. He wants the feelings and emotions plus the back story. All of which he patiently waits to hear. Experience has taught him the immediate response is not always the whole answer. He has learned to wait and let his subjects sort out their thoughts before he moves to the next line of questions.

"Great interview Jenny, thank you and your parents for allowing me to get your take on your experience." Eddy spoke with sincerity.

"Pack up folks," Eddy instructs his crew.

Off camera and while his crew were shutting down their equipment, Eddy walks over to where the family have congregated and says, "We have taken up far too much of your precious time than originally planned. Thank you so much Jenny and both of you, Mr. and Mrs. Wilson. We have really enjoyed having you share your Ben adventure and your most inner thoughts. Yours is a fascinating story. Many people are anxious to know more of the details surrounding this amazing dog, Ben."

"You will let me know about seeing Ben, won't you?" Jenny presses as she really does want to see Ben again. Jenny once again feels the emptiness that was left in her heart, since that day that Ben wandered off.

They shake hands, exchange more thanks all around, and then they are gone.

Mrs. Wilson watches Jenny as she is alone now and her body language shows her yearning to see Ben again. She puts her arm around Jenny's shoulder gives her a loving squeeze and says, "Sweetheart time is a great healer," she pauses then adds, "If Eddy does have a reunion you will see Ben, at least one more time."

Amanda – Chapter Eleven

Eddy works very hard to organize his reporters and sources for another of many sequels on the adventures of Ben.

He just knows this story is also the real thing. He mutters to himself, "I, like any good reporter, can smell it. After all these years you can't explain it. It just is."

He wants to make sure all goes well. He, as usual talks himself through the process, "I know I have covered all bases by mentally reviewing my plans and the questions for the interview over and over again."

"Tomorrow is my interview with Sam Garner the ex-hockey player. I'll take along my best reporter and photographer. We need to make sure photos are available for national stories. We will still need a video," he mumbles to himself.

"You can never go back or you lose momentum and the possibility that someone else will sneak in and grabs your story. I will leave no stone unturned. My motto is do it right the first time. The National TV News Shows are always looking for live feed for their broadcasts." He said more to himself than anyone within hearing distance, "I know that I have a reputation for having extensive conversations with people. This is good, and then no one thinks it abnormal to hear me talking away to myself when there is no one else in the room," he smiles to himself.

"We need feed for 'You Tube' just in case there's an opportunity," he adds.

"Every Tom, Dick, and Harry enjoys a good human interest story. We will have one, that everybody will fight to read, discuss with their families, acquaintances and share with their friends on Facebook, Twitter, heck all of the social networking sites," he says with obvious excitement in his voice.

Eddy's secretary Ruthie, tells Elli a cub reporter while he is waiting to see Eddy. "Bill Edwards, everyone knows him as Eddy, is a tall, slender, good looking young fifty-five years old veteran. His salt and pepper hair gives him the distinguished look he has always wanted since being a 'cub' reporter. He's a highly energetic person; I have trouble keeping up with him. I like that he is also extremely well organized, he'd deny it but he does have a photographic memory. His diplomas and photos on his office wall tell the story of his illustrious career, he claims to know everything there is to know, about Journalism and news business, and I believe him."

Eddy returns and invites Elli and Jessie into his office and says, "I have been preparing my whole life for this level of opportunity. I am confident that I will be prepared, and so will everyone else involved."

"We are ready. I believe we have every possible scenario covered," Eddy continues talking to them.

"Anything else I can do boss?" Jessie asks as he is eager to do his very best work on this story.

Eddy murmurs more to himself, "This is our 'Golden Goose.' We will make heaps of money for the paper and healthy bonuses for the reporters and photographers."

Eddy is salivating.

Amanda – Chapter Twelve

He telephones Amanda and asks, "Hi Amanda, do you have time tomorrow to meet another person, from Ben's past? He lives in Casper County. He tells me he has a very interesting story. He says a show and tell story. I have no idea what he has in mind. The reporter in me says it's real. He did specifically ask if we could bring along Ben."

She frowns and with real concern in her voice says, "I do not want to set Ben up, nor do him harm, bodily or otherwise."

"Amanda I will never let that happen on my watch," Eddy assures her.

"Let me check my schedule. I'll get back to you in a few minutes," Amanda hesitantly responds.

She hangs up and immediately phones her supervisor. "Trevor, I need some guidance from you," Amanda says with uncertainty and worry in her voice.

"There is another Ben story in Casper County. The guy wants us to bring Ben along. He said, it will be a show and tell and everyone will be pleased," She says looking for guidance.

"Amanda, I think it's time I had an out of office day. I will come with you." Trevor really wants the opportunity to spend time with Amanda.

"We need to be at the Blueberry Hill Diner, on Highway Fifty Two for two o'clock tomorrow afternoon," Amanda is pleased, and enthusiastic at the prospect of spending, out of the office time, with Trevor.

Amanda calls Eddy back, "We'll be there at two o'clock."

"Wonderful," Eddy happily responds while feeling his reporter's twitch in overdrive.

Amanda – Chapter Thirteen

Tom arrives at the Diner in the dark; he got up at 3:00 a.m. this morning. He's busy baking special muffins, and getting lots of coffee ready for the curiosity seekers.

By noon the atmosphere is electric at the diner. Staff and diners are primed and waiting for the arrival of the press and their hero Ben. "There's standing room only as the regulars are cramming themselves in, trying to grab their customary seat," Tom reports to Sam.

"Staff came in early. We have brought in extra servers to deal with the expected mass of people. Everyone is working hard to make sure we are ready, clean and able to serve the crowd," Tom shares with Sue.

The guys that were working in the parking lot report, "The barriers are set up at the parking lot entrances this will encourage car drivers to park on the streets. We have the tables and chairs in place, for the over flow crowd."

Tom made arrangements for speakers to be strategically placed outside. "This should please those sitting in the parking lot, our 'outdoor café'," he tells Sue pointing to the new extension to their diner.

"The technical crews are here with cameras, recording equipment, lights and microphones. There are way too many people here." Sue says to Tom as she observes the arrival of the curiosity seekers.

Eddy said to Tom, "I'll be in charge of the orchestration of the interview process. We pre-arranged the details with my staff."

Eddy exclaims, "I'm excited and pleased to see the celebrities are here, Ben, Amanda and Trevor," he approaches them with his hand extended, they shake hands, "Hello, thanks for coming and bringing our hero, Ben."

Ben is wearing his K-9 Patrol jacket. There is no doubt people will know who he is and how important his job is. Ben struts, looking around at the crowd. This looks like work with all of these people mingling around and all talking at once. There are some uniforms here too. Ben is now confused. Amanda isn't wearing her uniform plus she didn't say it's a work day, today.

The staff approach, the guests and say, "Hello, would you like a Muffin or coffee? It's on the house for everyone, today."

Tom gloats and tells Sam, "I am really enjoying this free publicity as the result of the exposure via free press.

People will come from miles away just to see The Blueberry Hill Diner; where the now famous Ben stayed."

Sam reports to Tom, "The parking lot is full actually over-flowing as people are coming from all over the county. They're mingling and talking to each other. The locals did a good job at spreading the word to so many people."

"The local newspapers carried the story yesterday. They even printed our name, The Blueberry Hill Diner located at highway Fifty Two, Casper County," Tom says.

"This is a big crowd. I hope there will be someone on crowd control, there is a potential for this to develop into an unsafe environment." Amanda assesses.

"No, these are local people, and I will testify they all live in and around our town. There is no danger here; believe me," Tom assures Amanda.

"Once the police and newspaper crews are satisfied, they settle in to work or watch the interviews, Eddy tells Tom.

Amanda – Chapter Fourteen

"Hi Sam, we are going to record our conversation today; this will ensure that your words are not misquoted." Eddy states.

Sam sighs and says, "I'm as ready as I'll ever be."

Eddy began with introductions, "Hello I am here at the Blueberry Hill Diner speaking to Sam Garner. This is part of our ongoing series about Ben a very special and heroic dog, now a member of the Bamberg County Police Force's K-9 Kennel Brigade. We are sitting here in a booth near the windows of the diner overlooking the parking lot. Due to the huge number of people interested in this event, the owners have setup a makeshift cafe outside taking up most of the parking lot. It has been created as part of the diner with rental tables and chairs just for this special interview. We can be seen by the folks sitting outside and hope they can hear us clearly." He waves to the outside diners and they wave back, confirming they hear him.

Eddy speaks directly into the microphone, "Hello my name for the record is Bill Edwards, Editor of the Bamberg Chronicle. With me again is Sam Garner."

"Sam, please call me Eddy, that's my nick name."

"Sam tells me he has a story about Ben that will be interesting to others. You call it 'Show and Tell.' Is that right, Sam?" Eddy sets the stage for Sam's introduction of his story.

"Yes I did. Is it okay if I just arrange it now?"

"Sure, the floor is yours," Eddy offers with a wave of his hand.

"Thank goodness for cameras. I'd appreciate it if Amanda would send or bring Ben into the room. Please trust me. I love and miss Ben. I will not cause him harm." Sam says mostly to Amanda, as she has concern written all over her face, plus to set the scene.

Ben is brought into the Diner by Amanda his handler, "It's okay Ben go see Sam."

Ben looking around the diner is cautious of the many people in the standing and sitting, but not frightened.

With a nod from Sam, Tom, the owner of the diner, opens the back door to let Molly and Harry in, "Come on guys. Go see Sam." They both obey.

Molly is a happy medium size mostly; longer white fur, with black fur on her back that resembles paint running down her sides over her white fur. She is furiously wagging her tail.

Harry her constant companion a small glossy black short hair cat, with yellow eyes, pink tongue and white teeth that show only when he snarls during a fright or when protecting his property.

"Come here Harry," Sam coaxes.

There was a tense feeling in the room. The onlookers were nervous and unsure. "What's happening here?" they ask.

This is amazing, Ben thought. He immediately saw Molly and Harry. All hell broke loose. Tails are wagging and heads are bobbing their bodies are twisting like the wagging tail motion is a rudder controlling their movements. Molly and Ben romp, bark, whine and play. Harry participates too. They are all so happy to see their old friends. It is like playtime all over again. As usual Harry acts like a small dog and joins in the activities.

Sam looks over at Amanda and says, "I really wanted them to see each other again. We spent some quality time together. I guess, I was just curious to see if they still remember each other. This couldn't have been better choreographed if I planned it myself."

Sam motions for the dogs and cat to rest while he talks.

"Stay. Now I'll tell my story. Ben and I met about three months previous to him leaving. It was a terrible stormy night. Lightning brightly slashed the sky and thunder cracked overhead. We shared a dingy protected hallway for shelter.

There were no words just an unspoken understanding. Next morning we set off together on a journey."

Ben remembers that night. That was a terrible storm. He also recalls this man. He wonders why the people are all so excited. He loves seeing Sam, Molly and Harry again. I wonder what's going on here.

"A journey? What kind of journey?" Eddy speaks into the microphone and questions.

"Well I don't really know what Ben thought, but I do know he seemed to have a purpose," Sam continues.

"Then early one morning we came across a very seriously injured dog, she had been hit by a vehicle. She was left on the shoulder of the highway, to die. Ben took a liking to her or he just thought she was worth saving. Stage left, Molly. Take a bow girl." Sam introduces Molly with the wave of his hand.

"No, we don't know how long she lay there but she was not in good shape. We flagged down an old truck driven by Farmer Frank. He was a real character also a very kind person. He helped us by driving Molly, Ben and I to a vet. She had a fractured back leg. She couldn't walk. They were going to keep her there and find either her home or a new home for her. But, Ben would not leave without her. We coaxed and pleaded with him. No deal he would not leave," Sam continues.

"Who was in charge?" Eddy asks.

"Ben. Absolutely he was in charge. It got to be so comical the people in the vet's office were placing wagers on who would win. Ben was the favorite."

"One man in the waiting room watched the little show and offered a solution."

"A solution?" Eddy wanted to hear more.

"Keep in mind these are dogs we're talking about here. Anyway this man offers us a broken down wheel barrel to transport Molly as she couldn't walk with a splint on her hind leg. Especially since Ben and I walked all day, every day." Sam had more to say.

"We were quite the traveling road show. People in cars and trucks stopped and offered money, comments and suggestions. Later that day we found a fairly safe place to bed down for the night. We decided to stay there, until Molly was able to walk distances."

"We found the dumpster out back, here at this diner to have great food that they throw away."

"You ate from the dumpster?" Eddy probes.

"Yes. What would you have me do? I had no money. Should I starve? How would I feed the dogs?" Sam asks raising his eyebrows and shrugging his shoulders.

"Incredible," Eddy said, he was starting to get real insight the life of a homeless person.

"It was on one of our visits to the dumpster that we found Harry, sweet little Harry. He didn't ask to be included he just joined the team. Then we were a quartette." Sam smiles as he is enjoying his interpretation of the events.

"This is a wonderful story," Eddy said as he loves these humanitarian stories.

"One day Tom and Sue, they own this diner asked me to fill in for a staff member who left. They gave me the apartment upstairs," Sam points to the ceiling to indicate where they live. "We were all so happy and finally enjoying three squares a day plus safe sleeping accommodation. Life was good."

"It was about that time that Ben decided to leave. He didn't show signs that he was ready to move on until we were settled in the place upstairs here. He acted like maybe he was out of sorts or ill. He was very attentive to me one day, I remember well. I guessed later – he knew he would be leaving. The next day he wandered away and I never saw him again . . . until today."

"How do you think he knew it was time? Why did he decide to leave at that specific time?" Eddy inquires.

"I don't know. Only Ben knows." Sam fighting back tears says, "I obviously don't have all of the answers."

Eddy volunteers, "If Ben were a person, believe me, I too would have asked by now. I interviewed a couple of people over in Casper County. It seems when Ben feels his work is done, he moves on. Is there anything else you want to add to this story?" Eddy is hooked and wants more.

"No, I'm good. I really wanted to know that he was in good hands. He has had a major impact on my life," Sam adds and smiles in Amanda's direction.

'Good story, Sam I can hear you still have questions. But only Ben at this point has the answers. Right? Thank you so much," Eddy was anxious to move to the next part of the story.

"May I ask you some personal questions so I can fill in some of the blanks and round out the story?" Eddy is now ready to probe more deeply.

"What else could I possibly tell you?" Sam's curiosity is aroused.

"Your story, I want to how and why you were in that place at that time to meet Ben."

"Can we take a break?" Sam feels the need for space. He knows what is coming and wants to mentally prepare.

"Sure let's have a short break. Then we'll pick up from here," Eddy responds as he knows, how to get the whole story.

Amanda – Chapter Fifteen

Tom brings out his great muffins and coffee again offering seconds to everyone, "Help yourself folks. It's on the house. Welcome to our diner." Tom is quite the host.

Sam walks over to see Ben; he pats him and says, "Hi Ben, it is so good to see you. I understand you are moving up in the world of crime fighting. You are such a great dog. We have read some interesting stories about your escapades. We miss you so much every single day. Love you and thank you Ben." Sam was near tears again.

Ben did his normal head bobbing and body twisting, also wagging his tail with glee. Sloppy kisses where always included in his greetings.

It's nice to see Molly, Harry and Sam again. I didn't forget them. I'm really happy to see them. Sam seems so happy to see me. I wish I could tell them I have a great life with Amanda.

Sam stood and left the area. He walks through the kitchen and out the back door.

Eddy approaches Sam on the back parking lot. He wants to get permission to ask the big questions, "I want to forewarn you. An important part of getting the whole story is asking the tough questions. Are you ready?"

"Yes, I think I am," Sam responds.

"I want to ask how you got here. You know those kinds of questions. By the way, are you wanted by the police? It is not my intention to cause you any legal problems."

"It's not unlawful, just terribly sad." He is ready to move on, "Sure Eddy, I'm ready. My past is just history now."

When Sam comes back into the room Ben greets him all over again. He wiggles, wags, licks and wiggles some more. He really does enjoy the limelight. He loves his people. Plus he knows he is loved.

Ben notices Amanda looking serious. She and Trevor are standing back just watching. He wants to tell her he likes working with her and he wants to go home with her. He didn't want her to worry.

Ben went to Amanda, licks her hand and sits beside her.

Amanda put her hand down, pats his head and says, "Good boy Ben."

Trevor states, "You're right Ben has had quite the life before he met us."

Amanda – Chapter Sixteen

"Okay folks can we have everyone seated or in place and silent – please. I would like to continue by asking Sam some questions about his life before Ben. This way I can fill in the blanks for me and my readers," Eddy knows he can dig for more details.

Reluctantly Sam begins; he takes a deep breath, drops his shoulders and head then begins. "This is always so difficult for me so I will abbreviate my story. It started a little over two years ago. My eldest little sister, Karen had a soccer match. It was a championship game and I had promised her that I would be there, but due to a change in my schedule, a stupid, silly photo op, I could not be present. I just could not change the appointment as it involved the whole team. It was one of those beyond my control situations," Sam said with lots of emotion.

"Sam we will go back to that but for my readers as I'm sure everyone here already knows you were a Professional Hockey Player, right?" Eddy prefers Sam tell this part of his biography.

"That's correct it seems so long ago. I was another person also a lot younger and fitter." Sam elicits a few chuckles from the crowd. He continues, "It was a dream life, lots of money, notoriety, a fast and fantasy life style. I felt privileged to be brought into the fold of this envied existence. I'm sure people thought '*what a lucky bastard he is*.' Yes, I was, but only for a little while."

Eddy asks, "Many people in your place would have also gotten into drugs. Did you?"

"No, on ice you would get creamed if you were not on your toes all of the time. I mean hurt, very seriously injured. I was lucky my parents lived a good God fearing life. They taught me well. I sometimes wonder if the most important lesson I learned from my personal tragedy is to live the life my parents wanted me to live. I'm not a Religious person but I truly believe in living by the Golden Rule. Treat others as you would have them treat you."

"Wise parents you had, Sam," Eddy interjects; he was playing to his audience. "Interesting background, would you mind continuing your story?" he asks as he wants the whole story.

"I carry so much guilt about missing her match." He fidgets in his chair and takes another deep breath, then continues, "Karen's team just won the County Title for Junior Girls' Soccer. They were jubilant, on cloud nine. It was a very happy time for them," Sam recollects, and then his tone changes. "While they were driving home after that soccer game a drunk driver hit them, head on. They all died instantly. They didn't suffer for long."

"My wonderful parents whom I loved so much were gone. I don't know why, I just couldn't make any sense of it then or now. I still miss them every single day. I'll never stop asking why," Sam says as his eyes fill with tears. Eddy offers Sam a Kleenex.

"Then, there's my youngest sister, Jenny. She was so sweet just three years young and cute as a button with her little turned up nose, clear glass blue eyes like a baby doll and her long curly blonde hair that bounced when she walked."

"Of course, Christopher, my little brother who idolized me so much, a little macho man just six years old. He so wanted to be a professional hockey player like me when he grew up. Little did he know he would never grow up," Sam pauses again to take a breath and fight back the hot lump growing in his throat. Sam knows he must continue.

"Then there was my other sister barely into her teen years. She was beautiful, competitive, and talented; Karen was the apple of my eye. I miss her smile and cheeky smirk she flashed at me when she wanted to win me over." Sam's voice now is cracking and his words are almost inaudible.

"All of them gone. Sometimes I wish I had kept my life together . . . but there was no way. I couldn't have continued to play professional hockey. It didn't mean anything to me anymore. That life had lost its importance for me," Sam states

Sam took a moment to compose and then he adds, "I was a mess. I stopped going to workouts. I was a well-paid professional hockey player. I lost my motivation to play. The team owners hung in for me as long as they could. Eventually my manager had to ask the dreaded question. When was I going to return to the game? Deep down I knew I never would," Sam said.

"I attended therapy for a while. Then the doctors offered drugs; but I was afraid that I would forget my wonderful family." Sam sighs deeply, that's my story, Eddy.

"Sam, did they ever charge the driver?"

"No, but he did meet his maker, in a horrific way, I would rather not talk about that here, if you don't mind," Sam adds.

"Was that your justice?" Eddy pushes.

"Let's just say another closed chapter in my life. I'm actually in a good place right now," Sam adds.

Eddy ends the interview, "Thank you all for being here. I'm convinced this is another happy ending of a story in Ben's life."

Amanda – Chapter Seventeen

As Eddy and his crew are packing their van, to go back to the newspaper after the interview, a weird looking girl approaches him.

"Hi my name is Sally; I want to tell you that I really enjoyed the interview today with Sam. I have another Ben story you might be interested in hearing," She shyly offers.

Bill Edwards says," Call me Eddy," as he shook his head for a reality check. He squinted at Sally to show his concentration, "You have a Ben story, too?"

"Yes, I have no idea about the sequence. I'm guessing about three months before that Jenny girl story you did last week," Sally replies trying to fit in the dates.

"Before I set up a formal interview, please give me a few specifics." Eddy's reporter twitch was once again going into overload.

"Ben and I met on the Fourth Line in Newberry County that's where I live. He had a piece of glass stuck in his paw. Short story my family took him to a vet etc. He got better he stayed for a while then left," Sally briefly recaps her story.

"I think it is important to say he helped me turn my life around."

"How did he do that?" Eddy asks with interest.

"So many ways, attitude, school marks, direction my life is now taking, and my relationship with my parents. I now have it all together." Sally was proud of her accomplishments and wanted to share her story.

"Wow, Ben is such an amazing dog. I wonder how many more people out there have met Ben. Then just being there he impacted their lives," Eddy was again reassured that this was the biggest story of his life.

"Please give me a contact number and I will call you Sally and set up an interview. Oh, I almost forgot, we are planning a reunion for those that Ben has had an impact on their lives. Would you be interested in attending?" He offers as he hands Sally one of his cards.

"Yes, that would be amazing. I always knew I was not the only person that Ben made a difference in their life," She replies.

"How many others are out there?" Eddy wonders out loud.

Amanda – Chapter Eighteen

Trevor said, "Let's go Amanda. We can chat on the drive back."

"That was so much more interesting, and touching, than I ever dreamed it would be," Amanda enthusiastically says, she is now a committed fan.

"Come, Ben, time to go home," Amanda said. They walk to Trevor's car. Amanda opens the back door and motions for Ben to get in onto the back seat.

Ben didn't mind the back seat because Trevor and Amanda are together.

He had many thoughts in his head on the way back home. He appeared to be in a very deep sleep . . . but he wasn't. Ben in his way is reminiscing. Molly looks well, all healed. She's very happy with Sam. She made the best choice for her. Harry, he is such a great cat and friend. He really is special. I know he is happy with his family. He still meows away to Sam, he'll never change. He's the best cat I've ever met. Sam seems very sad today but I don't think he is unhappy.

"I'm delighted we came to the interview," Amanda volunteers.

"Me too, it certainly was special." Trevor hesitates then says, "We should go places together more often," Trevor looks at Amanda, smiles and suggests, "I think we would get to know more about each other out of the office."

"I agree. I was very comfortable there today with you. We were just like other couples watching the event. It was special," Amanda adds, "I found the bonding of the dogs and I guess the cat too, quite amazing."

"I don't know how he did it but I've never seen a cat like him before, he really acted like one of the dogs. Harry that name suits him," Trevor chuckles.

"It was cute the way Sam called Molly and Harry, they both came right to him. I thought they would be timid or at least nervous with so many strangers around them. But not so," She adds.

"He seems to have a way with animals. I think it is because they trust him," Trevor agrees.

"He's a special guy alright," Amanda says.

"I'm also pleased that Ben was there with them. It was almost like a family reunion for all three animals." Her original hesitations were gone.

"Wasn't his story just the saddest? Wow, he must be so strong. Not everyone could survive that type of calamity in their life, and come out the other side solid, like he appears to be," Trevor said thinking more about Sam's situation.

"There was a complete change of job, scenery and people that's how he did it. Also not being doped up with drugs, so he is able to experience the deep sorrow, hit bottom, then he climbs back up knowing it is all about rebuilding his life," She adds.

"He's a very smart man," Trevor acknowledges.

"I would really like to know where he goes from here. A professional hockey player will not likely remain a bus boy at The Blueberry Hill Diner. I guess not for long," she replies, "I am very curious."

Ben listens to the conversation with interest. The tones in their voices were soft and friendly. He thinks they are doing just fine getting to know each other.

Trevor asks, "Would you like to get some dinner?"

Amanda looks directly at Trevor blushes, smiles then asks, "Are you asking me out on a date?"

Trevor took a deep breath, and then with a big boyish grin said, "Yes I am. Is that okay with you?"

"I would love to have a dinner date with you," She adds with a lilt in her voice that gives Trevor pleasure.

"I know a place fairly close to here. Their food is great, plus they serve vegetarian meals," He responds.

She raises her eyebrow, smiles then asks, "How did you know that I'm a vegetarian?"

"I know more about you than you realize. I have made it my mission. I told you the other day. I'm very interested in seeing if we have what it takes to be a couple," Trevor says in a very serious manner.

She blushes again and says, "I can't believe that, what you're saying is making me blush."

Trevor suggests, "Let's have dinner."

"Ben has his working jacket on so he will be allowed in the restaurant. By the way, is he a vegetarian too?" He banters.

"Definitely not, he loves steak," She adds. "He doesn't get it too often at my house, thought. Just for a *very* special treat. He has to work hard to earn his delicious steaks."

"We're here." Before Trevor opens his door he turns to Amanda and says, "I have really enjoyed our outing and drive back today. Thanks." He gets out of the car and walks to the passenger side then opens the door for Amanda and offers his hand to help her out.

Amanda gets out then opens the back door, and says, "Come Ben let's eat."

I think I heard steak. I hope they mean real steak. I think I worked hard enough today so steak should be my reward. They thought that I was sleeping, nope, not this time.

Wow, nice place. Yum! When I stick my nose up and sniff the air I can smell steak. Hmmm. I like these outings with Trevor.

"That's my beeper, just a minute," Trevor responds. "Where, Okay, I'll contact Amanda and Ben. Thanks."

Amanda – Chapter Nineteen

"There goes dinner. They need Ben immediately. There's a missing person," Trevor says with urgency in his voice but looking disappointed at having their date cut short.

Amanda switches into work mode. "Okay, Ben. Let's go boy."

Amanda responds to Trevor's sad facial expression and consoles him, "Sorry, I know you are fully aware that work will always take priority."

"Don't apologize; I know the priorities of this job," Trevor reassures her.

Ben left with visions of steak fluttering through his head. He also understood his priorities.

"We need to hurry. You know the first few hours are the most important in missing person cases," Amanda says, she is ready to work.

"I'm with you on that," Trevor replies.

Ben found this change of plans to be confusing. He thought he was going to eat steak. They put him in his cage so he knows he is going to work.

The drive to work was less than ten minutes. We're here already? Ben can see all the uniformed officers from his cage in the back of Trevor's vehicle, some are mingling and chatting. Others are investigating and looking for clues. One officer is speaking with a lady and taking notes. There is always too much talking from everyone at work. Ben barks, *Okay, I'm ready.*

Ben sees an older lady with short curly white hair. She is wearing glasses with thick lenses and wearing a colorful dress with a shawl wrapped around her shoulders. She is sobbing and crying, while wringing a handkerchief through her fingers and her hands. She looks very upset. Maybe her child is missing. Ben waits and watches. He sees Amanda's walking towards him. He barks to let her know he is ready to work.

Amanda opens the hatch door and says. "Come on Ben, time to work. Let's go boy," Amanda and Ben have this process down pat.

She gives Ben a sweater to smell, and then said, "Go Find, Find the Boy, Go."

Ben gets the scent he hesitates as he is confused. This doesn't smell like a child. This smells like an old person.

"Got the scent boy? Find Ben," Amanda instructs and points to the ground.

Ben has the scent and starts to run with it. It's very strong at first then it gets weaker and weaker then it almost fades away. There is just enough scent for him to follow. Ben wonders. *Did someone pick up the person?*

He gets the scent again it's a little stronger now. He runs across the street to the park then down a path to a riverbank. Now the scent completely disappears. He furiously runs around in circles continuing to sniff the ground and barking. He tries so hard to pick up the scent – but it is gone.

"Ben do you want the scent again?" She offers the sweater to him.

Ben sniffs for a while and gets his snout full of the smell. But the scent is not on the ground. He darts this way then that way, and barks, then sits down. He lost the scent at the river edge.

An officer suggests while pointing just west of them, "Do you think he crossed the river? Maybe we should cross over at that bridge."

"Sure," Amanda agrees. "Maybe Ben can pick up the scent on the other side."

Ben with a mind of his own wades into the chilly river, pulling Amanda in behind him. The river bed is soft and mucky also difficult to get a footing. He dog paddles to the other side. Amanda following him into the river did her best to not get bogged down in the mud.

Ben sees a few uniforms follow him into the water. Other less adventurous officers ran to the close by rickety wooden bridge to cross over.

When he gets out of the water, Ben shakes furiously spraying everyone within his vicinity. Amanda and Ben jog over towards the bridge where he searches again, barks to let her know he found the scent.

Ben thinks, *Yes, there it is.*

"He's got it. Find Ben find." Amanda encourages.

Ben with his nose on the ground runs across the grass to a road. The scent is weak but still there.

One of the officers that crossed the foot bridge just before Ben stops the traffic so Amanda can guide him safely across the road. He continues running and barking to the railway tracks. The scent is very strong here. He is locked in, running and sniffing the ground. He is confident he will find the person.

Ben suddenly stops. Sniffs around, but there is no scent . . . nothing. The scent is just gone.

Amanda suggests, "Check inside the railway cars. He may have fallen asleep. Also he may be ill as he has been without his medications for twelve hours now."

The officers shout to each other, "Let's break up into small search teams so we can spread out in different directions and check more railway cars."

Ben watches and listens as the officers look into car after car.

The officers call, "Hello, Malcolm . . . are you in here Mr. Weeks . . . Malcolm. Hello, anyone in here?" This procedure continues for almost thirty minutes.

Then they hear someone from inside one of the railway cars holler, "We found him. He's over here." An officer was hanging out of one of the cars waving to catch the medics' attention.

The medics run with their stretcher and emergency kit. Once they reach him they start checking his vitals. Observing his lack of alertness they ask, "Mr. Weeks are you okay?"

"Oh, groan," he moans and tries to speak but he loses consciousness.

"He's alive. We think he's going to be okay. You probably found him just in time," the EMT guys, tell the officers. They also determine he is in urgent need of medical attention. "We'll get help from the Emergency doctor on shift," The EMTs report while dialing into the local hospital's emergency department.

"He appears to be in shock or maybe a diabetic coma. Poor color and sweaty damp skin is a sure sign that he is in medical difficulty." The medics describe his condition and pass along information about his vitals to the physician at the other end of the line.

The doctor prescribes the appropriate emergency treatment. He instructs, "Hook him up to an intravenous drip. Get him here as quickly as you can,"

They put Mr. Weeks on the stretcher into the ambulance. One EMT runs and jumps into the driver's seat turns on the siren and flashing lights and then drives as quickly and safely as possible to the hospital.

"Mrs. Weeks, you can meet them at the hospital. One of the uniform officers will drive you there," Supervisor Trevor says comforting her.

"Before I leave can I thank your dog?" Mrs. Weeks asks.

"Sure he likes gratification. I think he's looking for a steak tonight though," Trevor adds.

"Well I can't cook him a steak but I would like to give him a hug and one of those treats you have there," she says pointing to the treats in Amanda's hand.

Amanda offers a couple of his treats to her, "Here Mrs. Weeks, he loves his treats. He understands they are a thank you for a job well done."

Mrs. Weeks bends over and pats Ben on the head then gives him the treats. "Thank you so much for finding my husband. He is not well and wanders off. He has Alzheimer's, you know," she says as much to Amanda as Ben.

Wow, treats. Ben is immaterial about who hands him treats as long as Amanda is there. He gently takes the treat from the elderly lady's hand, ate it in one gulp then nudged her hand with his wet nose looking for more.

"You are very welcome. Ben is very clever and does a good job," replies Amanda.

Trevor turns, looks at Amanda with raised eyebrows and then says, "Dinner? Shall we try again?"

"Yes please. I'm starved," she responds smiling at him.

"Steak for you Ben, because you did another great job," Trevor adds.

Amanda – Chapter Twenty

"Jessie, do you have the photos from yesterday's interview ready?" Eddy is eager to finalize his story and wants to choose the most appropriate photos.

"Sure boss, I'll bring them in for you." Jessie responds with enthusiasm as he has never been involved with such a high profile story.

Jessie enters Eddy's office with a stack of photos. "Jessie spread the photos out onto the story board. This way we'll be able to match photos with the text." Eddy says he has many years of experience and really knows his stuff.

"Not this one, I don't think Sam the athlete would like us running a photo of him sobbing. Doesn't matter how sad his story is." He pushes the photo out of his way, "This one over here is excellent. It shows his eyes full of tears, you can see the emotion but he's not totally out of control. Good stuff Jessie." Eddy excitedly states. He is pumped with enthusiasm for this story.

"Let me concentrate on matching these with the story. You know what they say. You only get one chance to make a first impression." Eddy says then he is gone; deep in thought.

"Sure Boss," Jessie's parting comment falls on deaf ears.

Eddy dialed a very familiar number then says, "Hello Cliff, have I got the most wonderful human interest story. Let me brief you," Eddy paraphrases touching on the highlights of his interview with Sam yesterday.

"Hello Eddy. Is this story still about that same dog? Cliff questions. They have been business acquaintances for many years. Cliff with his salt and pepper hair and expanding girth is a short man but has powerful connections in the news business he is also Eddy's mentor.

"Do you still have national wire service connections? This story warrants more than just sending it out on the wire service. It is worth sending it to specific people," Eddy says calling in a favor.

"Sure do and I think if the rest of your story is as good as your appetizer. Eddy you've got a great story that lends itself to sequels," Cliff is getting excited too.

"Appetizer?" Eddy questions, raising his brow.

"Yes the girl who had the car accident," Cliff continues.

"Oh, yes, Jenny, did you see that story? I ran it last week, about the folks in Casper County. Ben rescues a girl involved in a car accident. It only ran locally in a few counties. I don't think the wire services have picked it up yet. Though CNN did run the piece on the actual accident and Ben bringing help to her." Eddy smiles; he knows he has it all tied up.

"This story has the most unexpected but well known person front and center. He is an ex pro hockey player," Eddy goats.

"I expect you have lots of photos and documentation," Cliff is covering his bases.

"Sure, I have tons of photos, even a taped interview. If you are interested we also can run a video of the whole story," Eddy says with confidence and a chuckle. Of course Cliff is interested. Eddy knows him and his motivation for humanitarian pieces. They both are driven.

"You're joshing me right?" Cliff says as he is now also hooked.

"I'll have it ready to be released by noon. There are just a couple of little things I need to touch up. That is if I decide to include them in the story. By the way, I met another person, Sally, this is another follow-up story. I want to add that hook to the end of this story. You know wet their appetite." He smiles with confidence. He so wants his stories to be perfect.

"Does this new story fit; running it after the Casper County story?" Cliff asks, as they were both guilty of milking a story.

"Sure thing; I actually reference that story in this Sam piece. In reality it took place about two months prior to the Sam story but I just learned about it yesterday. People don't care they just want more stories about this dog." Eddy says clarifying the time line. He knows how to play the game.

"Good I'll make some calls. Talk soon," Cliff is on a mission.

Amanda – Chapter Twenty-One

"Amanda you and Ben are needed at Sharpe's manufacturing factory and warehouse, downtown on Queen Street. We have a volatile hostage situation taking place, right now. Please hurry," Trevor exclaims.

She hears stress and anxiety in his voice. "Come on Ben, let's go to work," Amanda summons Ben.

She opens the hatch and the cage then signals for Ben to get in.

Great we're going to work. He likes driving in the cage as this means work. Ben waits with anticipation. He enjoys working and especially the treats.

It didn't seem like they drove very far. *We're at work already? I don't know this place. No worry, Amanda always tells me what to do and where to go.*

Amanda calls to a group of about eight uniforms huddled in a circle discussing strategies, "Let me know when you need our help, Ben's ready."

There was lots of confusion. Loud panicky voices were hollering to each other. *I hear someone yell, "gun." That scares me. I know one thing for sure, I do not like guns.*

Amanda tells me to, "Stay!" Then she joins the blue uniforms gathered together on the parking lot, huddled behind several corralled police cruisers.

Ben waits patiently, he does not complain. He just wants to start work. Amanda walks towards the building then disappears. There is more excited talking and raised voices. Then Ben hears a bang . . . bang . . . someone is shooting.

"Shots fired! . . . Shots fired . . ." The officers shout.

Then Ben hears someone holler, "She's inside now. Amanda has been taken hostage!" Ben didn't know exactly what that meant but the stress in their voice makes him think that, this is not a good situation.

I'm ready, let me help. But no one came to get him. *Please someone . . . let me out of my cage . . . I can help.* Ben was bouncing around, whimpering, barking and sticking his nose through the wire openings of the cage trying to get the police officers' attention.

To Ben it seems like forever. He worries and waits for Amanda to return. It seems like hours went by, and all he is able to do is sit and wait for Amanda to return. He senses that the tense atmosphere just got more nerve-wracking. It seems to him that no one is in charge.

Ben wants to ask, *"Please folks. Where is Amanda?"*

He barks quite loud to remind the uniforms that he is still, waiting to work.

Finally, Trevor approaches him; he opens the hatch, then the cage. He talks to him but nothing that he said is understood by Ben, until he said, "Go get Amanda, find Amanda, go boy go."

Now I'm working. I know Amanda's scent. He runs as fast as he can towards the building, but he can't get in. He knows she's in there. He can smell her scent. He runs around to the back of the building, sensing danger he brushes the walls with his ribs and tries to make himself invisible. He worries that Amanda is in trouble. He smells fear everywhere. If he ever, is able to find someone; this has to be his best effort. Amanda's life may depend on him. *This is my most important rescue*, he thinks.

Again he heard gunshots. Bang . . . bang.

He senses danger all around him.

Ben shrinks his body and hides behind a big blue dumpster. This is when he sees the man in a strange uniform, wearing goggles and holding a big shield in front him. Ben watches for an opportunity. The man doesn't see Ben . . . so he waits keeping very still. The strange looking man wearing the goggles is walking towards the back door of the building. He looks around for the rest of his crew behind him. Ben keeps watching him closely. The man opens the heavy metal back door, but hesitates, as he hears a noise behind him in the parking lot. Still holding the door half open, he turns to see what is making the noise.

Ben is in a good position to take advantage of this distraction. He is able to carefully hug the wall as he creeps towards the door. Then he quickly slips through the slightly ajar door; he successfully gets inside, unnoticed by the man with goggles. He hid behind a stack of boxes. He instinctively knows that he must be very quiet and assess all situations before he moves any farther into the warehouse. Ben spots a man with a black hat that covers his face and he is waving around a gun. He can smell a very strong scent of fear in this big room with very high ceilings.

Ben worries for both his safety and Amanda's. *Where is Amanda?*

He sits behind the boxes only peeking out periodically into the huge room. He definitely didn't want to be seen by the man with the gun. He waits for direction, from someone, so he'll know what to do next. Just then he sees another man in work coveralls waving around another big gun. He knows from his training that he must at all cost; avoid this man. He continues to assess and patiently wait. He remembers that during his training he was told, *"There will be an opportunity."* He continues to patiently wait.

Then he sees Amanda. His first instinct is to rush over to her and smother her in kisses . . . but the scent of danger makes him hesitate.

He notices that the man with the gun is distracted, while he is talking on a phone.

He spots Amanda then he looks over in her direction she is sitting on the floor in a big circle with several other people. She sees him too. He watches her shake her head to say, no. He knows that is his signal to wait because she thinks it is too dangerous for him. Again he patiently stays hidden, waiting. He keeps Amanda in his sight line. He is sure she will tell him when to move.

Suddenly something changes, now she is shaking her head, yes. He carefully advances in her direction, still behind and hugging boxes until he reaches her. Amanda motions for him to go behind her and remove the ropes from her wrists. He creeps to where she is sitting then crouches down behind her and proceeds to chew through the ropes. He is being very careful and extremely quiet. He makes himself ever so small behind her. A couple of minutes later he frees her hands. She motions to him to shoo, with a hand motion. He knows this means he should go back to the boxes and hide again. Then in a whisper she says, "Go boy, go."

All of a sudden there are big fireworks. Amanda is holding her gun with sparks coming out of the end. There are lots and lots of sparks everywhere.

Ben isn't sure what to do next. His training didn't cover this situation. His instincts though are to hide, so he remains hidden behind the stack of boxes. There are lots more fireworks and a loud bang . . . bang. Yelling and shouting is coming from all directions. Ben is worried for Amanda's safety.

To Ben it seems like the shooting continued forever. He is surprised to see Amanda has now joined him behind the boxes.

"Good boy, Ben," Amanda whispers.

He watches the flashes followed by bang . . . bang. Then he hears more shooting this time coming from outside Then lots more fireworks, and suddenly, all is quiet and calm.

He senses that Amanda is more relaxed now, too.

"Good boy, Ben," Amanda praises him. "You're my hero."

Ben is delighted that once again he is the recipient of pats and ear rubs galore. He gives Amanda lots of mushy wet kisses. He is very happy she that she is safe, again.

There is lots of confusion in the room. People are running in and others are being escorted out. This scene is all a big mystery to Ben.

Ben notices Trevor entering the big room. He walks quickly over to Amanda and Ben.

Trevor greets Amanda with a big smile, "You okay? I was so worried about you. Amanda, how did you manage to get free?"

"Ben somehow found a way in, I don't know how, but he did. He is smart enough to assess a situation and not to expose himself, until he feels safe. I guess he sensed the danger," she speaks in a much happier tone.

"When I heard all the gun fire I worried about your safety," Trevor said, his relief shows with the now lack of tension, both in his body and face.

"He was quite amazing, he responded to the slightest head nod, from me, first 'no' then when they were distracted I nodded 'yes'. He cautiously approached me from behind. He chewed through the rope holding my hands. Then he left and found a good hiding spot and waited." Amanda proudly related the details to Trevor, she is very happy now.

"Good boy, Ben," Trevor gives him pats and ear rubs.

"They took my service revolver when they grabbed me. What they didn't know was I had my back up piece in my ankle holster. Lucky for me they didn't think to check there for a gun. I think there was too much going on."

"I was in communications with the task force and let them know when I saw an opportunity to turn things around. They were waiting at the back door for my signal. When I got the chance and the other hostages were out of my sight line. I shot one of the men with a gun. The other guy was shot by the Task Force fellas when they entered." Amanda quickly reports the scene and the outcome.

"Ben, thanks buddy for saving Amanda." Trevor was happy too.

Ben thinks that most times working is easy and lots of fun, but not this time. Ben hopes this is the last time he is this close to gun fire.

Amanda says, "Come Ben, we need to write up our report."

Amanda is approached by reporters when she gets near her vehicle. She says, "Ben came through again. He is really an amazing member of the K-9 patrol. His senses are so tuned in it just flabbergasts me," Amanda is Ben's number one fan.

When, Amanda is in the driver's seat and ready to leave. Trevor pokes his head through the open window and invites Amanda, "How about a celebratory drink?"

"That sounds good to me. Meet you at Cassidy's about seven? I must write up my report. See you later." Actually she needs to get the details of today's event on paper so she can mentally land.

They drive in silence to the office. Ben senses that Amanda's head is full of the incidents, of today's hostage situation. She is very quiet.

Amanda – Chapter Twenty-Two

Good thing about being a K-9 is your handler always keeps you close by. Off we went to Cassidy's. Ben took his place on the floor at Amanda's feet. Everyone shouts their 'atta boys' and 'good boy Ben.' He senses Amanda is also proud.

Ben hears Eddy's voice before he actually sees him.

As the reporter and editor for the Newspaper, he wants to crash the party so Eddy announces to the room of people. "Drinks for everyone, this round is on me."

That was welcomed with offers to, "Have a seat Eddy. Join us we're celebrating."

Eddy wants to scoop this story. He is chomping at the bit. "The past is one thing but the current story is worth so much more," he whispers under his breath. He drools when he thinks of the value of this press to his paper.

His tape recorder is hidden, but running. He isn't going to depend on his slightly inebriated memory. He clones himself as a friend. The more they drink the more they talk. "This is great stuff! How did Ben get in to help you?" He presses, "Who exactly was your captor? Did anyone get his name?"

Eddy is way too blatantly inquisitive. He is suddenly excluded from the group. He realizes that he pushed too much and the group is aware that he's actually interviewing. He is unsuccessful in trying to discourage the rejection of the group by saying, "I'm just curious, it's in my blood. I can't help it. I just like to know all of the details."

"Good night. See ya." Trevor waves him off.

"Dam, I pressed too hard," he mutters to himself as he leaves the bar.

Trevor and Amanda are the last to leave, maybe on purpose. "Amanda, want to get a bite to eat?"

"That would be great. I just realized that I am very hungry. With the occurrences of today I've worked up quite an appetite," Amanda says, but she knows she secretly didn't want the evening to end.

"Would you like a nice Italian meal at Tony's?' Trevor asks.

"Perfect, I love Italian. I'll just go to the Ladies Room to freshen up. Then I'm ready." Amanda is pleased and excited to be with Trevor.

A couple of glasses of red wine later, Amanda finally lands. "This is perfect Trevor. Thank for the great meal. Tell me, what are some of your other favorite restaurants," she wants to know more about Trevor as she has a huge crush on him.

They talk mostly about shop, peers and police work. Then as usual the conversation turns to Ben.

Ben's ears perk up at the mention of his name. He didn't really mind sleeping on the floor. Amanda drops some food for him. Then Trevor drops beef for him.

Trevor cautiously broaches the subject of them dating, "Would you like to go out on a real date sometime?" He held his breath in anticipation of her response. He has cared deeply about her for quite some time, now. He dearly wants to take their friendship to the next level. Trevor wonders, and hopes Amanda will agree?

Amanda pleased at the prospect of developing a relationship with Trevor says. "I would really like that. What do you think about the Police Department's policy of discouraging relationships with co-workers or in our case subordinate and supervisor relationship?"

"Amanda I know how I feel about you. Where is it going I don't know, sorry but I don't have a crystal ball? I'm open to finding out if we are compatible and can develop a relationship. Until we find out I don't think we're breaking any rules." Trevor rationalizes even though he knows that his reasoning is very fragile and would never stand up to scrutiny.

"Guess we have to keep in our sights, just what the decision would mean to each of us, should and if we become more serious," Amanda adds.

"Whoa! We're moving along way too quickly. I know there may be a time I will need to think about consequences, but not tonight, please. Let's just enjoy the company, finish dinner and maybe go for a walk." Trevor shows his pleasure, with a big smile, happy that Amanda is on the same page.

At the mention of walk, Ben's ears perk up, and then he sits straight up, as a signal he is ready. After all he has been lying around most of today. He wants and needs exercise.

Ben watches as Trevor pays the check. Amanda, Ben and Trevor leave the restaurant. They all saunter along William Street. Amanda and Trevor walk hand in hand, smile at each other and pretend to window shop, neither one was paying attention to what they actually saw. They are now strolling, arm in arm and coyly grinning at each other. Ben obediently walks next to them enjoying the positive vibes he is getting from his two favorite people.

By the time they arrive at their vehicles; they have already arranged a date, time and place to meet to test their mutual attraction. Once at their vehicles, they gently kiss.

"Good night," Amanda says softly.

Trevor wishes her, "Sweet dreams."

Ben watches as they part and get into their vehicles, they smile in the direction of the other one, and blow a kiss. Ben senses Amanda is very happy. He enjoys feeling Amanda's happiness. Driving home he sleeps peacefully on the front seat beside her.

He is aware that Amanda is softly humming all of the way home.

Amanda – Chapter Twenty-Three

Ben has never witnessed Amanda so edgy. He wonders what is going to happen. He watches while she gets dressed but not in her uniform. She must have a special date. She is looking great in her Green suit and flowered scarf. But, she goes back to the bedroom then returns with a totally different outfit in blue stripes with a coordinated jacket. She is fidgety, unsettled and nervous. Ben wonders if this is something he should also be concerned about? He wishes he could ask her. He has never seen her act this way before. She's on her way back to the bedroom again. Just then Ben heard the doorbell ring.

Ben as usual runs to the door when someone knocks or rings the doorbell. He wonders who is visiting. Amanda reaches for the door knob then hesitates and holds back. Why is she hesitating? He is really puzzled about her behavior.

Amanda takes a deep breath, and then answers the door. It's only Trevor. *Why is she anxious with Trevor?* Ben is now really watching with uncertainty. He senses he needs to be ready for something.

"Hi Trevor, please come in. Have a seat. I will get you a drink. What would you like, wine or rum and coke? She knows the latter is his favorite.

"Rum and Coke will be perfect. Make it weak though, thanks. I'm driving and hope to have some wine with dinner," Trevor responds.

With drinks in hand they both sit and sink into her cozy brown leather sofa. "How was your day?" Amanda inquires.

Ben watches them both drinking and chatting. Amanda is laughing; she is much more relaxed now. He joins them in the living room. He flops down on the carpet at Amanda's feet. His senses tell him; that everything is okay and normal again.

They get up from the sofa and Amanda says, "Stay, Ben. You can take care of the house for me. We'll see you later," Amanda and Trevor leave.

Ben is confused he still doesn't understand what just happened. More importantly, why did she leave him behind? This is different. He goes everywhere Amanda goes. *I don't understand why not tonight*?

He runs to the window. He whines and barks trying to get her attention. With paws on the window sill he sees them leave in Trevor's vehicle. Resigned to being left at home on his own, he found a comfy place, on the shag carpet, in the hallway near the front door to sleep. He will take care of the house and wait for their return.

Amanda – Chapter Twenty-Four

While walking to Trevor's vehicle he says, "You look great Amanda." Trevor sports a big smile that melts away any anxiety or doubts she has about the pretty blue outfit she finally chose to wear.

Amanda confidently smiles, and she smooths out her skirt with her hands then responds, "Thank you, I thought anything would look good, as long as it wasn't a uniform." They both laugh and shake their heads in agreement.

Trevor says, "I have to agree with that. I still think you look stunning; even if I am biased."

They climb into his SUV and drive for about twenty minutes. The casual chatting relaxes them both. "Here we are," Trevor says, he is elated and feeling nervous as a school boy on his first date.

"Tony's has great Italian cuisine. As a vegetarian you will have good choices. I hate recommending eating places as there are so many variables. Food, service, the company and so on. Therefore I will keep my opinions and survey results until we drive back to your place." Trevor was more nervous than he is willing to admit.

"Trevor I love the food, the service and the company. I think I'll give Tony's place five stars." She teases. She thinks the evening is going very well. The conversation is flowing; they have a similar sense of humor and interests. They each talk about their families and share a few interesting stories of family gatherings.

Driving back to Amanda's house, Trevor is trying to keep the casual stress free atmosphere they enjoyed at dinner, but the closer they get to her house the more tension he can feel.

At Amanda's house she invites Trevor in, "Would you like a night cap or coffee?" She asks, secretly crossing her fingers and hoping he says, yes.

"I would like that. We can finish tearing apart the new Employee Manual or just talk." Trevor does not want the evening to end, either.

The second Ben hears her voice. *She's home, she's home.* He sits straight up ready to welcome them with his usual wagging, barking and generally happy gestures. When she opens the door he put his happiness into action. Ben is making the biggest fuss over them both. He is so happy to have them back home.

"Hey Ben we were only gone a couple of hours. Down, Ben. Good boy." Amanda tries to settle him down.

Amanda admits, "It just struck me that this is the very first time I have left him home alone. No wonder he's so happy to see us."

"Really?" Trevor replies.

"Well, I take him with me everywhere I go, just in case I get a call. He's with me so I save time, because I don't need to come home, or go to the kennel to get him before going to our destination or job," She adds.

"That makes perfect sense to me. You've only been together a month and a bit. You two are still bonding," Trevor rationalizes.

"Speaking, of bonding; night cap or coffee?" Amanda wants to put the focus back on them.

"Brandy, liqueur, wine or coffee?" she so wants to extend the evening.

"I will have a coffee, thanks. I never drive if I have had more than one drink, it's not worth it. Especially in our jobs," Trevor says, alibiing his choice of beverage.

Amanda is so happy, she feels like they are two peas in a pod. They sure have a lot in common, besides the hot sexual tension between them. She says, "Trevor thank you so much for dinner. To be honest I was a little nervous because I wanted us to have a really good time."

They talked for another hour then, Trevor said, "Amanda, it's after midnight. I should go tomorrows a work day for both of us. Honestly, I'm having a wonderful time. I really do not want to leave. You are so easy to be with. I thoroughly enjoyed our first date."

They walk slowly totally engrossed in each other to the front door and linger there while they engage in a passionate kiss goodnight. "Me too," she whispers.

Amanda – Chapter Twenty-Five

A few days later, Amanda's phone went brrr . . . . brrr. She quickly looks to check the caller ID, then said, "Hello, what is it Trevor?"

"Amanda, are you close to the Devon River? I know you always keep Ben with you, we need Ben here quickly," Trevor anxiously requests.

"Yes as a matter of fact we're about two minutes away. Why? Trevor, what's up?" Amanda asks.

"Hurry, we need Ben's assistance. Please get here as soon as possible." Trevor says with dire urgency, almost panic in his voice.

"Come directly to the waterpark. We have a fella who is literally hanging on to the sheer rock wall by the tips of his fingers," Trevor is stressed and it shows in the insistence of his request.

"We'll be there in about one minute now. I'm literally just around the corner," Amanda consoles him.

"Please hurry. I don't know how much longer we can keep him from falling," Trevor worried.

"We're here. Where's the jumper?" Amanda says, "Ben is ready for work."

"He's not a jumper. He's a worker that was working up there on the edge of the cliff," Trevor points to a higher ledge, "When he fell. His safety straps for some reason gave way. He managed to hang on to a narrow ledge on that sheer part of the cliff. We can't reach him. He is not in a stable enough position to let go and grab a rope. Plus the helicopter won't be here for twenty to thirty minutes," Trevor fills her in.

"What is it you want Ben to do?" Amanda questions.

"Over here, look he's down there on that narrow shelf under the overhang." Trevor pauses and wonders how to encourage the hanger to continue to not let go of the ledge.

"Amanda, show Ben the man, and the distance to the water it's at least one hundred to one-hundred and twenty-five feet straight down. Of course the current is very swift this time of year. That's a really tough rescue for Ben," Trevor remarks as he shows concern for Ben's safety. "Do you think he would be able to jump down into that fast moving current?" Trevor adds.

"You want Ben to jump into *that* water? I don't know if he can do that," Amanda answers, she now worries for Ben's safety.

"It certainly will be a challenge for him. Have you trained him for a water rescue?" Trevor inquires.

"Yes, basic training but not in a real situation, and never from a height like this," Amanda responds.

"No time like the present. If the guy doesn't fall, there's no problem." Trevor assures her.

"He may not have a choice, though. He tells me his fingers are raw from trying to hold onto the jagged rocks. He says he is unable to get a solid shoe hold either. If this guy is forced to let go, there is very deep fast moving water down there. There's a possibility that he will not survive that jump or fall," Trevor replies.

"The subject fell into the river!" a uniform shouts. "Get help to him now!"

"Ben, I hate to do this to you," she takes Ben to the edge and points towards the water. "Go boy go." Amanda instructs. They watch Ben; he jumps straight out . . . for a few moments he seems to be suspended in midair, it felt like an eternity to the onlookers. Then gravity took over . . . he quickly fell into the turbulent waters of the Devon River.

"Look at him go! He knows what we want him to do, he just jumped," Trevor was surprised and in shock, "He really does understand his job. Does he know what to do when he catches up to Mr. Vincent?"

“I don’t know. His training taught him to pull the person to shore,” Amanda reassures.

“He’s in the water. That’s very choppy cold water, with a fast current. Be careful, Ben. I do hope he will be okay,” Amanda worries.

Trevor tries to assure Amanda. He says, “Ben is a very strong swimmer. I haven’t seen him swim before today. I’m impressed. He has almost caught up to Mr. Vincent. I’m amazed at how he is managing to swim against that strong current; and knowing where his subject is at the same time. This is truly mind-boggling to watch!”

“Amanda, he is a very special dog. I’m betting on Ben,” Trevor is becoming a huge fan of Ben.

The water is cold and the current keeps trying to push him in the wrong direction. Regardless Ben knows it is important for him to reach the man who fell into the water. He wonders why the man isn’t swimming. Maybe he is hurt. It doesn’t matter; Ben knows he can save him.

“He is very close now. Just a few more feet and he will be able to get a hold of him, and then pull the man to shore,” Trevor reports.

Then the man disappears. *Where did he go?* Ben couldn’t see him anywhere. He stops swimming and begins treading water. He holds his head out of the water and looks around in all directions for the man. That is when he sees an arm poke up through the surface of the water. Ben recognizes the arm as belonging to the man; he fights the current and swims as quickly as he can towards the arm. Grabs the arm in his teeth and tugs until he has a good grip. Ben pulls and pulls with all his mighty strength. He has to be careful to not injure him by breaking the skin on the arm with his sharp teeth. This is not easy as the current works hard at pulling the man away from him.

Ben is feeling very tired. He needs a short rest. He instinctively knows he cannot let go of the arm. He has to hang on at all costs. He might lose the man again, if he lets go. Ben positions his body in front of the man so that the fast current pushes the body against him instead of pulling him away.

Thirty seconds of rest renews Ben's energy so he resumes tugging and trying to get the man to shore. Just then Ben notices a couple of uniform officers coming towards him with a big round red tubular thing with straps that he harnesses around the man and helps Ben by pulling the man to shore.

Ben is very grateful for the help. He is far more exhausted than he realizes. The feeling of success in bringing the man to shore outweighs the intense feeling of exhaustion . . . but still he is very tired.

The ambulance arrives a minute before the helicopter. Trevor directs the EMTs to the rescued man lying on the shore. Trevor said, "They say he is barely alive and needs your help, immediately. Please hurry."

Trevor waves off the helicopter. "Thanks guys but we couldn't wait any longer." They give Trevor thumbs up to show they understand.

Ben is lying on the grassy shore on his side and panting violently. His whole body is shaking and shivering from the icy cold water. Ben sees Amanda and Trevor running towards him. He looks like a drowned rat as his soaked fur clings to his back and sides like a wet suit. He can't understand what they are saying but they look happy. He knows he is okay now.

"Ben you okay? Good boy, you did a great job, a super job, Ben," Amanda is ecstatic.

"Mr. Vincent will be fine in a day or two. Ben you were amazing and Mr. Vincent is very grateful," Trevor added.

He likes it when people are grateful. It makes the effort worth it.

Mr. Vincent looks very cold. He is visibly shivering when he waves to Ben as the EMTs put the stretcher into the back of the ambulance. The ambulance roars away with lights flashing and sirens screaming.

"Ben you really earned yourself a big steak this time," Trevor said, "A big twelve ounce steak and I'm even willing to pay."

Ben knows he did a good job. It was nice to have so many people show appreciation, on how well he performs his job. Ben is still recovering, but he nevertheless enjoys the hugs and kisses, from both Amanda and Trevor. He hopes that there are not too many more water rescues, though. This was a really tough one.

Ben catches his breath then gets his strength back. He stands on all fours and violently shakes and shakes his body. He is spraying the water in every direction soaking everyone and everything within ten feet of him.

Amanda and Trevor back off and holler, "Ben you're drowning us."

He finally gets most of the water out of his fur. *That feels so much better.* He even feels slightly warmer now.

They both laugh with the pleasure of a job well done, again. Trevor brings a soft fluffy blanket to help Ben dry his fur, and says, "We are so proud of you Ben. You are a hero. Thanks."

Amanda takes him to their vehicle. She put a dry blanket on the seat both for warmth for Ben and to keep the seat dry. "You have had a very busy afternoon. You went above and beyond our expectations this time. Good dog, you are the best," she is so proud to be Ben's handler.

Ben sleeps soundly all of the way back to Amanda's house, his home. First thing she does is cook him a big steak, fit for a king.

He meticulously cleans up his face after his favorite meal. Then wearily drags his fatigued body to his bed where he quickly slips into a semi-conscious like, very, very sound sleep for several hours.

Amanda – Chapter Twenty-Six

Eddy excitedly tells his reporters, "I've got a great idea. What do you think about having a reunion for all of those people, that we know about, and have had contact with Ben? We know some of the stories individually but what are the commonalities and out comes," he is full of questions and very few answers.

"These are the questions I have, at least to start," he continues. "Why were they at that place to meet Ben? What are the circumstances around their meeting? Where are they today and how did Ben impact their lives? Did they make any changes to their life as a result of their experience with Ben?

The offices of the newspaper are a buzz of activities. Eddy requests, "I want you camera guys to prepare for photos, videos, plus add sound," Eddy is ready for the group no matter which way the re-union goes. He adds, "There is no bad side to any of the Ben stories that I have heard so far. They are just that, stories."

"Ruthie, this is the final list of people that Ben has been in contact with, at least to the best of our knowledge," He tells his administrative assistant.

Ruthie excitedly telephones each person they have heard about. She says, "We are having a reunion at the Bamberg Chronicle, next Thursday. You and your family are invited to attend the re-union. You will meet and speak with others that have been impacted by their friendship with Ben. Do you think this something you would like to do?"

Invitations were extended to:

— Amanda and Trevor, Ben's handlers,

— Of course the Star of the Show, Ben

— Sam, Molly and Harry

— Sally, her parents Lil and Rob

— Jenny, Mr. & Mrs. Wilson

— Jarred and family

— Autistic boy Scott and his parents Pam and Lorne Hopper

— Mr. and Mrs. Sweets found him and saved his life.

— Mr. Doug Vincent – water rescue survivor.

Ruthie reports to Eddy, "The feedback, when I followed up with each person, is that everyone is interested in meeting other people, and most importantly to see Ben again. They each have already R.S.V.P.'d they will attend."

Eddy tells Ruthie, "I also invited my mentor Cliff. He has already sent me a R.S.V.P. Cliff has all of the important contacts for National and International News, Television, and the Wire Service."

Speaking to his reporters, Eddy states, "Here is a list of questions that I want answers to." He hands them the list for their reference.

1. Who are they?
2. Why them?
3. When and how did Ben help them?
4. What impact did he have on their lives?
5. Is everyone as happy with their contact with Ben we hear others are?

Eddy said, "There really are too many questions that need answers."

He invites an equal number of reporters as stories. "I am assigning reporters to the groups as specified on my list. There is a group or story for each reporter. This way we will have personal first-hand comments from each group," he says.

"Ruthie, I think we should include Willie, the reporter/editor for the Casper County Gazette. Assign him to just float, speak to people he chooses and gather information for us," Eddy advises her, knowing Willie will have his own slant on a few of the stories.

"I want you to hire professional caterers for the event; this way our people will be free to listen, watch and ask probing questions," he confidently adds.

Eddy calls Amanda and says, "I'm in the planning stage of the reunion. I would like you to bring Ben here about one half hour before our guests arrive. Thanks for taking the time out of your busy life to do this for us. Really, thank you so much."

"No problem, we will be there, I'm also very curious," replies Amanda.

She wonders, *"Will there be any surprises at the reunion?"*

Amanda – Chapter Twenty-Seven

Ben and Amanda go for an unscheduled visit to his groomer, Bob. She wants to make sure he will be a fine-looking specimen for his photo op today. He is given a bath, dried and brushed so his mostly black coat, pure white paws and a large area of white fur on his chest look fresh and clean. The groomer looks into the mirror and points Ben's nose in that direction so he can see how beautiful he is looking.

"Who is that handsome guy?" Bob says.

"Perfect," Amanda agrees. Amanda then put on his leash and said, "Ben you not only look good but you smell great too, no doggy stink for you."

Ben and Amanda then drive to the historic building that houses *Bamberg Chronicle*, which is a flutter of activity. They can hear the noisy grinding gears of the printing presses producing today's newspaper. Amanda screws up her nose as she smells the strong odor of the paper and ink wafting through the air and right up into her nostrils.

They wander through the hallway to the elevator; ride up to the second floor where they exit the creaky old lift. They make their way down the hall to the Conference

Room reserved for "Ben's Reunion." Amanda seems excited and nervous at the same time. She is happy, and displaying a wide smile showing her straight white teeth. She is humming a catchy tune that makes Ben happy too.

"Ben do you smell that food? I wonder how they plan on keeping the dogs away from the enticing fare," she says with a big smile as she envisions the dogs sneaking goodies off the tabletops."

Entering the conference room, Ben looks around and wonders what the fuss is all about because this definitely isn't work. He does have his K-9 coat on for the occasion, though. He wonders *why*? He is learning to be patient and wait, as Amanda always has his best interest at heart.

He heard Amanda say to Eddy, "Trevor is coming later."

Ben watches the reporters participating in horseplay, hanging around, munching the finger food, drinking the freshly brewed coffee and talking up a storm with their co-workers. This is all new to Ben. Not work and not play. *What then?*

Just at that moment he hears and smells someone familiar coming down the hall; he sticks his nose in the air trying to pick up their scent. He waits patiently watching the doorway. Trevor enters with a beautiful Golden Retriever. Her lovely gold fur is like soft feathers falling down along her side. The fur on her tail and sides ripple when she struts across the room. She has soft friendly warm brown eyes. She instantly gets Ben's attention. *WOW! Who is this gorgeous lady?* It is love at first sight. *I think she has stolen my heart.*

Ben is surprised to hear Amanda say that this attractive lady, Goldie lives with Trevor. He thinks *I should visit Trevor's house more often.* It is obvious that both Ben and Goldie have good training and indoor manners. They do not bark or romp too much, and only use their inside voices. Ben and Goldie rub faces and sniff each other for quite some time. They murmur back and forth to each other before lying down side by side, touching ever so slightly.

Ben is sure he is in love.

"Hans, Hans come here boy." Eddy calls his Dachshund.

Ben is intrigued with this dog. Hans sure is a strange looking dog to him, because he doesn't remember ever seeing a dog with such short legs. He certainly is a handsome creature with his shiny black coat and a touch of fawn on his brown eyebrows and paws. Ben wonders . . . *what happened to his legs?*

Suddenly Ben sits up straight, perks up and twitches his ears, and then tilts his head first to one side then the other, while staring, for what seems like an eternity, at the open doorway. There is something very recognizable about the man's voice and the scent of the dog approaching their room. He sits still as a statue with his eyes glued to the opening and waiting, oh so patiently. Then he saw Molly.

Amanda is engrossed in a conversation with Trevor, she is relaxed so she is totally unaware of the arrival of their latest guests, for this reason she is holding Ben's lead quite loosely. She is completely unprepared when Ben bolts for the door to greet Molly; he is almost dragging Amanda behind him clear across the room. It takes her a moment to mentally register what or who is getting Ben so excited.

He furiously wags his tail, playfully jumping up, indicating how happy he is to see Molly. She responds by murmuring and twisting her body showing her delight, it is clear she is also excited to see him. They play for quite a while just like they did when they lived together. Amanda encourages them to settle down. She firmly commands, "Okay Ben, down boy, sit. Good boy Ben."

Ben is aware of the other dogs in the room watching them play. He thinks they might want to get into the game also. He knows that would create mayhem.

Ben now turns his focus to Sam, and of course there is little Harry wrapped around Sam's neck like a scarf. Ben stands on his hind legs so he can sniff Harry; of course

Harry sniffs Ben, purrs and meows. The beautiful ebony black cat recognizes him too. He so wants to have Sam put Harry down on the floor. But, Ben is aware of the interest the other dogs have in Harry; so he agrees it will be safer for Harry to be held by Sam. Sam does squat down so Ben and Harry can renew their friendship. Harry purrs in recognition and Ben gives a low friendly growl to acknowledge him. After all, Harry slept curled up against Ben every night absorbing the warmth of his body. They were rubbing and licking faces for a while, just like old times.

"Hello Ben, you sure are looking handsome," Sam croons to Ben while he rubs his ears and strokes his back.

"Hello Amanda. Is Ben getting lots of work these days?" Sam inquires.

"Unfortunately, yes. He does a great job. He has found or rescued quite a few people lately. Some of them are here today," she reports.

"Is that right?" Sam replies raising his eyebrows to show his surprise and pleasure.

"You're a good member of the K-9 Kennel Brigade," she says patting Ben, "You do a great job, don't you?" Amanda stokes him and praises him again.

"He definitely is quite amazing," Sam adds.

Amanda says with a slightly furrowed brow and with concern in her voice, "Because, I now know, he has the habit of making friends, impacting their lives, then leaving that person, I sometimes worry that he will leave me, too."

"I hear you, I understand that feeling. I was very sad when he left us. When we took our customary walks, both Molly and Harry looked for him every day for weeks. They sniffed for Ben's scent in many of their usual play areas. I did not know why he left, nor did I ever successfully rationalize him leaving us. That is, until I started reading the stories in the local newspaper. Only then did I begin to get some insight into what Ben is really all about. It amazes me, when I think about how long he has been on his journey," Sam adds.

"I know, I would feel really bad if he left me any time soon," She states. "If I knew why he is here with me, maybe I would then have a warning that it is time for him to leave me. I could maybe emotionally prepare myself for the inevitable," she continues, "But I don't know."

Sam replies almost chuckling, "Sorry to tell you this, but, there will still be a vacuum in your heart, even if you prepare for him leaving."

"Let's change the subject. I'm not ready to think about that day, right now," She adds frowning, as she feels a lump forming in her throat.

"I understand from the interview with Eddy, at the Diner, you were in transition when you met Ben," Amanda said; it was more of a question than a statement.

"Yes, I certainly was feeling better by the time the interview took place. The night I first met Ben, I was not in a good mental space. I had been on the road for about two years, by then. My sadness may have been more intense, because it was a very stormy night. I think the bad weather may have made everything seem more dismal. Was the reason, we both chose the same abandoned hallway a force beyond my control? I don't know, but my life did take on a more positive direction a short while after our chance meeting." Sam is feeling melancholy just talking about their first encounter.

"Memories are good but sometimes they really hurt," Sam continues, "The story I told about my family being killed by a drunk driver is only part of the story."

"My God, Sam," she gasps, "What could you possibly add to that horrible story?" Amanda is surprised and a little curious about the rest of the story. She wants Sam to give her more details, but she doesn't want to appear too nosy.

"I was questioned about the death of the man who killed my family. For some reason the police gathered unrelated details and put them together manufacturing a bogus case that had me taking revenge and killing that guy, sorry Amanda no offense," Sam says volunteering more details.

"No offense taken, Sam," she responds and smiles.

"The police finally arrested the dirt bags that actually killed him, then removed his head and cut off both of his feet," Sam reports.

"Sam, that must have been horrible and an unsettling time for you. Did they apologize to you for putting you through that ordeal?" As a police officer she has heard stories when the suspect was never officially told they were no longer under suspicion.

"Oh yes, detective Mike met me at the diner a few weeks later and filled me in on the details of the arrest," Sam says with relief showing both in his voice and on his face.

"With all of that behind me I feel much better and more enthusiastic about life in general. I have a job, a place to live and proper food for me and my four legged friends. I believe Ben realized that too. How, I have no idea or about the why this happened to me and what is expected of me. I'm just happy to have been a Ben story." Sam adds.

"You still have Molly and that amusing little cat. They must be very comforting for you," Amanda teasingly says.

"You have no idea how these delightful caring animals have completed my life. When my family died the emptiness was enormous. I really do feel complete, once again," Sam shares.

"Are you still working at the diner?" Amanda asks.

"No, I accepted a job as a scout for one of the National Hockey League teams. I still live in the same area but now I live in a great house on a magnificent lake. The views just go on forever. It is heaven. Both Molly and Harry love it there too," Sam adds.

"How, wonderful that is for you. I can visualize your four legged friends having a good time there," Amanda jokingly adds.

"Yes, Molly swims every day and Harry brings me presents; a frog one day; a mouse another day, and so on." They both laugh at the vision. "He is a real hunter. Best of all he still continues to chat up a storm." Sam chuckles just thinking about Harry.

"Congratulations Sam, I'm pleased to hear you have been able to land on your feet and get on with your life. I'm sure we will hear only good things about you." Amanda is genuinely happy for him.

"Thanks," Sam said, "I'm very happy."

"I love chatting with you Sam, and getting an update, but please excuse me, I see someone I need to speak with," she offers her hand. Then Amanda starts to move on.

"It's been great to see you and Ben again. We will talk again soon," Sam said as they shook hands.

Ben turns towards the door and waits. Amanda tries to get his attention and direct him to one of the other guests. Ben wouldn't budge. His eyes were fixed on the door.

"Amanda, who do you think is coming down the hall? Everyone we invited is already here, I think," Eddy says.

"I have no idea. But, I do know Ben well enough, that if he recognizes a sound, a voice or scent, there is no distracting him . . . he just locks onto it," she adds, "Look at him, his eyes glued to the doorway."

Just then, a teenage boy and his parents walk through the door. Ben did recognize him. He runs to the door pulling Amanda behind him, to greet Joey. He so remembers this boy and their terrifying night together.

"Hi, Ben, buddy, wow you sure are a popular dog. I'm so happy we came," Joey gushes.

"When you left us, I really wanted a dog of my own," Joey adds while rubbing Ben's ears and hugging him. "Ben, I owe you my life. I have learned a lot about family, life and being responsible since that day. I do my chores every day, without even being told, well most days."

Amanda looks up to the man and woman who accompanied the boy, and says, "Hello my name is Amanda, Ben's handler. This is Eddy Edwards; he is the editor of the *Bamberg Chronicle*. I'm sorry but we don't know your Ben story," she says expressing surprise in her voice and on her face. Amanda is very interested in learning more.

Hi, my name is Joe Webb, this is my wife Betty and our son Joey," he said offering his hand to shake while introducing his family.

"Dad, don't forget Daisy," Joey said pointing to his golden Lab puppy.

"Of course, Daisy was an addition to our family after Ben made friends with our son. And we are so happy he did, because Ben risked his own life, while protecting Joey from a coyote that wanted to eat him for dinner . . . or to feed him to her cubs. We are so grateful to Ben. We saw the article in the paper and really wanted to be here and pay tribute to Ben. He is one amazing dog," Joe adds.

"I have not heard this story. Of course up until just a few weeks ago I hadn't heard any of these stories," Amanda responds with a welcoming smile.

"Are you telling me that Ben took on a hungry coyote?" she inquires.

"Yes. Absolutely! Joey balked at doing his chores that day. He chose to run away, instead. Unfortunately he got lost. He wandered onto some unfamiliar roads. You know these rural roads they can look very similar," Joe explains the circumstances that motivated Joey to run away.

"How long was he gone?" Eddy asks.

"He was missing for about twelve terrifying hours. We were really upset when he was still missing well into the pitch black night," Joe replies.

"We were worried sick," Barbara interjects, and then gathers Joey close to her and gives him a big hug.

"Mom — Ben and I were okay," Joey mischievously smirks and says, "Remember I told you, he got me lunch from a dumpster. Ugh! I couldn't bring myself to eat someone else's leftovers," Joey adds, as a shudder runs through his whole body and a look of disgust appears on his face.

"Ben seems to instinctively know what people need," Amanda adds.

Joey animatedly says, "Ben was ready to die for me. He didn't even know me, but he protected me. I was a silly irresponsible kid back then. I caused my parent a lot of pain and the searchers their personal time away from their families, looking for me. I learned my lesson, but that was last year, I was younger then," Joey proudly sticks out his chest, and then looks lovingly at his parents and winks at his mom.

"Well I think you as a family appear to be very happy now. It's great that you got to learn some valuable lessons without being seriously harmed. It must have been a terrifying experience for you Joey. What is it they say, 'All is well that ends well'?" Eddy adds.

"I can send you the write up, our local paper did on the whole story, if you wish," Joe adds.

"Yes, I would like that. I will add the story to Ben's Adventures scrap book. He has had quite a few adventures, I'm discovering," Amanda shares her pleasure at hearing Ben's stories.

"If you have a card I will send you a copy of the story," Joe replies. "Ben also helped Joey climb up a tree to safety. Oh I didn't mention Ben nearly got shot by the search team because they were under the incorrect impression that Ben was the coyote, as it was very dark and they didn't get a good look at him. He was lying down at the base of the tree when the rescuers arrived. He looked like a coyote to them in the dark. I'll send you a copy, it is really well written and a very good story." He adds.

Amanda hands Joe a card and says, "I look forward to reading it. Thanks. Thank you so much for coming today. All of Ben's adventures amaze me."

Ben checks out Daisy; she is quite the little beauty. She is a strong healthy looking dog. He observes that she is very fond of Joey. Ben is sure she will take good care of him. Of that he is certain. Ben thinks, *I hope she is never confronted by a coyote. I know I will never forget that day.*

Joey is down on his knees, giving hugs and kisses unrelentingly to Ben. "Thank you. Good boy. I love you." Joey says while pouring out his words of love and affection for his hero.

Ben takes it all in. He gives Joey several very wet licks up the whole side of his face as reciprocal kisses. He always enjoys attention.

Eddy offers his hand and says, "Thank you so much for coming. Everyone here has a Ben story and is very happy to share their story with you. Please circulate. We'll chat some more later." Eddy shakes their hands, and then he moves on.

Ben laps it up, as usual.

Ben and Amanda walk across the room to chat with another guest. Ben recognizes Mr. & Mrs. Wilson. He wonders if they brought their fat cat. He sees a handsome Sheep Dog, Mister he recognizes him to be a working dog just like him. Ben welcomes him with a gentle nudge and a sniff both their tails were wagging in a very friendly manner. Mister has a shiny black coat with pretty white fur on his belly. Ben likes Mister.

Eddy approaches the Wilsons, "Thank you so much for coming, Mr. & Mrs. Wilson," as they shake hands all around.

"I see you have a dog. Is this new?" Eddy inquires.

"Yes, isn't he beautiful? We missed Ben so much when he left that we went to the shelter and adopted Mister. He's part Sheep Dog," Mrs. Wilson volunteers.

"You have a ranch right?" Eddy inquires refreshing his memory.

"Yes, we do and yes, he is a valuable asset. He amazes us every day, he works so hard at rounding up the sheep and cattle and best of all I think loves his job," Mr. Wilson adds.

"That is wonderful. I'm happy for you," Eddy responds. "Is Jenny here, I haven't seen her yet?"

"Yes, over there with Ricky," Mr. Wilson says pointing across the room.

"Thanks, I will have a chat with them. I'm curious to see how she is doing. She is such a lovely young lady. I did enjoy meeting and interviewing her at your home a little while ago," adds Eddy. He starts to move on, he turns and says, "Help your selves to food and refreshments on the table over there," he points to the food table then waves good bye to the Wilson's.

Ben does not recognize Mr. & Mrs. Weeks at first; of course he didn't really see much of Mr. Weeks at that rescue, as he was ill and was taken to the hospital by ambulance. They have a cute Basset Hound his name is Chester. He is friendly enough. Ben is familiar with hounds and hopes he doesn't start howling. Ben sees that Chester is very attentive to Mr. Weeks. He follows Mr. Weeks just like a shadow. He wonders if he is a working dog too.

"Hello Mr. & Mrs. Weeks, how are you doing?" Eddy asks.

"We are doing very well thank you," she replies.

"I see an addition to your family," Eddy says bending down to pat their dog.

"Yes, ever since my husband wandered away and Ben was so efficient and quick to find him; we thought we should look into getting our own rescue dog. The alternative for Mr. Weeks would be to live in a guarded home as he really needs full time supervised care . . . I wasn't ready to do that after fifty-five years together."

"It must have been a very difficult decision for you," Eddy sympathizes.

"Yes, it was a tough decision, until we read how some dogs can be trained to help in this type of situation," she responds.

"I have heard some stories also," Eddy adds.

"One day we went to the Shelter and found this beauty. He is smart as a whip. He is also a sweet gentle dog. We asked if he could be trained like Ben. With an affirmative response we immediately hired a dog trainer to come to our home and teach Charlie to take care of my husband. Charlie is now trained to follow my husband and if necessary to find him. He has Alzheimer's, you know," She said while stroking Charlie.

"We didn't know how valuable and helpful a dog can be, that is until we met Ben. What an eye opener, that experience was for us. I would never have thought for a moment that a dog could be part of the solution," she says.

"That is a wonderful story and an excellent idea." Eddy said, "Thank you for coming and sharing your story. If you will please excuse me, I need to speak to another rescue of Ben's I just spotted. I suggest you circulate, have a bite to eat and speak with some of the other folks here. You will hear some very interesting Ben stories," Eddy continues, then points out a few people that might be of interest to them.

Trevor approaches with his hand out stretched and greets Mr. Vincent. "Hello, how are you doing? All recovered from your water rescue?"

"Yes thank you. Trevor? You're the one who brought that dog in to help me, aren't you?"

"Yes, to both questions." Trevor responds, "Have you met Ben since your rescue?"

“No, but I am eternally grateful,” Mr. Vincent answers.

“Let me get Ben for you. He likes to see people he has had a hand in rescuing,” Trevor said and walks across the room to Amanda and Ben.

“Amanda can I borrow Ben for a few minutes?” he asks.

“Sure, if you can pull him away from Goldie,” she replies.

They both smile and look at the contented dogs, Ben and Goldie together, just hanging out.

“Come with me Ben I have someone who wants to meet you,” Trevor said.

Ben and Trevor cross the room to see the man with the little dog.

Trevor did the introductions, “Mr. Vincent this is Ben a member of our K-9 Patrol and your rescuer.”

Ben thinks Mr. Vincent‘s dog looks like a rat. The people were saying Chihuahua is his breed. What a silly name he has, Taco Bell. Who would name their dog, Taco Bell? That man should have a Water Spaniel as he was my first and only water rescue.

“It is really good to finally meet you, Ben. Good boy . . . Thank you so much. This time it’s under better circumstances then the last time. I’m happy that you were such a good swimmer. I don't know how you managed to keep me afloat in that rough water; but I am very thankful that you did." Mr. Vincent sincerely says as he pats Ben's head.

"You are really quite handsome aren't you?" Mr. Vincent continues still rubbing Ben's ears and stroking him. "Thank you so much, you are my hero."

Ben seems to smile; he is taking in all of the praise and enjoying the affectionate stroking. He is happy to see these people again.

Ben wonders why anyone would have a dog so small. Taco Bell spends all of his time being carried around. What kind of life is that? Harry is bigger than Taco Bell.

Trevor offers his hand and says, "Thanks for coming, please circulate and speak to the other folks here, as there are several people here that are also Ben rescues."

Ben heard a noise then looks towards the door. Here comes the boy in the chair with wheels. He has a dog too. I hope he doesn't ignore his dog like he did me. Why is he pulling the hound's ears? Good grief, that dog sure needs to be patient. His mother and father are here too.

On his way back to Amanda, Trevor stops to speak to the Hopper's. "Thank you for coming. Your family's experience with Ben was a very interesting story. It's unfortunate that your son didn't respond to Ben in person."

Pam replies, "No he didn't, but we are encouraged by Scott's awareness of this new dog. We named him Buddy because Scott can vocalize something similar to that. This is a big step forward for Autism in general. We are hopeful for more progress."

"That is great. It sounds like he just needed an animal to relate to," Trevor adds.

"Yes, aren't animals truly amazing?" Lorne agrees,

"You got that right and they are far smarter than given credit," Trevor answers.

Pam says, "We have been following the stories about Ben in the newspaper. He's quite the dog."

"He sure is," Trevor adds, "Good luck; I hope you enjoy your new dog."

Buddy, Scott's hound dog brushes Ben and murmurs to him. He is telling Ben he loves his new home. He likes helping the boy and is proud to be a working dog too.

"Please feel free to meet the folks here; pretty well everyone here has a Ben story and best of all they are happy to share," Trevor said encouraging them to circulate.

Trevor waves, and then leaves to return Ben to Amanda.

Ben wasn't sure what he did or didn't do in that situation. It seems there was lots of disappointment at that house. He remembers the flashing lights and those sticks with balls on the end being pushed into Amanda's face. He is also recalling how irritated Amanda was with that crowd. I remember that someone stepped on my paw. That really did hurt. He was not having good memories or feelings from that experience.

Wow! Another handsome all black dog, just arrived. This new dog is with Jared. The dogs sniff each other, and then wag their tails in a friendly manner showing their approval. Blackie, the Labrador has a sleek black coat of short bristly hair. He has good manners, and lots of confidence as he proudly struts close beside Jared.

Ben remembers Jared; he's the person he convinced to follow him so he could help the girl in the red car. He didn't know he had a dog.

"Hi Ben, you're looking good. I think you have been to the groomers." Jared teases while he rubs Ben's ears.

Ben sits up straight, ears perked up and wags his tail waiting for the loving pats that seem to be the order of the day.

Trevor laughs, "Yeah you know these photo ops."

Jared looks at Trevor and says, "After my encounter with Ben, I got to thinking how nice it would be to have a dog again. When my kids heard I was thinking about a dog; they literally hounded me every day until we finally made the trip to the shelter. It took two trips before we found this beauty." He fondly rubs Blackie's ears and brushes his beautiful ebony coat.

Ben thinks that Blackie is feeling loved and really likes his new home.

"We are fortunate to have found Blackie. He is wonderful with the children and they absolutely adore him. It's like we have added a new member to our family. He is always ready and willing to run, chase and retrieve anything the children throw in his direction," Jared adds.

"Labs are perfect family pets," Trevor adds.

"Please socialize with the other folks here," he said with a wave of his arm to indicate the people scattered around the room. "They each have interesting and different Ben stories."

Please excuse me, I need to get him back to Amanda," Trevor says as he points to Ben then moves in her direction.

"Sure, no problem we'll be fine. I would like to hear some of the other stories. I see the Wilsons are here too," Jared replies.

"Ben . . . Ben . . . hello Ben, how are you doing? It is so good to see you again." Sally shouts almost screaming as the tears of joy are running down her face and she begins sobbing uncontrollably.

Sally? Ben didn't recognize her at first as she no longer has that crazy messy and wildly colored hair.

Wow! Ben thought. Look at that proud German Shepard. What a magnificence canine she is, he immediately likes Sissy. They sniff each other with their long pointy noses. While frantically wagging tails they rub faces and murmur back and forth. Ben sees that Sissy is trained to stay close guard to Sally.

Just then, Amanda arrives to rescue Trevor.

"Hello, Sally is it?" Amanda asks.

"Yes, I am so grateful to have met Ben. He helped me appreciate my parents and I learned the benefits of caring for others."

"Hi my name is Amanda, I'm Ben's handler. He's now a member of the Police Department's K-9 Brigade," She introduces herself, "Tell me more about your contact with Ben," she adds.

"Well, I was a troublesome, irresponsible teenager, when I met Ben. I had silly fights with my parents, friend and others. No one could tell me anything. I knew it all, and resisted everything. If they said black, I said white. I drove my parents crazy. What an ungrateful brat I was in those days. During Ben's stay I learned some significant life lessons," Sally confesses.

Amanda says, "I don't know your story with Ben. Please tell me."

"That day, the day I met Ben, I was once again, having a major temper tantrum. So I went for my usual walk to cool off, like always. There was Ben. He came from nowhere he just appeared in front of me on the Fourth Line. He was limping because he had a piece of glass stuck in his paw. We made friends. I carried him home. He sure was heavy. My parents agreed to take him to the town vet where they removed the glass. I nursed him back to health and it was during this time we bonded. It was good for me to focus on someone other than me. He healed and we played lots, then a few weeks later he just up and left."

"Almost like he had a purpose for being there at that time and place, right?" Amanda offers.

"Yes, precisely," agreed Sally. "It was like he was there to help me get my act together."

"Sally if you were to talk to others in this room you will hear more Ben stories but none are exactly the same," Amanda says then continues, "I am intrigued. I believe you will be also."

"I am very happy to have made your acquaintance, Ben," she said as she bent down and tousled his fur again.

"Thanks to Ben, I have made an important decision about my life's work. I have applied for and been accepted to work as a Veterinarian Technician. We'll see where that goes, I might end up being an actual Animal Doctor," Sally proudly states holding her head high then continues, "I had no idea how much I would truly love working with animals. Since my experience with Ben I began volunteering at the local shelter. That's where I met and made friends with Sissy here. She is the best dog ever, well maybe not a Ben but darn close."

"That's wonderful Sally. A really good Ben story," Amanda was delighted with this story and impressed at how Sally has turned her life around.

"Thank you so very much for coming," Amanda responds smiling, "Please circulate, listen to others and share your story. Please help yourself to the table of goodies over there," Amanda points in the direction of the spread, "I must move on myself. I am happy to hear things are going well for you. It's lovely, to have met you." They hug and move in different directions.

Ricky and Jenny arrive with their handsome Water Spaniel, Winston. Ben admires Winston he looks sturdy like a strong working dog. Ben wonders; *who's the handsome guy with Jenny.* He didn't remember him.

"Hello my name is Amanda I'm Ben's handler, this is Eddy, editor of the Bamberg Chronicle newspaper. I believe you two have already met," she says introducing herself and Eddy as he had just joined them.

Jenny responds, "Yes Mr. Edwards interviewed me several weeks back. Amanda, my name is Jenny Wilson and this is my fiancé Ricky."

"Good to meet you, I think I heard you have a very interesting Ben story," Amanda probes, "Please tell me more."

"They, the doctors, told me I would have died if not for Ben. I must admit I had very little faith in Ben, and I still feel so bad about that. Who would have believed that an unfamiliar dog would respond to my cries for help, or that he could actually bring help back to me? I was trapped in my car way down a ravine, totally out of site, and jammed between two trees," Jenny recalls.

"That is amazing; you must have been so frightened?" Amanda marvels.

"Yes, I was slipping in and out of consciousness. I didn't learn until later the details of my rescue." Jenny adds.

"It is a good thing you fought to stay alert," she says.

"Have you met Jared?" Jenny asks.

"No." Amanda answers.

"Ben somehow found Jared, and then amazingly, made Jared understand that he needed to follow him. Ben then showed him where I was so I could be rescued. Thankfully Jared drove his truck to the accident. Then he called 911. When the EMTs got there, Jared using his tow truck and helped free my car from between the two trees. Yep, Ben saved my life." Jenny recounts her experience.

"You make it sound so simple but I'm sure there is a lot more to your story," Amanda caringly suggests.

"Of course, then there was the drive around the county to find the truck that side swiped my car, forcing me off the road. Ben brought my attention to the fender of the truck that had paint from my car smeared on it." Jenny adds.

"We were also great detectives as we, Ben and I, made it possible for the Sheriff to arrest a cattle rustling ring that involved the same people that hit my car. We were heroes for weeks after my story broke," Jenny proudly reports. "We won't talk about my sleuthing that got us, Ben and me, into a lot of trouble with some unsavory characters. That is a story for another time," Jenny adds, lowering her head and eyes looking and feeling a little sheepish.

"That is a wonderful story. You must be happy she survived, Ricky," Amanda elicited.

“I am very, very happy. She tells me I was one of her last thoughts just before she went zigzagging down that steep ravine,” Ricky shyly responds.

“I understand there will be wedding bells ringing in the future for you two,” Amanda teases.

“Yes, we are engaged but we’re not planning to get married until we graduate from High School next year. A near death experience can really impact your life choices. That is the reason and that we are in love, Ricky and I decided to commit to each other,” Jenny adds.

Amanda hugs Jenny and shakes hands with Ricky then says, “It has been great meeting you two. Good luck to you both. Sorry but, please excuse me, I need to speak to some people before they leave.”

They shake hands all around then Amanda, Ben and Eddy head towards the doors and say good bye to those leaving.”

Amanda – Chapter Twenty-Eight

Once everyone left, Eddy, Amanda, Trevor, the reporters and photographers, sit around reminiscing and recounting Ben's stories as they were related to them by those attending the reunion.

"Absolutely unbelievable a few months ago I would have brushed off the idea that a dog could actually be trained to catch people and find others. I admit I was wrong. Today we heard and saw proof. That is all I can say on the subject," Doug, one of the reporters enthusiastically comments about his observations to the group.

"That sums it up for me too," Stephaney, another reporter, adds, "Eddy, thank you so much for including me in this reunion. It was very interesting but mostly heartwarming. I love hearing their stories."

"We have recorded and photographed the visitors from all directions and groupings both human and canine plus one feline; we mustn't forget Harry the cat," Eddy says, "I'm confident that this story has to be the story of the year for us. I can't wait until it is all put together."

"Sure Eddy, everyone knows you're the master of writing stories that people love to read," Doug teases.

"Every person here today, had a story with a different element, twist and result. Each one on their own is a great story with the most gratifying and positive ending," Eddy muses, as he is very happy. His reporter twitch is once again operating in high gear.

Amanda, thinking out loud says, "Did you notice how each one of the people involved with a Ben story, now have rescue animals?"

Trevor adds, "Yes, and they all seem to be so devoted to their new master. They appear to be very happy and contented in their new homes."

"You know, that is a very special detail that links everyone together." Eddy notes.

"Ben positively impacted their lives. This gave them the desire to have their own loving, loyal canine friend. That's really great!" Amanda marvels as she mentally remembers the various conversations she had with the folks that attended the reunion. "Ben showed them what a great, faithful friend a dog can be."

Amanda turns to Trevor and quietly asks, "Do you think Ben's mission was to bring us together?

"If that was his purpose, thank you Ben," Trevor

responds and smiles at Amanda. He takes her hand and squeezes it.

"We probably, would not have spent good quality time together out of the office, if not for the interview with Sam regarding his experience with Ben," she said.

Trevor responds, "I think you're right. I wasn't sure just how I was going to approach you about seeing you away from work. Going to The Blueberry Hill Diner proved to be the perfect venue for us. No pressure."

Amanda's face turns serious, "Do you think he will leave us now?" She speaks out loud her greatest fear. Deep in thought she wonders how she will feel if Ben leaves her. "I would be very, very sad for sure," she says, then goes silent thinking about this conversation in the privacy of her mind.

Trevor started to answer, "No — " But when he looks at Amanda and sees the distant, deep in thought look, on her face, he feels his words will fall on deaf ears.

Goldie and Ben are lying side by side resting. Ben is listening to the conversation between Trevor and Amanda. He didn't want to make Amanda sad. But he is on a journey to find his people family. He wonders. *Is my people family sad because I'm not with them? Is it time to continue my journey? Being a pet is great, but being a working dog is different because I have responsibilities and people depend on me. I really like being a working dog.*

Amanda looks at Trevor smiles, and justifies why Ben will not leave her by saying, “Ben is my rescue dog, and I chose him from an array of dogs that were picked up by the Animal Control Unit. I’m worrying about nothing. Ben *is* a rescue dog . . . *my* rescue dog.”

BEN BOOK EIGHT

Ben – Chapter-One

Ben's torn. He thinks about his current family, Amanda and now Trevor and Goldie. Everything's great here. *How I would like to stay here. But, I get this nagging feeling that it's time for me to continue my hunt to find my first people family. I think about Mom, Dad, Roy and Molly a lot. They took really good care of me, regular vet visits, groomed me and made sure I had enough tasty dog food, I really do miss them.*

Roy is such a typical thirteen year old, black hair, brown eyes and skin. We would romp around on the grass and pretend to fight and play. I pulled and tugged on toys with my teeth that Roy held onto. He's lots of fun.

My Molly is the real reason that I wanted to call my dog friend Molly, I miss this very pretty sixteen year old girl with lovely brown eyes, black curly hair and soft brown skin. She's so cuddly and always smothered me with kisses.

My Dad is tall and slender with beautiful shiny ebony skin. He is kind and takes good care of me. He has a soft calming voice.

Mom has the prettiest brown face with huge brown eyes and a tall lean body. She is the person everyone comes to as she is smart and kind. She is appreciated for her ability to settle conflicts.

I'm so lucky to have people that care about me.

They must be very worried about me. Dogs don't usually get the opportunity to make choices about where they stay. Maybe I have the ability to choose right now.

Ben found that lately he's more and more pre-occupied with these thoughts. It is not like he's unhappy or ill-treated. It's that feeling that something is missing; it just keeps nagging at him. It will not go away. *I'm thinking it is time to go.*

Ben – Chapter Two

"Mom . . . Mom," Molly screams, "Oh my God Mom. You had better sit down. This article here in the morning paper is a huge surprise and very exciting – wait until you read this," Molly yelled as she runs into the kitchen holding the newspaper up like a torch.

"What's so shocking, honey?"

"Sit. I can't believe it. Look at this story, I just read. They had a reunion or something for a dog. Look at the picture of the dog. I'm pretty sure it's *our* Ben. He's alive!"

"Really? Let me see," Mom said pulling out a chair and sitting down at the kitchen table, and then reaching for the newspaper.

Molly thrusts the paper at her Mom. Looking over her shoulder they read the article, about a K-9 dog. *Bamberg Chronicle* had a reunion for people that were rescued or their lives were impacted by a dog named Ben. "Do you think he's *our* Ben? This dog is a famous K-9 dog. What would Ben know about being a police dog?" Molly asks with some doubt creeping into her enthusiasm.

"I don't know, Molly. I guess with the right dog they can train them to be a K-9 dog."

"Mom, Ben has a microchip if this is our Ben why didn't someone call us and say they found him?" Molly asks, walking around the table now facing her Mom.

"Sorry Molly, with all of the confusion and settling into our new house it didn't occur to me. I will look in my papers, find his Microchip number and then call and update his information. How silly of me. I should have thought of this before. I promise. I will update his information today, for sure," Lori comforts Molly. She is feeling guilty for not having updated the National Registry previously.

"Where's Roy?" Molly asks.

"Your brother's at the park playing soccer with his new friend, Peter."

"He will be so happy to know that Ben is alive and well. He was sure that Ben would have been injured or killed because he wouldn't know how to survive in the wild. Roy told me he believes Ben could never stay alive on his own, because he has always lived with us, in a house. I think he has come to terms with the fact that Ben is gone and he will never see him again."

"Molly, I think we should be cautious and confirm the details of this story first, before we get Roy's hopes up. I will find the contact information for our newspaper; maybe they will tell us who to call at the Bamberg Police. Of course I will share our story with them and why I think he's our dog. I'll ask to speak to the person they refer to in the article as Amanda, his handler. I hope she will give us some details. I want to confirm that *their* Ben and *our* Ben is the same dog," Mom cautions.

"Mom, this is so exciting," Molly shouts, "Hurray . . . Ben's coming home. Isn't this great news Mom?" Molly was already running out of the kitchen.

Mom calls after her, "Molly, please contain your enthusiasm until we confirm the identity of the dog . . . *please*."

"Hello, I would like some information about the article in today's paper about the K-9 dog working for the *Bamberg Police Department*," Lori, Molly's mother said.

"Sure I will connect you to our editor's assistant, Peggy," the receptionist advises then transfers her call.

"Peggy Black, how may I assist you?"

"Hello, my name is Lori Charles. I read the article in today's paper about the K-9 dog, Ben. Can you tell us how to contact someone at the *Bamberg Police Department* or whoever is the contact for more information?"

"May I ask why you are so interested in the story?"

"Yes, of course. During our move to this house, we stayed overnight at a motel. That's when we lost our dog, Ben who looks remarkably like the dog in the article."

"Oh, that's a wonderful story. May I get some details from you so we will be able to run a follow-up?"

"Actually I think it would better if I first confirmed that he is *our* dog. I don't mind you doing an article. But first, I need to know if he is *our* Ben."

"I understand. Mrs. Charles will you give me your phone number? You know bosses. If I don't get your phone number my boss might be upset with me, as we may miss out on a great humanitarian story."

"Okay, just use the number that is showing on the call display. Who can I call to confirm the identity of the dog?"

"I'll put you through. You will save on long distance charges plus the folks at *The Bamberg Chronicle* are more likely to give out information when my boss's name shows on their call display." What Peggy didn't say was transferring the call from her phone allows her to listen in on the actual conversation for her boss.

It only took a few seconds then Peggy heard, "*Bamberg Chronicle* how may I direct your call?"

Peggy had already told Lori that she would get the correct person on the line for her as she knew the folks at that paper quite well. "Eddy Edwards, please."

The phone was answered after one ring as if he was waiting for her call. "Edwards here."

"Hello Eddy, this is Peggy at the *York Sun*. I have a lady, Mrs. Lori Charles on the line with me. Mrs. Charles is pretty sure that the dog in your reunion article is the dog they lost about a year ago, when they were moving to this area. I'll let you speak with her directly."

Eddy said, "Thanks Peggy. Hello Mrs. Charles, if you don't mind repeating your story to me, I would like to hear more about your lost dog."

"We love our Ben very much. We had actually given up on ever finding him again. I really just want some information to confirm he is *our* dog Ben and that *your* Ben is the same dog," Lori pleads, "My daughter, Molly, saw the photo of Ben in this morning's paper. She is so excited. I don't want to get her hopes up until we determine he is *our* dog. The children have been devastated with his loss. If we can arrange to see him, I know he will recognize us," Lori continues, "I don't mind telling you our story, but first, let's determine if he is *our* lost dog."

"Okay, I will call his handler and make arrangements for you folks to meet with Ben. This might be a very sad story as I know how attached Amanda is to *her* Ben."

"Thank you, Peggy has my number. Bye" Lori hangs up. She has a knot forming in her stomach, as she is now anxious to know if he is their missing dog.

Ben – Chapter Three

Eddy can't believe his good fortune. He thinks, "What are the chances that Ben's original owners call me and are willing to tell their story?" his reporter's twitch is working in high gear.

"Hello Amanda, Eddy here, I just had a very interesting telephone conversation with a woman over in York County. I understand that they lost their family dog during their move to their new house. They saw the newspaper article and the photo of Ben. She is pretty certain that *your* Ben and *their* lost Ben is the same dog."

"No way, how can that be?" Immediately her emotions start to run out of control. Deep down she had always feared this day, she needs time to digest this news flash. "Wow . . . I have so many scenarios whirling around in my head, right now." Amanda's heart ached with the dread of losing Ben.

"They would like to see Ben."

This comment was like dropping a bomb in her lap. "Eddy, give me some time to breath. I'll call you back in a little while."

"Sure. We'll talk soon." Their voices were strained as they both hang up. Amanda's mind was racing. She feels muddled with thoughts about, "*Now what? Where do we go from here? What do I do, now?*"

Ben watches Amanda as she sits at her desk too stunned to move. He moves closer to her, sits up and puts a paw and his head on her lap and murmurs. He wants to comfort her; he senses that she is upset.

Absent mindedly she reaches down and strokes his head as much to comfort Ben as herself. "Good boy," the lump in her throat and the tears gathering in her eyes prevent her from uttering more words.

Ben – Chapter Four

"Dinner's ready. Don't forget to wash your hands kids," Lori calls out. Once they're seated to eat their evening meal.

Molly blurts out her big news, "Ben is alive and working as a K-9 with the police force."

"Molly, we don't know that for sure," Lori tries to downplay the story.

She turns to her husband, Fred and explains, "Molly is so excited about the news. I did ask her to not tell Roy about the dog but her enthusiasm has taken over her common sense."

"Sweetie, do you have a plan to check out the details of the story? The children are getting excited and as you point out he may not be *our* Ben," Fred said as he looks over at Lori. He reaches over under the table and gently squeezes Lori's knee and smiles.

Lori blushes and shyly smiles back, then says, "Yes I called the *Sun* today and they transferred me to Eddy Edwards. He's the editor of the *Bamberg Chronicle*. He wrote the story and knows the Police Officer and handler of *their* Ben."

"Mom, when can we go to that place and get Ben? I really want him home, now. I miss him a lot. Please, Mom, when?" Roy demands with the eagerness of a thirteen year old who is missing his playmate and pet.

"Roy we don't know for sure the police dog is *our* Ben. Sorry you just are going to have to be patient," Fred says trying to reason with Roy.

"Why? Of course he's our Ben. Just look at his picture. I hope they aren't going to tell us that we can't have him," Roy passionately demands.

"Patience honey, I will try to make arrangements for us to see him as soon as possible. This is exactly why I didn't want Molly to mention the story to you," Lori states and looks over at Molly, and then frowns admonishing her for not obeying her request to *not* tell Roy until they were sure.

Roy explodes. "That's not fair! He's *our* dog. *They can't keep my dog*," Roy leaves the table in anger, and kicks at the door jamb as he storms out of the room.

Trevor says as he hugs and kisses Amanda, "Hi honey. What's for dinner? Mmm . . . sure smells good, I'm guessing one of your great seafood dishes."

"You're correct, salmon with a delicious dill sauce. If I wasn't a vegetarian I would be tempted to join you,"

Amanda offers hoping to activate his taste buds through his nose.

"Hello to you too Ben," Trevor smiles then grins in Bens direction. He pats Ben as he is prompted to pay attention to him due to his constant nudging by his pointy nose.

"Trevor, would you like a glass of wine? This will help you wind down before dinner? Amanda suggests.

"That sounds perfect to me. Today was crazy," Trevor responds. They quietly sit side by side, holding hands and sipping their drinks.

Over dinner, Amanda and Trevor discuss their day. "Trevor you are never going to guess who I got a phone call from today."

"Anyone I know?"

"Yes, and no, Eddy, he received a call from a lady in York County that claims Ben is *their* dog they lost about a year ago."

"No way, what took them so long to find him? What do they want?" He stops eating and put down his utensils, so he could give Amanda his full attention.

"It was the article about the reunion in the paper. Eddy told us it would go national. I was so worried about that.

I feel empty inside like someone has snatched out my heart." Tears started to roll down her cheeks.

"Wait, please don't cry, he may not even be *their* dog," he held her in his arms, stroking her hair, consoling her. "We can use our resources to protect our investment in Ben. He is a valuable asset to the force."

"It's more than just business, Trevor. My heart is breaking and I have only had Ben a few of months. It must be awful for a family that raised him from a puppy, and then lose him. We have to think about their feelings too."

"Let's have a meeting with these people. We'll bring Ben along with us. They can see him and we will know if Ben recognizes them. What do you think about that idea?" He is hoping this proposal consoles her.

"Sounds good, up to the point of what happens if he does recognize them?"

"Maybe we can negotiate something with them."

"Okay, let's just sit back down and eat, I just can't think about this right now."

Ben watching Trevor and Amanda wonders what they are talking about. He is sure it has something to do with him because he heard his name mentioned several times.

Ben – Chapter Five

"Hello Amanda, Eddy here. I followed up with the lady, Lori Charles that phoned me yesterday regarding their lost dog, Ben. The Charles family live approximately sixty-five miles from here. They want to drive here. I have arranged the meeting for their convenience next Saturday about noon. We can meet here at the Chronicle. I will put on a spread, keep the atmosphere homey. I hope you have no other commitment for that time and day."

"Thanks Eddy. Yes, I'm available to meet with them. I wish we were meeting today but at the same time I wish it would be five years from now. I am so nervous about this meeting. Do you know anything about the family?"

"Of course, we've have done some back story, checking to see who they are. They're a family of four, a 13 year old son, Roy, a 16 year old daughter, Molly, plus a stay at home mom, Lori and dad Fred, a techie guy. They live in a well maintained Victorian era home in a great part of town. This is a typical middle income family, living within their means."

"Now *I really* feel they are going to take Ben," Amanda sighs deeply trying to ignore the pain she is feeling in her stomach, "The boy probably is eager to get *his* dog and go home."

After terminating the call, she sat with her hand still on the receiver, she thinks, I'm a smart person and have been told that I'm very astute when it comes to the psychology of both people and situations. I need to think this through and plan my strategies. The K-9 group is depending on me. The boy wants *his* dog. I appreciate that. How, can I turn this emotionally charged situation into a, win – win?

Ben – Chapter Six

Ben is not sure what exactly is happening. Amanda is very cuddly these days. *I love to cuddle with her, but she seems so sad. I hope it's nothing bad.*

"C'mon Ben we're going to the groomers this morning," Amanda is suited up in her navy blue dress uniform with brass buttons and gold braid trim. Her slim taut body shows a poster-perfect police officer. She wants to impress the boy with her official position. She is also trying to be upbeat, but inside, her stomach is twisting and churning. She needs to keep busy until her meeting today with the Charles family. Going to the groomers will help her put in time and give her something to think about other than her fear that this may be their last visit to the groomer.

Both the groomer and Amanda fuss over their handsome canine friend. Amanda hugs and smiles at him, then says, "Ben, you look especially good today. Everyone will be impressed by your soft, great smelling fur and freshly filed nails." Amanda is trying desperately to be optimistic and does not want to think about the possible negative outcome of today's meeting.

When they leave the groomer's Amanda put on his K-9 coat. Ben wonders, *are we going to work? We usually go to the groomers after work.* He doesn't worry about the change in routine as he knows she has his best interest at heart. He trusts Amanda to always do what is right for him.

The drive to *The Bamberg Chronicle* is solemn no singing or humming from Amanda, this morning. Her quiet manner hints to Ben that something very serious is about to take place. *What is so special about today?* Ben ponders the events that have taken place so far this Saturday morning.

When they arrive at the newspaper building, Ben recalls the smell of newsprint and ink. Then he remembers, *we were here with Sam, Molly and Harry. That was a fun day. It sure was good to see them. Maybe I will see them again today.*

They ride the creaking old elevator in silence to the second floor, and then they slowly walk down the long carpeted hall to an office. There's a man he recognizes sitting in a black leather oversized chair behind a big wooden desk. Ben *remembers Eddy.*

"Hi Amanda," Eddy stands offers his hand and they shake. Then sitting down he says, "How are you holding up? I'm so sorry you're going through this. I guess we always knew Ben belonged to someone previously. We have learned that he does have a history. Hang in there, Amanda." Eddy tries to console her.

"I know. I just wish this wasn't happening. I have been on edge all week. I can't imagine what the Charles family is going through. It must be horrible for them. For me, it's the boy and *his* dog thing."

Ben is lying on the plush carpet in Eddy's office snoozing. Amanda nudges him because he is dreaming. He shudders, shakes and snorts when he dreams. Suddenly he's wide awake and quickly sits up straight, perks up his ears and stares at the doorway. He hears something familiar but he's not sure why he knows those voices.

Roy and Molly burst through the door opening and smother Ben with their joy, "Hi Ben, it's so good to see you. We thought we would never, ever see you again. Oh we're so happy," Roy and Molly spoke in unison while patting him. Then they stop, step back and look at the dog in front of them. They hesitate as they are waiting for and expecting the usual very wet face licks and frolicking from the dog. They do not know why, but this isn't happening.

Surprised, Roy says to Molly, "Maybe he is not *our* Ben after all." They both turn and look at their parents and Amanda.

"Hello, I'm Eddy Edwards, Editor of the *Bamberg Chronicle*," he said offering his hand to shake, "Hello again, Lori, we spoke last week on the phone." He turns and faces the man, offers his hand then says, "And you are?

"Fred Charles," he put out his hand to shake. He says in a very calm controlled voice, "As you can imagine we are looking to a quick resolution to this issue, as it is very unsettling for all of us."

"Yes that is our goal too." Then pointing to Amanda he says, "This is as you probably have figured out by now, Amanda, a decorated member of the Bamberg Police K-9 Department and Ben's handler." They acknowledge each other then while still standing they enter into casual chatting.

Ben did recognize Roy and Molly but he also knows from his training that he must refrain from greeting the visitors until Amanda gives him permission to relax.

Roy and Molly try to assess the unexpected greeting from the dog. "Mom, Dad, we think that maybe this dog is not *our* Ben, or is it possible that he has forgotten all about us already? It's only been a year. I don't understand Mom," Roy said while tapping his mother's arm to get her attention. "Why doesn't he recognize us?" Roy is stymied.

Ben appears to be ignoring them, but he wasn't really snubbing them nor had he forgotten them. He wanted to greet Roy and Molly but he didn't have permission from

Amanda. He sat and queried her, with his ears perked up and head tilted, waiting for her instructions.

Amanda notices out of the corner of her eye that Ben is just sitting and patiently waiting, just like his training taught him. She stops chatting with the parents and says, "Excuse me for a moment." She walks over to Ben. "I'm so sorry, Roy. Ben is well trained as a working dog, to not make advances to people until I give him permission and remove his K-9 coat.

Amanda bends down, unfastens the coat and removes it, and then she pats Bens head, smiles at Molly and Roy, and says, "It's okay, Ben. Go see Roy and Molly, go Ben," Amanda gives the command allowing Ben to greet the kids.

Amanda's permission is exactly what he is waiting for. He ran to Roy, rolling over to have his belly rubbed, and then gets to his feet so he can furiously wag his tail and lick Roy's face again and again. Then he runs over to Molly and puts on the same performance for her.

Wow, I never thought I would see Molly and Roy again. I'm so excited.

Elated, almost giggly, Molly says, "See Mom, Ben is *our* Ben that we lost. I told you so," Molly states emphasizing the '*our*.'

Roy asks, "Are you Amanda the police officer and Ben's handler?" He gives her the once over seeing her decorated uniform. He's somewhat impressed.

"Yes, I am. Ben is now a member of the Bamberg Police Force in the K-9 Unit and I have been assigned to be his handler."

"Is it true that Ben finds people and catches bad guys?" Roy questions. He is eager to quickly learn as much as he can about Ben's job

"It certainly is true. I have a book I call, 'Ben's Adventures' would you like to see it?" Amanda asks and picks up the scrap book impressively stuffed with newspaper articles, photos and awards.

"Hey, Ben. You're a real cop, cool. I can't wait to take you home and show you off to all of my new friends and tell them what a great life you've had. Sure I'd like to see his adventures book." Roy says as he is getting enthusiastic about the new life of *his* Ben.

Amanda's heart sank hearing Roy's mind set. She wonders if she can change his thinking. She's committed to trying her best. She takes her place in the middle of the sofa, in Eddy's office, Molly and Roy sit on either side and Mrs. And Mrs. Charles stood behind, so everyone had a good view of Ben's Scrap Book. Amanda presents a brave demeanor then begins, "This was Ben's first search for a young boy who was abducted while at the County Fair with his parents. Ben not only found the boy safe, but he led us to the abductor who took the boy." Amanda wants to share some aspects of Ben's life, that as civilians, they wouldn't know about. She really hopes they will be agreeable to letting Ben stay with the force.

"Look Mom, Ben is a real working dog," Roy happily announces.

"Yes Roy, he has a very exciting and rewarding life, now," Lori said preparing Roy for the possibility that Ben might have to stay with the police.

Amanda flips to the next page then before she can tell them who this person is Fred asks, "Is that Sam Garner, the hockey player?"

"As a matter of fact, yes it is. He and Ben had quite the adventure. Sam's whole family was killed by a drunk driver. He was very sad and thought his whole world had fallen apart," Amanda responds.

"I heard something about his family all dying. That must have been terrible for him. I always wondered what happened to him. It seemed like he just completely disappeared," Fred said, "Roy and I closely follow hockey, specifically Sam's team." He leans forward reaching for Roy's shoulder and affectionately squeezes him. "I read something recently in the sports pages, that he is scouting now for his old team. Is that right?" Fred questions.

"Yes, he is happy and settled down and says he owes it mostly to Ben, because he gave Sam something else to think about. Just being there helped Sam get his life back. That's what he told me at the reunion," Amanda was happy to share the stories with this great family. She likes them.

Ben – Chapter Seven

Eddy approaches the group and announces, "I ordered some food and have it laid out in the conference room down the hall. Are you kids hungry?"

"Yeah, sure am, I hope you have some real food," Roy responds

Lori says, "Roy, watch your manners."

Eddy says, "Follow me, I will show you the way. I think we did okay with our choices, that'll appeal to you younger guys. Amanda please bring along Ben's Scrap Book. There are lots of adventures in that book. I'm sure you want to share."

Ben watches as everyone walks to the Conference Room. That is everyone but Roy. Ben senses that he is full of nervous energy, plus the excitement of finally seeing him again.

"Come on Ben, I'll race you to the food," Roy says in a voice a few octaves higher than normal due to his excitement and elated mood. He runs with a peppy step almost bouncing off the floor. He is several feet ahead of everyone else and encourages Ben to keep up with him.

The adults continue talking about the circumstances around losing Ben, most of the way to the food. Amanda asks, "Tell me how you lost Ben while driving to your new home. I'm curious."

Lori starts, "Well, it was early morning; we were packing up the car after staying the night at the motel. We had left Ben sitting at the car minding the luggage while we checked out. We told him to 'stay,' he usually was good at obeying our commands. Roy and Molly were supposed to be standing by the car, too. Out of nowhere, so the story goes, a big beautiful ginger colored cat appears. Apparently, it just sits there observing Ben and the children. I think Molly said something about the cat dared them to chase it. Sure thing," she chuckles and rolls her eyes back, "Roy proceeded to walk towards the cat, and then the cat turned and started to run. Of course, so does Roy and right behind him was Ben. Roy stopped at the edge of the parking lot, but Ben was in for the game and continued to run after the cat. We waited around for over an hour calling him but Ben did not return. We left our contact information for the new house with the motel manager should he return."

Fred continues the story, "We never heard from the manager. We telephoned him a few weeks later, but he said, he never saw our dog."

"We notified the local Animal Control but they had not picked him up, either," Lori interjects, "We also advertised in the local paper, but there was no response."

"That motel is almost a hundred miles from Bamberg County. Ben has travelled a very long way. No wonder no one saw him around the motel," Fred says. He wants to make sure that Amanda knows, they did make an effort to try to find Ben.

Roy is fussing over his found pet, patting and chatting with him just like old times. "Ben you are still my buddy. I have missed you so much," Roy fondly says. "Amanda, I like Ben's K-9 Coat. Does he have to wear it all of the time when he's working?" Roy asks he is curious about Ben's current life.

"Yes, that is how everyone knows that he is working. Otherwise they would not let him near a crime scene. Something else, you may not know the lab people know Ben's DNA. This allows them to separate his from any other DNA that they gather for testing," Amanda reports.

"Dad, did you hear that? That's so neat. He's just like a real cop," Roy says, as he reaches down to tousle Ben's ears again, "You're a very important dog now."

Ben – Chapter Eight

"Mmmm – pizza I can almost taste it from here, this is my very favorite meal. How did you know? I must be really hungry as it smells so good." Roy gushes.

While Molly and Roy eat their pepperoni pizza and drink their soda pop they play with Ben. They chat mostly about Ben and taking him to their new home. Molly says, "You know Roy, Ben is different now. He isn't just a pet any more."

"I know but he is still *my* dog. We've had him since he was a puppy. We trained him, not *her*. I'm not going to let *her* keep him," Roy emphatically states, with a clenched fists, with determination in his voice and resolve on his face."

Molly says, "I agree with you, but you need to think about Ben. You are at school all day and at soccer four or five evenings every week. What is he going to do, just lie around the house waiting for you to come home? He will quickly get out of shape, fat and bored. Considering both games and practices, you're hardly ever home. This year coming up you will be away even longer days because you will be busing back and forth to high school. He's with

Amanda all day and night," Molly tries to argue in Ben's favor by pointing out some of the realities of Roy's life.

"Stop talking. Molly, let's just play with Ben," Roy says, he does not want to be convinced, least of all by his sister. Roy turns to Molly and defensively asks, "Whose side are you on anyway?"

Amanda and their parents chat. "Mr. And Mrs. Charles, Ben has been a very valuable asset to not only the Police Force but those he has rescued. We spend more time together than we do with family or friends. That's part of the relationship; we must emphatically trust each other."

"Amanda, I would love to say Ben should stay with you. From our point of view it really is Roy's decision. We have done our best to coach him to do the right thing, but in the end we have given him permission to make the ultimate choice. He hasn't slept a whole night since he thought Ben would be coming home with us," Lori shares trying to explain their awkward position.

Lori hands Amanda papers. "Amanda if there is any question about Ben originally being *our* dog, here are the papers from the National Registry to confirm we first registered his Microchip four years ago."

"Thank you Lori. Let's see if we can settle this dispute in the best interest of everyone," Amanda adds, "I'm not looking for conflict I prefer to settle issues amicably. As a trained police officer I do know it is necessary that I keep these papers. I hope the legal department will not need to use them to verify Ben's ownership." They watch as she carefully puts the papers into her uniform pocket.

Lori then whispers to Amanda, "Maybe if you convince Roy about Ben's value and the exciting and sometimes dangerous life he has now, Roy may agree that Ben should stay with you. You can see that Roy is really excited about and enjoying Ben's adventures."

"Thank you. I just want to know how much resistance I'm facing and from where. We on the Police Force value Ben so much. I'll show you some of his awards that he has earned." She must make points in Ben's favor.

Amanda calls to the children, "Molly, Roy, would you like to see more pictures and stories of Ben's adventures?" She picks up the Ben's Adventures book and starts flipping pages again.

"Roy, did you know that being a handler, like me, we spend twenty-four hours each and every day, with our K-9 partner? The bond is so strong that when a handler is mortally wounded, that means gets shot and dies, they normally retire the dog," Amanda says. She can see that she is starting to break him.

"Really? Why would they do that?" Roy asks. He is interested and starting to understand the relationship.

"Because we are so close and they are so loyal to us, the dogs trust us to be their leader and have faith that we will look out for them, in turn they look out for us. We, Ben and I, bonded very quickly. He is a natural, and he loves his job. Remember earlier today, he hesitated greeting you until I gave him permission, telling him it was okay to come out of training mode."

"Yeah we were scared that he didn't remember us," Roy offers.

"Based on his age you told me earlier, he is five years old. He probably has six or maybe seven years of service left before he must retire. He does his job so well; he makes me look good to my superiors," she continues impressing Roy.

"Something else you might not know, there is a National Police Canine Association, also known as NPCA, and they annually present awards to the K-9 force for bravery. The NPCA publish a monthly magazine where they have photos and stories about the K-9 dog's successes and awards that they receive. I can arrange to send you a subscription of that magazine. They'll mail the magazine to you on a monthly basis, if that is something you would like," Amanda says, sharing more aspects of the K-9 world.

"Yeah! Thanks that would be amazing. If Ben stays with the police I bet he'll get one of those awards for bravery," Roy says as he is un-expectantly gaining more appreciation for the complexity of Ben's Police Force job and the emotional attachment between *him* and Amanda.

"Ben and I were summoned to a hostage situation. During the initial investigation I let myself be taken hostage. The S.W.A.T. team gave me an ear wig so I could communicate with them. In the meantime Ben found me and the other hostages sitting on the floor in a circle, by sneaking through a partially open door. He hid out of sight behind some cartons until it was safe. He waited for me to give him the 'go' signal. Then he carefully made his way behind me, and successfully chewed through the ropes freeing my hands. The hostage situation changed completely due to Ben's astute ability and senses. He knows how to do his job," Amanda says, sharing her personal rescue story.

"Look Roy, this photo is Ben with the Mayor. He is giving Ben the Mayor's Medal for Bravery," Amanda turns a few more pages then says, "This photo was taken in Casper County, by the date of the newspaper article, and I can see this happened about six months before I met Ben. He saved the life of a sixteen year old girl, Jenny." Amanda hesitates a moment and looks over at Molly because she is the same age as Jenny then continues, "Jenny would have died if Ben had not brought help to her. "Aren't you proud of Ben?"

"Wow, Dad look at him in this picture. Amanda is he flying?" Roy exclaims pointing at the photo and looking directly at Amanda, with big eyes.

"No, one of the officers at the site took that photo with his cell phone. Isn't that a great photo?" she chuckles, "This assignment was a very dangerous one. He jumped off a hundred and twenty-five foot sheer cliff down into the Devon River. It's known for its very strong current so it was *extremely* treacherous. He didn't hesitate for a moment. He showed us that he's a strong swimmer even in that fast moving water. Ben saved Mr. Vincent's life by holding onto him until the police officers could secure him with ropes," Amanda is feeling confident that she is doing an outstanding job at impressing Roy with the photos and stories.

Ben is very happy to see Roy and Molly. He is lying on the floor at their feet while they look at his book and talk about his success. *What am I going to do? I wonder if I get to choose. Will I decide to stay with Amanda and work, or go with Roy and play? Now that I have had a taste of fame, will I be able to be just a pet again?*

Ben – Chapter Nine

Lori approaches Amanda and says, "Would you give us about twenty minutes, we need to have a family meeting."

"Sure, take as long as you need. Ben and I will be just down the hall in Eddy's office," she says trying to be casual but that was not how she was feeling. Amanda is hoping for a positive result.

The whole Charles family sits around a table. Fred begins, "Roy, tell me what you are thinking."

"I miss him so much. I really want to take him home so we can play together. I do see how important his job is too *but* he is my dog," Roy emotionally whines.

"We know you must be confused about what is the best decision, for everyone. We are counting on you being mature enough to make the right choice," Fred consoles him.

"Doesn't the fact that he's our dog, mean anything?" Roy stubbornly asks raising his voice in frustration and anger, and then slapping his hand on the table spilling his drink.

Molly adds her two cents to the conversation, "Roy, remember our discussion earlier today? You are hardly ever home these days."

"He's *my* dog."

"We know, but we want you to think beyond your personal wants. Please consider Ben and the people's lives he saves," Lori adds.

Fred said, "We took care of him and loved him for four very good years. Think of it this way, all the time he was with us, we were grooming him for this important job he has now." Fred is pulling out the big guns.

With tears running down his cheeks, Roy says, "If, and I said *if*, I were to let him stay with *her,* do you think that she would let me visit Ben" every so often?"

"Sweetheart, I'm sure that can be arranged. Remember though that he has been a very busy crime fighter. His life doesn't run on a prearranged schedule. There is no set time frame when he would be called on to catch bad guys and find people. He might not always have free time." Lori pitches, she didn't want to make promises she didn't think would be easy for Amanda to fulfill.

"I'm going for a walk down the hall. I want to think this through all by myself," Roy is feeling very sad and isn't quite ready to give in — not just yet, even if he does eventually.

Fred, Lori and Molly, sit in silence during Roy's absence. Then Fred says, "I'm all out of arguments. If you have another approach, give me a hint. I think Ben should stay here but it's not my decision. We made it clear to Roy he gets to make the final choice."

Amanda is pacing back and forth quickly wearing a path into the carpet in Eddy's office. "The longer it takes for them to make their decision, the more worried I get," she tells Eddy, shaking her head in despair.

"Not necessarily," Eddy says trying to be positive. "I'm thinking that based on their comments the parents are trying to convince Roy to do the right thing."

"Eddy can you believe this whole debate is over a dog, a very special dog, but still a dog," she says sitting down on the sofa putting her head in her hands and elbows resting on her legs. She is experiencing an enormous amount of frustration. With her mind a million miles away she reaches down to rub Ben's ears, and wonders just how much longer she will feel his soft fur in her hand.

For some reason Ben is very aware that he is right smack in the middle of these discussions. He doesn't understand exactly what is at stake but, he does understand and feel the tension in the room.

"If it wasn't for the boy and his dog thing, I think I would leave and let the legal folks resolve the issue. They may have to get involved anyway. Especially, if the Charles family decides that they want to take Ben. After all, the taxpayers have invested a lot of money in his training. I was advised to go the legal route instead of appealing to the boy and the family's good judgment. I really hope that I'm not wrong. I have always trusted people to eventually choose to do the right thing."

Eddy says, "Wow, this could get interesting. I didn't think about that part, the cost of training, every body's wages and the cost of Ben's food, vet bills, groomers and so on, never mind your salary, Amanda." He is thinking about how he will include this additional information in his already exciting story. His reporter twitch is pushing his thoughts into an altered story line.

Ben – Chapter Ten

Roy returns to the conference room and stops in the doorway. He stands motionless as if he is a statue. He looks at his family for an indication of what they are thinking. He searches their faces. There is no clue. Everyone has a neutral expression on their face. He asks, "Do you have any advice?"

Fred beckons Roy with his hand, then pats the chair and says, "Come here and sit down Roy. My last piece of advice is you must make your decision with your heart. You know the right thing to do. You just need to come to terms with the option you choose."

"Have you made a decision, Roy?" Lori asks.

"Yes, I'm pretty sure I know what I want to do. Is it okay if I talk it over with you?" Roy asks.

Fred says, "I know you will choose the right path for you and Ben."

Roy continues, "I don't want to make a mistake I will regret for the rest of my life. Please help me I love and missed Ben so much. I don't want him to think that I just abandoned him. That would make me so sad. Mom, Dad,

I really need your input." Roy seems hesitant, but there is hint of some resolve evident in his facial expression.

Fred says, "Take your time and tell us what you are thinking. We can talk about your decision once we know where your head is at."

"I am very impressed with Ben's adventures, the people he has saved and others he has found. I would never in my wildest dreams have thought this is where he would end up. But he has. I thought he was dead or lost from us forever. I'm very happy that he is alive. I would love to have known about his whole trip over the past year. I think that would be amazing. Who would have guessed Ben is a natural for the K-9 patrol. For sure, not me." Roy has tears in his eyes. He is hinting that he might be leaning towards letting Ben go . . . but he is not a hundred percent – yet.

Lori has tears running down her face and she is very emotional when she responds, "Are you saying that you are ready to leave here today without Ben?" She takes another tissue from her purse and wipes away her tears along with her smeared eye makeup.

Roy exhales a big sigh then scrunches up his face. Running his fingers through his hair, he is gathering the courage to give his answer. He is desperately fighting back more tears. "I want you to know first of all, that my decision is not what I really, really want to do. I'm thirteen now almost fourteen, so I think everyone wants me to make the tough decision. By the way, Dad, maturity sucks! Let's talk to Amanda. I want to give her my answer."

"Are you not going to give us a clue?" Molly asks as she wants the inside scoop.

"No I'm not going to tell you. It's my decision. I want to be the one to tell Amanda," Roy is feeling better and a little more confident now.

"I'll go and get Amanda," Molly volunteers, quickly jumping up from the table, she rushes out of the room and jogs down the long corridor.

Molly blasts into Eddy's office and announces, "Amanda, we have a decision for you. My family is still in the Conference Room." Molly likes being the messenger, even though at this point, she's not sure if she is the bearer of good news or bad.

Amanda, looks at Eddy then at Ben with a painfully serious look of fear, hesitation, and oh so wishing it was already tomorrow. "The jury is in, are you ready to hear the verdict, Ben?" Amanda makes it sound like she was not going to like Roy's decision.

Molly, Amanda, Eddy and Ben solemnly walk down the hall, hesitant to walk too quickly. Why rush for bad news? "This hall feels so much longer now than it did thirty minutes ago," Amanda says as she exhales because she has just become aware that she has been holding her breath. Then she says, "Whew, this walk seems to be taking forever. Molly do you have any idea at all about Roy's decision?"

Ben is almost overwhelmed with the stress he is sensing from Amanda. He has no idea why she is so upset but senses it is important to him.

"Nope, he wouldn't even tell my parents. He just said he wants to tell you his decision," Molly shares.

"Okay, I guess a couple more minutes and I'll know." Amanda applies the logic she is famous for in her job. She is trying so hard to not be too emotional.

The trio plus Ben arrive at the doorway of the conference room. They look in for an indication of the decision. But they only see three stone faces. "Hi folks, I'm here and anxious to hear what you have to say," Amanda put on her police officer face. She decides to not reveal her emotions. She is hoping that no matter what the decision is, she will be able to control of her feelings.

Fred says waving his hand like he is introducing him to the audience, "Roy, you have the floor."

Ben – Chapter Eleven

Before Roy speaks there is severe tension obvious in the room, Ben can feel it. Roy walks calmly over to him; he kneels down wraps his arms around him holding him tight. He pats hugs and kisses him.

What Roy doesn't tell the people in the room is he is stalling to gain control over his fragile feelings. He stands up, clears his throat then speaks, "I guess everyone is waiting for my decision." He let out a big sigh."

Ben is looking at everyone with his head cocked to one side and a crumpled brow. *What is happening? I wish I could understand.* Ben wonders if they are aware that he is tuned into their emotions and he isn't getting good vibes.

"Amanda, if I were to decide to leave Ben with you would you send me some of the articles about Ben's adventures?" Roy asks tentatively.

"Roy, I will not only send you articles, but I will arrange to send you the magazine I mentioned earlier about the K-9 dogs," Amanda promises with a cracked voice and tears start to trickle down her face. She is not sure at this junction, if she is crying with joy or grieving her loss of Ben.

"Good, I would really like to show my friends what Ben does," Roy is pleased and it shows in his body language.

"Roy is there anything else?" Amanda asks with her voice cracking then quickly adds, "So far I think everything is doable and the K-9 Department will be able to live with this bargain."

"Yeah, just, one more thing, I want one of Ben's K-9 coats as a souvenir and for me to remember him," Roy continues to negotiate.

"Oh." Amanda draws in her breath, hesitates a moment because she doesn't know if this will be a deal breaker for their negotiations, but she must draw the line here. "Roy, if it were up to me I would emphatically say yes, please take it with my blessing, but it is not. Of course you probably are not aware, but, first, his coat is not mine to give away. Secondly, these coats are official and only actual K-9 Patrol dogs are allowed to wear them. I don't think you would do this, but if the coat gets into the wrong hands, there may be some legal issues. You might want to think about this request a little more. I'm sure you don't want to do something that is illegal." Once again she found herself holding her breath.

Roy reveals a crooked smile exposing a dimple in his left cheek, and then he looks over at his parents. He says, "Oops! I guess I overstepped my boundary with that request.

Lori with a grin, says, "Well Roy, can you please tell us your decision now? This is just too much drama for me."

Molly says, "Yeah! C'mon Roy. Please don't keep us in suspense any longer. What have you have decided to do?"

"This was the most difficult decision I have ever made in my whole life. That's all thirteen, going on fourteen years of it. Thank you for allowing me to make my own choice. I have decided . . . to have Ben continue with his job as a working dog for the police." Roy gave a big sigh of relief, and then he actually appears to be far more relaxed. The pressure and stress he was experiencing left his face and body.

Fred and Lori jump up shoving their chairs back and rush to Roy and hug him. They say in unison, "We are so proud of you honey. We believe you made the right decision for you, us and Ben.

Ben watches as everyone looks over at Amanda.

She now knows that her tears are tears of happiness. "Thank you so much. I *really* do appreciate your decision, Roy. I have no doubt about how difficult it was for you making this choice. I think you might be braver than me. If I could speak for Ben I think he would also say, *thank you Roy.*

Molly takes her turn then Mom and Dad. They smother Ben in hugs and kisses.

Does this mean that I'm going home with you?

Why is Amanda crying? Wait, what's happening? I'm so confused. Will someone please tell me what's happening? Ben whines questioning his brow furrowed, and he is moving his head back and forth, and whimpers.

Ben glances towards the door and observes the Charles family congregated at the conference room exit. Amanda has taken a position opposite them, standing with her arms crossed hugging herself. Both groups say something to Ben, which makes him tilt his head again from side to side. He is filled with uncertainty.

He softly barks. *What are you saying to me?*

Roy approaches Ben, gets down on his knees beside him. He wipes tears from his eyes with his very wet sleeve. He kisses and hugs Ben again, and says, "I love you so very much . . . I missed you a lot when you were gone . . . We all are so happy that you have such an important job. I now understand that people depend on you. Seeing the great pictures of you working and the appreciation they show towards you, makes me feel so lucky, to have known you.

"It would be selfish of me to keep you as a pet because you are so good at catching bad guys and finding lost people . . . sob.

"I want you to stay and continue to work with the K-9 Kennel Brigade."

"Amanda has . . . given me some souvenirs. She has also . . . promised to send me clippings of your successes." Roy has difficulty with the words as he is blubbering. He knows he must continue even though his voice is strained. He needs closure. "I will tell my classmates and friends about the great job you have and show them a photo of you so they will know what you wear when you work . . . They will be so jealous, and I will be so proud of you," Roy says wiping away the flood of tears still streaming down his cheeks. He hopes, by pouring out his heart-felt feelings that Ben understands that he is loved, he is not abandoning him and most of all everyone only wants what is best for him.

Ben looks up at Amanda with his soft brown eyes, she still has tears in her eyes but now she is also smiling at him.

He looks over at the Charles family, they smile back at him, wipe away tears and wave good bye, they look so very sad as they start to walk away.

Brrr . . . Brrr . . . Amanda's business line is demanding her attention. "Excuse me," she said as she picks up her phone and holds her hand in the quiet please position, "I have to answer this call." Amanda with her official business voice says, "Amanda K-9 Brigade."

Roy turns to Molly and mischievously whispers, while he is waving good bye to Amanda, "Wouldn't it be neat if we could see Ben at work?"

Lori looks at Fred, rolls her eyes back and groans. She says, "Not a chance Roy. Don't even think about going there."

"Hello." Amanda listens then says, "Yes — our ETA is twenty minutes." She puts down her phone, straps on Ben's K-9 coat, and then says with a happy lilt in her voice, "C'mon Ben, it's time for us to go to work."

CPSIA information can be obtained at www.ICGtesting.com
Printed in the USA
LVOW080313250513

335467LV00001B/1/P

9 781458 208606